Praise for **Sco**

"[Gordon's] exploration of mental illness is fearless and without artifice, portraying not only the debilitating effects on those afflicted, but also the trepidation, helplessness, anger, neglect, scorn, and occasional love returned to them by family and strangers. Mikey is an engaging protagonist, and all of his charges emerge as distinct characters . . . Readers will find themselves caught up in the journey, cheering for Mikey and his team . . . An absorbing, uplifting tale of finding light and self-worth in adversity's darkest depths."

**—*Kirkus Reviews* (starred review)**

"*Head Fake* is about how laughter can save us. It's a jab in the ribs, reminding us that even in our worst hour, laughter and connection can be the flashlight in the dark, guiding us toward healing and redemption."  **—Chris Rock, comedian, actor, writer, filmmaker**

"*Head Fake* is an inspiring addition to the literature of sport, the literature of long odds and underdogs, the literature of mental illness, the literature of overbearing fathers. Scott Gordon writes with profound candor, wit, and empathy about people on the edge, people who could just really use a few wins."

**—Chris Bachelder, author of four novels,**
**including National Book Award finalist, *The Throwback Special***

"*Head Fake* is a wonderful read on so many levels. The writing is superb, as the characters and each storyline kept me from wanting to put the book down. The topics of mental illness are hit with such brutal honesty and woven into a team taking its roller coaster ride through their basketball season with a rookie coach. So many themes touched me: coaching/support; team/togetherness; hanging in there/standing strong in the face of adversity; and mostly love and dedication. I highly recommend it."

**—Nick Nurse, Head Coach, Philadelphia 76ers,**
**2019 NBA Champion, 2020 NBA Coach of the Year**

"Like all the best novels that revolve around sports, *Head Fake* is much, much more than what happens on the basketball court. This is a novel that explores mental illness and offbeat youth with a warm heart. You won't soon forget Mikey Cannon and his under-dog journey as he comes to realize that not everyone can play for the Lakers but anyone, in fact, can make a difference. *Head Fake* is nothing but net."

—Mark Stevens, author of *The Fireballer*

"Mikey Cannon and his eclectic basketball team are not just charac-ters, but complex and fascinating humans who will leap off the pag-es and nest inside your psyche long after the final point is scored . . . This is not your typical 'dude helps troubled' kids story. This story will gut you, and change your perception of those we deem outcasts forever. Scott Gordon weaves an absolutely brilliant and authentic tale that set me on a roller coaster (the thrilling, yet frightening, up-side-down kind) of emotions. It's been ages since I've read a story that can have me cackling one second, then bawling my eyeballs out the next."

—Eve Porinchak, bestselling author of *One Cut*

"*Head Fake* accomplishes a rare feat; to make me care as much about the protagonists as the game they play. The truth under the mental illness subject matter could've come off as medicine in lesser hands, but Scott's ability to merge character development without slowing plot is simply amazing. I love this book! You will too!"

—Rodney Barnes, Writer/producer, *Winning Time: Rise of the Lakers Dynasty*, *The Boondocks*, *American Gods*

"Gordon writes with humor and compassion about a courageous team of characters as they navigate friendship, contend with their demons, and play some hoops. *Head Fake* is a masterful debut."

—Gary Lennon, writer and executive producer of *Euphoria* and *Power*

"Tonally reminiscent of *Up in the Air*, *Sideways*, and *Fargo Rock City*–the engrossing *Head Fake* can be simultaneously profound and hilarious. Scott Gordon's highly accessible writing exhibits ir-reverence and pathos, with a deep empathy for his richly drawn characters. I was cheering along with their small victories, laughing along with their absurdities, and crying along with their traumas. Don't wait for the inevitable film adaptation–you know the book is always better! Bring on the National Book Award."

—David Wolthoff, producer of *Concussion*

"I've never even watched a basketball game, but I eagerly turned the pages in this heartfelt, funny, wise book like a rabid fan standing and cheering for my team from the stands. Of course, this story's not about basketball. It's about not giving up. On anybody. Not even yourself. Scott Gordon accomplishes a true literary feat in this masterful debut novel. I loved it!"

—Staci Greason, award-winning author, *All the Girls in Town*

"Despite its heavy subject matter, [Head Fake] is full of genuine laugh-out-loud moments, not just from Mikey's frequent wise-cracks but also the team's antics as they forge unlikely bonds that help them cope with the heartbreaking challenges they face at school, at home, and within their own mind. Gordon's precise, detailed writing not only brings each character's inner world into sharp relief, it also captures the team's growth on the court . . . This persistently honest look at the difficult realities of mental illness avoids any sugar coating but still offers an uplifting tale full of warmth and humor. Funny, honest story of teamwork in the face of mental illness."

—*BookLife* by *Publisher's Weekly* (Editor's Pick)

"Readers who navigate Mikey's world and the uncertainty of his pathway to success and mental health will find *Head Fake* a rousing story of failure, success, and connection . . . a wry tone of ironic humor permeates the novel, lending it just the right flavor of insight and fun to keep readers enjoying and thinking. The result is a late-stage coming-of-age story; a foray into mental health and re-covery; an examination of intergenerational relationships; and an uplifting success story that navigates mine fields of failure before achieving its goals."

—D. Donovan, senior reviewer, *Midwest Book Review*

"*Head Fake* is a wonderful and timely story that illustrates in the most basic and profound ways the absence of connectivity and understanding between young people in crisis, their families, and the very institutions designed to help them. *Head Fake* is inspiring, moving, and meaningful."

—Gil Bellows, actor and Emmy Award-winning producer of the film *Temple Grandin*

"*Head Fake* made me laugh and cry in equal measure—sometimes simultaneously."

—Doug Kurtz, story coach and author of the novel *Mosquito*

"*Head Fake* offers a suspenseful and emotional journey that's full of passion, conflict, drama, and resilience . . . an unforgettable, heart-warming, and lifelike book. I strongly recommend it!"

—*Los Angeles Book Review*

"Scott Gordon's uplifting novel *Head Fake* combines humor with emotionally charged storytelling to explore themes of self-worth, perseverance, and the inner strength we can find when we need to fight for our team . . . The author's deep compassion for his cast of underdogs and misfits is infectious, and readers will quickly find themselves cheering for the team's successes—on and off the court."

—*IndieReader*

"Gordon's characters were so well drawn and realistic, they jumped off the page and begged me to get to know them . . . This is one of those books that you will think about and wonder how it will end, and then when it does, you will miss the characters as they will have found a place in your heart."

—Leslie A. Rasmussen, award-winning author of
*After Happily Ever After* and *The Stories We Cannot Tell*

"Inspiring, deeply emotional and uplifting, are just a few simple words to describe a truly wonderful work that reminds us to never judge and to never give up."

—Nigel Daly OBE, ex-chairman BAFTA LA, publisher of *THE LAB MAG* and
president of Screen International North America

# HEAD FAKE

*a novel*

Scott Gordon

Brooklyn     Los Angeles

Brooklyn     Los Angeles

Copyright © 2023 by Scott Gordon

For information about special discounts for bulk purchases, please contact Maxwell Street Books sales at business@maxwellstreetbooks.com.

Cover and interior design by
David Ter-Avanesyan/Ter33Design LLC

Cover image by Shutterstock.com

ISBN: 979-8-9901035-2-8 (hardcover)
ISBN: 979-8-9901035-1-1 (paperback)
ISBN: 979-8-9901035-0-4 (ebook)

FOR SAMANTHA

**To:** chey%@gmail.com, tobikenobi@gmail.com, smurft-hepit@gmail.com, sociokiddie@gmail.com, donniethe-counter@gmail.com, adderallandbeam04@gmail.com, nubbintillet@gmail.com
**Subject:** Where I'm coming from
**Attachment:** Mikey.doc

Hey Dream Team,

I want you to know I've read and re-read your assignments countless times, the memories and break-downs you were afraid to share. Every time I read them, I get more respect and love for you. I know your day-to-day isn't easy. I know it all too well.

I feel like I owe you my story. I'm gonna tell you how a major depressive with impulse control disorder and ADHD, one of the biggest losers you've ever met, went from being homeless to championship basketball coach. My story is part warning that we're all just a bad turn away from allowing our worst self, the one we keep hidden in the shadows, from emerging and taking over. But it's also a reminder of when this does happen—and it will—there is someone you can go to who's traveled similar roads before and has come to realize that with a little pivot, you can see the humor of life glimmering through the pain.

Coach Cannon

# ONE

**Father of the Year said that if I didn't get this job,** I was back out of the house and living on the street . . . tomorrow. Based on my interviewing skills, my time indoors was running out.

It was almost three. I noticed a few tatted and pierced students sucking on smokes and playing with their phones by four yellow buses parked in the school's drive. The buses looked like every other I'd seen, only three-quarters the size. A driver was dozing in the front seat of one. The way he slept without a care in the world, he just had to be the one quitting. I hesitated to rouse him, but I wanted to know why he was leaving and if he had advice on how to land this gig, so I rapped on his door.

His eyes fluttered open, focusing on me as if I were a madman. He swung open the door. "Can I help you?"

"You the one quitting?" I asked, ascending the first step. I peered down the aisle, which appeared to have twenty seats. The driver, a lanky dude, all knees and elbows and pointy chin, nodded. By his feet sat a six-pack of Coke and a brown paper bag with grease spots that smelled of tuna fish, which reminded me of childhood lunches with my mother.

"About to take my final run, quit two weeks ago, and they still haven't found anybody stupid enough to take the job."

I couldn't win. "What's bad about it?"

"Just wait about thirty seconds and see for yourself."

On cue, the school's doors opened, releasing fifty or more kids. As a group, these kids looked rough, the kind of rough you would avoid by crossing the street. Some headed toward the buses, others played grab ass, and most lit up smokes. The mentally ill loved their cigarettes. The sticks gave their hands something to do and the tobacco whipped their wandering thoughts in line—at least that's why I used to smoke. I don't anymore 'cause you gotta be kidding me at a buck a loosie and eight a pack.

Suddenly a six-foot girl with a red mohawk launched out of the school like a guided missile. "Gonzalo!" she wailed. "You stole my phone!"

A Mexican kid began bobbing and weaving through the crowd to avoid her.

"Give me my phone! You know that's the only phone I can speak to Darnell on!"

"Darnell's her dead brother," said the driver.

Gonzalo had some moves, faking left and darting right, but she homed in on him like prey, flinging some poor rag doll of a girl out of her way.

I didn't want to look, to see this poor kid having a psychotic episode, but I learned in the ward to keep my eye on people in the middle of a break—their movements were unpredictable and dangerous.

"I'm gonna beat your raggedy ass, Gonzalo!" she said, swinging her arms with the abandon of one of those advertorial air dancers you see in front of car dealerships, until she finally connected with the back of his head, knocking him to the pavement. She leapt on him and patted him down. She yanked his backpack off his shoulder and emptied it, but there was no phone. "He gonna call any second."

A Black mountain, maybe six-six and three hundred-plus

pounds, who looked like an angry linebacker, bolted out of the building. He pushed his way toward the fight, which escalated into the girl now banging Gonzalo's head on the pavement. The Mountain was fast for a big guy and snatched the girl off her prey, putting her in a full nelson as she mule-kicked his shins. "I know he got it!" she cried. "He got my special phone."

As Gonzalo stood and brushed himself off, I noticed he had 5150, which I knew to be California code for "involuntary psychiatric commitment," tattooed on the side of his neck. He started putting notebooks, pens, and books back in his backpack. "I'm outta here. That *puta's* off her meds," he said to nobody.

"Gonzalo, hold up!" issued a voice that started at the Mountain's feet, taking sand and gravel with it on its way up to his mouth.

The bus driver turned to me, shrugged, rested his case.

"I don't got anything," said Gonzalo, as he backed toward me, absently touching his back pocket, which had a white phone peeking out of the top.

"Gonzalo, stop. Now!" said the big man, still holding the struggling girl.

But he kept moving, looking like he was thinking of bolting. The students watched in silence and my heart tore in half for this girl—I would've killed to have a phone I could call my mom on. I'd be dialing right now.

"Hey, Gonzalo," I called out, stepping off the bus. "She can talk to her dead brother on that phone. You gotta take that into the equation."

Both the kid and the Mountain stopped and regarded me. "Who the hell are you?" they asked in unison.

"New driver, maybe, hopefully."

"Office is that way," said the Mountain, thumbing over his shoulder to the door.

"You the gym teacher or something?" I asked.

"Security."

Gonzalo slung his backpack over his shoulder, knocking the phone for me to clearly see it—it wasn't his. "Hey, playa, you a big Hello Kitty fan?" I called out.

Gonzalo turned and mad dogged me. "What you say, *cabrón*?"

"You gotta cat in an adorable red ribbon sticking out of your pocket."

"Bring the phone here now," called out Mountain. "Now!"

The gig was up, and Gonzalo moped his way to the big man. He handed the phone to the girl, who burst into tears.

The Mountain looked over to me. "Yo, you better get your narrow ass inside you want that job."

I turned to the driver, who was finishing his Coke, then back to the girl sitting on the ground talking on her phone.

"You still want it?" asked the Mountain.

"I'm going. I'm going."

• • •

Inside the Mary Friedman Alternative High School was a reception area like at a doctor's office in which a thirty-something Latina, in jeans and a Mickey Mouse sweatshirt, sat behind a large desk.

"Hey. I'm Mikey Cannon," I said. "I have an interview for the driver position."

She gave me the once-over and leaned back in her chair, unimpressed. With a pen, she gestured to a couch on which a girl with short hair and a nose ring sat hugging her knees, whimpering. "Have a seat. Dr. Tambori will be right out."

I sat next to the kid and smiled, prompting her to sob louder.

"Everything OK?" I asked her, but she ignored me. "What's this Dr. Tambori like, anyway? A hard-ass?" The girl shrugged. My first therapist said one of the most positive coping mechanisms was humor. Of course, another shrink told me I used humor too often

6

as a defense mechanism. Figure it out, people. Anyway, my coping mechanism, CM, known by most as my moronic wit, lurched for the wheel. I turned back to the secretary and said: "A bus got what, drive and reverse?"

The secretary looked up and pursed her lips with all kinds of attitude, but the whimpering girl emitted a sound that was sobbing and laughter pushed together, like when you laugh and snort soda out of your nose. That sound was worth the price of admission right there. Something told me she hadn't laughed in days, maybe weeks.

I was working on some material to keep the girl laughing when this petite Indian woman with medieval green eyes—their attention made me feel naked—stepped into the waiting room. She was a few years older than me with thick black hair pulled tight into a ponytail, a blouse buttoned up to her neck, and a stylish and pressed pantsuit, all of which made me run my hand over my wrinkled button-down to straighten it out.

"Follow me, Mr. Cannon," she said in a posh English accent. I almost curtsied.

I trailed her down a hallway, past a few students, a doctor in his white coat and stethoscope, and a room that said, *Occupational Therapy*, to her office.

Man, I'd never seen a room so organized. It was like a show-room. Everything had its place, even the paper clips were little soldiers dutifully facing the door. Every therapist I met—and I've met a plethora—had issues. One of my shrinks would absently shove her fingers under her armpits and then rub them on her chin as she listened to my problems.

Dr. Tambori sat, spotting a rogue pencil that rolled off and returned it to its holder, and with *her* OCD in check, she looked up at me with those probing eyes.

"OK, Mr. Cannon, you brought your CV, I presume?"

"I love your accent. Where you from, Pennsylvania?"

"You don't have your CV, I take it?" She was a very serious woman.

I buried my hand into my pocket and extracted a folded piece of paper and handed it to her. I could tell from the look on her face *I* should unfold it, so I excused myself, took it back, unfurled it, and presented it to her like a proud Japanese businessperson's card. "Sorry about that," I said.

She placed it on the desk and smoothed it out with her palm. Her fingers were thin but not at all frail. Her fingernails were painted white, which seemed all that much starker against her brown skin. "You do know this is a school for juvenile offenders with mental illness?" she said, studying me for a reaction.

"Are the kids big tippers? 'Cause the salary is a little light," I said, trying to be funny, my way of keeping myself one step removed from a conversation to keep an ear open for catastrophic lies whispering in my head, lies like *I'll be dead on the street in a month*.

She clicked her tongue as she perused my curriculum vitae. "You've moved about quite a bit, performed five jobs in the last year."

"Most of those I quit. I didn't get fired. I mean I got fired from the last one. But most of the others I quit," I stammered. "I'm better than that résumé suggests. I haven't found the right fit is all."

"What have you been doing the last four months? I don't see anything here," she said, turning over the paper in front of her.

"I was sick." I thought keeping it vague was better than telling her I was homeless for most of that time, that I had been on and off the streets for years, and that the only reason I was showered, shaved, and in semi-clean clothes was I had gotten bronchial pneumonia and collapsed onto my father's doorstep three weeks ago. It took begging, but he let me in.

"I see you *have* driven a school bus before."

"I love school buses," I said, degenerating by the second into more of a buffoon than usual.

"You mean you love to drive them?"

"Yes, I love driving them because . . ."

She waited, but there didn't seem to be any thoughts willing to risk exposure. I swallowed, feeling the mucus go down my throat. I was blowing it, like I always do. I couldn't even focus on an interview long enough to get a bus driver position. I would be back on the skids, dead by pneumonia or worse by the end of the month. There is no chance to avoid getting sick when you're homeless. None. My father was right about me. I was such an incredible loser.

"Mr. Cannon, are you OK?"

"Yes," I said, realizing she'd caught me twirling and yanking my hair between my fingers.

"Can you give me an example of overcoming some obstacle while driving the school bus?"

"Like swerving?" I said, sitting on my hands.

"I'm sorry, Mr. Cannon, it appears I should be more literal. I meant an issue with one of the students." She took the rogue pencil back out of its holder, and with its tip hovering over her notepad, she prepared to write down my reply.

My ass sat in the chair, but my mind floated around the ceiling, keeping a safe distance from the disaster below. My ADHD was in overdrive. For years, I tried every med you could think of for my symptoms, but the cure felt worse than the disease. I'd been off all meds for at least a year, which was good because I didn't have insurance and couldn't afford them anyway.

I took a breath and forced myself to concentrate. "Obstacles. Let's see. There are many. I was always overcoming obstacles. Obstacles, obstacles, obstacles . . ."

She furrowed her brow.

I couldn't think. I started talking. "OK, I got one. I had this kid on the bus, a real bully. He was picking on this little towheaded girl, wouldn't stop, made her bawl."

"What did you do?"

"I stopped the bus, had him sit right behind me."

"Right," she said, leaning forward, rubbing her nose as if she had an itch.

"And then I had the rest of the kids make fun of him, call him fat and stuff. See how he liked it." I couldn't help myself. That was the thing with me—I always went for the funny, even when the result was self-sabotage.

"Mr. Cannon, you put me in a very difficult position here. You see, my boss informed me that if you passed your background check, I should hire you no matter how unqualified you were, that it came from above."

"God?"

"No, Mr. Cannon, not God—a board director of the hospital, a friend of your father's as I understand it. But you see, you're horribly wrong for this opportunity. These kids need stability, normalcy, someone who can maintain order on that bus—someone who can be taken seriously."

She spoke with the kind of confidence that comes from knowing your place in this world, and that self-assurance coupled with those piercing eyes killed me, and I had to stop myself from falling for her. "OK," I said. "My bad—I joke around too much when I get nervous."

"Why did you leave the bus driver position?"

"I was let go for attendance issues," I said, omitting I'd called out for a month straight due to sleeping.

"Do you have any experience with mental illness, Mr. Cannon?" she said, absently tapping her fingernails on the desk.

Wow. That was a question and a half. I wanted to tell her everything: about how I could hardly pay attention to what she was saying, how at times I had trouble controlling myself, about the negative thoughts, the depression, about wanting to sleep my life away, the horror show that was my father, about living both tired and wired, about how my hands wouldn't stop sweating, how if I didn't get this job I'd die on the streets. But if the floodgates opened, everybody in this building would drown. Besides, she might think it a bad idea to hire a crazy person to drive around crazy people. "Not really."

"Well in full disclosure, this position might be emotionally draining in a way none of your previous posts have been. For instance, you may be forced to deal with violent or emotional outbursts while driving." She clicked her tongue. "This job isn't for everybody. Are you certain you even want it?"

"I do."

"Will you pass your background check?" she said, those eyes on my wrinkled shirt.

I dried my wet palms on my jeans. "I'm clean."

"Right then, thanks for coming in, Mr. Cannon," she said, standing, extending her hand across the desk.

"That's it? The interview is over? I blew it?"

"Actually, the interview was a formality. As I stated, if you pass the background check, you have the position. Luckily for you, it didn't matter what utter rubbish you spoke here today."

"That's great," I said.

"Is there anything else, Mr. Cannon, you want to ask me?"

I couldn't believe I landed this job.

"No?" she asked, as if I should be asking questions.

"Oh, yes, I do. How long have you been a doctor? You look young."

She took a deep breath and tilted her head. "Why do you want this job?"

Her question was so sincere it knocked me off balance. "I'm looking for a job I can get jazzed about."

"And you believe you'll be *jazzed* to drive our school bus?"

"I don't know," I said, her sincerity inspiring my own. "I don't know what gets me excited anymore. I can't remember."

"I'm in my second year of residency," she said. "For those who truly invest themselves, Mr. Cannon, working with this population can be fulfilling."

I wanted to ask her how she got into the doctor game, about what got *her* jazzed, but she opened the door and stared at me. It was clear she was kicking me out.

As soon as I exited the school, the relief of getting the job was replaced by the fear of losing it. I'd never kept a job longer than three months. Driving mentally ill kids who had been arrested for God knows what would be difficult for a normie. For me, it would be impossible. I had no idea what to do if a kid had a *violent outburst*. What if a student attacked me while I was driving? What if I lost control and veered into oncoming traffic and killed the kids? I couldn't live with that.

A police car raced by, to the emergency entrance of the Friedman Psychiatric Hospital, which shared a parking lot with the school. The officer got out and led a cursing, handcuffed man inside. The familiar odor of disinfectant and iodoform escaped through the automatic doors and reached across the parked cars and ambulances with memories of my time spent there. I was admitted to Friedman at sixteen, nine years ago, before The Mary Friedman Alternative High School existed.

My hand wandered up to my hair and I forced it back to my side. Every instinct was telling me to get as far away from this school as possible, but I knew down in my bones that if I had any chance to make my twenty-sixth birthday, I needed to keep this job.

# TWO

**I walked the forty minutes from Friedman Psychiatric** to Vinton Avenue in Palms, where my grandparents moved in the early '60s. Vinton was a combination of apartments and older, single-family houses and as diverse as any street in LA. In a half block, we had six Black families, five Mexican, three Guatemalan, two Japanese, one Filipino, one Korean, one Jamaican, one Kenyan, a biracial gay couple and us—my mother, Jewish and my father, Irish Catholic. My mom wasn't religious, but every year she would have a Passover Seder with the neighbors, a Seder that included sushi, *carne asada*, jerk chicken, and noodle *kugel,* and once a mariachi guitar, and yet another time a sitar player.

"Mom, I'm home," I called out, seeing my family's old two-bedroom shoebox with its asphalt roof still stained from the parrots of Palms, who for years built nests on our roof. There were many origin stories of the parrots, but they all came down to one commonality—somebody raised parrots and they escaped and had baby parrots, and forty or more of them lived high above us in the palm trees, on telephone wires and roofs. When life became too gray, you had to only glance up to their tropical faces watching over you like squawking angels. But I didn't see any angels now. I sure didn't.

Every time I got near the front steps, a feeling seized me that my mother was watching me, or that she might suddenly open the door and run down the cracked sidewalk and hug me. She'd been gone ten years, but there wasn't an hour that went by I didn't think of her.

As I approached, the two deadbolts unlocked and the door opened, revealing my towering old man with his Frankenstein's-monster shoulders and gorilla arms, skin that was becoming loose under his chin, and blond hair going gray at the temples. It was as if age was slowly climbing up his face and hadn't yet reached his youthful eyes. Andrew Cannon, my father.

"Please tell me you didn't screw up the interview," he said.

"If I pass my background, I'm in. I'm a little worried my trips to the bughouse might surface."

"Akheem, who got you the job, said they don't do that kind of background for bus drivers." My father looked at his watch and retreated into the house. "Follow me. Quick!"

For most of my childhood, family photos hung in the hallway of the three of us—my mother, my father, and me—downing a bucket of shrimp at Neptune's Net in Malibu, eating ribs at a neighbor's barbecue, of my pops and I playing hoops at the rec center, of my first haircut at a year old. Sometime since I last lived with my father two years ago—a disaster I was trying my best not to repeat this time—my father replaced them with several shelves covered in basketball trophies, the last one empty. I longed to once again be embraced by those memories, my mother's joyful face.

I followed him into the family room, which, since my mom passed, could only be called the TV room because all my old man did in there was watch sports. He'd watch anything competitive: b-ball, football, tennis, golf, poker, anything with a winner and a loser. I challenged my father to checkers when I was about eleven, thought I could beat him, but he whooped me, smack-talking the whole game like we were on the courts. He even made me cry, which put my mother out of sorts, causing one of the biggest fights I remember them having.

"It doesn't work," he said, jabbing the air in the direction of the TV.

"Looks like it works to me."

"*It!*" he shouted, reaching over, and slapping the DVD player.

"I told you last night, you record on your cable box now."

"I need it on DVD to keep it. It's starting. Quick. Fix the moronic thing," he said, dropping into his well-worn lounge chair, which over the years had moved closer and closer to the TV; now it was three feet away.

On the TV, a beautiful Hispanic broadcaster with a practiced smile was about to interview him. I hit record on the cable remote. "I'm here with Andrew Cannon," she said, "who's been coaching basketball at Westchester Private High School for the last twenty years, and who is poised to break a major record."

My father leaned forward, his elbows on his knees, a smile so big it ran out of face. Looking at him on the TV, I had to grin, too.

Instead of talking into the newscaster's mic, my father took it from her and faced the camera. "All I have to do is win every game, plus the division title, and then the first tournament playoff game, and I have the most consecutive wins in US history by a high school coach—160 straight wins. Ernest Blood, who coached in Passaic, New Jersey, had a run of 159 consecutive wins from 1915 to 1924."

"Wow, that record's been on the books a long time," said the broadcaster.

"Mine will be on longer."

"You sound confident," she said, talking into what was now clearly my father's mic.

My pops nodded both on the TV and in his chair.

"What do you attribute your success to?" she asked.

"Hard work and talent," my father said on the TV. "You have to have both."

We stared at the TV until the weather report started.

"My pops on TV—pretty cool," I said, trying to keep his attention on his greatness and not . . . me. "How come you didn't mention the record to me?"

He shrugged. "It's over. Did you record me?"

"Sure did," I said, rewinding the image on the TV, which I instantly regretted.

"On the DVD? You *did* record it on the DVD, didn't you?"

"No. I told you. On the cable box."

"I said I wanted it on the DVD."

"What's the difference?"

"You don't *listen* is the difference."

"I didn't have time. It was already starting. You know that! Why didn't you tell me before I left this morning?" I shouted.

"Always full of excuses. Kid's always full of excuses," he said to the ceiling. "You never change. I don't even know why I bother with you. How long do you think it'll be before you're fired from *this* job? Or you quit?"

"What do you want me to say to that?"

"I got you a full ride to one of the top high schools in the country. Ninety percent of the students at Westchester Private go to college, to Ivy League schools, but not my boy. You blew it like you do everything else. Remember last time you moved in? Remember what I said to you?"

"I do." Two years ago, after losing my job and apartment, I had the great idea to move back in with the Führer. I got so depressed I stayed in bed for a month. Lost forty pounds. He said I wasn't a man and would never be one until I could stand on my own. Now that I was healthy again, I wondered which was worse: sleeping in a park with lots of cats—in LA you either have cats or you have rats, and I couldn't sleep with rodents—or having to spend time with my father.

"You should be embarrassed having to come home to daddy like this. You're twenty-five years old, Mikey. Thank God your mother isn't here to see you."

Fire crept from my gut to my neck, and I was unsure if the explosion would produce rage or tears.

"How's the apartment search going?" he asked.

"The *apartment* search?" I snapped. "I don't technically even have the job yet."

"We had an agreement about your staying here. You remember that?"

"I do."

"Last time you made a big show of telling me exactly what you thought of me, that you didn't need me. I don't see you for two years, and then you waltz in here like nothing."

"I hardly waltzed. And I *need* your help. I won't survive on the street again. I won't. I can feel it. It's all I can think about."

My father stood and turned toward me, squaring off. With the heel of his hand, he popped me in the shoulder—hard.

"Why did you do that, Dad?"

He then lowered himself into a defensive position like he was guarding me on the courts, as if we were going one-on-one.

"Get by me, and we'll talk."

"What?"

"You gotta show me something, right here and now, that makes me believe you got it in you to turn things around. Come on, boy." He banged his hand on his chest.

I usually walked away when he was like this, but he was going to regret this little challenge. I pretended like I was above this game—that is, until he let his guard down. I faked left and darted right, then charged him, but my father was too big and too fast, and he kicked out my feet, sending me crashing into a kitchen chair and then onto the floor.

"I'm still the king, Choke Artist."

I looked up at my old man towering over me, beating his chest.

"Choke Artist. I haven't heard that one in a while," I said, remaining on the floor.

"You showed me something now," he said, extending his hand. "You went for it, tried to get by me."

I took his hand and he helped me to a standing position. "I can stay?" I asked, trying the *soft close* I learned at a call center hustling pills for making dicks bigger. They didn't. "For two months?"

"You lose the job and you're gone. I won't enable you. Got me?"

"I got you."

My father slapped my hand. Apparently, I'd been twirling my hair, a habit my first shrink, Dr. Collins, said was connected to my hair pulling. I played with my hair all the time. I absently twirled it, patted it, rolled it, and pulled it. One time I shaved my head, but I only ended up playing with my eyebrows and incessantly folding my lip, which was worse.

"And no episodes. Sleeping all day and night, pulling your hair out. All that stuff should be behind you already."

"A thing of the past." Might as well sound confident.

My old man crossed his arms. "If you don't turn around your life now, you're never going to. I've seen it all over this hood. Eventually, a man becomes indistinguishable from his bad decisions—even to himself."

• • •

My bedroom was like stepping into a time machine. Posters of Fergie, Beyoncé, and *Superbad* were still thumbtacked to the walls, and an old *Call of Duty* video game sat propped in the corner under a Nerf hoop. *Sacred Hoops* by Phil Jackson and a Kevin Durant biography sat among old schoolbooks and Spider-Man comics on my bookshelf. As a kid, I breathed hoops. I watched every UCLA and Lakers game I could on the TV, and at least once a month my old man would take me to see the blue and gold and, if I was lucky, the purple and gold. At these games, I would don my father's old Lakers jersey, number

62—my pops played two seasons for the Lakers before blowing out his knee.

My dream, as a kid, was to continue where my father left off and play for the Lakers—maybe even don 62. But what do you do when you stop growing at fourteen, and you're not even six feet, and you got no springs? You realize you're nothing but a pickup baller at Pan Pacific or Hoover Park. Besides, pro athletes don't yank out their hair to stop their thoughts from burying them in a hole. I never had the stomach for that kind of pressure.

I picked up a photo—my mom sitting in the Walkers' yard at a high school graduation party, laughing. My mom, with her hip-hugger jeans and fashionable light-blue sweater, had been so much fun back then. She was the main reason the neighbors got together. They used to call her the mayor of Vinton Avenue.

My parents met at some Lakers party at James Worthy's house after my father was drafted. Of course, he soon blew out his knee. But then I came along, and he needed to get a job, and after trying insurance sales, car sales, Amway, and a host of other things, ended up coaching high school ball, where he went on to break every record Westchester Private had. Sometimes a person plans their whole life to be one thing and it doesn't happen. Then from out of nowhere, something changes that puts you on a different trajectory, and that turns out to be your calling. At least, that's what happened to my father.

My mother never found her calling. Instead, when I was seven, she was diagnosed as bipolar with severe depression. My mother, who had been so much fun, started to stay up all night in the kitchen chain-smoking, staring at nothing. I never asked her what she thought about during those sleepless nights, but God I wish I had. Did she think about me? My father? Her life? The questions we have for the dead haunt us like unfinished dreams. I missed that woman.

And I was a lot like her. I escaped the bipolar, at least so far— my mother wasn't much older than I am now when she was diagnosed—but of course, not the depression. After she died, I spent countless nights studying my own dark thoughts on my bed, in this room, and now I was back, and so were the thoughts, the obsessional thoughts. *I'll be driving kids who are going to have violent outbursts or psychotic episodes . . . or worse. No way I can handle it. No way.* Panicked, I jumped up from bed and began to pace my room. I couldn't allow myself to fall down the rabbit hole.

I paced the length of my room back and forth for I don't know how long, maybe an hour.

I flopped onto my bed, and I turned onto my back, and I stared at a crack in the ceiling that had grown wider and deeper over the years. Closing my eyes, I felt my head fill with the pressure of falling, as if I'd stepped off a cliff and was plunging through space.

# THREE

*"It's time to get up. It's time to get up. It's time to get up in the mor-ning,"* my father sang in a tone that could best be described as passive-aggressive supersized. He was mocking the tune my mother used to rouse me gently from slumber, and I loathed him for it.

In the kitchen, I grabbed some coffee and sat across from my father, who was reading the sports page.

"I don't know anything about driving these kinds of kids," I said, hoping he would offer some advice, some nugget that would quell my anxiety.

"You drive the bus, that's all. You'll be fine."

Not exactly what I hoped for, but it would have to do. "Thanks for hooking up the job, Pop. I *do* appreciate it."

"Yeah, don't embarrass me."

"Do you think I could borrow a few hundred for a cell phone? I lost mine when I was living on the street. I'll pay you back with my first paycheck."

"No," he said, snapping the paper as he turned the page. "Your Clips blew it again, Choke Artist. They led the whole game, then blew it in the fourth. I'm beginning to see why they're your team."

I took a sip of coffee, wondering how I was going to find the students' homes without my cell and navigational app, when I looked at my watch. I had to go.

• • •

I picked up the school bus at Mary Friedman, where I was told that in the future, I could park it at home overnight. It took a half hour, but after some embarrassing grinding of gears and lurching, I remembered how to drive the cheese box. I cleaned the Coke cans and candy wrappers from the aisle and under the seats, and even culled an empty dime bag from the crack between the pleather cushions. I was ready to go. I was going to keep this job, at least until my true calling came.

My route was West and East Adams, Jefferson Park, and Palms. I had ninety minutes to pick up the students and get them to school. My handbook stated that if a student spent more than ninety minutes one way on the bus, the school could be fined—a city law. It was a good route, all three parts of town close together and not too far from the Friedman School. On a good day, the route was supposed to take seventy minutes, but 6:45 a.m. on a Monday was a hassle with traffic. I wished I had my cell to use Waze to avoid the crush.

A woman in a Tesla cut me off and then flipped me the bird. I did not miss driving in LA. Nope. Anxiety sizzled on my skin as I tried to get comfortable in my squeaky seat.

Finally, running about twenty-five minutes behind, I made it to what my list said was Gonzalo Garcia's house, a low-rise off the 10 Freeway and Crenshaw behind the Rosa Parks Villas. As I pulled up, I saw the kid who stole the Hello Kitty phone. I should've known he would be my first pickup, with my luck. He stood in the driveway studying two girls walking by, as I popped open the door.

He called out something to the girls, who flipped him off. Then he bounded onto the bus and looked at me and shook his head. "*Chupame la verga.*"

"Really? You want me to suck your dick, Gonzalo?" I knew most of the curses.

He smiled. "*Pendejo.*"

"Come on. Let's move it. We're late."

He took a few steps down the aisle. "I was gonna give the phone back. I was just fucking with her 'cause she needed to be fucked with, not that it's any of your business. Honestly, I knew she was off her Lithium. She and I are tight."

"Yeah, well unless you have a death wish, you might want to leave her alone."

"You don't know jack. I had things way under control."

"You did, huh?" I said, examining him to see if he was messing with me, but he was hard to read. "Take a seat so we can get going."

"Where's everybody else?" he asked.

"You're the first pickup."

"*Soy el tercero, güey,*" he said, taking a seat in the middle of the bus and sliding to the window.

I looked at my route sheet. Fuck! I missed the first two kids. I had thought they were part of the document's heading. "Hey, Gonzalo, can you sit up here? I lost my phone. Could use some help finding the next stop. Please?"

"Fuck no, *que chingas*. Find it yourself."

"There's five bucks in it for you," I said, desperate. I would never be able to focus long enough to get us back on track. No way.

"Forget five bucks. Twenty."

"Job pays five. What else are you doing?"

"Fifteen. I know the shortcuts."

"Five. Come on, we're already late."

"Why would I help you?"

"Four."

"*You* need *me*. We're supposed to get there by 7:30—the latest. First period starts at eight, and without my directions, we'd get there at 8:15 and that's if everything's thumping."

"Shit."

"Shit is right. Some teachers are cool but Dr. T locks her door at

8:05, and if you're late you get detention and if you're late three times you gotta take the class over next semester. Half your pickups are in that class, and if they even think they gonna be late it's gonna be chaos."

"I take it Dr. T is Dr. Tambori?"

"She's by the book, *güey*."

"You expect me to believe she would punish students for the *driver's* mistake?"

"Yeah. 'Late is late,' is what she says. Life lesson or some nonsense. But honestly, your real problem is if you're late, you're fired. Last year, we had a driver who was late on his first day—never saw him again. So really, *güey*, without my help, you're done—sucks to be you," he said, threading his hands behind his head and leaning back against the seat.

He was right—it did suck to be me. I didn't know if I was more afraid of being fired or the chaos. "OK, OK, ten—final offer."

"Fifteen."

"You win—twelve. Now can you come up here?"

"Let's see it," said Gonzalo, still sitting.

I grabbed three bucks out of my wallet and nine more from my socks, while Gonzalo made his way toward me. My time on the street taught me to keep a few bucks in my wallet and to spread the rest around. Muggers never checked your socks. They'll steal your shoes, but they won't check your socks. I handed him the roster along with twelve singles. Gonzalo sat in the seat behind me, beaming.

"What are you cheesing about?"

"Never made any money off a bus driver."

"I'm gonna take it back, we don't get there before 8:04."

Gonzalo flashed me the OK sign with his fingers, which meant *fuck you*, but he was good to his word. We circled back to grab the two kids we missed, who both entered the bus and sat in the back without saying a word, then made our way toward La Brea. It was now 6:53. "Any of these kids we're picking up dangerous?" I asked.

"Hell, yeah," he said, chuckling.

"Steal your wallet dangerous? Or weapons of mass destruction dangerous?"

"Some fucked dudes go to this school. We got antisocials, bipolars, psychotics, avoidant personalities. We got kids who've attacked cops, teachers, and more than a few drivers. You gotta always watch your back. Your next pickup, Donnie, super cracked—bipolar with psychosis. His place is on your left up there," he said, pointing to a dilapidated Victorian, which needed a new roof. "Donnie's mother cooked crystal before she was sent up. Made Donnie hide it in his locker."

"He was selling it?"

"His brother was, used to deal from Donnie's locker, so when the shit went down, Donnie gets busted, and his brother gets off clean. Oh shit, you better open that door, *güey*, no joke."

A blond kid with a big head on a tall skinny body that made him look like a lollipop hauled ass down his driveway toward the bus, not slowing one iota as he approached. I reached for the handle, but it jammed. "Shit." I shook it, but the door wouldn't open as Donnie picked up speed.

"Open the door, *güey*!"

He was going to smack right into the door. Fuck it! I punched the lever, and it sprang open just as Donnie's foot hit the first step.

"Jesus, kid. You're lucky I got that door open."

"You're the new driver?" he asked, his eyes wide and his narrow shoulders hunched forward as if bracing to be hit.

"Nothing gets by you, Donnie," said Gonzalo. "Yo, driver, it's a left at the light."

"Did you do your group-therapy assignment?" Donnie asked, sitting beside Gonzalo, and taking some papers out of his backpack.

"Hell no. If Dr. T thinks I'm going to write down a memory I'm afraid to share, and then turn it in to *her*, she's high."

"After *she* reads it, you have to share it with at least one person from group—*at least* one."

"Yeah, well I ain't sharing shit that happened to me."

"It's due today," Donnie said, waving his papers in front of Gonzalo's nose.

"What you write about?" asked Gonzalo.

"I don't want to talk about it," said Donnie.

"Then stop waving it in front of my face," said Gonzalo.

"Dr. T said we don't have to share it with anybody from group until we are ready, and I'm not ready, and you can't make me talk about it if I don't want to."

"You're cracked, Donnie. I swear to God."

"Shouldn't use God's name in vain," said Donnie. I glanced at him in my rearview as he turned to the window with finality. "Besides, I was just saying."

Gonzalo took us down streets I didn't know existed. I wasn't sure he was saving us time, but he kept us moving, and I didn't think my nerves could have handled standstill traffic.

The next kid Gonzalo thought worth mentioning was Otis Washington. "Right up there by the Volvo, see that kid," said Gonzalo, pointing to a six-foot, three hundred pounder, who looked thirty-five with the same iconic fro Dr. J sported in the '70s, lumbering toward us. My copilot informed me Otis was bipolar with psychotic features and was arrested for breaking a guy's legs by throwing him off a bridge onto the dried-up concrete of the LA River. He was the most dangerous kid in the school.

"Hey look. I'm just the driver. You don't gotta tell me all this," I said, opening the door.

"I like the look on your face when I do," he said, shrugging. I made a mental note to control my face around this "population," as Dr. T would say.

A sturdy-looking woman in her sixties hurried down the driveway, carrying a paper bag lunch. "Otis, Otis, you forgot your sandwich and pretzels." Otis stopped but didn't turn around, looked straight ahead at me, while the woman, who I guessed was his grandma, placed the lunch in his hands.

"That's his foster," said Gonzalo. "His bio mom raised him in an abandoned warehouse downtown before she got sent up for Mexican tar."

There was something about the way Otis moved that felt like a jack-in-the-box about to spring as he entered the bus and cleared his throat, which sounded like a grunt. He then lumbered to the last seat, where one of the kids I originally missed happened to be sitting. There were some words exchanged before Otis grabbed the kid and threw him into the aisle and took his seat, then looked at me to see what I was going to do—which was nothing, failing my first test. Our eyes met in the rearview, but I didn't have time to start anything now. Besides, the kid sat in another seat; the whole thing seemed to work itself out.

"I remembered that today would be Otis's third late," whispered Gonzalo. "He's gonna lose his mind if you don't get him there on time, *güey*."

"Drive!" screamed Otis.

It was 7:18 and anxiety slithered its nasty tentacles up and down my neck as I put the bus in gear. "All right, there's another fin in it for you if you get us there on time."

"All right, my friend," he said, shuffling in his seat, "you upgraded to the premium directions."

Gonzalo became all business. He pointed and I followed, and we picked up eight more kids in record time. We still had one stop left, and we were looking at getting to school, according to Gonzalo's calculations, somewhere between 8:02 and 8:09. This meant a good chance first period was going to start without my busload of kids, which meant I would have to explain to Dr. Tambori I was too stupid to read a roster. It also meant I would most likely be murdered by a student on my first day.

As we pulled up to the last stop, I spotted an altitudinous Black kid in b-ball shorts, a six-foot-five beanpole with self-inflicted cuts up and down his arms and legs standing in front of a run-down apartment complex. The scabs were in various sizes and patterns, but he seemed to favor the shape of an *x*. I was never a cutter, I knew a few, but they all kept their scars covered. His were on display.

"That's Toby," said Gonzalo. "Borderline personality disorder with suicidal ideation. Put two cops in the hospital during a manic. They stopped him for being Black and crazier than shit in the bougiest part of Hancock Park."

By the mailboxes stood what looked like this kid's mother. She was still in her slippers and robe sucking on a cigarette, which bounced on her lips as she read from the *Enquirer*.

"See ya, Momma," he said, rubbing his bald head before stepping onto the bus.

"What?" she said, continuing to read the magazine that had a giant-sized slug and spaceship on its cover.

"I said, I'll see ya is all."

She kept reading, blowing a stream of smoke, some of which entered the bus with Toby as he walked by me as if I didn't exist. Gonzalo directed me to leave the neighborhood almost the way I came in.

"Yo, what up, G?" he said to Gonzalo, as the two performed an impressive handshake. I almost hit a mailbox watching it in my rearview mirror.

"Hi, Toby," said Donnie.

Toby patted Donnie on the head, mussing his hair as he sat behind him. "Yo, what up, little man?"

"Did you finish your assignment for group?" asked Donnie.

"Hell yeah. I ain't trying to have Dr. T come back on me."

"We don't have to share them until we're ready," said Donnie. "I might share mine with you, Toby, but not today because I'm afraid. OK?"

"Me, too, believe that. I wrote about my baby bro, and you know I don't talk about him *ever*," he said, kissing a silver bracelet on his wrist and pointing to the sky.

"Gonzalo didn't do his," Donnie stage whispered.

"I'm not trying to share something personal with Dr. T or *any*body. It's the stupidest assignment she's ever given us, drop it!" shouted Gonzalo.

"I can totally talk about it if I want to," said Donnie.

"You can, buddy," said Toby. "You talk all you want, for real. Besides, Dr. T's gonna make G do it."

Gonzalo shook his head. "I ain't turning anything in," he said to himself.

"Come on, G," I said, pulling up to a stop sign. "We got eight minutes to get to Friedman. Which way do I go?"

"Chill," he said. "It's a left at the next light."

"Do you mind if I call you G, Gonzalo?"

"I'm as G as can be," he said, cheesing.

I put the bus in gear, and we were off, and man, everything just clicked. Every light was green, and Gonzalo and I were in sync, and we pulled into the parking lot at 7:59 in the a.m. where the security guard, the Mountain from the Hello Kitty incident, was waiting for us.

The students got off, except G, who hung back, tossing some crumpled paper in the trash can mounted to the floor by my feet, waiting for the fin I promised him. Good to my word, I slipped him his well-earned cash. He winked at me before slinging his backpack over his shoulder and leaping down the two stairs past the security guard.

The guard stepped onto the bus. "Name's Tyrone. How was your first run?"

"Stressful as hell—Gonzalo told me about being late to Dr. Tambori's class."

"What did he tell you?"

"That she locked her door at 8:05 and any kid that wasn't there got detention."

"That boy's full of it." He shook his head, smiling.

"What?"

"First off, none of the teachers lock their doors. And second, the doctor would never give somebody detention for being late. Kids are late all the time at this school."

"What about being kicked out for being late three times?"

"Boy played you good."

I looked through the windshield as Gonzalo gave me the finger before entering the school.

"Don't worry about him. Pull your bus around back and get it cleaned up. You represent the school now. Bus has got to shine."

# FOUR

I pulled my cheese box around back to where another driver was throwing garbage in a dumpster. After he was finished, he began to unravel a hose. I parked my bus, and I started to gather up trash from the aisle and seats. It was amazing how much garbage these kids generated in such a short time. There were a couple Red Bull cans under one seat, an Egg McMuffin wrapper under another, and a half-eaten Twinkie on the floor in the aisle. I was about to toss everything in the trash, when I spotted the crumpled papers Gonzalo had tossed in. Curiosity got the better of me, and I pulled them out.

On the top page was printed: **STORY I AM AFRAID TO SHARE BY DONNIE HELLER.** I sat in the driver's seat and straightened them across my lap. The front page had ketchup stains and smelled like maple syrup. The writing was half script and half printed letters with whole sections crossed out and rewritten. Of course, I should've run right in and handed the pages to Donnie but once I started reading, I couldn't stop. I just couldn't.

## DONNIE'S ASSIGNMENT

The personal memory that I am afraid to share is when the girl I am in love with realized she hated me. It was the worst day of my life.

First, I have to tell you about the best day of my life so that you can understand the worst day of my life. The best day of my life happened at bible study after school. Jessica was sitting right next to me in the pew listening to the pastor, who was standing up front. He was talking about how we had a war going on inside us. That both Jesus and the devil were trying to get into us.

Jessica whispered that she had heard the pastor give this exact speech about a quadrillion times. She then crossed her eyes, making fun of the pastor. It was funny. I mean it was the funniest thing I have ever seen in my WHOLE life. I put my hand in front of my mouth because I couldn't stop laughing and I didn't want to get in trouble. Everybody wanted to be Jessica's friend. She was popular. I really sucked at having friends and stuff because kids called me the general of the short bus brigade.

The Sunday after the best day of my life is the day I don't like to talk about. Except now I have to because of this assignment. My mom and I went to church like we always did before my mom had to go to jail for dealing drugs. We were sitting in the back, and Jessica, her sister, and her grandma were sitting in the row in front of us.

It was hot inside, and Jessica reached back and lifted her hair off her neck and fanned herself with her other hand. I imagined what it would feel like to touch her skin. I wondered if it would feel like normal skin or if it would feel better, like softer maybe. Then I wondered what it would be like to kiss Jessica. Right when I was thinking all that, Jessica turned around and smiled at me and then crossed her eyes like she did at bible study. She really is the funniest, most beautiful person I have ever met in my whole life. She could totally have her own YouTube channel. I would definitely watch it all of the time. Her grandma made her face back front toward the priest.

Then suddenly, my left hand started to itch like crazy. I scratched and scratched but I couldn't stop the feeling. I tried sitting on my hand, even slapping it with my other hand, but the feeling grew into an angry butterfly flapping inside my hand.

Oh yeah, I forgot to tell you about the devil's angel. For the whole week before this, I kept seeing one of the devil's angels in my bedroom. He looked like a small devil with wings like a bat. He would buzz around my computer and my closet and hover right over my face when I tried to sleep. He had the reddest eyes I've ever seen in my whole life. I know now that the devil's angel wasn't real, but at the time I thought that he was.

My mom asked if I was OK. But I couldn't hear her because it sounded like a bunch of people were whispering in my head, which happens sometimes. Anyway, the itching was like a thousand times worse than when I had poison ivy all over my body. I nodded that I was OK so my mom would stop asking me if I was OK. It would be embarrassing if Jessica saw my mother asking me if I was OK like I was a little kid.

That's when I realized that the devil's angel had somehow gotten into my hand. It was obvious. At the time, I thought it must have gotten in through my fingers when I was sleeping. Now, its wings were flapping so fast that it burned. It was like fire spread up my shoulder and to my left ear. I pushed my fingers into my ear, but I couldn't reach him.

Finally, I couldn't take it. *I have a fallen angel inside me,* I whispered to my mom. *He's hurting me. Really, really hurting me, and his wings are so loud. He's going to kill me from inside my head,* I said.

Mom looked at me like what the heck was I even talking about. Jessica turned around again, and I wanted to make a funny face like when she crossed her eyes at me, but I was in too much pain. So much pain that I screamed! Jessica pulled back and stared at me like I was a TOTAL freak. I knew right then that she hated me.

I had to get the devil out of my head. I picked up a bible and hit myself on the side of my head, thinking maybe I could knock him out through my ear. *Mom, help. Please. He's right at my ear!* I kept hitting my head with the book over and over and over until a man jumped on me and pinned my arms to the floor, which also hurt.

I could feel its wings beating against my actual brain. I really could. My mom yelled for someone to call an ambulance, while I was shouting, *The devil is killing me! His wings are destroying my brain!*

The tiny devil was officially freaking out. He was SLAMMING against my skull like a scared bird. It hurt so bad. I banged the back of my head on the floor, trying to like crack it open to free the devil. I remember Jessica watching me with her hands over her mouth like I was such a disgusting freak. She hated me. It really was the worst day in my life. The reason I am so scared to share this memory is in case whoever reads this decides to hate me too. Please don't. That's all I remember. I might remember more, but not now.

• • •

I read Donnie's assignment straight through without looking up, without taking a breath.

I'll never forget my pops and I finding my mom in the park by our house in full conversation with some squirrels. I was seven years old. She was sitting cross-legged on the grass giggling as if one of her furry new friends had said the funniest thing. Hoopers on the nearby court gaped at her through the chain-link, while a young woman scooped up her kid and hurried out of the park like my mom was dangerous. An ambulance pulled up and a paramedic rushed over to my poor mother, who began to scream, a scream I still hear in my dreams and during those dark times when I am too afraid to move. It sounded as though she were howling in pain, like she was being mauled by something invisible. It was a scream like the one I imagined Donnie let out as his winged devil *slammed* against his skull.

Even though the episode only lasted a few hours, my mother was forever changed, like she lost a part of herself in the park that day. She smiled less, laughed less. She began to chain-smoke all night, to sit on our porch or in the kitchen in the dark while my father and I slept. And there were more breaks after that, each one stealing another piece of her, of the light, fun mom she had been.

Donnie was young. No kid should have to walk around afraid of devils invading his head. Looking up from the pages, I saw Donnie's blond hair through the bus-door window. He stood there as if willing it to open. I tried to collect my thoughts and put on a poker face like I hadn't read the papers in my hands. I shouldn't have read his assignment. Here he was, terrified to share such an intimate memory with people he knew, let alone somebody he'd just met.

Opening the door, I handed the pages to him. "They were in the garbage," I said, pointing to the can by my feet like this explained everything.

He nodded, examining me before turning and running back to the school, the pages held tight against his chest as though he could once again keep his story private.

# FIVE

For the rest of the week, I studied my route and memorized the roster, did my pickups, my drop-offs, listened to my pops go on and on about how his team now was the best he's had, about how the record was in the bag, and I slept about fourteen hours a day and still dragged ass.

The only incident I had on my bus the first week was handled by one of the students. Donnie had a panic attack and ran up and down the aisle obsessively touching each seat, agitating each student he passed. The more the students protested, the more frantic Donnie became, hyperventilating, his breaths sounding somewhere between coughing and choking. I couldn't find a spot to pull over, so I just kept repeating, "Sit down, Donnie, sit down," which was like throwing dry leaves on a brush fire to put it out. Finally, I spotted an empty curb to pull over when Toby yanked Donnie into the seat beside him. "Yo, look me in the eyes, Donnie. Don't look away. Focus on me, my eyes, for real." Donnie tried but couldn't seem to manage it, so Toby took his head in his large hands and forced Donnie to lock eyes until he calmed, then he put his arm around Donnie and the two remained that way for the rest of the trip. Toby was so much bigger than Donnie that it looked like a father helping his son. I wished I didn't have to drive to watch this show of love, the kind of love I wished I had in my life. My pops could take a chapter out of Toby's book.

I expected to feel lighter not having to worry about a place to live or money, but I didn't. I wasn't sure if it was living with my father, having to drive a bus, or the type of kids I had to drive, but a feeling of impending doom sat on me, and I was afraid the weight would become unbearable.

With my Friday afternoon drop-offs completed, I drove downtown to find the only person who could help me when I felt this unhinged. Alvarito and I met the first night I spent on the street. He saw I was scared and took me to McDonalds, where we drank coffee until morning. He was forty but the ten years on the street made him look older. The skin on his cheeks sagged and his wild eyebrows reached up his forehead in every direction, causing his face to look as though it was trying to escape itself. He had traversed hell and appeared with an understanding of life I didn't possess. When I felt hopeless, I would go to him and he would tell me stories about Guadalajara or, more recently, from his time as a laborer here in LA.

I drove to Winston Street, where he'd been staying, but he wasn't there. He sometimes hit the skids under a bridge by Walt Disney Concert Hall. I headed there, desperate to see his gummy smile. From my school bus, I scouted the little Calcutta of shopping carts, tarps, tents, ratty suitcases, bicycles, and cardboard boxes for my friend, spotting somebody familiar sitting on a camping chair holding court.

"Yo, Ace, how are you?" I called out of the window.

Ace was somewhere between fifty and sixty, from the Midwest. He came to town to be an actor, even landed a small gig on the original *90210*, but ended up on the skids. He was sober, as honest as you can be living on the streets, and a friend of Alvarito's. Ace had two guitars and Alvarito knew how to strum a few tunes, and the two of them would wail their stories of heartache to the sounds of sirens, shouting, and the occasional gun shot. A few blocks away, the pros played their concerts at Disney Hall.

"Who is that? Oh shit, Wag, is that you? Damn, Wag got himself a school bus!"

Ace gave everyone in the encampment street names. I was Wag because I was always making people laugh. I think it had something to do with the wagging of a dog's tail, but I never got a straight answer.

"I'm looking for Snapper," I said, using Alvarito's street name.

"Saw old Snap couple days ago. I said hello and he spat at me. I mean, I call him Snapper 'cause of his short fuse, but I'd never seen him this angry."

"Where was he?"

"All the way by Eighteenth and Hope. Ever since everybody and his brother's been moving downtown, us bums are getting shoved to the outskirts of the city. Hell, they'll keep pushing us until we're living in the burbs." This line got some chuckles from a few of his cronies.

"Thanks, Ace. You need anything?"

"I need a damn school bus is what I need."

"You want to drive kids to school?"

"I don't want to drive kids. I want to sleep in it."

"Are you sure? I could put in a good word, get you all set up with a job—401K?"

He stage laughed for the camp. "See, that's why I named you Wag. Always saying the craziest things."

A woman stepped out of a tent cradling a small, white dog carcass. "Who's a good *girl*?" she said, petting the dead animal. "Who's a good *girl*? Are you a good girl?"

The gathered dispersed, except for Ace, who turned toward the woman. "Jada, what do you say you and I go walk Peanut together."

If you had a predisposition toward mental instability, you needed to keep a roof over your head, because crazy just flew out of people living on the street.

"Are you ready for a walk, Peanut?" said Jada. "Are you, girl?"

"Let me help, Ace," I said, turning the bus off.

He waved me off. "It's better if it's just she and I. I already dug the hole. And tell Snapper to come by. We miss him here."

I thanked Ace and drove on, but I couldn't stop thinking about poor Jada. I felt somehow contaminated by her break with reality, as if I were next.

I needed to find Alvarito. Now.

I continued driving until I saw the Hippie Kitchen van by Hope Street. I spotted Cat, a former nun who fed the homeless, keeping hundreds of the city's forgotten alive, and pulled up beside her and asked if she saw Snapper. She said she hadn't seen him in two days.

The sounds of a couple mutts snarling and barking caused me to turn around in my seat. About fifty yards ahead in an empty parking lot, a reedy guy with gray hair pushing out from under a fishing cap was shouting, "Get away! Shoo!" and kicking at some dogs. There were always stray dogs and cats around the homeless encampments. They gave freely of their souls to anybody who would love them.

"What's with that guy over there?" I asked Cat, turning back around.

Cat shrugged. She was busy. The line by her van was growing.

I parked and headed to the abandoned lot to see what was what and saw he was kicking at two mangy, snarling pit bulls. "Get away from him, mongrels!" he shouted. "Get away or I'll take a bite of your ass, show you how you like it." One of the dogs bit at the man's shirtsleeve, so I busted over to help, clapping my hands and shouting my head off until the dog released the guy and turned his attention on me—not one of my smartest decisions.

"Get!" I yelled to the dogs. "Get going!"

"They were eating him. Fucking dogs," said the guy in the fishing hat, following my lead by clapping his hands and shouting. "You're the only one come to help me. Nobody wanted to lose their place in line."

I picked up a Coke bottle and threw it between the dogs, the breaking glass causing them to scatter about fifteen feet. They glanced back at us with wolf eyes, as if their own time on the streets had reverted them to their origins. I screamed, "Get! Get!" putting my hands over my head to make myself bigger—something I saw on Animal Planet you were supposed to do with mountain lions. It worked. The mutts slunk off and took to biting each other.

I saw spots of blood on the fisherman's hand. "You got bit?"

"Yeah," he said, wiggling his fingers. "One of those mutts got me pretty good. I think I got a piece of him too. Kicked him right in the snout."

"You should go to the E.R.; dog could have rabies."

"I probably gave rabies to the dog. Anyway, I'm doing better than that guy," he said, pointing to a man lying face down on the buckled pavement, a trail of blood beyond him.

I thought I recognized the soiled and stained Lakers hoodie, but this was LA and many people had them. I squatted down and turned the poor guy over. Half of his face was missing, his jawbone pushing through ripped flesh. Even with his cheek missing, I recognized the wide-opened, milky eyes—it was Alvarito, or what was left of him. I turned and vomited.

"I told an officer a few hours ago, but nobody came yet. I'm just staying with him for there to be something left of him to bury. If nobody picks him up by tonight, rats will finish him off. I'd rather fight off some dogs than rats."

I knelt on the pavement beside Alvarito and touched his chin, looking into his eyes. "What happened to him?"

"Got me. I came here, he was already gone."

I wondered if my friend had a heart attack. The homeless were always dying of heart attacks, the street having more than one way to break your heart. But Alvarito was healthy. Or was he? Why had he spit at Ace? I reached for his hand and saw dark, almost purple blood on his shirt cuff. Turning over his hand, I saw a ragged gash in his wrist. By his elbow sat a shard of bloody glass. My best friend, my mentor, my savior, had checked himself out.

"Alvaro," I said, feeling a retch burrowing up my chest.

"You knew him?"

"His name was Alvaro Martinez," I said, wiping my eyes and mouth. "He was a dentist in Guadalajara. He came here to settle and then send for his family. Only by the time he did, his wife had met somebody else."

"That's a bad hand. No wonder he's in the streets."

Why had my friend lost hope? *He* was the one who had it together. Only a month ago when I was sick, *he* took care of *me*. I felt a wave of loneliness, and it occurred to me why I had really come downtown to see Alvarito. When I was with my old man, I experienced the most painful kind of loneliness, one you only felt when trying to connect with somebody who kept you at a distance. It wasn't only Alvarito's stories I had driven downtown for. I craved the company of someone who *wanted* to tell me his stories, who wanted to teach me how to cope, who appreciated me. Reckless, unstoppable tears burst from my eyes.

The gray-haired guy stood and watched me.

"I love you, buddy," I sobbed.

"Well, he's gonna get his ass eaten if we don't get him some-where," he said, looking at my parked bus.

I choked, tasting my own bile. I took a deep breath, trying to grab hold of my sobbing.

"You OK there, buddy?" the gray-haired man asked.

"Yeah. I'm not crying, just got something in my eye."

A laugh bloated with grief exploded out of my new friend. I was always making them laugh.

• • •

The guy in the fisherman hat was named Burton, and he helped me load Alvarito onto my school bus, and we took him to the city morgue because I didn't have money for a proper burial.

Trying not to look at his exposed jawbone, I lifted my buddy from under the arms. Burton took his feet and we walked him inside, where an attendant came out from the back with a gurney, and where over his shoulder I could see into the back room, the rows of the bagged-and-tagged.

"What's gonna happen to him?" I asked.

"We hold him for a month, then if nobody claims the body, we send him out, and he gets cremated," he said, helping us get Alvarito onto the gurney.

I didn't know if Alvarito wanted to be cremated or buried or what. My guess was he didn't put a lot of attention on the question.

"Hold off," I said to the attendant. I stood over Alvarito, and Burton took off his fishing hat. I thought about what to say for my friend, but I couldn't think of anything profound. "I wouldn't have made it through my time on the street without you. You took pity on me, showed me the kitchens, where to bed down. Remember my first night? I was too terrified to sleep. We drank coffee until morning, and we learned more about each other than most brothers ever do. I mean, who am I gonna see when I'm lost and lonely? Who's gonna make me feel right? I'm sorry your wife left you, Alvarito. I'm sorry you had to live with that kind of hurt your last years. I hope you found some peace, my friend."

Burton placed his hat back on his head, shook my hand, and walked out the door. I thought to ask if he needed a ride somewhere, but my knees buckled, forcing me to the floor.

"Hey, I can't have you doing that here," said the attendant.

"I just need a second," I said, rolling from my knees to a sitting position.

The attendant reached for my hands and hoisted me to a standing position. "I'm used to lifting dead weight," he said.

"How long you been waiting to use that one?"

"About a year."

# SIX

**It was two in the afternoon, and I was still in bed,** having been assaulted by nightmares for fifteen hours. I'd spring to a sitting position, images of Alvarito's torn face begging me for help, or the dogs fighting over his cheekbone. Once awake, I'd relive turning over my friend's hand, seeing his torn wrist.

I got up to pee and became frightened to get back in bed. Of course, it was an irrational fear, but I couldn't convince myself I wouldn't die if I got back into that bed. My father was traveling with his team for the weekend. I turned on the TV hoping for distraction, but I couldn't stop picturing my own death. I pictured myself decaying in the soil, bugs eating my eyes. I needed to get out of the house and see if the sunlight could save me.

I dragged my thousand-pound body toward the door. If I couldn't pull myself together now, I wouldn't be able to make it to work Monday, I would lose my job, my father would kick me out of the house, and I would suffer the same fate as Alvarito. All the signs were there—the headache, the upset stomach, the back pain, the lethargy, the anger, the picturing my own death. I was slipping into the deadened silence, where the only sound was my mind insisting, *I will never know happiness again.* It was what led to the hair pulling, to the thoughts of the Dutch, and ultimately to the ward. I looked at the door handle and shook my head, picturing my friend's wrist, the ragged cut, and I forced myself to stand.

• • •

I didn't know where I was going, only that I needed to keep my feet moving. One of my friends, Clarence, drank Drano on his sixteenth birthday. He was the first person I knew who lost his drive to survive. I'd known others who did the Dutch since then, but I never got over Clarence's death, and I still think about him, about who he would've grown up to be.

I came upon the park where I used to play ball, the same park my father and I found my mother laughing with some squirrels. A few hacks were running up and down the court, and I stopped and looked through the chain-link to see if it was a game worth watching, when one of the players turned.

"Mikey?"

"Yeah," I said. The big guy looked to be six-four with the body of a retired football player who'd let himself go.

"No shit, is that you, Mikey?" he called out, jogging over. "Shit, man, you look like ass. You OK?"

"Gerald?"

"Fuck yeah, it's Gerald. Who do you think?" he said.

"I haven't seen you since fifty pounds ago," I said.

"Fuck you," he said, smiling, rubbing his belly. "It's been two years shithead, and this is baby weight, what we call sympathy poundage. I got myself a kid coming."

"Sympathy poundage, my ass. Looks like KFC to me."

Gerald lived down the street from me my whole life. We went to school together right up until high school, when I went to Westchester because of my father and Gerald went to Hamilton.

I congratulated Gerald, even tried to put on a smile. Gerald was having a kid, building a life, while I was trying to keep living.

"How's your old man?" asked Gerald.

"An asshole."

"Glad to see nothing's changed."

"Where you at now?" I asked. "You living at home?"

"Fuck no. I bought the Brown's place across the street from my mom. My father passed from colon cancer last year."

"Oh man, Gerald, shit, I'm sorry to hear that. Fuck," I said. Images of his father ran through my head, the age spots on his face, his booming voice echoing down Vinton Avenue yelling for Gerald to get his butt home for dinner. I didn't know how much more death I could take.

"Thanks, Mikey. It was a surprise. I'm sorry I didn't reach out. My pops really liked you."

I kept shaking my head, cramming down images of the newly dead.

"Mikey, I wanna catch up, but we're running fives, and I got fifty on the win."

"Yeah, yeah, don't sweat it." I didn't want to let Gerald go. "I'm gonna watch a few rounds, see if old age made you any smarter."

"Look, we're getting slaughtered here. Can you do your thing? Like the old days?"

I nodded, not knowing if I could focus long enough to help him. Gerald ran back to the game, while I swung around the fence and leaned against the jungle gym and watched to see if I could spot weakness on the other team. When we were kids, Gerald and I played at courts all over the city and, sometimes, depending on what part of town we were in, I'd be the only white boy and Big Gerald would vouch for me. I had an average shot, but I could set up plays like a pro. I earned respect by spoon-feeding guys easy buckets.

I watched them as I twirled my hair with my pointer finger,

absently pulling out a couple of strands as I tried to concentrate. After a few rounds, the game came into focus, and I called Gerald over. With my life such a mess, it felt good to see something clearly, like putting on glasses first thing in the morning. B-ball was always the one thing I saw precisely.

"What do you think?" said Gerald.

"You see that Snoop Dogg-lookin' dude?" I asked. I gestured with my chin to a tall, skinny guy.

"Yeah, he's killing us."

"Can't go left. Fakes it every time."

"That guy's got skills."

"When you see those limbs bob left, step to his right, he'll hand you the ball with *a gin and juice*."

"You sure?"

"With the *gin and juice*."

"All right. I'll give it a try."

Gerald trotted back onto the court and switched with the guy who was defending Snoop. Snoop sized up Gerald, tossed him the ball, and Gerald tossed it back—a check.

"I gotta baby on me now?" said Snoop.

Gerald smiled. "You better get a screen on me, 'cause I don't get crossed up."

"Which way am I gonna go?" said Snoop. "Nobody knows."

Snoop did some fancy dribbling between his legs, some more hotdog moves, then faked left and drove right into Gerald, who stole the ball and swung it out to one of his teammates. He took it coast-to-coast for an easy bucket.

"Cookies!" I screamed to Gerald, which is something said when someone stole a ball—like Cookie Monster swiping cookies. The cloud was beginning to lift, and I could feel the LA sunshine on me now. The tide turned—Gerald owned Snoop—and with every bucket Gerald and his crew made, I felt lighter. I even called out some more plays, which Gerald implemented, and when my old friend sank the final bucket, I pointed to Snoop and sang, "Beautiful, I just want you to know, you're my *favorite* girl."

It felt good to feel a little bit like my old self. After Gerald collected his money, he hugged me. I had the urge to let loose and tell him everything that was going on for me—but he pulled away, and I said nothing. I really wanted to, but I was embarrassed that things had gotten so bad. We swapped numbers, and I swore I'd come around and see him soon.

# SEVEN

**My morning pickups were silent,** the kids reflecting my somberness back at me. A few students complained of a strange smell on the bus, which was, of course, from Alvarito's chewed-up body. I thought about my friend decomposing in the back room at the city morgue, his half face staring into the whiteness of the sheet covering him. Would he still be alive if I hadn't gotten sick and gone to live with my father? Alvarito and I spent so much time together. I could've sensed if he had become too tired of the fight. I could've kept him from Hope Street.

After I dropped the kids off at Friedman, I visited a car wash and scrubbed the seat we laid my friend on until all I could smell was disinfectant. On Mondays, Wednesdays, and Fridays, my afternoon drop-offs consisted of two runs: one was my regular run and the other, two hours later, was for the b-ball team after practice, and for any other students who stuck around for counseling or to see doctors.

That afternoon, I pulled into the school and saw the kids scrimmaging four-on-three on the rim next to the building. These kids didn't have a gym, so they practiced outside, making it look more like a pickup game than practice. Not one of these kids seemed to be able to set up a play. They were all hogging the ball as their coach, whistle and all, sat on the sidelines looking at his phone.

The only one watching practice was a girl from my bus, Chey, a lanky blonde with a streak of pink in her hair and thick black eyeliner. She was sitting by a palm tree alternating between looking at her phone and rolling her eyes whenever someone made a bad pass or missed a shot. Gonzalo picked up the ball and inbounded it to some beanpole I didn't recognize, who swung it out to Otis, who missed a shot off the backboard.

"Nice shot, Le-*brick*," said Toby, who had a fresh *x* cut into his shin.

"What you say?" said Otis, lurching at Toby, but Toby was too quick and evaded him.

The coach, a stodgy-looking guy with a high and tight military crew cut, blew his whistle. "Dammit to hell, boys! Can't you run two consecutive plays? You lost your first two games to the worst teams in the league. You're *pathetic*, all of you."

Otis stopped chasing Toby, turning his attention on the coach.

Donnie screamed, "Oh no! No! God, be my fortress."

Otis lunged for the coach, flinging him to the ground and jumping on him, grabbing his throat with a monstrous hand, as the rest of the team gaped. Tyrone raced across the yard, tackling Otis and putting him in a headlock.

By this time, I was standing by Chey. "How's practice going?"

She looked up at me. "Are you a moron? I want to know."

"I've never been diagnosed, but I wouldn't be surprised."

Tyrone dragged a struggling Otis into the school, leaving the coach lying on the ground coughing and massaging his throat. I went over to him, extending my hand. "You had that coming, Coach."

"No, I certainly did not," he said, ignoring my hand, still hacking.

"You called that kid pathetic. What'd you think was gonna happen?"

"I've been coaching for twenty years, and I've never been attacked by a player. I take this job as a *favor*, and I get attacked not once, but twice."

"You call *me* pathetic, I would've put you on your back, too," I said, my hand still extended, the team watching us.

"Who are you?"

"Bus driver."

Donnie bounced the ball at the top of the key before shooting a perfect arc hitting nothing but net. Toby grabbed the ball and fed Donnie, who shot from his hip, Steph Curry-style, the ball sailing in another perfect arc toward the rim, making a perfect swish.

"Get away from me, *bus driver*," said the coach, shoving my hand away and standing before turning his attention to the team. "What are you guys looking at?"

"One sorry ass motherfucker, *güey*," said Gonzalo.

The rest of the team laughed. I must admit, I chuckled. Don't raise a question to which you don't want to know the answer.

"That's it. I've tried, but you boys are uncoachable. You're not basketball players. You don't listen. You can't follow a play. You can't pass. I'm not going to risk my life to try and teach you something."

"A little dramatic, don't you think, Coach?" I said.

Chey looked up from her phone at me. "So, I don't bet anymore, 'cause apparently it makes me psychotic, but let's say I still did. I'd bet you a yard Donnie splashes the next bucket."

"I don't bet kids as a rule, but in theory I'd take your hundo 'cause no way he drops three in a row."

Chey extended her hand, and we shook, a sort of gentlemen's bet.

"What's wrong with you? You can't bet a student!" said the coach.

"You're not the boss of me," I said, which prompted a smile from Toby, who fed Donnie the ball again at the top of the key. Splash! "Damn," I said, shaking my head. "That boy's putting on a clinic."

"Each time Donnie shoots, there's a ninety percent chance of it dropping. Odds are the same every time—three in a row or not. And so, yeah, welcome to school," said Chey.

Toby passed Donnie the ball again, only this time he rushed

him, got in his grill, waving his arms, prompting Donnie to hand him the ball.

"Odds go the other way if he's guarded," said Chey.

Dr. Tambori, all five-foot-two of her, her hair pulled painfully tight in a bun, bolted out of the school and past me over to the coach. "Are you OK? I heard what happened. Bloody awful."

"I'm done," muttered the coach, shoving stuff into a gym bag. "I've tried, but these boys aren't capable of competing in a league. They're a hazard."

"I apologize. We can of course suspend Otis from the team for his inexcusable behavior."

A balding guy in a suit, maybe fifty with kind eyes and freckled skin, exited the school and pulled the coach to the side of the court, out of the way of the game that had spontaneously resumed. I pretended to watch with both ears on the men. "John, are you OK?"

"I'm fine, Dr. Lipschitz."

"Come on, call me Paul. I heard what happened. It won't happen again. I promise."

"Paul, you told me this job would be easy and rewarding. You told me these were basically good kids with some behavioral issues. These kids have got real problems. They're dangerous, and quite frankly, it's not safe to have them play other schools."

"Look, John, I know you're upset Otis attacked you again," he said quietly, putting his hand on the coach's shoulder.

"Damn right I'm upset!"

"Otis hasn't had an easy life," said Dr. Lipschitz. "But he's making some good strides. We have to be patient with him."

"I'm used to coaching college ball, not . . . this," said the coach, shoving the doctor's hand off his shoulder.

"Can you just stay on until we find somebody?" asked Dr. Lipschitz. "Team sports are great therapy and socialization."

"You don't need a coach, you need a prison guard," he said.

"What kind of man quits coaching 'cause some kid attacked him?" I asked, having had about all I could take from this guy.

Dr. Tambori jerked her head; it's miraculous it stayed on her neck.

"What did you say to me?" asked Coach John.

"You really afraid of getting hurt by some kid?" Of course, I was afraid to get hurt by the same three hundred-pound kid, but I didn't think that pertinent to this conversation.

"Not that it's any of your business, but I tore my ACL last season, and it's still healing."

"You never coached college hoops," I said. "No way."

"Why is the bus driver still here?" asked John.

"You don't got the balls for it."

"Mr. Cannon, is there not something you should be doing right now?" asked Dr. Tambori.

"Not really. I'm just waiting to drive Chicken Liver's team home."

"I got an idea—mind your own business," said Johnnie Boy.

"You gotta kid who can shoot ninety percent from the top of the key, and you think he shouldn't be in a league? Are you serious?"

I could feel Chey standing beside me.

"You don't know anything about it," said John. "Stick to driving the bus."

"I know plenty about it," I said, not really knowing what I meant.

"Mr. Cannon, please excuse yourself," said Dr. Tambori, the muscles in her cheeks tightening.

"Hold on," said Dr. Lipschitz. "I want to hear what he has to say."

"You ever coach?" asked Coach John.

"Yeah, I was just coaching Saturday." A lie but a little tiny one.

"Really? Where?"

I could feel Chey's eyes on me. The team had stopped playing ball and moved in closer.

"Woodbine."

Toby smiled and nudged Gonzalo—these kids obviously knew the court I was referring to.

"I don't know what that is . . . a school?"

"A whole lot of teachin' goes on there, you can believe that," I said.

"Well, I've never heard of it."

"You're Andrew Cannon's son," said Dr. Lipschitz. "One of our board members asked us to hire you."

"My father's about to have the most consecutive wins in US history by a basketball coach," I said as if laying down a royal flush.

"I'm Dr. Lipschitz."

We shook hands. "That's a great name, *Lipschitz*. You part of the tribe?" I asked.

"Yes," he said, smiling. "I'm Jewish."

"My mother was Jewish."

"I went to Yeshiva University High on Pico when I was a kid. The rabbi was our basketball coach."

"My mom had her Bat Mitzvah at Wilshire Temple," I said. "Stacy Cannon. Actually, her name was Stacy Gold back then."

"Of course, right down the street from Yeshiva," he said. "Can't say I know her—Stacy Gold."

"She never went back to temple after her Bat Mitzvah."

"And what about you?" said the doctor. "Do you know basketball?"

"Better than anything else."

"And you'd like to coach these kids?"

"What?" I said, turning to the team, who was staring at us.

"I can promise you just by looking at this guy, Doctor, that he doesn't know the first thing about coaching," said John.

"How about it, Mr. Cannon, you have any desire to be our coach?" asked Dr. Lipschitz.

I wasn't a coach. I was barely holding it together. My every thought was to drop these kids off as soon as possible so I could get in bed and sleep.

"Who doesn't have the balls now?" asked John.

"Follow me, Mr. Cannon. Let's talk."

● ● ●

If importance was measured by how many square feet your office was, then the doc was an important dude. Dr. Lipschitz's office was twice the size of Dr. Tambori's with a whole wall of framed certificates and honors. The corner of the room was set up like a living room, where the doc sat across from me on a club chair and where I wiped my sweaty palms on the leather couch. Coaching was my father's business, and it took energy and focus, both of which I had in short supply. Not that coaching these kids would be the same thing he did. My father was a championship coach for an award-winning high school, and this . . . would be different.

I would've said no and put this ridiculousness behind me, but my mind kept finding its way back to Gerald in the park, how good it felt to lose myself to the game. If I could rekindle something akin to that feeling, even for a couple hours a day, then this coaching thing might save me from a darkness that could put me on a path that ended with dogs chewing off my face. On the other hand, coaching might be too overwhelming and could put me on a different path that ended with dogs chewing off my face.

"So, Mr. Cannon, pretty exciting stuff about your father, huh?" Dr. Lipschitz said, leaning forward.

I nodded. People were always excited about my father.

"How confident is he about that record?"

"My dad wipes his ass as if nobody's done it better."

"And your father taught you to coach?"

This question hit me like a gut punch. My father stopped teaching me anything when my mother died. My old man, the one who lived in my head, chimed in: *You'll never be a coach, Dingus. A coach is a leader, a winner in the game of life. What you are, son, is a choke artist.*

Of course, I knew the answer Dr. Lipschitz wanted, but it would've been too painful to lie about my old man being some kind of teacher to me. I used to sit in the stands choking down jealousy like broken glass as I watched him with his arm around some player's shoulder, teaching him the game. "Let's just say, nobody knows coaching better than my father."

"This really is so fortuitous," he said, nodding like he'd reached into his pocket and found a lost billfold. "The team is new. It began in recreational therapy five years ago. A therapist thought it would be beneficial to have the kids scrimmage the staff, and that worked so well he somehow convinced a small league to let us join. But that therapist retired and the team never took off, which is too bad because I believe team sports teach young people a lot about dealing with conflict and different types of relationships, and about having some damn fun. I don't have delusions of being a championship team—although I have to say, it would be nice to win a game."

Of course, I didn't have life skills and knew even less about having fun, but I could show them how to D-up or run a play off the stack. Besides, the doc had low expectations, which was right down my alley.

"So, Mr. Cannon, do you want to coach the Mary Friedman Alternative High School's basketball team?"

As I was about to say yes, a succession of three knocks interrupted us, followed by a piping-mad Dr. Tambori. "Paul, I know what you're thinking, but no. It won't work."

Dr. Lipschitz looked from Dr. Tambori to me, eyebrows up. "Why's that?"

"Mr. Cannon is not suitable to be the coach," she said, those green eyes slapping me into place.

"That's a serious statement," he said. "Why would you say that?"

Dr. Tambori looked at me. "Paul, can we please hold this conversation in private?"

"This is about Mr. Cannon, he should be here."

"Call me Mikey."

"Fine," she said, folding her thin, brown arms across her chest and sitting in the chair across from me.

Of course, she was right—my father was the best high school coach in the country, and my polar opposite. What this school really needed was a young version of my old man—not me. But now I wanted this—perhaps even needed it—and I wasn't about to lie down.

"No offense to Mr. Cannon, of course, but coaching these students is a difficult post, one at which many seasoned professionals have been unsuccessful," she said, her metered accent making her sound highly informed on the subject. "We've had three coaches come through here in the last two years, and they've all resigned. It's essential that whomever we hire know more than basketball. We need someone who knows this population. Also, half the team has abandonment issues, and I don't want to add to that by knowingly giving them a coach who isn't going to stick around. The person we hire needs to be, above all else, *stable*."

"Do you think Mikey unstable?"

"Mr. Cannon's track record at keeping posts has been, shall we say, less than stellar."

Dr. Lipschitz turned to me.

She made a great point. If I took this position, I would have to stick around—at least for the season. Could I really commit to that? What if I just couldn't get out of bed? I caught myself playing with my hair and pretended I had an itch before placing my hand back at my side. "I've never quit a coaching gig."

The good doctor looked back to Dr. Tambori, who blinked and bit her lower lip.

"Mr. Cannon," she started.

"Please call me Mikey."

"What kind of adult goes by *Mikey*?" she snapped.

"You can call me Dr. Cannon if it makes you feel better," I said.

"He doesn't take anything seriously. He's what we're trying to prevent these kids from becoming!"

Dr. T was no nonsense. She was a slugger, and what she said sounded true—they *were* teaching these kids to manage their illnesses to have a normal life and grow into responsible adults, i.e., avoid becoming me. "Dr. Tambori and I have a complicated relationship," I started.

"We do not. We do not have *any* relationship."

"I think we just need to get to know each other better is all. I tend to grow on people."

"Bollocks. There's nothing you can possibly tell me that would convince me you have the maturity or depth for this post. This isn't a game, Mr. Cannon."

"Of course, it's not a game. Basketball is *definitely* not a game," I said, raising my voice. I was done letting her speak to me like some schlep.

"You really have no idea what you'd be taking on, Mr. Cannon. If you did, you'd most certainly run from this opportunity."

"Like your last coach?" I asked. "Who found that gem?"

"Hiring Coach Johnson was a sound decision. He is an experienced collegiate coach."

"His name is Johnny Johnson?" I asked.

"Yes," she snarled.

"And you have a problem with my going by Mikey?"

If I didn't know any better, I'd say Dr. Lipschitz was enjoying the back-and-forth. He watched with a bemused smile.

"Please, Paul, you have to believe me. Making Mr. Cannon our coach would be disastrous."

"Given your history with Johnny Johnson, perhaps you should let somebody else choose the next coach," I countered.

"Dr. Tambori, may I ask *who* you were thinking about hiring as coach?" asked Dr. Lipschitz.

"Well . . . nobody yet."

"So, it's fair to say that Mikey here really is our only choice."

Dr. Tambori took a deep breath. "I strongly protest this."

"Your protestation has been noted," he said, turning to me. "Mikey, look, I have a lot of respect for Dr. Tambori, and if she feels this strongly that you shouldn't be our coach, then you shouldn't."

"I get it," I said. And I did.

"But we don't have another choice. We are already two games into the season. It's either you or we have to go the year without a team, and I don't want to do that. I said earlier that I thought team sports taught life skills, but it's much more than that here. Being on a team can show these kids not to give up, how to keep going in the face of adversity. You can't walk off the court if you're losing. You have to continue to play. You have to continue for your teammates and your coach and for yourself. I have seen too many students with mental illness give up when things got bad, Mikey. We have to teach them that no matter what you're dealing with, you go on." Dr. Lipschitz leaned toward me. "What do you say?"

Both sets of eyes were on me. I thought about Otis jumping Johnny Johnson. I thought about Gonzalo, and how he'd burned me on my first run and couldn't be trusted. I thought about my old man and how he would ridicule me for taking on something so far above me. But I also thought about Donnie splashing ninety percent from the top of the key. And I thought about Alvarito at the city morgue. And I wondered if being on a team could teach someone how to go on.

"Will you coach our guys, Mikey?" said Dr. Lipschitz.

"Let's give this thing a shot," I said.

Dr. Lipschitz stood and shook my hand, prompting Dr. T to huff out of the room.

# EIGHT

**That night I dreamt I was sitting on my front porch with my mother.** She was in the rocking chair she'd inherited from Grandpa Howard, which had Hebrew writing pressed into the wood, translation: *The Lord speaks to us in our affliction.* She was rocking back and forth smoking a joint. She exhaled a rush of smoke, and we both watched it dissipate. I didn't say anything for some reason, just watched her take another hit, but when she turned toward me half of her face was missing like Alvarito's.

I was still shaken by the dream when I pulled into the parking lot of the school and saw Dr. Tambori waiting for me. I'd just finished my afternoon run and was about to begin my first team practice, which I had no idea how to do, and seeing this highly intelligent, furious woman who would love nothing more than to kick my ass to the curb gave me the jumps.

"You waiting for me, Dr. T?" I asked, getting off the bus.

"Yes, I was, and please don't refer to me as Dr. T. That is reserved strictly for the students. And whatever you may think, Mr. Cannon, you are not one of the students."

"Duly noted."

She took an exasperated breath. "I wanted to inform you that, moving forward, basketball practice will be from half four to half six instead of half three to half five to allow you enough time to return to school after your drop-offs. Your second run will be made up of your players. Another driver will take home the students who had doctor's appointments. Your team's parents have been notified of this change."

"OK," I said, running my fingers through my hair, looking past her at the team scrimmaging on the court. Brian, a Filipino kid from my bus with shoulder-length, shaggy hair that covered his face like a mask, was dancing by the foul line, sprinting in place as he did the Running Man. Gonzalo gave a head fake and popped a jumper, but Brian stopped dancing long enough to hack him in the arm, the ball smacking Donnie in the head.

"Sorry," said Donnie. "Sorry, sorry, sorry."

"Donnie, stop apologizing!" screamed Toby. "For real!"

"Sorry."

How did my pops begin his practice? My mind was jangled, and I just couldn't remember. Maybe I should watch them scrimmage to see each player's strengths? Yeah. That sounded good. I could take notes. Of course, I would need something to write on. I turned to Dr. T. "Do you have a notebook I can borrow?"

"Mr. Cannon, did you even hear what I said?" she snapped.

"Of course. You said something about changing something. Um . . . I also need a . . ." I couldn't remember the word for pen. To make matters worse, I begin to write in the air as if on an invisible chalkboard.

"OK, Mr. Cannon, I'll retrieve you a notebook and *pen*, but for now let's introduce you to your team," she said, leading me to the court, past Chey, who was kicking it on the grass watching practice. "Are you sure you can handle this?"

"Hells to the no. I'm not sure of a thing."

She stopped walking ten feet from the court and turned to me with eyes that raised my self-doubt to toxic levels. "Before I introduce you as coach, I need to know you're going to give this endeavor the seriousness it deserves. If you're not going to *try* here, then I have no problem finding another coach."

"What is it about me you hate the most?" I asked.

"I'm not in the sodding mood, mate."

"Look, Doc, I'm gonna give it my all here, and we'll see how it plays out. OK?"

"You want to know what I don't like about you?"

"I've changed my mind. I don't want to know."

"It's that you're not right for the job of driver and certainly not right for the position of coach, but because of your father and *his* accomplishments and connections, you're now both. I deplore nepotism. It's the absolute retardation of progress."

"No. That can't be it. Is it my ears? Are you saying I have big ears? 'Cause that's mean." CM, my coping mechanism, tried to protect me, but Dr. T calling me out for riding my father's coattails stung more than she could have realized.

She started up again toward the court. I followed.

"OK, please gather around, boys," she called out to the team, who stopped play and straightened up. "I have some bad news."

I looked at her like, *what the hell, dude?*

"I'm sorry to say that Coach Johnson has informed us that he has a personal matter to attend to and won't be able to serve as your coach for the remainder of the season."

"Surgeon giving him a new set of balls?" asked Gonzalo.

I laughed, couldn't help it. The kid had a nice delivery. Dr. T shot me a look, and I apologized.

"Gonzalo, please pop by my office for a chat tomorrow morning before class."

"Fuck," muttered G.

"Mr. Cannon has graciously agreed to fill in as your coach."

"For real? The bus driver?" asked Toby, his voice finding an impossible soprano as if this was a dastardly joke. "That's happening?"

A tall kid I didn't recognize snatched up his gym bag. "Fuck this. I'm up outta here."

A shorter kid followed suit. "Me, too. I quit."

Dr. T said, "Of course that's your choice, boys, but Mr. Cannon does know about the game of basketball. I ask that you give him a chance."

The tall kid gave me the once over. "He's not a coach. He's a joke."

Kid had me dead to rights. Took him two seconds to sum up my whole life. As the two boys stormed off, Otis whipped the ball at me, hitting my shoulder.

"Good pass, big man. My bad."

Dr. T extracted a radio from her jacket pocket. "Tyrone, please run Otis."

Tyrone appeared at the school's door. "Otis, you and I gotta date with two miles."

Otis shook his head and began to jog. He knew the drill.

Toby clapped the ball between his hands. "Dr. T, come on now, you can't be serious. The bus driver, for real? I was hoping to win *one* game this year. I was looking forward to that shit."

"I know how you feel, Toby. Believe me, I do. But please give him a chance? Please."

"Fine," said Toby, rubbing a scab in the form of an *x* on his arm. "For you, Dr. T, against my better judgment."

"Right then, let's see what you can do, Coach, and I'll go retrieve that notebook," said Dr. T, heading back to the school.

I looked down to Chey, who blew a purple streak of hair out of her eyes and studied me.

"I think she likes me," I said.

"She totally beyond hates your guts."

"Thin line."

There were four kids on the court, all from my bus: Toby, G, Donnie, and Brian. With Otis, we had five, which was technically enough to play ball. But with only five, the players would have to run the whole game without subs, which would be exhausting, and if a player fouled out we would have to run four against five or forfeit. We needed at least one more player. I turned to the kids who quit, who were walking away, gym bags in hand. "Yo, guys, give me a week? If you still think I'm a joke, you can quit then."

The taller one flipped me the bird.

"Well I guess five is technically enough."

"Technically," said Chey.

"OK, team," I said in a voice I hoped was authoritative. "Let's continue to shoot around, I guess, to see your game."

"My pops plays pro ball in Germany, *güey*, if you need any pointers, I'm your man," said G.

"Thanks, G," I said, rolling my eyes, fairly sure he was kidding me.

"He does," said G. "Right, guys?"

Donnie nodded, and Brian busted out a body wave, rolling his head, neck and ass.

"I'm not lying here," said G. "Truthfully, he's out of the country now, but he comes back once a month. Coach Johnson didn't want any help, but my dad offered."

"OK. How would your father start practice?" I asked G.

"Fuck if I know."

"Thanks for the help, G. Can you at least tell me where we play our actual games?"

"We practice here and play at other schools," said G, who bricked a shot off the rim.

"One of the many problems," said Chey. "You can't win when you got no home court and no fans. Home teams win 61.7 percent of the time in hoops, and the average they win by is 3.62 points. It's like you got the psychological support of the crowd, refs siding with the home team, and the peculiarities of the court. I made more cheddar on that info when I had my book than anything else. People don't get the importance."

"Your *book*?"

"I was tagged for bookmaking and running a gambling house from Foot Locker at the Beverly Center."

This girl was a genius. "You go to the games?" I asked Chey.

"Yeah . . . no. I'm not even allowed to watch sports on my phone. Dr. T thinks it would set me off."

"That sucks, I can't imagine not watching hoops." I clapped my hand over my mouth. "Sorry, I didn't mean to say that."

"I can't even with you right now," said Chey.

"Thing is, I could use your help. You know the guys, the game."

"You want to know your chances of winning a game this year?"

"Zero?"

"Zero. Besides, read my file. I'm a loner, don't like going in for team stuff."

I twirled my hair in my fingers, and as I was doing so, I noticed Brian doing the same thing with his thick black hair. I wondered if he ever pulled any out, if he was a brother in trichotillomania. I didn't see any bald spots. I was hopeful his was only a nervous habit. I had no idea where to start. Donnie dribbled the ball and was about to shoot, when G got in his face and blocked the shot, screaming, "Not in *my* house, *cabrón*!"

"First thing I'd do is get a fifth guy," said Chey.

I looked at the court to double-check my math—there were four on the court, plus Otis. "Otis is gonna play, right?"

"Oh yeah, Otis'll play. It's Donnie you got to worry about. For the last three years, Donnie has quit the team before the third game, which is tomorrow. He's about to skirt right now. Look at him."

Donnie was muttering to himself, "Nope, nope, nope, nope."

"You OK, Donnie?" I asked.

"No!" screamed Donnie. "I quit. I definitely quit. I'm sorry. I can't take people screaming at me all the time."

"G!" screamed Toby. "What is wrong with you, for real? You know you can't scream at Donnie."

"It's not my fault," yelled G. "He quits every year!"

"Come on, Donnie, we can't run with four," said Brian, twirling his hair between his fingers before raking it out of his eyes. "We straight need you, bruh."

Donnie shook his head. "You guys can't make me play. I quit. I definitely quit." He sprinted away from the court to the parking lot, as I watched in disbelief.

"Should I go get him or something?" I asked Chey, who seemed to be the expert on . . . everything.

"He's done," she said. "Your season lasted about two minutes. Nice job, Coach."

"I'll talk to him," I said. "You guys . . . keep doing what you're doing."

"He's not gonna play," said Toby, rubbing his bald dome. "Why can't one thing ever go right?"

*I feel you, kid. I really feel you.*

●  ●  ●

I followed the crying to my bus, where Donnie was sitting against the front tire, his head tucked between his lanky knees. My first few minutes as coach and half the team quits. I wanted to cry, too, to just say forget it and bawl like my little friend here, but these kids needed this team as much as I did, and there was no way I was going to tell them the season was over because of me.

"Donnie, how you doing there?"

Donnie wouldn't look up, just kept bawling, his face still hidden between his knees.

"You got one excellent shot, kid. I mean the best I've ever seen."

Donnie's waterworks downgraded to a sniffle. He was listening.

"I don't know anything about most things, but I promise you, Donnie, if you can shoot in a game like you do on the rim over there, we'll win one this year."

Using his fingers, Donnie counted to five. He then repeated the count on his other hand.

"What are you counting, buddy?"

"Nothing."

"You look like you're counting something."

"No, I'm not."

"Look, if you want to tell me to mind my own business, go ahead. But don't lie to me. I get enough of that from Gonzalo."

"*The Lord detests lying lips.*"

"Hell, yeah, She does."

He looked up.

"I read your assignment, Donnie. I shouldn't have, but I did. It was a stupid thing to do, and I hate myself for doing it."

"Gonzalo stole it out of my bag," he said, looking at me.

"I'm really sorry I read it without your permission."

He blinked his eyes at me.

"It must've been scary what happened to you."

Donnie nodded. "It was. It was scary."

"I'm sorry you had to go through that, Donnie."

Donnie looked back at his hands. "I'm counting my fingers. I have to count to keep myself from freaking out—*really* freaking out."

"Does counting work?"

Donnie nodded.

I sat beside him and began counting my fingers, and we both worked our digits, his fingers playing the air like an invisible piano, for about three rounds each. You could see by the way he strained his forehead and shook his head that he was having a hard time keeping it together. All the action on the court was probably just too much for him. As much as I needed him to play, there was no way I was going to add to his stress. "Look, Donnie, do me a solid and hold off on telling Dr. T you quit."

"Why?" he asked, his fingers settling down.

"I need to find another kid to have five players. Then you can tell her."

Donnie's counting picked up again at a furious pace.

"What scared you back there? G yelling?" I asked.

Donnie didn't say anything, just continued to count.

"Come on, Donnie. You've put me in a hard position here with only four players. At least tell me why."

Donnie stopped counting and looked at me again. "The other coach yelled at me a lot. And the other team, they like always yell at me. Even my own team yells at me because all my shots get blocked. Everybody yells at me. I try really hard to shoot and score, but the other team won't let me. I get way frustrated. *Way* frustrated. With all the yelling going on it's hard to think, and I have important stuff that I have to think about all the time. Every second of every day, I have to keep track of stuff. It's like literally impossible."

"What's this stuff you have to keep track of?"

"I don't want to talk about it, and you can't make me."

"Ok, but I understand having stuff going on. I got stuff up to my eyeballs."

"Like what?"

"You really wanna know about my stuff?"

Donnie nodded.

"OK. You asked for it. You ready?"

Donnie tilted his head at me.

"To start, I can't tell you the last time I had a date, 'cause I can't keep a job, 'cause that's how it works, Donnie. Women. I'm talking fine women like Dr. T, they don't date losers, and I'm a loser. I'm a grown man living with his father."

Donnie's attention fell to his lap, as if my problems were too small to bother with. From where we were sitting, I could see across the parking lot to the hospital. I needed to show this kid he wasn't alone. I needed to go deeper.

"I get so anxious sometimes I hyperventilate. Other times, I get so messed up, I can't eat or sleep. It's either that or I sleep the whole day away. Also, I've done a few stints at the hospital over there," I said, pointing. "I'm not a frequent flier, but I've done my time."

Donnie didn't say anything.

"And my best friend just died, which makes me feel that much worse about the world. And don't even talk to me about antidepressants because I've tried them, and they don't do it for me, so I'm ruined."

"That's bad, but mine is worse."

"It's not a contest, Donnie. Let's say you and I got some stuff going on."

"I have more," said Donnie. "*Way* more."

"Maybe you do, but about this yelling—I'm gonna help you with that. If anybody raises their voice at you, they're gonna have to deal with me. That's done. Today. I mean how you gonna keep track of what you gotta keep track of if people are all up in your face, yelling at you? So, you'll get me, right? If anyone yells at you?"

He closed his eyes.

"*That* I can help you with. It will make me feel good to help you, and I need to feel good about something."

"OK, I'll get you," he said, opening his eyes and looking at me.

"You promise?"

"*He who speaks falsehood shall not maintain his position before me*," said Donnie, holding up his hand as if taking an oath.

"OK. And, Donnie, you can't tell anybody about my hyperventilating or being in the hospital across the street and stuff. I gotta rep."

A little smile curled Donnie's lip, and man, that smile filled the moment with lightness and simplicity, as if Donnie and I were just two normies sharing a light conversation on a sunny afternoon.

"You don't think I got street cred?"

"No."

"That's cold, Donnie. I got mad street cred."

Donnie shook his head, his smile becoming a giggle. I reached over and patted his shoulder in camaraderie, prompting him to scream out as if he'd been attacked.

"Oh shit, sorry, brother," I said, startled, as Donnie rushed back to his counting, his skinny fingers dancing like mad.

• • •

As I made my way back to the court, I thought about how to help Donnie. I wasn't sure what kind of stuff he had to keep track of *every second of every day*, or why he screamed when I touched him, but I sure hoped he would get me if someone yelled at him. I just wanted to make his life better in some small way. His daily existence seemed too hard, and I knew what that was about. You just try to get through the day. The small stuff—waiting on a bus, eating, having a simple conversation—is too much to bear, and you fight to make it through the next minute without screaming. You look around at people going about their day—smiling, laughing, having meaningless encounters and conversations as if living was effortless, and you curse yourself and your mind and you wonder if someday things will get easier, and you become terrified of what will happen if they don't.

At least I got a smile out of Donnie. I hadn't seen him smile before. That was something. When I reached the court, the guys were waiting for me. "I'm sorry, guys, Donnie's out."

"Fuck!" screamed Toby, shaking his head, picking at a red, swollen scab. "We can't catch a break. Come on now."

"Let's just make those *putas* who quit play," said G.

"I'm not trying to make some sorry-ass scrubs play, believe that," said Toby.

"Hey, Donnie, what's up?" said Brian, wiping the sweat off his forehead and looking past me.

I turned to see Donnie approaching. "You OK?" I asked.

Donnie shrugged. "Are you really like gonna stop people from yelling at me?"

"You know I am, buddy." I turned to the team. "Nobody yells at Donnie. Got it?"

The team was quick to agree.

"This is *your* team, Donnie. Nobody's gonna yell at you here."

"So . . . like what if the other team yells at me?"

"We got you," said Toby. "Me, Coach, and the boys gonna make sure nobody yells at you, believe that."

"Yeah, we all will, brah," said Brian, once again pushing the hair out of his eyes.

"All right, then. I'll play."

"Really?" asked Chey, standing, eyes wide. I don't think she was used to being wrong.

"You're gonna play?" asked G. "No shit?"

"And we will win one this year, 'cause you promised," Donnie said to me. "And a promise is a promise."

Whoops. "You're gonna have to work with me. You gotta learn to shoot with somebody on you."

"But if I do, then you guarantee we'll win one this year, right? 'Cause that's what you said."

What was wrong with me? I just open my mouth and trash pours out. "Yeah, buddy, I guarantee it. We will win one this year."

"That is like gonna be so great," said Donnie, his eyes coming to life.

The rest of the team looked at me to see if I was serious or if I was channeling my inner Gonzalo, but I was for real. I didn't know how, but I was going to give Donnie something to feel proud about, a reprieve from all the stuff he had to keep track of. We were going to win *one* game.

I followed Donnie's gaze to Dr. T as she approached the court in short, quick strides, notebook in hand. "How's practice progressing?" she asked.

"Team and I were just working out some deets," I said.

"Coach promised me we'd win a game this year. He promised."

Dr. Tambori turned to me. "You did?"

I nodded—guilty as charged.

"Well, the coach shouldn't make promises he might not be able to keep."

"We will win one this year," I stated. "Right, Donnie?"

"That's right," said Donnie.

"It's not always about winning," said Dr. T.

"Yeah, it is, dude," said Brian.

"That's what's up," said Toby.

"You play hoops to win," I said, knowing if we had a chance to take a game, these guys had to think like that.

Dr. T looked at me, crinkling her forehead and shaking her head. "Coach, can you pop around my office for a chat tomorrow morning?"

My first day as coach and I was already in trouble with the principal. It was a good thing I was their only choice.

"You can go after me, Coach," said G.

"Thanks, G."

# NINE

**During breakfast the next morning,** I wanted to tell my old man about being a coach, to ask his advice, but his reproach was so distinct in my head—*Son, you're no coach, and that's not a real team*—that I didn't feel the need to play it out in the real world.

Instead, I listened to him wax on about his record, about how he had it in the bag. Here he was telling me how he couldn't lose, when all I could think of was how my guys had never won. It all felt too familiar. My father was the winner, and I was the loser. In an effort to stop feeling sorry for myself, I counted my fingers under the table. *One, two, three, four, five. One, two, three, four, five.* I wondered if Donnie beat himself up like I did. Maybe that was what he was up to when he talked to himself? On my last trip to the ward, I shared a room with a guy who argued with himself. He told me his brother lived in his head and was always picking on him. To see somebody give himself the middle finger is to see mental illness.

· · ·

Another kid was added to my route—actually, reinstated. He'd spent the last fourteen days at Friedman Psychiatric on a mandatory hold, a 5250 under California Code, for being a danger to himself.

"I heard he locked himself in his bedroom for five days," said Gonzalo, who had resumed his role as my morning copilot. "That's why he got all 5250'd."

"Because he didn't come out of his bedroom?"

"I heard he wouldn't eat, that he pissed and shit in a bucket."

*Poor kid.* I couldn't imagine things getting so bad as that.

"His father called the cops. Dude would probably still be in there if they hadn't busted his door down."

For a second, it occurred to me that Gonzalo might be lying, but something in his tone told me he wasn't.

"Turn here," said Gonzalo, pointing.

My copilot brought me into one of those neighborhoods of five bedrooms and three-car garages. We pulled up to the biggest place on the street, a gray-and-white monstrosity with a fountain of a cherub in the middle of a large cobbled driveway. In the side yard was a paved half-court, lines and all, where three athletic-looking kids were shooting around.

"You see that tall Black kid in the middle? That's Tim Tillet," Gonzalo said, as if I should know him. "The best baller in the state—got moves like LeBron and a full ride to UCLA next year—gonna go pro."

I honked and waved to get this kid's attention.

"What are you doing, *güey*? Kid like that doesn't go to Friedman, goes to Westchester Private."

"No kidding." Here was the kid who would be standing beside my old man when he won the record. I pictured them both being lifted onto their team's shoulders, and I hated to admit it, but I felt jealous of this kid, who was too handsome for his own good.

"We got his brother, Nubbin, the bucket-shitting *hombrecito* over there," he said, pointing to a squat kid who couldn't have been over five foot five, walking toward us.

"I think his name's Gordon, but everyone calls him Nubbin

'cause he short. Avoidant personality disorder—truthfully, that kid's got nothing to say. Mute."

G was speaking the truth. Nubbin entered in silence, his gait the soft glide of an athlete. As soon as he sat, he began to bounce his leg, which prompted me to do the same—our sewing-machine legs doing double time like our anxiety was powering the bus.

We got stuck at the first light, where a tricked-out Navigator pulled alongside me, and the window rolled down revealing Tim Tillet, Mr. Best Baller in the State, who flipped me the bird.

"Nice," I said.

He looked at me over his shades like I was a servant who dared to address the king directly, then leaned out the window and yelled, "Hey, psychos!" to my bus, ignoring me. His friends joined in, screaming, "Retards!"

My students didn't react. Gonzalo shrugged. "People call us names all the time."

"Yo," said Tim, getting my attention. "Do everybody a favor and drop those aborted crack babies back in the garbage. Seriously."

I looked back to Otis with his disco fro, who could've eaten two of them for dinner with fava beans. With both hands, he grabbed the seat in front of him and shook it. "Drive!" he screamed.

• • •

I was just about to rap on Dr. T's door when it opened, producing G and that 5150 tattoo on his neck.

"G, any advice for a newbie?" I asked.

"Look her in the eye and nod like you're a bobblehead. Pretend like whatever nonsense she's spinning is gold. Truthfully, therapists lap that up."

"Word."

"Good luck, Coach."

I liked that—*Coach*. I could get used to that, although I probably shouldn't.

Dr. T wanted to rebuke me for making promises I couldn't deliver, and she was of course right to do so. I shouldn't have promised Donnie we'd win a game, but I didn't know what else to do. What I did know was that I needed some intel on Donnie. I'd spent the night trying to think of a way he could get open to shoot, but I needed to know more about him to do that.

Dr. T gestured for me to sit in the same chair from my interview, which was still warm from G. "Let us talk about expectations," she said, strangling her every metered word as if this conversation pained her. "When working with *this* population, you have to be very careful not to make false promises."

I nodded. I used to have a car that had a Kobe bobblehead on the dash that nodded approval with every pothole.

"You cannot tell Donnie that he's guaranteed to win a game. You cannot guarantee something like that, can you?"

"No."

"Donnie is a sensitive boy who's been lied to his whole life."

"By who?"

Dr. T looked at me and chewed her lip. "Do you really want to know this type of information?"

"I do," I said, sitting up straighter.

"OK," she said, leaning forward on her desk. "His mother has been in and out of prison his whole life."

"Right, she made Donnie hide meth in his locker."

"How do you possibly know about that?"

"G told me."

"G . . . *Gonzalo* told you?" she asked, eyes wide.

I nodded.

She straightened some pens on her desk and sniffed in a quick inhale. "Yes, well . . . Donnie's mother has given him many unreasonable expectations. She's downright lied to him."

"About what?"

"For one, she told him that if he tried really hard, he could *make* himself *better*."

"Fuck," I said. "Sorry, Dr. T. I mean, Dr. Tambori. That sucks."

"Yes. It's utter bollocks. Point is you have to be careful what you say to this population. You cannot say whatever you believe sounds good. Do you understand the importance?"

I nodded.

"You promised Donnie that if he played better, he'd be able to win a game. First, that's an extraordinary amount of pressure to put on him. Second, if he does improve and you still don't win a game, it'll be that much harder for him to trust somebody."

"We'll win one."

"I need you to understand what I'm saying. These kids have all been lied to by adults, and it's up to us to show them that there are adults who can be trusted, that people can be trusted. For some-one like Donnie, it could make all the difference in how he views the world, and that could be the difference on how successful he becomes at navigating it."

There was such intelligence and warmth in her eyes. The way she spoke, that voice, that accent—man, she had class out the wazoo. I tried to picture her at five years old, but all I could summon was this serious little brown girl in a pantsuit organizing her dolls by height. I wondered what she was like outside of work, if she ever let loose, if she had a secret wild side.

"Mr. Cannon, are you listening to me?"

"Yes." I bobbled.

"I invest a lot of time and work with these kids, and I don't want you to undo any of that. I cannot allow you to make my job any more difficult. So, please be mindful of what you tell them, and if you have any questions about what you can or cannot say, my door is always open."

"I was thinking about Donnie last night. What's his deal?"

"His deal?"

"You know, what's wrong with him?"

"He's bipolar with obsessive compulsive disorder, psychosis, and severe anxiety."

I looked at her pens, five red, five white, lined up by color in front of her. "Yeah, I know, but like what's his deal?"

"His *deal*? I'm afraid I don't understand the question."

I thought about how to rephrase. I needed him to push off on a defender to get open. "You know, like what's his *deal*?"

"Mr. Cannon, *please*."

"I need to get him to push somebody."

"No, Mr. Cannon. We don't want Donnie pushing anybody. We don't want him raising his anxiety level. He has a hard time dealing with stress. It's something we're working on, so please stick to basketball."

"I gotta toughen him up to hold his own on the court. To back some people down to get him that win."

"Mr. Cannon. Please do not *toughen* Donnie up! Teach him basketball."

I wanted to explain that toughening Donnie up was the first lesson in teaching him hoops, but I could tell by her tone we were done talking about Donnie. I also got how much she cared for him, and that tenderness really touched me. I hadn't had tenderness in my life for many years—since my mother.

"I am glad you're taking an interest in Donnie. I am. I just want you to be careful," she said, holding my gaze.

"What's *your* deal?

"Me?"

"Yeah. Why did you want to be a shrink?"

"Why don't we stick to your players?" she said, folding her manicured hands in front of her.

"You know a lot about me, about my father, my job history. I want to know. Please."

She bit her lip, deciding whether I was worth this info. "When I was a child, my father was clinically depressed," she said, crossing her arms on her chest as if giving herself a hug. "He spent quite a bit of time in and out of hospital."

"That's rough. How's he doing now, your old man?"

"Unfortunately, he's not with us anymore," she said, looking down at her pens.

"I'm sorry." I spent a lot of time apologizing to Dr. T. "When did he die?"

"During my first year of uni, he died by suicide," she said, moving a coffee cup from one side of her desk to the other.

"I'm sorry."

"After his death, I switched my specialty from general pediatrics to pediatric psychology."

Dr. T, like the rest of us, was wounded, which made me want to walk around the desk and give her a hug and tell her I had her back, that she could tell me anything. I didn't, but, man, I really had to stop myself.

"OK, Mr. Cannon, I imagine we're through for the day," she said, standing.

"I'm sorry about your old man."

"I appreciate your sympathy, Mr. Cannon, but that was a long time ago already," she said, rising.

"If you ever want to talk about it, I'm your guy."

"Thank you," she said, ushering me out with a hand on her hip at her open office door.

# TEN

**I couldn't stop thinking about Dr. T** and how she must scrutinize her patients for signs she missed with her father. I wondered how close she and her father were. Did she switch her major to learn more about him or to prevent others from following in his footsteps? Both?

The idea of doing the Dutch existed in me like a spy with a cyanide capsule sewn in his uniform—every so often he will absently touch his collar, making sure it's still there. I knew a kid who put his father's 9mm to his temple and squeezed the trigger, another who chased a bottle of pills with a forty, and another who took a dive from a hotel balcony. Two friends of mine drank themselves to death before they turned twenty. How did Dr. T's father do it? I pictured an Indian man, who I imagined looked like Ben Kingsley as Ghandi, putting a handful of pills in his mouth, and I began to sweat and felt as if I might pass out.

· · ·

That afternoon was my first game as coach, and I had no idea what to expect either from my guys or our opponents, Ernie Kovacs, or why the high school was named after the comedian from the '50s.

From what I could gather on the drive, my guys played in a division of pocket-sized inconsequential high schools, schools my father probably never heard of. I decided no matter how long it took, I wasn't going to tell my pops about coaching until I won a game. I hoped winning would make him proud, a thought that made me want to kick my own ass.

We drove down the 405 to the 101 past Warner Bros. into Burbank, the Media Capital of the World, where I prayed my debut as coach wouldn't be a slaughter. Dr. Lipschitz asked one thing of me: not to embarrass the school. It turns out a petition circulated last year to remove Mary Friedman from the league because of some embarrassing incidents he refused to tell me about. The school was able to fight it off, but the doctor didn't think we had another life in us.

Thanks to Gonzalo, I parked the bus in the principal's spot but, at the behest of an orange flag-waving janitor, had to move it. I was jumpy and looking for help, but I needed to learn not to trust this kid.

I never paid attention at my father's games to what a coach does when he first enters the gym. Does he check in with somebody? How does he know which bench is his?

The small gym was half-filled, and it was no problem recognizing which bench was ours, because behind one bench the stands were packed with students, faculty and parents, behind the other sat a few stragglers I guessed were Kovacs overflow and only sitting on the visitors' side to avoid standing.

The comedian's movie posters hung on the walls along with photos of Kovacs with Sinatra, Jack Lemmon, and Shirley MacLaine. One night when I couldn't sleep, I caught a Kovacs marathon on A&E, and he had me laughing into the morning. I mean, the guy wrestled a jaguar on live TV for laughs—he was a guy who always went for the funny—a kindred soul. He was looking down now, gathering his cronies and popcorn, preparing for what had the makings of a huge belly laugh: my first time coaching. My mother was up there, too, sticking up for me, telling old Ernie not to count his chickens.

Kovacs warmed up in choreographed layup drills. Their coach, a middle-aged guy in a polo shirt and a permanent snarl, blew his whistle, and his team, in military precision, began running a give-and-go drill. These guys played with a crispness that would've impressed my old man. Turning to my guys, I saw five dudes wearing white T-shirts with numbers written on them and different styles of blue shorts—they didn't have uniforms—standing by our bench as if they were strangers waiting for a bus.

"OK, guys," I said, clapping, "let's do a layup drill."

"Like those *pendejos*?" asked G.

"Fuck that," said Otis, plopping his bulk down on our bench.

"Like . . . what do you guys usually do before a game?"

"Truthfully, we just shoot around and warm up," said G.

"OK, go do that."

Four of the guys trotted onto the court, while Otis stayed on the bench.

"Big man, aren't you gonna warm up?"

"Nope," said Otis, clearing his throat.

"OK. Sounds good." I wasn't about to push my luck—yet.

I made my way to the coach and extended my hand, which he inspected as if I might have a prank buzzer, before granting me a handshake. He pointed out the five consecutive Division 1A championship banners on the wall behind the Visitors' bench. Great. We were playing the division champions, this league's version of my father. Perfect.

A student film crew entered, and a girl wearing a T-shirt that said, *Ernie Kovacs—The Future in TV and Film*, shoved a microphone in my face. "How does it feel to be the worst team in the league?"

"Now I get the whole Kovacs thing," I said, gesturing to her shirt. "You guys study TV here."

"You didn't answer my question: how does it feel to be the worst team in the league?"

"Does Jerry Springer teach at this school?"

"You have only five guys?" the coach scoffed, watching my team miss shots. "You have seven on the roster."

"We had a couple call out sick," I said, for some reason wanting this guy's approval.

The coach shook his head. "Doesn't matter. Your team hasn't won a game in three years. You guys should pack it in, if you ask me."

The likeness to my old man was uncanny. The camera swung in front of me. I hated being on camera. During my time on the streets, I was always getting hassled by guys with cameras trying to tell my story—in LA, doc filmmakers were a bigger problem for the homeless than rats and dogs and people stealing your shoes.

As I made my way back to our bench, someone hollered, "Nice uniforms, chodes!" Students began chanting *retards* over and over, while some adults attempted to hush them. My guys continued to shoot, ignoring the insults, as some cheerleaders bounced into the gym, shaking their pom-poms. Gonzalo, the team Lothario, took interest in one. "Your legs are tight. Cheerleader muscles. I'm super *serio*." She smiled as he bounced the ball off his shoe and yelled at Donnie for making him mess up. Donnie apologized.

The ref blew his whistle and the other team gathered at their bench. It was game time. I summoned my guys and called out their positions. "Toby, you're center. Otis, power forward. Brian, small forward. Gonzalo, point. And Donnie, you're our shooting guard. Let's see a lot of passing, and feed the ball to Donnie if he's gotta look. All right, let's talk to each other out there," I said, mimicking something my father said before every game.

Gonzalo looked at me. "What are we supposed to say?"

"I don't know, G, ... communicate with each other."

"*Que pendejo*," said G.

Across the court, their coach clapped his hands and said, loudly, "Make them regret ever joining this league."

The game hadn't started yet, and my fight-or-flight was flaring. I fantasized bolting, turning on my heels and hauling ass. Toby stood center court across from their center, and the ref began the game by tossing the ball between the two boys. Their center won the jump, tapping the ball to their point, who swung it to their shooting guard, who sank a reverse layup. I could see why these guys were champs. I clapped, wondering what my guys would do with their first possession.

Toby inbounded the ball to G, only the Kovacs point guard stripped it and bounce passed to their center, who sank an easy layup—four to the goose egg.

"It's like playing my daughter's team!" their coach called across the gym, prompting some laughs from his players and the stands. "She's five."

Their point guard, a tall kid with some impressive dribbling skills, took the lane for another deuce.

"You haven't gotten around to showing your guys defense yet?" asked their coach. I hated this guy.

Kovacs put a few more points on the board before my guys were able to set up their first real play. G dribbled the ball at the top of the key, while Toby pushed off his defender and was wide open under the basket.

"Toby's open in the paint!" I yelled.

"Let's see you block this, *güey*," said G, smack-talking before driving the lane and getting stuffed.

"G, you gotta pass, you're not the Black Mamba," I called out, as Kovacs point once again pushed the ball down the floor for an easy bucket.

"You guys are worse than you were last year," the coach yelled.

Brian brought the ball up the floor. Otis, in an effort to get open, bumped his defender, knocking him halfway across the court and onto his ass. Somewhere in the stands behind me a parent said,

"Our kids shouldn't have to play this type of team." Somewhere higher up, in the clouds, Ernie Kovacs giggled and my mom flipped him the bird.

The first quarter went like this: Donnie got every shot blocked. Gonzalo shot every time he got the ball. Toby, who had some mad skills, scored a few baskets without much help from his team. Otis, for his part, fouled people, and Brian busted dance moves and played with his hair and barely touched the ball, while I tried to get my guys to set up plays and pass by yelling stuff like, "Guys, set up a play," or "Pass the ball!"

Just when I was about to give up, sure the game would continue unraveling, my guys did something Ernie Kovacs won't soon forget. Toby got wide open for an easy shot, and Otis ignored him and bricked the ball off the backboard.

"Come on, Otis, Toby was wide open. Pass the ball!" I shouted, four ticks beyond frustrated.

"Yeah, jagoff, pass," said Toby.

"What you say?" asked Otis.

"You heard me, jagoff."

"No!" screamed Donnie. "No. No. No. No. No. No."

Otis lurched at Toby, the two landing in a loud thud on the floor. The ref blew his whistle as the two boys kicked and punched each other. I ran out and tried to yank the prodigious Otis off Toby. Gonzalo and Brian, God bless them, jumped in to help me, and the five of us bounced around the floor like a circus act. It was the first sign of teamwork all night. Donnie, for his part, screamed for everyone to stop fighting, while the other coach, the players, and the stands filmed us on their iPhones in horror.

The ref blew his whistle repeatedly until we all stopped moving. "Game over. Forfeit," he screamed, pointing at me. "I'm calling the game for fighting."

"Ref," I said, shoving the tangle of players off me and jumping up. "You can't call the game for a team fighting themselves."

"I can and did."

"It's my first game," I said to the retreating ref. "Just give us one more chance."

"Good call, ref. This team and their coach are an embarrassment to the league," chirped the Kovacs coach.

I turned to my guys in their disheveled T-shirts, as they picked themselves up from the floor.

"An embarrassment," the coach repeated.

The father who lived in my head joined in, *All you were asked to do was not embarrass the school, and you couldn't even handle that.*

• • •

I hustled my guys to our bus like we were outlaws who'd robbed the town's bank—that is, everyone but Otis, who lumbered as if on a summer stroll. By the time he reached us, the players were onboard, and I was by the door. "Come on, Otis, let's go, let's go," I said, at the end of my tether with this kid.

"You best step off," challenged Otis.

"You best get on this bus, Otis. Right now."

With speed I'd never seen on such a big guy, Otis pinned me by my neck to the side of the bus. Instinctively, I kicked out his feet and jumped him so that he hit the ground and I landed on top of him, grabbing him in a headlock. He yelled and swung around as the rest of the team jumped off the bus and helped me, pinning his arms and legs to the ground. He bucked and punched and kicked as we held on for dear life until he gave up, leaving all six of us sitting there on the ground in front of the bus, in front of the championship school, panting, as the custodian waved to the exit with big orange flags.

"You done?" I asked Otis, watching his eyes gathering steam for a second go. This kid had worse impulse control than I did. We would never get through a game let alone win one if he couldn't control himself.

"Otis? What do you think? Can we get on the bus now, or are we going another round here?"

Otis turned to the custodian flapping the orange flags. "You and I be continuing this later, Coach," said Otis.

"OK. Later it is," I said, standing. "Everybody on the bus."

# ELEVEN

**On the ride home, I kept my eye on Otis,** who sat two rows back, rocking back and forth grunting to himself. He stared at his reflection in the window and shook his head, working something out. He was built like an NFL lineman, like a walking, talking wrecking ball. If I could somehow mold that power and anger into something resembling a ballplayer, we'd be on to something. Of course, I could see my own reflection, as well. My first game as coach, and what do I do? I get into a wrestling match center court. How was I going to explain that to Dr. T and Dr. Lipschitz?

• • •

At my father's house, I walked the trophy-lined hallway where the wall was discolored in shapes of picture frames no longer there, and I heard my pop's voice in the kitchen.

"My wife's passing broke me. It took me forever to rebuild." Who was he talking to? Was he on the phone? I'd never heard him speak about my mother's death. Not ever.

"It was in a car crash, correct?" chimed in another voice. Someone was with him, but he never had people over. Had someone broken in? Some crazed psychiatrist helping people at gunpoint?

I cracked open the kitchen door and saw the back of some bald guy's head, which obscured my old man sitting across the table.

"It was after the crash," my father said. "She died from internal complications."

I froze, feeling as if I'd happened on a secret bearing of the soul. Whose shiny black dome was this? Mr. Brooks, the neighbor? No. He moved to Lancaster three years ago. Was it a new neighbor, friend?

"When was that?" issued a voice deep and nasal and familiar.

"Ten years ago, March 13."

This guy kept moving so at times I could see my father and at times only the back of this dude's shaved head.

"I'm sorry. Thinking about my wife is painful," my father said, looking down at his huge hands and fidgeting in his seat until he stood. He looked too tall and too big, as he towered over this average-sized guy.

Not wanting to miss the smallest expression of pain, I stood, too, smacking my head on a trophy shelf. With lightning speed, I caught the gold statuette of a player mid-shot, but the shelf smacked the floor, making a noise comically loud in the now-silent house.

"Mikey?" called my old man. "Is that you?"

"Hey," I said, entering the room as if surprised to see someone with my father, picking up on the scent of Aqua Velva, the cologne of old men in barbershops.

"How long you been out there?" asked Dad.

"Just got home," I said. Over my dad's shoulder, a tall woman with the toned arms of an athlete and a short Afro peered into a camera. My father was doing an interview.

"Hi, I'm Richard Knowles from E:60," the man said, standing.

"Right! Richard Knowles from ESPN. I loved your story on Griffin," I said, shaking his hand, looking straight into the camera.

"Pretend it isn't there," said Knowles.

The camera swung to me, as I brushed my hands through my hair and straightened my collar. My father's most intimate, painful memory, something he would never share with me, he was willing to mine for ESPN.

"I'm doing a documentary on your father and his chance at the record."

"Why are you carrying my trophy around, boy?"

"What?" I said, confused, looking down at the gold man still in my hand.

"First, you eat my steak, now you're screwing around with my trophies?"

"Don't worry about me," I said. "Go back to your interview or whatever it was you were doing."

"I asked you a question, boy."

The camera swung to me, which had the opposite effect it had on my old man. I guess if you're good with your life you don't mind letting the world have a go at you. Knowles did an in-depth story on Magic, and even he suffered some bruises. I liked the shadows.

"Well?" asked my father.

"I was starving. It was in the fridge . . . I'll replace it, OK?"

"Here I am looking forward to it all day. I come home, open the fridge—no steak."

The camerawoman popped the camera off the tripod and walked it over to my father for a close-up.

"Should we talk about it later?" I said through gritted teeth, gesturing to the camera, now a foot away from my old man.

"Let's talk about it right now," he said, nodding to the camera, his new confidant.

"I'm gonna head upstairs," I said. I didn't remember an argument about steaks in Magic's doc.

"Mikey, we want to talk to you, as well," said Knowles.

"I'm good."

"I heard you're a bit of a coach yourself," he said, nodding to the camerawoman to move in on me.

"Mikey couldn't coach a dish from the sink to the dishwasher," said my old man.

The camera pushed in a foot from my face, allowing me to see my distorted reflection in the lens, which felt about right. This wasn't how I wanted my old man to learn I'd encroached into his sacred world.

"Little birdie told me you were coaching," said Knowles.

"I drive a bus for the Mary Friedman Alternative High School, and their coach quit, so I'm just helping out—no big deal," I said, attempting to lessen the blow.

"What?" said my pops pushing off the counter. "You're doing what?"

"Do we really gotta do this now?"

"You're coaching?" asked my father.

"Can we please shut off the camera?" I asked.

"Your father granted us full access."

I turned to my dad. "I was gonna tell you. It's no big deal."

"You're always looking for ways to embarrass me," said my old man.

"As I understand it, you coached your first game tonight," said Knowles.

"How do you know all this?" I said.

"I do my research," said Knowles. "I sent one of my colleagues to the game tonight. He said you had to forfeit."

"I've never forfeited a game," said my old man. "You are so predictable."

"Really? You could've predicted my whole team would be expelled from the game for fighting?"

"With each other, as I understand it," said Knowles.

"Appreciate the assist," I said.

"Pathetic," said my gem of a father. "Only you."

"See, that's why I didn't tell you. Because I knew you would react like that."

"Like what?" asked my father.

"Like calling me pathetic."

"What word would you use to describe a coach who lost his first game because his team got in a fight with themselves?"

"This is great," said Richard. "For the doc, I mean. Coaching—the family business."

"I'm done talking," I said.

"And you still live at home, Mikey?" asked Knowles.

I took a deep breath.

"He can't make it on his own."

"I'd really like to interview you."

"Nobody's interested in a grown man eating his father's steaks."

"ESPN's gonna love your son's a coach."

My father took a step toward me and so did the camera. "A coach is a leader, someone people want to follow. Not some mule head who eats another man's steak."

"I'll replace the fucking steak!" I shouted.

"Damn right you will!" screamed my old man.

I stormed from the kitchen, the camerawoman a crazed shark feeding on the bad blood in the water, following me until I slammed my bedroom door in her face. Outside, Knowles asked if she got the shot, and she said she had, that it would play well.

• • •

The next morning my father and I clomped around the house ignoring each other until we both were in the kitchen looking for coffee. I'd spent the night hiding in my room thinking about fathers and death. I wondered about Dr. T's dad and how unbearable it got before he threw it in, and I thought about my old man, who opened up to ESPN about my mother's death. I'd tried over the years to speak with my father about the night my mother passed, about the complications that killed her, but he always shut me down. I don't even remember him crying. Maybe we never get to know our fathers, not really.

"I'm sorry, Pops. I was gonna tell you about the coaching," I said, pouring some joe into a Lakers mug.

"I've been waiting my whole life for something like this, and I don't want you to squander my chance at recognition like you do everything else," he said, sitting at the table. "ESPN—you don't get bigger than having ESPN do a story on you. They did one on Bird."

"I'm not the one messing it up. I don't remember Bird going off on his son for eating his steak."

"I've seen hundreds of these docs. They don't put stuff like that in there. And even if they did, I'm not going to change who I am for E:60. The world should know what makes a winner."

"You know best."

"Damn right I do." My father eyed me. "Tell me again, how'd you end up coaching?"

"Like I said, their coach quit, and it was between me and calling the season."

"Tough choice."

"You told ESPN about mom's death?"

My pops took a sip of coffee, examining me over his mug.

"I heard you talking about her when I came in." My father didn't say anything. "How'd you keep going after she died?"

"I don't want to talk about this."

"What? I gotta wait for the doc?"

"It doesn't do any good bringing all that up. Knowles has got a way of making you talk about things you don't want to talk about. Believe me. You should stay away from him. God only knows what he'll have you blubbering about."

"He wouldn't get me to talk about Mom."

He grunted. "Just stay away from him."

"He wants to talk to me. What am I supposed to do?"

"The documentary should be about how I started in the pros, blew out my knee, and went on to coach. It shouldn't be about how my son's a coach one day and then gets fired the next. Doesn't send the right message."

"I'm not looking to play the loser in your life story, believe me."

"Good. You'll stay away?"

"Miles away." It was the first thing in memory my old man and I agreed on, but it hurt that I was the part of his life he didn't want to share with the world.

# TWELVE

**When I got on my school bus that morning,** something caught my eye—some papers were jammed between a seat and the wall. Extracting them, I saw it was Otis's assignment. At first, I wondered if G lifted the papers from Otis's bag, but Otis sat by himself after the game, and besides, G wouldn't dare risk stealing from him. Of course, I was curious about Otis, about what he would be scared to share with the group, but I felt so guilty for reading Donnie's assignment that I stuffed the papers back where I found them and sat in the driver's seat.

But then I got to thinking. Did the papers just fall out of Otis's bag? And if they did, how did they become stuffed between the seat and the wall? Something didn't add up. There had to be another explanation of how they got there. I turned and looked at the lined paper sticking out between the pleather seat and wall. Did he mean to stuff them there? Did he not want his assignment anymore? But why put them *there* and not just throw them out? Was it possible he left them for me to read? He knew *I* would find them, as I was the only one who cleaned this bus. If that was the case, I had no choice but to read them.

Of course, I knew this was a leap, a monstrous rationalization, but it was a good enough one for me to go pick up his pages.

Unlike Donnie's, nothing was crossed out and the penmanship was flawless, each letter perfectly positioned between the lines.

# OTIS'S ASSIGNMENT

This here assignment is bout how my only friend is a dog. It ain't really a secret cause I ain't embarrassed bout it, just never had a reason to tell anyone.

At first, I hated that dog on account he keeps me and my foster mom up all night. Made me angry cause Ruth is a nurse and she need her sleep. One day, I get to thinking maybe the neighbor need to be taught a lesson bout messing with people sleep. He shouldn't let his dog bark all night without stopping it. So, I go over and knock on the neighbor's door but nobody answers, just the dog barking his damn head off in the backyard. I look over the fence and that dog be snarling at me through his chain-link cage like he wants at my throat. So, I bark back at him. Don't know why I bark at that dog. I just do. I mean, I never bark before. Got no reason to, I guess, but I let loose, and it feel pretty good, this barking, and I see why he be barking all the damn time. And all the while, he barking right back at me. He don't care if I human or dog, he don't like me barking at him, especially in his own damn property. But I getting angry at that dog, like we in an argument. I start screaming. Not words. Just sounds like a lion or some damn thing. Really screaming and he barking right back, not scared of me, not even a little. We go on like this for some time.

Next day at school I thinking of that dog, thinking what he be doing now, if he barking all day or he wait for me to come home to start up like that. When I get off the bus, I don't bother knocking on my neighbor's door, I go round back of the house to see the dog, and he there barking at me. He barking all right, but not crazy barking. He barking like he know who I am. Like he remembering me. So, I start talking to him. I say, Hey dog, why you barking all the damn time?

He cocks his head like he trying to figure me out, like he interested in what I saying. Then he barks at me like he talking, like he got something on his mind. I wanna get closer to him. I ain't worried about being attacked. If he attacks me, I attack him right back. Then we see what is what. But he be in his cage anyway, so I open the gate and I enter the backyard and he show me his teeth, like a warning. I go over to his cage, and I look at him, just look him in the eye, not threatening, just looking. He doesn't bite at me or anything, just put his head down between his shoulders like he a wolf or something. We take account of each other. I just standing there. And he just standing there. We go on like this for some time. Then he starts barking, he had bout enough of me being in his yard, I guess. I respect that, so I let him be.

Next day, I wanna take this here thing to the next level cause I don't always like being by myself after school. I wanna see what would happen if I open the cage, see if he bite me or if he and I got an understanding. So I open it, and he dart out to the opposite side of the yard and he bark at me. I don't care if he attack me or not, just wanna see if he will, but he don't. He just make a lot of noise. He not saying he want business with me, he just telling me he ready if I push it there. But I don't push him, cause I don't want that kinda business with him either. He and I just look at each other a long while, not making a move, just being with each other. Then he find a nice place in the sun and he lay down. He closes one eye, but he got the other on me, making sure I ain't changing my mind bout attacking him.

Next day, when I let him out his cage, he head to the other side of the yard and he curl round like he finding just the right situation to get comfortable, and then he sit, so I sit. He not barking at all this time. He know me now. Then he gets up and come over to me and sniff my ear like my ear maybe smell funny. Then he go back to where he was at, bark a little, and then curl up again on the ground, looking at me, keeping a eye on me. I just sit there. I like this dog, and I think he be OK with me too. He thinks, why this boy sitting in my yard. I'd tell him, but I don't know. I guess I like his company.

That day in algebra, teacher call on me to see if I do my homework. I know the answer, I did my work, but I shrug, don't say anything. I tell this dog all bout it, how I don't know why I don't say anything to the teacher, considering I did my homework and knew the answer. He snorts a little, kick up some dirt with his breath. He listens, not judging, just listening.

Next day, I go back, and he curl up again and he sit and look at me and I'm thinking the shrinks and advocates and judges always talking to each other how I'm unreachable, how nobody be able to get me, lost cause and all that, but me and this dog, we doing fine.

A few days later, I go back to the yard, and we do our thing, me and this dog, then he come close to me and do his circle before he plops down right beside me. He *right* next to me. We almost touching, his back and my leg. We not touching, but we close to touching. One thing for sure, he just fine sitting beside me.

I look down at him, then across the yard to Ruth's fence, where she and I living. I just sitting there and the dog, he yawning. Like maybe he happy I there. His face got dirt on it, and his nose all black and wet. I nod. I don't know why I nod but I feel good. The whole world outside, they be running crazy, but me and this dog here, we OK. I reach out to him, and he lick my hand. First one lick and then he licking my hand like mad, like he ain't licked a hand in a long while, like he thankful he got my hand to lick. I pat his head one time. His head feel sticky like he got some sap from a tree on there. It feels good, his dirty, matted hair. I do it again. I like petting this dog.

Next day, same thing, only he put his head in my lap. His whole big head be in my lap, and I don't move, cause I don't wanna ruin how comfortable he is. My leg falls asleep, but I ain't bout to move it. I like this feeling I got, like he and I understand each other. He be barking at the damn world, ready to pull the throat outta it, but with me, he and I, we OK. My shrink always be asking me if I like visiting my mom in prison. I tell her it be OK. That all I tell her. But I tell this dog I don't like visiting her. She recalls all the bad stuff I got in me. I look at her and I don't care if I ever see her again. Let her die in that damn place. She messed me up good cause the crank. She got no reason living in a warehouse with a two-year-old, doing drugs, forgetting to feed me. I don't know why anybody think I wanna see her, anyway.

The dog licks my hand, slow and thoughtful. I not saying he understands me . . . completely, but he get something off me, cause that lick feels like he telling me he got me. It being a slow lick, like he understands where I'm coming from. My eyes burn and I sniff, and that dog, he sits up and he licks my face, and this make me cry, and this dog, he be licking my tears. His warm tongue licking my tears and I let loose. I cry like I never cry before, and he keep licking me like he trying to heal my pain, like his tongue got magic on it. And it does a little, cause I feeling pretty good. I cry and he be healing me.

Then I hear the bell on the gate, and I see this white guy enter the yard. He sees me sitting with his dog in his yard and he start in screaming bout why I in his yard. He starts dialing his cell, making a big show of it, telling me the police is coming. I tell him I live next door. I'm just petting his dog. He doesn't believe me and he tell the cop on the phone that I'm breaking into his house. Then he picks his-self up a shovel and begin swinging it at me like he gonna do me some harm. Things go black and my whole body explode in heat before I jump him and take away that shovel and grab him by his neck. But the dog leap on me, start biting my arm, bite it real hard, and I punch the dog, and he cry out. I hurt him, and he run back inside his cage.

I throw this guy down and I hurry over to that cage and I apologize to that dog. I tell him I didn't mean to hit him. I tell him I sorry. I shouldn't have lost control of myself. I tell him I will never do that again. I should have never raised my hand to him. But he back away from me against his cage. He scared of me now. I make calm sounds and tell him he a good boy and invite him over to me with my hand, but he too scared now. He no longer trusts me. I think to turn and kill that guy for ruining what the dog and I had. We connected, but not now. I think to do that, but I don't. I am too sad bout the dog, and I thinking bout some consequences like Ruth say. If I put this guy down for good, I be put away, away from Ruth and away from this dog here, so I go back next door, cause I ain't bout that kinda trouble just now. I ain't saying this guy not gonna get his. I just saying I ain't bout all that just now. That's all I saying.

The police come over, but Ruth is home then and she explain who I am to the cop and the neighbor, and he won't press charges but he don't want me in his yard any more. He says if I in his yard again he gonna report me to social service and they gonna take me away from Ruth. My body shakes when he says that. I don't ever want to be without Ruth. Ruth looks at me and she shakes her head like she doesn't want me to do anything. I nod to Ruth. She and I got an understanding concerning this here conversation. They ain't taking me anywhere. I stay right here. The cop go and the neighbor go back next door, and Ruth and I don't say anything, cause we already say it without words.

I look out the window, and I think bout the dog behind the fence screaming at the world. I get why he bite me. He a dog. But me. I shouldn't have hit him. I gotta be better than that. I look at Ruth and then back at the fence. I gotta be better. He my best friend.

# THIRTEEN

When I finished reading Otis's assignment, I put the pages back where I found them, and when he got on the bus, he hurried to his seat and slipped them in his backpack. He then looked out the window at a few kids walking by, never even glancing at me. I began to doubt my rationalization. Maybe they did really slip from his bag. I felt criminal for reading something so heartfelt and personal without permission, and I decided never to cop to it.

After my morning run, I cashed my first paycheck and used all of it to get myself an iPhone. That afternoon, I was summoned to Dr. T's office, where she showed me on my new phone an Instagram post of my Battle Royale center court. Oddly enough, that wasn't what she wanted to talk about.

Her face was strained, a small vein lifting on her forehead. "I heard Otis attacked you."

"From who?"

"One of your players. It came up in a private session this morning." She leaned forward, her elbows resting on her desk. "You're the third staff member he's attacked and there's a three-strike policy. We don't have a choice, Otis will have to be sent to a residential facility."

I was in a hard place. I didn't want to lie to Dr. T—I respected her too much for that, but I couldn't say something that would remove

Otis from his foster home. I knew how much he cared for his foster mother and would never do anything to compromise that relationship. What if while he was in residential psych his foster got another kid? No. I couldn't chance it. Perhaps this three-strike policy was why Otis left me those pages. Were they his way of apologizing and asking for my help? My rationalization was back.

I could tell by how quiet Dr. T was, she didn't want to put him there, either, but she didn't have a choice—she was a rule follower. Not to mention, if I lost Otis, I would have to find another player. What everyone needed was for me to give Dr. T a reason to avoid putting Otis in a place where he would get angrier at the world. She needed me to lie.

"No, he didn't attack me, but I understand the confusion."

"Really," she said, leaning back in her chair. "Why don't you enlighten me?"

I needed to concoct a reason Otis and I would be rolling around the ground that wasn't us beating the snot out of each other, and I guessed cuddling wasn't gonna fly. "Otis isn't the tallest player, but he's bulky, and in hoops that's OK, as long as you know how to use your heft to get position. So, I was . . . uh . . . showing Otis how to use his body and how to control his aggression." It was more of a plan than a lie, as I was *planning* to show him these things.

"You were showing Otis how to control his aggression?" she asked, her raised eyebrow telling me she needed more convincing.

"Right. I was showing him how to box out."

"Box out? What may I ask is that?"

Recognizing an opportunity to loosen her up, I leapt up and slid my chair to the corner of the room.

"Crikey, Mr. Cannon. Please sit this instant."

"Stand up, so I can show you what happened," I said, advancing around the desk.

"I need you to return to your side of the desk, instantly. I am more than capable of standing on my own."

I returned to my side, while she rose and stood in a stiffness normally reserved for royalty or planks of wood.

"You gotta come over here or else I won't be able to show you, and I'm guessing you gotta describe what happened in some report or something."

She narrowed her eyes at me.

She didn't trust me, and of course I *was* lying, but still, a little trust would have been nice. "Please come over here, for the sake of Otis. Do it for the children, for the little children," I said, smiling.

"Can you not explain what happened using words?"

"I'm not good at explaining things," I said.

She was fearless and strong, but appeared fragile as she approached, and I couldn't help picturing Otis attacking her, which would be like an elephant attacking a squirrel, but something told me he wouldn't—that above all else, he also respected Dr. T.

"OK, your coatrack is the hoop," I said, flinging her jacket from the rack to the chair. I snatched a piece of paper off her desk and crumpled it up.

"What was on that piece of paper?" she asked.

I shrugged. I was on a roll. "OK, so this paper is the ball. A player shoots. Both you and I want the rebound, but I'm taller, so how you gonna get it?"

"I am sure I do not know," she said, placing her hands on her hips.

"By getting position," I said, turning so she was standing behind me. "Ball goes up, you gotta box out. You get in front of the defender and back 'em out." I threw my paper ball in the air and then lowered my ass and backed into her hips, forcing her to take a step backwards as I caught the piece of paper. "See, whoever has position, gets the ball. You try it—get in front of me, and back that ass up."

"No, I don't think so."

"Are you sure?"

"Quite. I still don't understand how you two lads ended up on the ground fighting."

"I was showing him this, and when he backed me out, I stumbled and grabbed a hold of him to break my fall, and he fell on top of me. So that's what I'm guessing this person, whoever they may be—let's call him Donnie—witnessed."

Dr. T rehung her jacket on the rack, unfurled my paper ball, examined it and sat back in her chair. "I do appreciate your perspective on the incident, which I'll write up as an accident."

Of course, I couldn't be sure, but I saw in her statement a sort of wink, as if we were complicit in saving Otis from a res psych ward, at least for now.

"Do you believe Otis will benefit from being on this team, Mr. Cannon?" Dr. T asked.

Did she want my opinion? I thought a lot about winning a game for Donnie, but I hadn't thought much about how ball would help Otis. "You can call me Mikey."

"I'll call you Mr. Cannon, thank you very much."

"I stopped playing ball my sophomore year, and I wish I hadn't. I'd hate for Otis to look back and feel like he made a wrong move and missed out on something important."

"Why did you stop?" she asked.

"It's a boring story."

"Humor me." Those piercing eyes settled on me.

"I had a chance to win the championship game for my old man. If I made my two foul shots, we won; if I made only one, we tied. I missed both. I quit."

"Because you missed those shots? Or was it something else?"

"My father calling me an embarrassment in front of the entire school might've had something to do with it."

"I'm very sorry that happened to you."

Her compassion made me feel closer to her but not enough to tell her my mom had died seven months earlier, and missing those shots was the tipping point that put me in Friedman across the street. What I wanted to ask my old man wasn't how *he* made it through my mom's death, but why he hadn't helped me do the same.

"Thanks for sharing that information, Mr. Cannon. It was helpful on multiple fronts. Also, whatever that rubbish was I showed you on Instagram—please don't let it happen again."

"You have my word."

· · ·

I walked out of Dr. T's office to see Otis leaning against the wall mean-mugging me as if he might attack. "What's on your mind, big man?" I said, bracing myself for anything.

"You tell me, *Coach*," he said, gutting me with the word, pushing himself off the wall. "Dr. T need to see me. Know anything 'bout that?"

"I sure do," I said, holding his stare. "I know a lot about it." No matter how on edge he put me, I wouldn't show it. If I could get *him* to respect me as coach, I might even be able to see myself with a shiny new whistle.

"I knew you'd rat," he said, his attention falling to his feet, his hard expression losing its grip on his features, allowing me to see the kid who loved that dog.

"I'll see you at practice, Otis."

"I ain't thrown outta school?"

"No, you're not."

Otis brought his attention up to my eyes to see if I was playing him.

"I still on the team?"

"You are. If it should come up, I was showing you how to box out, and we slipped," I said. "That's how you and I ended up on the ground after the game. *Comprende*?"

Otis cleared his throat, appearing dazed.

"Isn't that how you remember it?"

"That be how I recall it," he said, something that could almost pass as a smile twisting his lips.

It was the first time I saw Otis not play it so hard, and I took the opening. "Look, we're gonna work on setting screens today, which is right up your alley if you can keep your head."

"Why it up my alley?"

"'Cause if you do it right, you get to knock people on their ass without getting kicked out of school. But it's not gonna work if you can't get control of yourself. 'Cause if you attack another teammate, you're on your own. You feel me?"

The door opened, producing Dr. T. "Otis, please come in."

"You feel me, big man?"

"I'm down, Coach," he said.

"What are you two discussing?"

"Listen here, Ms. Nosy Pants, that's none of your beeswax," I sang out.

"I believe there may be something fundamentally off in your general makeup, Mr. Cannon. Otis, please come in before I say something to your coach that I most definitely will regret."

Otis looked at me and nodded before entering the office.

"Mr. Cannon," said Dr. T in a conspiratorial whisper, glancing back at Otis and pulling the door mostly shut behind her. "I appreciate that you're attempting to help Otis, and I also appreciate how you protected him here today. He doesn't have many advocates in his life. His behavior has even soured the most hardened staff toward him. But you need to be careful both for his and your sake."

"I gotcha, doc."

"I'm rooting for you both, Mr. Cannon."

"For me, too?"

"Yes. But please let's not make a big deal of it."

"Of course not. Let's just say, I'll pick out curtains, but put a hold on them, unless of course they're the only ones left on the rack."

Dr. T retreated into her office, shaking her head.

"Do you have a favorite color or pattern?"

The door shut, but I could feel her grinning on the other side.

# FOURTEEN

**That afternoon, as I parked my bus and walked** by one of the school's therapists speaking in an important voice on his phone, by orderlies leaning against busses sucking cigs to the sounds of ambulances whining across the street, toward our court, I thought about Ernie Kovacs and their gym and their cheerleaders and film crew, and I wondered if maybe we didn't belong in this league. I mean, if it rained, I had to cancel practice. Of course, it only showered a few weeks a year in LA but still I felt outclassed. When I reached the court, I noticed my guys were still in their street clothes—they must feel the same way. I had to change the way we saw ourselves.

"You're as useless as every coach we've had, *güey*," said G.

"G and I are out," said Brian, pushing his hair out of his face. "It's straight up embarrassing losing every game."

"I totally don't want to quit," said Donnie.

"I'm not gonna lie to you guys. Last night was embarrassing," I said. I knew they needed motivation, but as much as I tried to recall a coach quote, the only one that surfaced was, *If lessons are learned in defeat, our team is getting a great education*, by the old Big Ten guy, Murray Warmath.

"That's all you got, Coach?" asked Toby, touching a fresh scar on his arm. "For real?"

"I'm thinking," I said, the team watching and waiting.

Toby turned to the guys. "You all gotta stop trippin'. I would lose my shit without hoops, believe that."

"I hear you, brah," said Brian. "When I played for my old school, it was lit."

"It's time for the cops to lay a sheet over our sorry asses, *cabrón*," said G.

"You boys better stop pitying yourselves, and infuse some mojo back in your game," I said. "Or she'll drop you like she never knew you."

"What does that like even mean?" said Brian.

"I used to *breathe* hoops," I said. "I was good. I played varsity when I was a freshman. But when my mom died, I stopped playing. The only thing that could've saved me, I turned my back on. Biggest mistake of my life."

"You turned your back 'cause your mom died?" asked Toby.

"'Cause I didn't have someone telling me to fight for it. The game's *yours*, boys, don't let others steal it from you."

"Wait, whose stealing what?" asked G, rubbing the 5150 tattoo on his neck.

"I never got it back," I said. "Game left me forever."

Toby shook his bald head. "Man, that's some heavy stuff you're dropping, Coach."

"Wait, I don't get it, *güey*. Who's stealing from us?" repeated G.

"The other teams calling you retards, coaches telling you you're not good enough to even be in this dismal league—they're trying to take the game. You gotta fight for what's yours."

The guys were contemplating my words when Otis, wearing shorts and sneakers, his '70s Afro seeming to stand even higher than usual, lumbered onto the court. "Where you want me, Coach?"

Everybody went silent, looking at Otis, who was all business, something I don't think they'd seen before. I led him to high post and picked up the ball and began to dribble at the foul line. "Brian, guard me," I said, waving him over.

Brian watched Otis, unsure. "Otis, G and I are thinking of killing this thing. It's straight up embarrassing losing every game. What do you think?"

"Do what the man say, Brian," said Otis, very much a command.

Brian turned to Gonzalo, who shrugged.

"I ain't tryin' to ask you again," said Otis taking a step toward Brian, who decided it was in his best interest to guard me and walked over.

"Otis," I said. "Plant your feet. No matter what happens, hold your ground."

Otis hunkered down like a hydrant.

"No matter what, just stand there—do *nothing*."

"Come on, Bri, strip it," said Toby, clapping. "Coach ain't got nothing real."

The team moved in closer.

"Deny him," said G. "Don't let Papi Van Douchebag score."

I dribbled in front of Brian, putting the ball just out of reach as he swiped at it. "That's all you got, son?"

Brian shook his head, serious. "Try me, brah," he said, banging his chest.

"Step on his sorry ass," said G.

Brian swiped at the ball a few more times, while I performed some fancy dribbling, hotdog stuff. I threw a head fake and dribbled toward Otis. Brian stayed with me like a shadow, unaware I was leading him straight into Otis, who stood there, feet planted, and Brian bounced off the big man and hit the ground like a bag of twigs, while I took a step and a two-point silencer. By just standing there, Otis set the perfect screen. Brian, from the ground, and Otis, still holding his position, both turned to me.

"That legal, Coach?" asked Otis.

"If you plant your feet and keep cool, then yeah—it's not only legal, it's good ball."

"Let's go again," said Otis.

Toby stepped forward. "Yo, Bri, switch out."

I turned to Otis, who rubbed his hands together and stretched his neck as he tracked Toby onto the court.

"You try that with me, Otis, I'll drop you, for real," said Toby, kissing his bracelet and pointing to the sky, coming up on me. "And you—let's see what you got, Papi Von Whatever Gonzalo said."

Chey, from seemingly out of nowhere, stepped up to the court—closer than I'd seen her before—and bent down, hands on her knees.

"Otis, same thing, just keep cool," I said. "Keep your feet spread, hips down and knees bent."

Toby winked at Otis, prompting the big man to clear his throat, while I dribbled the ball at the top of the key, praying there wouldn't be a murder. Toby struck the ball, knocking it from my hands. This kid was lightning. "I think you lost this, Coach," he said, handing it back to me.

I turned my back to him and signaled with my head for Otis to change position. Otis moved to the opposite side of the court while Toby checked me, his hand on my shoulder. I faked left and dribbled right, leading Toby straight toward the hydrant. Toby, not realizing Otis moved, smacked into the big man and fell back on his ass. Otis never even lost his balance. Most players were reluctant to set hard screens, to sacrifice their bodies, as they were afraid of people ramming into them—Otis, on the other hand, enjoyed it. He reminded me of my old friend, Gerald, who used his size to make up for his lack of skills, something I would have to work with Otis on.

"All right," said Toby still on his back, his hand raised in the air. "Otis, a little help?"

You could tell Otis didn't trust Toby—probably because he didn't trust anybody—but he reached down, and the two boys clasped hands, and Otis yanked him up as if he weighed twenty pounds. "You're a strong player, Otis. That's what's up."

Otis nodded to Toby then turned to me.

"Everybody line up," I called out. We were gonna have a little fun. I set the guys up to take turns running each other off Otis, and each time a defender hit the ground, the team screamed, "*Damn*!" and they winced and laughed, and that laughter was contagious. I wondered if Otis ever made up with that dog, if he would tell him about today, about me.

Then I introduced the give-and-go, which was the same play only when the player bounced off Otis, Otis rolled down into an open space and the shooter, instead of taking the shot, passed him the ball for an easy bucket, which the guys executed easily, giving us two plays and a foundation to build on.

As the guys continued to run these plays, Dr. T approached and spotted Chey standing beside me clapping every time a player sank a shot. "Chey, you and I agreed that you'd stay clear of sports for the time being. You know they're a trigger for you."

Chey shook her head, all engagement and fun falling from her eyes. "I'm just watching. It's not like I'm betting on anything."

"I don't feel that's a good idea," said Dr. T.

"I feel fine. No voices."

Voices? Of course, I knew Chey had some form of mental illness, but I never would've guessed she heard voices.

"It's not the voices I am talking about, and you know that. We both know sports helped put you in here."

"It wasn't sports, it was betting," said Chey, catching me staring at her.

I put my attention back on the court.

"All the same, we need to do some more work around controlling your anxiety and compulsive behavior before you return to watching sports."

Donnie ran G into Otis, and when G went flying, Dr. T winced, her attention darting to me. I gestured to her that it was OK, that I knew what I was doing, while Otis rolled down into the paint, and Donnie fed him the ball for an easy deuce. Chey looked back and forth between Dr. T and I, eyebrows raised, and I can't say I blamed her there. I couldn't believe we were in cahoots, either.

"Wasn't that a great play, Dr. T? Otis kept his cool," I said, prompting her.

"Sorry, Dr. T," said Otis.

"Why are you sorry, Otis?" she asked.

"Knocking Gonzalo down."

"It looked to me like you made a good shot," said Dr. T, smiling a little too eagerly as if to make even herself believe it.

Otis rocked back and forth, clearing his throat, looking to bury his hands in pockets that didn't exist. Maybe I'd have to teach him to take a compliment.

"Really!" shouted Chey. "So, you're like OK with Otis knocking these fools on their ass, but not with me *watching*?"

"Chey, please follow me, for you and I to have a private word. Team, I'll let you all get back to practice. Coach, please be careful."

"Dr. T, my eyes are up here," I said, pretending she was checking out my ass, attempting to break the tension of Chey's outburst.

Dr. T shook her head. "You really are a blooming trial."

• • •

I still wasn't sure we belonged in the league, but we were gonna stick it out, at least for now. I knew hoops, how to see the court and everybody on it, but I didn't know the first thing about coaching, and I needed a crash course. The next afternoon, against my every instinct, I drove my short bus into the parking lot of my alma mater, where I missed those two foul shots and where my father spent his time turning water into wine. I needed to watch my old man practice, study what it was that made him the best coach in these United States.

I hadn't been here since I graduated, and even with the new *Home of the Rams* sign out front, I felt like I was stepping back into the old hurt. My muscles ached and the heaviness I felt all those years ago doubled down as I remembered my friends laughing outside the cafeteria, ignoring me after my crackup. For years I hated them, but it wasn't my former friends I hated. I left all that was light and fun in the hospital, and I hated the tortured kid who returned to this school, the loner who knew too much about loss, the weird boy who pulled out his hair and flew off the handle at the slightest provocation, the boy who almost failed out of school because he couldn't concentrate. Did Chey also feel changed after hearing that first voice? Did Donnie loathe himself, as he counted to gain control of the world? Did Otis give up on people when his mother was sent to prison? My team was too young to shoulder their burdens, just as I had been, but life doesn't care much about that.

I entered by my old locker out of habit, and I continued down the hall to the gym where a shrine to my father sat behind glass, where there was no trophy for the year I missed those shots.

My father and his assistant coach, a thirty-year-old, muscular crew cut of a guy, were huddled over a clipboard. I recognized Nubbin's brother, Tim, and the Filipino and white kid from Tim's Navigator. I snuck to the back of the gym by the workout room, where a few students were jumping rope and horsing around, and sat on a gymnastic mat.

My father ran some rebounding drills, telling his players a game can be won or lost in the few feet below the hoop, something he'd been saying since I played for him. He put three players under the hoop and shot the ball. The drill was simple and good. The player who gets the rebound becomes offense and shoots, while the others try to grab the rebound, all of this done feet from the hoop. It was your standard drill, and I began to wonder why I was here. Did I really believe some drill or phrase would turn me into a coach? Or was I still trying to connect with him and gain his respect? Had any time passed? I was still the kid who missed those shots, who lost his mother and then his father. Yeah, it was on this court I learned there was more than one way to lose a parent. I became conscious of rubbing my hair between my fingers until there was only a single strand, and I yanked it out and flicked it to the floor.

Next, he ran a shooting-off-the-dribble drill, where the player takes a jumper off his weak side and then again off his strong-hand side. A little too complicated for my guys now, but I took notes. The white kid from Tim's Navigator made a strong move to the hoop, but bricked a shot off the backboard, prompting my father to blow his whistle. "You have got to make those shots," said my old man.

"I slipped," said the kid.

"I don't want excuses. You gotta make those gimmes every time."

The back door opened, letting in some kids in track uniforms, catching my old man's attention. I thought to hide but it was too late. I waved, a gesture he did not return. Instead, he blew his whistle and signaled his team in.

"I want to talk end-of-game pressure," he said loud enough for me to hear. "Great games come down to the last shot. Your Kobes, your Jameses, your superstars, they want that shot. They want the game on their shoulders."

Did any of my guys have superstar potential? Toby was good, but he couldn't do it alone.

"They live to be on the foul line, down one point, two seconds left on the clock, knowing they must sink both shots to win."

This speech was for me.

"Tim, head to the foul line."

Tim, who was a few inches shorter than my old man with the chiseled face of a model, followed the instructions, and then the best high school coach in the US told his team to get in his superstar's grill and taunt him, to avoid touching him or blocking his vision, but to dig in and make him bleed. It was clear by their confusion this was a new drill.

"Come on, Pussy Cat Dolls, get in his face or I'm getting in yours!"

My pops started them off, getting inches from Tim's nose. "You miss this shot and you're benched next game. I don't care how many UCLA coaches are here to see you." Tim's eyes widened. "Let's see if you are worth all the hype. You miss this shot, and you'll know you don't got what it takes for the Show."

Tim tried to appear as if these words weren't rattling him, but his flustered eyes betrayed him.

"If you miss, you'll never be anything real, a loser who will never be able to hold down a job," said my father. I felt the heat on my face.

Tim swallowed, fighting back emotion as the rest of the team got in on the action, telling Tim to suck their collective dicks. Then my father screamed, "Shoot!" And Tim did, he shot the ball. I was standing holding my breath. Tim was indeed a champion, and his shot landed, grabbing nothing but net.

"That's why Tim is the captain," shouted my father, turning to me. We locked eyes, and then I stormed out of the gym, slamming the door behind me.

# FIFTEEN

**Our next game was against Mitzvah High,** a Jewish high school in Beverly Hills. A mural of a white-haired, wind-blown Moses, staff held high, clearing a path in the Red Sea for the skedaddling chosen people, covered the wall behind our bench, and I hoped Moses kept it up, so the sea didn't crash down on this Jew, the slow one lagging behind the others. *Please allow my team to make it through the game without being disqualified. Amen.*

The Mitzvah coach kneeled and his players huddled close, which gave the impression of a tight-knit team. "Let's huddle like those guys," I said.

"We don't huddle, *güey*," said G.

"Come on, let's at least move a little closer to each other."

My guys took a small step closer, which still looked like strangers on a corner, but perhaps ones collectively glancing at a map. The ref approached and pointed at my guys' T-shirts. "Your team doesn't have names on their jerseys."

"They have numbers," I said.

"Rules state they must have names on the back of their jerseys."

"They've never had names before," I said.

"Actually," said Toby, "we stopped writing them on because the schools wrote smack about us in their papers and websites or whatever, using our names."

"Yeah, no way, dude, I'm not putting my name on my back for them to kick," said Brian, wiping sweat off his brow. "One player called me *Charles* on his feed, basically calling me Filipino trash, using my actual name."

"We need names," repeated the ref, "or I'm going to have to disqualify you."

"You got a marker?" I asked.

The ref happened to have one in his pocket.

As the ref moved off, I turned to Toby. "Gimme a name. Doesn't have to be your real name."

Toby shrugged, while just like our last game, students shouted vitriol at my guys. One girl screamed, "What time you due back at the loony bin?"

As I smoothed out the back of Toby's shirt, I couldn't help looking at the tick-tack-toe board he'd cut into his bicep, the scab was bright red and still new. "Why tick-tack-toe?"

"My bro and I used to play all the time," he said, kissing his bracelet and pointing to the sky.

"Who used to win?"

"Nobody wins at that game."

"True that," I said. "OK, what name?"

"*Cutter*," said Toby. "That's what the people up in here see anyway."

"You sure?" I asked.

"If you think it'll come back on you, I get it. You make up a name."

Number five's name was Cutter.

"Put *Psycho* on mine," said Otis in solidarity, nodding at Toby.

By the time I wrote *Psycho* on # 22's back, the rest of the guys had picked names: #1, Gonzalo, was *Mentiroso*—Liar in Spanish; #6, Donnie, was *The Counter*; and Brian, #00, was *Adderall*, one of his meds. I should've written *Major Depressive* on the back of mine.

The crew went out for the jump, while their coach stormed to me on the bench. "What are your players wearing?"

"Basketball uniforms."

"Get them some real uniforms."

"Right away," I said, searching under our bench until he huffed off.

I heard someone say, "That guy's a total noob," behind me. Turning, two rows back, I saw Chey messing with her phone.

"Chey," I called out. "Does Dr. T know you're here?"

She ignored me, and I thought to climb up to her, but the ref blew his whistle.

The game started by Mitzvah making a ten point run before G got the ball and executed our practiced play. He drove his defender into Afro Wall, and the defender hit the floor, but G missed his jumper. But that was OK. We set up a play.

"Gonzalo has to play it off the glass from there," shouted down Chey.

"You're not ignoring me anymore?" I said to her over my shoulder.

"You're sensitive."

"Come down here, Chey."

"Why?"

"I'm lonely by myself on the bench."

The student sitting beside her checked her out. "You go to Friedman?"

"My eyes are up here, bro," said Chey.

"Please, Chey, I need your help," I called back.

Chey climbed down the two rows and sat beside me and began messing with her phone.

"What are you doing, texting?" I asked.

"Working the percentages keeps my mind off . . . things."

"Can I see?"

Chey turned her phone to me. In the notes section, next to each of my players' names were computations I couldn't make out.

"What's it all mean?"

"Gonzalo shoots seventeen percent higher from the right side of the court. That shot he just bricked—thirty-five percent higher if he uses the backboard."

"I wasn't being nosy when you were talking to Dr. T," I said.

She hit some numbers in her phone. "Everybody thinks I'm texting or whatever at practice. I'm not."

"But you're not supposed to be watching the game, right, Chey?"

She shrugged.

"Why you here?"

"Please don't tell Dr. T," she said turning to me, eyes pleading. She broke my heart, but I was done lying or keeping info from Dr. T, who was doing everything she could to help these guys.

"You can't watch sports because you're addicted to gambling, right?" I asked.

"It's my psychosis you have to worry about, not my gambling addiction."

On the court, Donnie's defender shoved him.

"I'm gonna have to tell her, Chey."

She looked out at the court. "My father and I used to watch games together. He would tell me about the players and his theories, and I would talk to him about percentages. It was our thing. I even started going to my school's games. Actually, I did that to watch the players running up and down the court in shorts, but I got into it. I mean, I've like read at least twenty books on the game. The gambling got me all manic, not ball, but Dr. T doesn't get the difference."

"I feel you, Chey, I do, but I don't know anything about the voices. Only Dr. T can help you with that, and if she thinks sports is gonna make it worse, she's probably right."

"Sports don't have anything to do with my psychosis. That starts on its own. Most of the time, a voice will kick in quiet, like static in the background from out of nowhere. If I ignore it, it usually goes away after twenty minutes, but if it doesn't it could be with me for a while. Thing is, sometimes when I get manic, I forget and I follow one of the voices down the rabbit hole. That's when I end up in the hospital or arrested or whatever."

"You don't gotta tell me this stuff."

"I know when I'm starting to go off, so you don't have to worry about me losing it during a game. Thing is, I've been watching the team practice for two years. The other coaches ignored me—some girl watching boys run around, but you got me right away. You *saw* me. That's why you asked me to coach with you. You totally knew I could help."

"You told me, no."

"I changed my mind. Let me be your assistant coach."

"I can't."

"I'm a lot smarter than you," she said. "I can really help."

"No doubt."

"Why don't you call the guys in, and I'll talk to them about setting up a give-and-go, while you chat with Otis?"

"Otis?"

"Yeah, to help Donnie shake the punk throwing elbows every time the ref turns around. Come on, you know you've been thinking it. It's a good idea." It was like she was in my head. "I don't know what you said to Dr. T to keep Otis in school, but you definitely said *something*."

I didn't agree or disagree. What I did do was call a time out, and while Chey chatted with the team, I pulled Otis and asked him what he thought about putting a scare into Donnie's defender, if he thought he could do it without getting booted from the game. He said he would try, and when he trotted back on the court, I said a little prayer.

For the next few plays, Otis kept cool until he found himself in front of our bench, the ref facing the opposite direction down the other side of the court, and he took this opportunity to shove Donnie's defender over our bench into the first row. The ref blew his whistle but didn't have any idea how the boy ended up in the stands.

Otis leaned over under the guise of helping Donnie's defender up. "You push The Counter again, I'll pull your spine out your mouth." The defender, a tall kid with goggles, nodded as Otis helped him to a standing position.

The very next play, not surprisingly, Donnie got open and Brian bounce passed him the ball, but Donnie bounce passed it back. Brian, in turn, passed it back to Donnie, who quickly returned it. The next play was a replay of the previous with Toby.

"Come on, Donnie!" I shouted. "He's giving you room. Take the shot."

Donnie wouldn't look at me as he counted his fingers.

"I had a lotta friends and a boyfriend before I got arrested," said Chey. "I got nothing now. At first, there was a girl at Friedman I was tight with, but she OD'd. Now, it's me and the lovely voices."

Many people with mental illness were loners. I had a lot of friends before my first break, but I couldn't keep a relationship after. It was hard to be present with somebody when, as Donnie said in his assignment, you had to keep track of so many things. I was too busy keeping track of the catastrophic whispers in my head to be a real friend. "I'm not promising anything, but I'll talk to Dr. T."

"You'll ask her if I can coach with you?"

"I will, but don't get your hopes up."

"That stuff about you giving up on the game when your mother died."

"Yeah?"

"Is it true?"

"It is."

"Good."

I don't know what she meant by *good*, but Chey needed this team, and this team needed Chey.

"I gotta plan to get Donnie to shoot. You see if you can get Donnie's head together and I'll talk to the team," said Chey.

I realized I needed Chey. I signaled the guys back in, extinguishing another timeout. "Donnie, you OK, buddy?" I asked.

Donnie shook his head, his fingers playing the air, his eyes darting back and forth between his defender and my mouth. "*Jesus, be a fence around me.*"

"You're doing great. Otis put the fear of God into your guy, so you can shoot. Can you shoot, please?"

"No," said Donnie.

"Why?"

"Because if I miss, then everything is ruined, and everyone will quit the team, and you won't be able to coach, if that makes any sense." I wasn't the only one who suffered catastrophic thinking.

"Donnie, don't worry about making the shot. Take it."

"I can't."

While I spoke to Donnie, Chey talked to the team, and I thought about my father and his assistant. We weren't gonna break any records but seeing Chey talking with such passion fueled me—and that's what I needed. I needed that kind of excitement beside me on the bench.

Brian took the ball down the right side of the court. All five defenders shifted right. Toby, Otis, and G also shifted, leaving Donnie standing by himself on the left side of the court. Donnie's defender left him alone since he wasn't shooting and not a threat. Brian then whip passed to Donnie before purposely dropping to the ground so Donnie couldn't return the ball. Desperate to unload it, Donnie looked for someone to pass to, but the rest of the team had also flopped to the wood in vaudevillian brilliance. Donnie, to dump the ball, shot. Swish! Nothing but net! I loved this kid. I really did. I'd never seen anyone with such raw talent.

The team showered Donnie with high fives, and G almost knocked him down with a chest bump. I held out my fist to Chey, but she just looked at it in pity. "Nobody fist bumps anymore, OG."

I picked up her hand and forced contact, which prompted her to wipe her knuckles on her jeans.

The next play, G ran the guard off the immovable Otis, who rolled down, caught G's pass and shot. The ball bounced around the rim but didn't land.

"Ten feet is out of his zone," said Chey. "Anything under seven is a total gimme."

"Why you telling me? Tell Otis."

"You tell him."

"No, you."

"Do you really think Dr. T will let me coach?"

"I'll give it a shot, Chey."

"But she totally beyond hates you."

"I'm growing on her."

"Like fungus you are."

"You're pretty funny."

"Funnier than you."

"Wait, no way you're funnier than me."

"You're so not even that funny."

Donnie landed a few more buckets, two of them threes, and my guys were getting pumped and starting to hustle. For the next five minutes we matched them basket to basket, and we started the third quarter with the score thirty-eight to nineteen.

That's when Mitzvah's coach subbed Donnie's defender for the Missing Link, a big hairy kid who outweighed Donnie by seventy pounds. As soon as the ref turned his back, the Missing Link shoved Donnie to the floor.

"Come on, ref, number eleven mugged my guy," I said, sounding like a coach, startling myself. Would my old man have said the same thing? I thought to ask him about it later but hated myself for the thought. I didn't need his help.

The ref ignored me, but on the next play, the defender caught Donnie's wrist, and a shrill whistle pierced the air.

"Nice call, ref. Keep an eye on that kid. He's a thug."

"Watch yourself, Coach," said the ref, gesturing for me to get off the floor and back to my bench.

The next play started with Brian inbounding to Toby, who threw it to G, who pushed it up the floor. Donnie's defender kept bumping him, not allowing him to get open, until Otis came up to set a pick, and Donnie's defender rammed into him, the two boys falling to the ground.

The ref blew a whistle and called a foul on Otis because he moved his feet. If Otis remained planted, the foul would've been on number eleven. "That's OK, Otis, just remember to be the Great Oak."

Otis picked himself up and waved, letting me know he understood.

The next few plays, Donnie's defender shoved him whenever the ref turned around. I called to Donnie to see if he was OK, but he shook his head, his fingers dancing, all of which got the attention of Afro Wall.

"Coach," I yelled out. "Your guy, number eleven, he's playing cheap ball."

Mitzvah's coach ignored me.

The score was sixty-eight to thirty-nine at the start of the fourth when Toby performed a great no-look bounce pass right into Donnie's hands. Donnie turned to shoot but his defender tomahawked him in the head. Like a linebacker, Otis charged, knocking the Missing Link into the air so that when he landed on the wooden floor the entire stands winced. I charged out to break up the fight, but Otis jumped up and reached for the sky as if being arrested.

"Number twenty-two, Psycho, is gone!" said the ref, blowing his whistle and pointing at the door.

"Are you kidding me, ref? What about the flagrant on my guy?"

"If you would have let me finish, I was going to say that number eleven is also out. I will not have this kind of play on my court."

"How about you give the boys a warning?" I said. "What if they say sorry and shake hands? We got only five players."

"Not my problem," said the ref.

Chey was in my ear, asking me to call the game. I thought we should continue without Otis, but she made a good case against losing the gains we made by going four against five and getting blown out the last quarter. I trusted her instinct and called it, then helped Donnie up and asked if he was OK, which he was, just rattled. We both turned to Otis, as he stared down the Missing Link. "Otis," I called out, trying to get his attention. "Otis!"

He turned to me. "That boy gonna get got, he messes with Donnie again."

Donnie smiled.

"Come on, guys, let's hit it," I said, gathering up the team. Donnie slid up beside me and my instincts took over, and I placed my hand on his shoulder, eliciting a blood-curdling scream.

"Sorry, Donnie. I forgot."

# SIXTEEN

**That night Gerald and I went to a pub in the hood to catch up.**
My old friend showed me pics of his new baby on his phone like a
proud papa. I told him about Alvarito and my being homeless—and
how even with all that history, it sucked to need help from my pops,
considering the kind of trash my old man still pulled, like what he
did at practice.

"I mean, here I am *coaching* of all things," I said, "and I can't
even ask my own father, *the best coach in the US*, for help."

Gerald shook his head. "I hear you. It's messed up."

"When he looks at me, all he sees is a failure. A failure whose roots
can be traced back to missing those foul shots all those years ago," I said.

"Well, I love you, buddy."

"The only thing that could come between us was Brandi Johnson," I said.

"I remember her! We didn't talk for months."

"And she never dated either of us," I said, shaking my head. "Her
loss, now that we are both pillars of the community."

"Speak for yourself, my baby girl's gonna change the world one
day," Gerald said with a grin. Then Gerald hit me with something I
all but forgot about. "Remember in seventh grade, you always had
that b-ball, carried it everywhere with you."

I smiled. "My mom used to make me wash it every night before dinner. I would eat with it on my lap."

"You'd hold the ball with one hand, hold your dick to take a piss with the other."

"Remember Ms. Peshotta would try to steal it from me in the hallway between classes?"

"She did a few times, too," said Gerald. "She was a good hooper."

"Yeah. She was a great teacher. To Ms. Peshotta," I said, raising my glass.

Gerald and I clicked our pint glasses together and drank.

"As I recall," I said, "you made fun of me about that ball. You were relentless."

Gerald smiled. "But I envied your ball control. You were unpredictable on the court. You know—you play with guys enough, you know their tells. Remember, Jamal?"

I nodded. "Used to purse his lips before he shot."

"*Every time.* Or like some players favor one side of the court, or they always shoot with their right hand. Not you. Nobody ever knew what you were gonna do. I miss watching you ball, brother. Matter of fact, I'm looking forward to seeing your kids play your unpredictable style of hoops."

"Gerald, I missed you, brother."

"Me too, Mikey. I'm sorry I didn't know how bad things got for you."

"That's on me. I'm sorry I lost touch."

Sometimes old friends see you better than you see yourself. I didn't need to learn from my old man. I was going to coach my own way, with, I hoped, an assistant who hears voices by my side. First thing though, I needed to pick up five basketballs.

• • •

The next morning, I pulled up in my school bus to Nubbin's where he was playing ball alone, jawing to himself like I had as a kid whooping Kobe in my driveway. Little guy had some skill, dribbling well with both hands and pulling up some impressive three-pointers. I was about to blow the horn when his brother trotted onto the court to guard him. Nubbin put the ball to the floor, throwing a head fake and putting his bro back on his heels. Nubbin was good. Only when he went to shoot, Tim swatted the ball away.

"Don't even think about it, *güey*," said G.

"What?" I asked.

"Nubbin's cracked," said G turning his Dodgers hat around on his head so it was facing backwards. "He shit in a gym bag."

"Come on, G, he didn't shit in any bag," I said.

"And he blew up a car, stuck some dynamite in the tailpipe or something. Truthfully."

"Chey, is G talking trash?"

"You're going to talk to Dr. T about my coaching today, right?" she asked, single focused.

"Yes. Like I said when you got on the bus, I will try."

"Nubbin is a straight up mumbling psychopath," said Brian, twirling his hair between his fingers. "He's worse than Donnie. No offense, Donnie."

"Don't do Donnie like that," said Otis, clearing his throat.

"Yeah," said Donnie. "Don't do me like that."

"Are you guys kidding me?" I asked. "You're judging him for mumbling. I mumble to myself all day long."

"We hafta deal with you, Coach," said G.

On the court, Tim shoved Nubbin, who shoved right back, and the two were about to pop off when I honked, causing both boys to turn.

"We need a sixth," I said. "Otherwise, we'll end up forfeiting every game. I'm gonna ask him to play."

"Boy does got some talent, for real," said Toby. "I've seen him pick up the ball at school when he thought nobody was watching, but he's got no interest in other people."

"Besides shitting in their bags," said Brian.

"Besides that," allowed Toby.

"Dude walks like five hours a day," said Brian. "I've seen him— ambles around LA talking at himself. One time in downtown Culver, I called out to him, but he straight canceled me, brah, just walked right by. He's seriously not right."

"He's probably walking to clear his mind. Nothing wrong with that," I said.

Nubbin entered the bus head down, silent.

"Nubbin," I said, as he walked by me like I wasn't there and sat in an empty row. "We need another guy on the team. How about it?"

Nubbin just stared out the window at his brother shooting.

"Total hater," said Brian. "Psycho Midget doesn't care about helping us out."

"Shut up, Brian," said Chey from the seat behind me.

"Forget you," said Brian.

"Suck my dick," said Chey.

"Whip it out," said Brian.

Nubbin just stared out the window, blinking and raising his eyebrows.

"Nubbin, you in there?" I asked. "You had your bro back on his heels, but you telecasted your shot."

Nothing.

"Think about it. We could use someone with your skills."

Nubbin shook his head at his lap.

"The man's talking to you, *güey*," said G, turning his hat back around so it was once again facing front.

I drove for a bit before turning on a busy street, when a Coke bottle with clear liquid smashed against my windshield—from the inside! I slammed the brakes and pulled over to the side of the road to avoid a major accident, as the kids leapt up screaming like they were on fire, the bus instantly reeking like skid row.

"Yo, what happened, Nubbin!" screamed Toby.

"Extra!" yelled Brian. "You still want him on the team, Coach?"

I tried to catch my breath, my hands shaking.

"Open the door, Coach," yelled Toby. "It stinks in here, for real!"

I swung open the door and Nubbin bolted by me into the busy street, darting between cars like an expert back across the avenue. He had some major issues, but speed wasn't one of them.

"Is everybody all right?" I asked the bus.

"You got piss all over you, Coach," said G, up in the aisle.

I looked down. Not only was urine all over my shirt and hair, I now had to tell the school I lost a kid.

# SEVENTEEN

**I pulled up to the school, and my gagging kids sprung from the bus** with the histrionics of theater actors playing for the back row. A fellow driver, Angie, perhaps thirty with the face of an actress and a pear-shaped body perfect for sitting on bus seats approached, shaking her head. "Look who done popped his cherry," she said through the open door. "No, didn't take you long at all."

She onboarded and we examined the spider crack in the windshield from the bottle crashing. "You know your bus smell like pee, right?"

I shared my morning with her.

"That's nothing. I had one kid, he gets off the bus right here, and he turns and throws a big rock at my windshield. In case you ain't notice, this ain't exactly a quarry up in here. Kid must've been carrying a two-pound boulder in his pocket. Now, I ask you, what you gonna do with that? No. I'm asking you?"

"Don't know."

"You get your windshield fixed and fill out an accident report, and tell someone who look smarter than you about it, and then you put it behind you."

"One of my kids bolted."

"Let me guess, Nubbin?"

I nodded.

"You let the doctors worry about Nubbin. You don't get paid for that kind of worry. They double my salary, I worry about a kid going jackrabbit, but until that time, I punch out at 4:30, and I go home and see my babies. 'Cause if you take it home with you, it will keep you up all night—take it from me. You gotta shake it off," she said, massaging my shoulders like a coach getting a boxer ready for the match.

"I was prepared for fighting or whatever, but not for pee. If he didn't want to hoop, he could've said no."

"Don't you even try to get in their head. I'm serious. Not if you wanna stick. Let me hear you say you're not going to try and get up in their head. Say it."

I told her I heard her, but I couldn't stop thinking about Nubbin. I feared what he might do next. If a kid is willing to whip a bottle of pee at a windshield, what else was he capable of?

• • •

A patient man would have taken two trips, but I snatched up the five balls I'd gotten from Santee Alley, a low-end market with anything from piñatas to three-piece suits, and scuttled toward the court for afternoon practice like some overwhelmed juggler when I noticed Dr. T, her inky-black hair yanked tighter than usual in a bun, approaching in long, deliberate strides. I still hadn't talked to her about Chey coaching. I was afraid she would say no and that would be that.

"Are you OK, Mr. Cannon? I heard about your morning bus ride."

I rehashed the incident and handed her two balls, which she dropped, prompting me to reach down and drop the other three, which took off in every direction like excited puppies.

"When I was a kid," I said, chasing a ball, "I used to carry one of these with me everywhere—I mean, *everywhere*. It gave me good ball control. Some of my teachers would even let me bring it to class. I got to thinking, if I got them each a ball, maybe you would let them bring it to class."

"They have a difficult enough time focusing in class without basketballs," she snapped. She picked up a ball and threw it to me, sending it over my head.

"You did that on purpose," I said. "You upset I didn't tell you about Nubbin or something? I didn't want to bother you with it."

"No, Mr. Cannon, what I'm cheesed off about is that during her morning therapy, Chey informed me you made her the assistant basketball coach," she said, raising that ancient eyebrow of hers.

"No. No. No," I said, my hands up in a defensive position, the balls left to scatter. "I told her I would talk to you about it."

"Did you tell her not to let me *steal* basketball from her?"

"I did mention something like that," I said, backing up, my innocent hands still raised high.

"Because I'm not attempting to steal anything, Mr. Cannon. What I'm attempting to do is help her control her anxiety and compulsive behavior, and we took a great big step backwards in that regard today because of this coaching business."

"What happened?"

"She threw a wobbler when I told her she couldn't coach."

"She said you wouldn't get it," I said, picking up the ball she threw.

"This population can be masters at staff-splitting. And whether you recognize it or not, mate, you're a staff member, and you must always be aware that these kids may be pitting us against each other."

"She needs the team."

"You could not possibly know what she needs."

"And the team needs her. *That* I know."

"I don't want to insult you, Mr. Cannon, but what Chey is dealing with is very complicated. It's hard enough to be a young woman under normal circumstances, but to compound that with compulsive behavior and psychosis and a difficult family situation is challenging. Any stimulus that could provoke her anxiety and compulsion should be eliminated now, do you not agree?"

I was once again carrying five balls. "She told me she's lonely, that she doesn't have friends anymore."

"She told you she's lonely?" asked Dr. T.

"Can you grab a couple without winging them over my head?" I asked, gesturing to the balls spilling from my arms.

She begrudgingly took two again, and we continued toward the court where my guys were getting ready for practice by whipping a ball at one another. "When precisely did she tell you she was lonely?"

"During the game. And she said she used to watch ball with her old man. I guess she doesn't talk to him anymore."

"I'm sorry. Did you say she told you about her father?"

"Yeah, so?"

"I've been attempting to get her to open up about her father for over a year—since the divorce. How did you get her to talk about him?"

I shrugged. "Dunno."

"And she went to the game last night?" said Dr. T, stopping. I did the same.

"Oh, she left that part out, did she?"

"In group therapy," began Dr. T, "I asked the students to write a personal memory they feared sharing, one they would eventually give to at least one fellow student from group. It's a crucial exercise in trust. Chey never even bothered to complete the first part of the assignment, to turn her work into me. She doesn't share herself, and I've been trying to get her to do so for some time. It's a very important step in the coping process for her."

"Why's it important for her to share herself?"

"Our secrets lose their stranglehold on us when we share them. Things we think expose us as different show our similarities."

"Has anybody shared theirs?"

"Only Donnie and Otis have completed the second part of the assignment, and they chose to share with the entire group."

"Why? They only had to give it to one kid, right?"

"They wouldn't or couldn't tell me why, but I was thrilled they did."

"Chey brought up her father when she was telling me why she should coach," I said.

Chey exited the school carrying some papers. "Dr. T," she called out. "I thought about what you said this morning. I wrote my thing and put a copy in your box."

"You did?" asked an astounded Dr. T, looking back and forth between the approaching Chey and me. "Brilliant, Chey. I appreciate how difficult it must've been for you."

"I wasn't looking to relive my first crackup, *thanks* for *that*."

"I will read it straight away, and when you're ready you can share it with somebody from group. You'll feel a great weight lifted, I promise," said Dr. T.

"Yeah . . . no. I'm not sharing it with anybody from group," she said, as she stopped a few feet away from us, shaking her head. "It's totally beyond personal."

"Not now. When you're ready."

"I'll never be ready."

"The exercise was to develop trust, which is something you and I have been working on for a long time. I do feel strongly about this, Chey."

"I feel *strongly* you should let me coach." She ran her hand through her hair. "I made a copy for Mikey."

Dr. T's attention swung to me. "Why are you OK with sharing your story with Mr. Cannon and not someone from group, some of whom have shared their own with you?"

"Because if you change your mind and let me be Mikey's assistant, he and I are going to have to trust each other," she said. "We'll have to know what the other is thinking at all times."

I nodded. I didn't mean to, but I couldn't stop myself.

"Chey, did you do your assignment to convince me to let you coach?" said Dr. T. "Are you attempting to manipulate me?"

Chey handed me the pages, which I took as if they were a priceless document, letting the balls drop and bounce away.

"Chey?" asked Dr. T.

"I did them," she snapped. "You wanted me to do it and I did it. OK?"

By this time the team approached.

"What's with the papers, Coach?" asked Brian.

"They plays or something?" asked G.

I looked at Chey. I didn't mean to give her up. It was just a reaction.

"No way, is that your story, Chey?" asked Brian, wiping his hands on his shorts.

"Don't even worry about it, because you guys aren't reading any of it," said Chey.

"I'll straight give you mine if you give me yours," said Brian.

"Mine be all kinds of embarrassing," said Otis, clearing his throat.

"Yeah, it was," said G. "You and that poodle."

"Coach, I be in my right to beat his ass."

"G, I'm a second away from beating you myself," I said.

"Chey," said Donnie. "Nobody laughed at mine, and you know mine was weird."

I looked at Dr. T. She was watching the interaction like a scientist observing a chemical reaction.

Chey shook her head, overwhelmed.

"Yo, Coach, so what's with the balls?" said Toby.

"Right," I said. "Everybody gets one."

Everybody grabbed a ball.

"Dr. T, guys would love if you could watch practice," I said, hoping she would stay long enough to see some benefit for Chey and change her mind.

"I wouldn't love it," said G.

"You gonna love it just fine," said Otis, showing G his fist.

Dr. T looked at my hands as I folded Chey's pages and slipped them in my front pocket. "For a few minutes," she said.

"Great. OK, guys, the ball you're each holding never leaves your side. You eat with it. It goes to the bathroom with you."

"Balls can't go to the bathroom," said Donnie. "They don't have penises."

"Donnie," I said. "Did you make a joke?"

Donnie giggled.

"My man, Donnie," I said. "That was a good joke."

"Thanks."

Dr. T allowed a small smile.

"This ball should feel like an extension of your body," I said, feeling Donnie's smile smack me from halfway across the court. "Like an arm, Donnie. And. . . . I want you to tell your friends, teachers, parents, probation officers, doctors, lawyers, case workers, whoever, to try and steal it. I want you guys to learn to protect that ball."

"Like we do our own balls?" said Donnie, giggling.

"Don't force it, Donnie," I said.

"Sorry, Coach."

"We can keep them?" asked Brian, tossing the ball in the air, performing a quick arm wave, and catching it.

"They're yours, unless someone steals it."

Donnie hugged the ball to his chest.

"I'll make your teachers and the staff aware that they should attempt to steal the ball away from you. You can even take them to class," said Dr. T, changing her tune. It felt good Dr. T thought my idea had merit, the kind of good I hadn't enjoyed in eons. Now I needed to change her mind about Chey coaching.

"Really? We can bring 'em to class?" asked Otis, palming the ball in his meaty hand.

"You can," said Dr. T.

The guys looked as if they'd won something.

"OK," I said. "Let's talk about all the shots we missed. Easy layups, jumpers in the paint. We gotta get better at shooting if we're gonna win a game. Donnie, put your ball down."

Donnie shook his head.

"OK, we'll use your ball," I said, realizing he was not putting his ball down, not ever. "Pass it here. Come on, Donnie, I'm going to pass it right back."

Donnie turned to Chey, which caught the eye of Dr. T.

"It's OK, Donnie," said Chey. "Coach is gonna give it right back. He's gotta plan." She was already the assistant.

"All right, Donnie," I said, passing him back his ball. "Shoot!"

Donnie grabbed it and sank an easy deuce.

"OK, Donnie, do it again in slow motion," I said. "The same exact thing, and I want everybody to watch the master."

"Come on, guys, bring it in," said Chey.

The team circled Donnie.

"Everyone watch what he does," I said, again passing Donnie the ball. "How he holds his hands, how he turns to the hoop—his eyes aren't on the ball. They're on the front of the iron."

"And his elbows are in," said Chey.

In comically slow motion, Donnie shot.

"Good spin, good spin, and swish," I said as the ball sailed through the rim grabbing nothing but net. "Everybody takes turns shooting. Donnie, you give pointers."

"Do me first, Donnie," said Otis. "Tell me what I do wrong."

Donnie watched Otis brick a shot. "Your elbows are all the way out here," said Donnie, flapping his own like wings.

Toby nodded at me, as if we were on the same page. "Yo, Chey, those plays you thought of last night were dope."

"See, Dr. T, Toby knows I can help."

"I'm serious. You need to think of some more, girl," he said.

"Mikey asked *me* to coach," said Chey, "not the other way around."

"I'm sorry, Chey," said Dr. T. "Maybe later in the season we can reevaluate."

"Team needs me now!" she shouted.

"Yeah, Dr. T," said Toby, rubbing his dome. "That's what's up."

"Why can't you give me a chance? Please?" said Chey, grabbing Dr. T's hand.

"I'm sorry," said Dr. T, yanking away her hand as if Chey crossed a line. "You're not ready."

"You just don't get it!" screamed Chey, looking to me for help, and when I didn't say a word, she bolted, ran off. I wanted to fight for her, but I just couldn't, not in front of the team.

Dr. T reproached me with a subtle shake of her head before hurrying after Chey.

"You asked Chey to coach with you?" asked Toby, dribbling between his legs and around his back.

I nodded.

"Word on that," he said, banking a soft shot off the backboard.

"I'm also shopping for a captain," I said, "Someone to lead *on* the court, help me get these boys to pass. What do you say?"

"Me?" He stopped dribbling. "No way, Coach."

"You got leadership skills, Toby. You must know that."

"I can't be trusted to look after people," he said, rubbing the stubble on his shaved head in a front to back motion. I wondered if he was talking about somebody specific.

"I need someone guiding them on the court, and the guys already look up to you." I turned to Otis. "Otis, what do you think about Toby as team captain?"

"Fine," he said, making a shot as Donnie watched.

"You're not gonna get a more ringing endorsement than that," I said.

"Donnie, I made one," shouted Otis like a kid after his father's approval.

"Good work, Otis," said a very serious Donnie.

"Don't do me like that, Coach," said Toby, his eyes growing distant as he touched his bracelet. "I'm not who you think I am."

I clearly hit a nerve. "Think about it is all I ask."

"I said no, Coach. Leave it! For real!"

• • •

After dropping off the last student, I pulled the bus to the side of the road and pulled Chey's assignment out of my pocket. I unfolded the papers and, with my palm, straightened them on the steering wheel. Her memory was written in pen in perfect script. Wondering if Dr. T read her copy yet, I prayed there was something in these pages, some nugget, I could use to convince her to let Chey coach.

## CHEY'S ASSIGNMENT

My memory is from the day my former best friend and I stopped being friends. We'd been besties since second grade and now we don't talk at all, which is *so* depressing.

Selene and I were like the same person. When we weren't together, we were texting. We talked the same, dressed the same. We decorated each other's lockers on Valentine's Day in case one of us didn't get any cards. I was the only person she talked to about saving up for plastic surgery on her flat butt. One time I dreamt that my father got hit by a car, and I called Selene at three a.m., and she calmed me down.

Anyway, the day in question, Selene and I were at the Grove in line at the Veggie Grill, which is last-meal-before-the electric-chair good, and which we called Snack Grill, because all the boys that worked there were hot. The line was super long. I hadn't been feeling well for a week, and this head-ache started, like the school bell was ringing in my ears. Selene said, "I'll go get you Advil from my car if you buy my falafel burger."

As soon as she walked away, I heard this guy calling my name: "Chey! Chey!" as if he were a few feet away but out of sight. He sounded like my dad's age—forty or whatever. I turned in every direction to see who was calling me, but I didn't see anybody, which was weird. The Market was packed. I started to get dizzy like I might puke, and my fingers began to tingle, which was random, and I began to bite my fingernails, a lovely new habit of mine. Of course, I understand now what was happening, but that was the first time I ever felt weird like this and had no idea an attack was coming. This was my first attack.

I thought I saw one of my neighbors, a guy who was always checking me out, but I couldn't tell. I sort of doubted it, since he was an ortho and not the type to call my name and skate. Maybe what I heard only sounded like somebody calling my name? TBH, I was over the whole thing now.

The lady ordering was taking her sweet time. I mean, you don't have to be in Mensa to choose between guacamole and hummus. I'm all like, the struggle is real, lady. Then I caught this man's voice again, only this time he seemed closer, as if he were a few people away like some creeper or something. "Where are you?" I said out loud, feeling like a tool. A girl and her mother in front of me in line turned around and the mom asked if I was talking to them. I said no sorry, but I was thinking, stay in your lane, lady. And then I heard "Chey!" again.

I spun around, but I still didn't see anybody I knew. I was like WTF right now. I mean, it felt like he was standing beside me, but there was no one there. I literally felt like I was dexing, sweating and dizzy and disgusting. If I didn't need to order Selene's food, I would've taken off.

I texted Selene to see how far away she was. At the exact same time, the voice returned: "Chey, I need you to do something."

"Where are you, anyway? If this is some kind of joke, it's not funny. I'm beyond serious right now." For a second, I thought Selene might be messing with me, but then this invisible dude was all like, "Don't worry about that." And I'm like, "How come I can't see you?" And he's like, "You are going to have to kill your brother."

"What?" I shouted. "You did not just say that to me!"

"You need to kill your little brother, Stephen."

I was like out of there right then. I bolted, shoving some tourists out of my way. I was officially shook, like way beyond freaking out. I ran through the crowd in the direction Selene had gone because I needed my best friend. I tripped over a little kid who was bent over tying his shoe, causing me to smash into a cotton-candy cart. The voice was all AGRO, shouting in my ear: "Kill your brother or I'm going to choke you to death!"

I felt hands tighten around my neck. I was losing my breath—not because I was running but because super large, Shaquille O'Neal hands were tightening around my throat. "Kill your brother, and I will let you live." I grabbed my throat but there were no hands there. I rounded a corner, knocking over a whole magazine stand. "*Kill* your brother or I'll kill you." I was being murdered by an invisible man.

That's when I saw Selene. "Selene," I called out. "Help me!" She didn't hear me right away. I screamed, gave it everything I had but the hands were choking me. "Selene! Selene! He's killing me!"

"Kill Stephen or I'll kill you!"

"SELENE!"

This time she saw me. I'll never forget the look in her eyes. Terrified. I collapsed onto the floor and was thrashing around like I was having a seizure or something. People were all staring at me like I was crazy, as I screamed, "Selene, help me, please! He's trying to kill me!"

But she was frozen, beyond freaked out, staring at me as gawkers started snapping photos on their phones. It was the most embarrassing day of my sixteen years of life. I don't know how long I stayed there like that until some stranger called *Paul Blart: Mall Cop*. Selene disappeared, never even checked on me to see if I was okay. She didn't visit me for the whole two weeks I was in the hospital either. I texted and called but she never answered. And when I finally returned to school, she got up and changed tables when I sat down next to her at lunch. I used to think that Selene and I would be best friends forever. I thought she was my ride or die. When we were little, we talked about how we would get married on the same day and live next door to each other and babysit each other's kids. I don't hate her. I really don't. Believe it or not, more than anything else, I miss her.

# EIGHTEEN

**I shut my eyes, allowing Chey's terror to get into my blood** and swim through me. I swallowed, feeling monstrous hands squeezing my Adam's apple, causing me to gag. To clutch at murderous hands that aren't there is to question reality, the one thing a person should be able to take for granted.

Chey's issues were much more debilitating than mine. I felt pathetic that my trouble easily upended me.

I wished I could tell her I read the pages, and everything was going to be OK, but it wasn't. It wasn't going to be OK. She would continue to walk around knowing the horror waiting in the shadows to pounce on her. I couldn't imagine her fear. How many of these episodes had she suffered already? And it wasn't only her—how many times had Donnie fought against winged devils? And Otis? Did he have breaks like Donnie and Chey? Did the others? A pain that ran from my forehead to my clenched jaw caused me to dry heave.

Coaching could cause Chey to become so anxious and compulsive that she would miss an oncoming psychotic episode. Why would she risk that? Did she love the game that much? The camaraderie? Even if I could convince Dr. T to let her coach, should I? What if she hurt herself, or worse, on my watch?

And Toby? Why was he so against being captain? I would never get Donnie his win unless Toby became captain and Chey my assistant. My erratic breathing plus the pain in my head made me disoriented. I needed my bed. I fired up the bus and drove, as the wind from the open window chewed at my face like wild dogs.

• • •

I pulled up to the house to see Richard Knowles, the ESPN reporter, shooting hoops with my father in the driveway. I hadn't said boo to my old man since the stunt he pulled at the gym, and confronting him now would be disastrous in ways I couldn't imagine.

I felt like I was lying in a ditch with shovelfuls of dirt raining down on me. I couldn't let my father see me like this. He'd seen the signs of a breakdown too often not to notice them, and worse, what if ESPN wanted to put me on camera now? No. I needed to slip inside without anybody seeing me, so I parked up the block and waited for an opening.

The camerawoman continued to film my father taking foul shots while Richard rebounded. Finally, after waiting for God knows how long, the ball took a bounce off Richard's shoe into some shrubs, and when all three became distracted, I hurried to the front steps.

But it didn't work. Richard turned and shouted, waving me over. "Mikey, I want to talk to you." Life's funny—a month ago, if you would've told me Richard Knowles from E:60 wanted to bend my ear, I would've told you to stop being such a tool, but now he did, and all I could think to do was avoid him. "Come here, Mikey," he called out.

My head was now a bag of sand that prevented me from moving without falling. My father screamed out my name, reminding me of the million times my mother would call me home from these steps. She would stand here pointing to her watch as I dragged myself home, wishing I could stay out with my friends. What I wouldn't give to be able to speak to my mom about Chey. She could tell me what it was like to have a psychotic episode, how to help her. "Richard wants to talk to you, boy!" yelled my father. I'd also like to ask her how my old man was able to take life in such stride, not to mention why he was contemptible.

"Sorry, *Ellen* just started," I shot back, pointing to my naked wrist.

Richard, having retrieved the ball from my neighbor's tree, was now trotting back with it. "I have a few questions for you."

"I can't now."

"Mikey, your father's made thirteen foul shots in a row," he gushed, passing the ball to my old man, who sank another shot. "Come on, Mikey, join us."

"Cast of *Atlanta Housewives* is gonna be on *Ellen* today. It's a must-see TV type of situation," I said, my keys jangling in my trembling hands. I was so close to the dark sanctuary of my room.

"Mikey, it's important for your father's documentary to get you on camera," said Richard.

My father sank another shot and turned to me, his face puckering as he saw the familiar struggle in my eyes.

"You want me to come over, pops?" I asked. "You sure?"

Richard turned to my old man, confused as to why I would raise such a question. "Of course, he wants you to come over. Right, Andrew?" he said.

My pops did the type of nod where you barely move your head. He had to pretend he wanted me in this doc. The pain in my forehead and jaw surged, but as upset as I was at him, I wouldn't ruin his sixty minutes of fame. We would never get past that. Not ever. I hoped when I finally had enough cash to move out, my old man and I would be on better terms than when I arrived. My mother was gone, and he was all I had. As I trudged over, the dizziness unbearable, I heard my father in the middle of one of his favorite diatribes:

"Nowadays, you can't tell the winners from the losers—everybody gets a trophy, a pat on the back. *Hey, you did your best, son.*

*That's all anyone can ask*. That kind of nonsense gonna kill the game, turn this generation into a bunch of pissants."

"What do you think about that?" asked Richard, the camera swinging over to me.

I was adrift, a prizefighter searching for his footing after a wallop to the head.

"What do you think about the everyone-gets-a-trophy generation?" Richard continued.

"I guess I don't think *everybody* should get one," I managed.

"You agree with your father?"

"No. I don't agree with my father," I snapped. I didn't agree with him about anything. "There's other smaller victories, like a kid who overcomes the fear of shooting. I'd like to see that kid get a trophy."

"Horse piss. You shouldn't get a trophy unless you win the championship—end of story," he said, making another shot. "A kid who's scared to shoot should be on the bench."

"As a coach, would you not want to work with that kid to overcome his fear?" I said, wanting to know.

"The kid who is scared to shoot?" asked my father.

"Yeah," I said, as the camerawoman took a step closer to my old man.

"I'd work with him," he said, looking at the camera, "but not at the expense of the team. You don't get to where I am by playing kids who have no reason to be on the court. It's hoops, not a charity."

"It's not the pros, either," I said.

My father bounced the ball, then turned to Richard. "I tried to teach Dink over there to be a winner, but it was like teaching a turd to be a flower," said my old man. "Mikey, tell Mr. Knowles about your moment in the sun, about your shot at greatness?"

"You can't help yourself, can you?" I said, coughing, still trying to catch my breath.

Richard fed my father the ball.

"Like I said, there are winners and there are losers, and my boy lives on the wrong side of things," said my father.

I watched him dribble the ball three times, something he always did to set his rhythm, a rhythm now making me wild with anger and vengeance. "No way you make this shot. No way," I said, challenging him. Let's see if he could pass his own pressure test.

My father turned to me and smiled, as I stepped up on him. I was a foot away. I would show him how Nubbin's brother felt with everybody in his face. "Which are you, Dad, a winner or a loser? I'll bet you a hundred bucks you miss this shot."

"You don't got a hundred."

"If you miss, everybody who watches ESPN will see you choke. Famous coaches, players, your precious Larry Bird."

Richard signaled the camera to push in on my old man as he stepped back and shook his head at me. "You're pathetic," he said. Then he re-approached his spot and bounced the ball three times.

I turned to the camera. "My father can't stomach weakness, isn't that right, Dad?"

"Don't embarrass yourself, son," said my old man, shaking his head before going back to bouncing the ball.

"You want to know about my old man, I'll tell you," I said, the camera pivoting to me. "There were times my mother suffered crippling depression, and my old man—the *winner*—didn't help her, let her suffer alone. She would sit up all night long smoking cigarettes, staring into space, unable to even speak, and what did he do—nothing."

"Nice try, but it's not going to work, boy," said my father, his eyes on the rim.

"He told you my mom died as a result of a car crash," I said. "Did he tell you that years before, she tried to kill herself?" I surprised myself I was willing to take it this far, but I was feeling wild.

My father turned to me. I'd gotten to him.

"She took pills."

"That's enough!" he shouted.

"But she changed her mind and called the ambulance herself, all while my old man, coach of the year, slept. You didn't think I remembered that, did you, Pops? But I do. I remember her sticking her fingers down her throat in a panic, and how those same fingers trembled as she dialed 911. I was ten years old, and I remember screaming for you to wake up, Dad, screaming at you to save mom. I remember."

My father's Adam's apple jumped as he turned his head from side to side as if stretching his neck. He then bounced the ball three more times. While the camera pivoted toward him, my father shot, the ball hitting the front of the rim and bouncing up in the air, hitting the backboard and then landing. "*Nothing* rattles me," he said to Richard, who nodded.

"Good for you, Dad," I said.

"Winners don't choke!"

"I think we've had enough afternoon fun," I said.

"Mikey," said Richard, sharp eyes on me, "you owe me an interview."

I turned to my father as he prepared for another shot. I saw a man I not only didn't get, but one I didn't like. "Richard, why is it important to interview me?"

"To help us understand your father."

"Not sure I'd be much help there."

"We're going to speak to a lot of people—old mentors, former players who went pro, rival coaches—but your perspective will be important in helping round him out."

"Good," I said, my father sinking another shot. "But I'm gonna tell you about the real Andrew Cannon. The one I know."

Richard smiled.

"We'll see if you're still smiling after my interview," I said, huffing off.

• • •

That night I couldn't sleep, rattled that I told ESPN about my mom's suicide attempt. I never spoke about it, not even to myself. After struggling to nod off for a few hours, I finally got up and knocked around the cabinets looking for some sleeping pills, but my father apparently slept like a baby and didn't need any. I settled on some expired Benadryl and went back to bed, but after an hour I still couldn't sleep, and to make matters worse, the Benadryl gave me the jumps.

I made my way to the living room, which looked exactly the same as it had the night my mother swallowed the bottle of pills. The leather couch still faced the window, beside which sat a phone on an Indian-looking end table. I recalled being at the top of the stairs watching my mother stumbling around this very room, how I ran up to her as she dialed 911. I remembered being terrified as she clawed at the curtains and fell to the ground. I recalled screaming for my father, the terror on his face as he raced down the stairs, how he shook her and screamed for her not to fall asleep. And I recalled the red ambulance lights flooding our house as EMTs and firefighters invaded our living room and rushed my mother onto a gurney and out the door. I remembered the neighbors all coming out of their houses as my mother was sped away.

It was now three a.m., the time when night pushes into morning, your chance at sleep gone, when you feel as if you're the only one awake in the world. I saw a lot of Mom in myself. She too would stop eating and sleep for days at a time and then be unable to for as long. I saw myself going to the cabinet and downing a bottle of pills and letting the calm warmth inch through my body until everything went quiet. My father didn't have sleeping pills but there were enough painkillers to put down an elephant. The thought scared me because I knew I could swallow those pills.

I needed to stop thinking about that night, about my mother

stumbling around the living room. I went back upstairs. I opened my father's door and saw his huge bulk sleeping on top of the covers fully dressed, snoring, half a bottle of Jameson on the bed beside him. I picked up the bottle and took a pull, then placed it back beside him and went to the kitchen to brew some coffee.

# NINETEEN

I pulled up to Chey's house, but she wasn't at her usual place at the end of her drive, so I tapped *The Simpsons* theme on the horn and waited. I didn't know what to say to her about the pages. I took a gulp of my fourth mug of coffee and tried not to think of my mother clawing at the curtains. Why had she changed her mind and picked up that phone? Was she struck with a reason to live or was it the fear of dying that saved her? I hoped I would be able to sleep that night. I pictured my father's Oxy in the cabinet, and I became afraid of what would happen if I couldn't.

Chey still hadn't come out, so I upped my game, hammering on the horn as fast as I could, which began to annoy even me. That's when what looked like Chey's mother stepped out of the house and threw her arms in the air. She was gaunt with dirty blonde hair like her daughter and the still-beautiful face of an ex-model with some tough years behind her—not a unique look in LA.

I hopped off the bus as she approached. "Hey, I'm Mikey."

"Alex," she said. "Can you tell Dr. Tambori Chey's ex-friend took up with her ex-boyfriend and that Chey's not taking it well, that she's not going to make it in today?"

Toby popped off the bus. "Yo, everything OK, Coach?"

"Chey's taking a sick day," I said.

"She OK?" Toby asked Alex.

She didn't answer. She looked confused at the six-foot-five Toby.

Donnie appeared at the door. "Tell Chey we are going to miss her at practice today."

I told Donnie and Toby to get back on the bus and to shut the door.

"Who are those two boys?" Alex asked, shielding her eyes from the sun as she looked back at the bus.

"Toby and Donnie," I said. "Friends of Chey's. She's gonna be OK, though, right?" The idea of her having an episode caused me to break out in a sweat.

"Friends of *Chey's*? I thought Chey didn't have any friends."

"She's friends with the basketball team," I said.

"Since when?" she said, her tired eyes waking up.

"Yeah . . . I might've asked her to be the assistant coach."

"Sports put her in Friedman," she snapped, grabbing a pack of Marlboro Reds from her sweatpants' pocket and looking back at the open door to her house.

"Chey told me it was betting that spun her out, not sports."

"It was gambling on *sports*," she said, lighting up a smoke. "And what does Dr. Tambori say about it?"

"She didn't think it was a good idea."

"And who are you? The driver-slash-*coach*?" she said, the edge in her voice sharp.

"I think she needs the camaraderie," I said, realizing I sounded like a crummy after-school special.

The front door opened and out walked Chey with her school bag. "Come on, Coach, let's bounce."

"Honey," said her mother, rushing to her. "You're staying home sick today. You can't go out when you're like this."

"Yeah . . . no. I'm not sitting home all day bawling," said Chey. "I gotta talk to Dr. T about something."

"About you assistant coaching?" asked her mother.

Chey continued to the bus.

"It's a bad idea."

Chey whipped around on her mother. "My life's a mess. All of it. Nobody'll date me 'cause I'm fucking crazy. Even my old best friend hates me. And all I ask is to be the assistant coach. That's *it*. Not such a big deal."

"Dr. Tambori doesn't think it's a good idea, either."

"She's not God. She doesn't know everything," said Chey. "I can help the team win a game. And they haven't won a game in three years, right, Mikey?"

"Hell yeah she can, brah," said Brian, whose head was now sticking out of the window. With that, Toby and G poked their heads out their respective windows.

"Chey, *tu mama's* fine!" said G, snapping his fingers.

"Yo, Chey," said Toby. "What up, girl?"

Donnie shoved his head out G's window.

"Get your own window, *puta*!" screamed G, shoving Donnie back into the bus.

"What if you have an episode?" asked Alex. "What then?"

I turned to Chey. I needed to know the answer myself.

"What if I do? Four months ago, I thought I was a vampire," she said, shrugging. "I can't live my life scared of having an episode. I wouldn't get out of bed. That's what I'm going to tell Dr. T today, Mikey. I'm willing to risk it and so should she. She must know there will be some benefit from my being on the team, unless she's a complete noob."

I could feel my head nodding, as I caught Chey's fortitude like wind in a sail, as I pushed past my lack of sleep and thoughts of my father's Oxy to wanting to help Chey. She was going to be the assistant coach.

"Straight up!" shouted Brian. "I got a session before yours. I'll prime her."

"Me, too. I'll lube her up, and you can slide right in, Chey," said G, winking at Chey's mother as Brian giggled.

"G, get your head back in the bus," I said.

A giant hand appeared in G's window and yanked him back in the bus, followed by a loud thud and some screaming.

Alex's attention volleyed between Chey and the talking heads. "Those boys are your friends?" asked Alex.

"Hell yeah we is," said Toby, "and that's a fact. Don't worry, Chey's mom, if she freaks out, we got her."

Chey looked at Toby, unblinking. Alex threw her cigarette on the ground and stubbed it out with her slipper. "There are certain things you can do if Chey has an episode, Mr. coach-slash-bus driver. Do you want to hear them?"

"I sure do," I said, feeling hope for the first time since I'd read Chey's pages.

"I'll come in to school today, and we can talk about it with Dr. Tambori," she said, looking back at the bus.

Chey hugged her mother, who squeezed her eyes shut and stroked her daughter's hair. I thought of my mother and how she would squeeze me so tightly I would have to scream for her to stop. Alex loved her daughter—you could see it all the way down to her pink slippers. She and I were going to convince Dr. T to let Chey coach. I was even beginning to think such a thing possible.

"*Nos vemos* at school, *ama*!" shouted G from somewhere on the bus, followed by another thud.

• • •

I spent the morning obsessing about Chey, about her first episode, about her ex and ex-best friend hooking up, about her need to be assistant coach, and about how her mom and I were gonna ambush Dr. T to change her mind about hoops. I played out scenario after scenario in search of the right angle, but none finished with Dr. T acquiescing, and I hoped Alex had a plan because otherwise Chey was out of luck. For the moments I was able to put Chey out of my mind, I thought about Donnie's devils and Otis's dog. I also wondered about the rest of the team, about their assignments. I wanted to read them but was terrified they would make me even more depressed.

Alex texted Chey that I was to meet her at Dr. T's office at high noon. At 1200 hours, I put my ear to the doc's door—it appeared Alex hadn't shown yet. Dr. T was probably eating at her desk, like she did every day at this time.

"Mr. Cannon," said Dr. T from behind me, startling me. "May I inquire why your face is pressed against my door? Have you forgotten how it works?"

"I was going to . . ."

"Are you all right? You look especially knackered."

"My mind was doing somersaults all night."

"It appears my noon appointment is late. Can we have a brief chat?" she said.

I followed her inside.

She asked if I'd read Chey's pages, and I told her I had. "You understand why she simply cannot coach," she said, turning to me, her eyes owning mine.

I kept my head still, but I yearned to shake a defiant *no*. I felt guilty teaming up against Dr. T, but I wouldn't be able to convince her to let Chey coach on my own. That was even clearer now.

"I hope the story of her first episode was enlightening, and that you've a better understanding of what Chey is dealing with. There are times when she cannot distinguish reality from her psychosis. In fact, I wish I could share the rest of your team's assignments with you that you may learn more about them."

I nodded. "I've read Donnie's and Otis's."

"What? Did they give them to you?"

"Not exactly. They were left on the bus, and I couldn't help myself."

"Mr. Cannon! You had no right to read those—none at all."

"I know. I know. But even you said you wish you could give them to me."

"But I wouldn't. I would never forsake a student's trust, and neither should you."

"You're right."

"Promise me you won't read any more without their explicit permission. I need you to promise me."

"I promise."

"Because the second part of the assignment—sharing them—is about trust, and I don't want you to compromise that. Trust in the staff and with each other is vital. It's the foundation on which everything else is built. Without it, we can't help these kids."

"Chey's mom wants her to coach. That's why she's coming," I blurted out. "She wanted the three of us to speak."

Dr. T shut her eyes and took a deep breath. When she opened her eyes, she placed her pens in order of color in front of her. "Was this your idea, Mr. Cannon?"

"It was Alex's. Although, I guess I led her to it?"

"We need to get on the same page here, Mr. Cannon. We need to be a united front for Chey as well as for her mother. Otherwise, Chey could end up getting hurt. She's the only one on your team who's suffered recent episodes. We're still working on finding the right balance of medication for her."

"I see something in Chey. She's . . . inspiring."

"*Inspiring*?" questioned Dr. T as if I hadn't a full grasp of the word.

There was a knock on the door and since I was blowing it on my own, I let Alex in. After a few pleasantries, she sat next to me across the desk from Dr. T and launched into Chey's emotional morning, while Dr. T scribbled on her notepad.

"Chey did something today I've never seen her do," said Alex. "In the midst of her hysterics, she forced herself to calm down. When I went out to tell Mikey here that Chey was going to take a sick day, my daughter was inside screaming and crying and pounding her hands against the wall. A few minutes later, she emerged from the house ready to go to school. This kind of agitation would usually put her out of commission for days. Come to find out, she pulled herself together to plead with you to let her assistant coach. I've never seen her want anything this much."

The doc was all poker face. "It's great to hear that Chey was able to overcome her emotions around her ex-boyfriend. I know their severing was difficult for her."

"She never would've pulled herself together if it wasn't for the possibility of coaching," said Alex.

"And I agree that pulling herself together is a positive change in behavior," Dr. T said, leaning forward in her chair, her hands steepled on the desk.

Both Alex and I were nodding like metronomes.

"And then to see how she interacted with the kids on the bus," said Alex.

"The team," I pointed out, trying to be helpful, my hands sweating in my lap.

"Yeah, the team," said Alex, welling up and dabbing at the corner of her eye with her finger. "She hasn't had friends in so long. These kids seemed to care about her."

"They do," I chimed in.

"I think she wants—needs—to be a part of something bigger than herself," said Alex, taking up my after-school special approach.

"I *have* seen her interact with some of the students on the team, and I agree that I do see a positive change in her interpersonal relationships, but sports put her in a manic state, which caused her to miss the signs of oncoming episodes, one of which put her in here."

Alex nodded.

"I believe we've made great progress in teaching her to manage her illness. Although she has had a few episodes recently, their severity has decreased significantly."

"That's true," said Alex.

"I'm afraid we would jeopardize that progress by putting her in a situation she might not be able to handle. Not only that—we're still playing with the doses of her medications."

"I understand," said Alex. "It was that I got excited when I saw her with friends, but of course, you're right. I wouldn't want to jeopardize Chey or her improvement."

"If we continue to see this sort of progress, perhaps next year she can be part of the team?" said Dr. T. "It'll give Chey something to work toward."

Alex was giving up, and I couldn't let her. "*No*," I said a little more forcefully than intended, catching them both off guard. "We jeopardize her progress by *not* allowing her to be on the team."

Alex turned back to Dr. T.

"She wants to be part of the team because she needs some purpose in her life besides working on herself to get better," I said.

Dr. T looked at me. With one look, she scrutinized my expression, my body language, somehow absorbed my thoughts. It was unsettling. "Someone said those same words to me once," she said. "Those same words. Uncanny."

"Who?" asked Alex.

Dr. T waved it off. "Please continue, Mr. Cannon."

"Sometimes, when you're lucky," I began, "when life is dragging you out past the last buoy, you get thrown a life preserver and you grab onto it with everything you got, because you know it's your only chance to stay afloat."

"You feel the team is Chey's life preserver?" asked Alex.

"I know she has you two, but that's not enough. She needs friends. Purpose. I know. I've been without purpose for too long."

Dr. T lifted her hand over her eyes, and I couldn't tell if she was frustrated or having an emotional reaction to what I was saying.

"She knows coaching could cause her an episode, and she thinks being a part of this team is worth the risk," I said. "She plans to tell you this herself later today."

Dr. T lowered her hand, her eyes moist but steady on me.

"Give me a chance to work with her," I continued. "If she has an episode then at least we tried, and she'll know she's not ready."

"When we were talking earlier," said Dr. T, "you said Chey was an inspiration. What did you mean?"

"She knows what she wants, and she's willing to risk everything to get it. I don't know about you two, but I need to learn me some of that."

Dr. T turned to Alex, who was smiling and biting her lip, then back to me. "Unfortunately, the school doesn't have the funding to send a nurse along with you to games in case something does happen. You would be the one to have to sedate her and to call the ambulance if she has an attack."

"Show me what to do, and I'll do it," I said.

"I can go over the early warning signs of an episode," said Alex. "And the nights I can get a sitter, I'll come to the games."

Dr. T shook her head. "OK, Mr. Cannon, if you're willing to take on the responsibility of learning the signs of an attack and what to do if one should occur…you have yourself an assistant coach. But if she has an episode or appears to become manic, she'll have to be taken off the team—no questions."

"Hells to the yes," I said.

Dr. T nodded, looking lost in thought as her eyes wandered to the window.

Alex grabbed my hand. "Thank you, Mikey."

• • •

As Dr. T and Alex gave Chey the good news, I strutted out the front door of the school like I owned the place. Alex had looked at me with such appreciation, and Dr. T listened to what I said as if it was insightful and mattered—as if *I* mattered.

Looking at the empty court, I wanted my team to share this feeling. We all needed to strut through the school like we were all that. My guys needed to know what it was like to feel victory. I needed to think of something they could win at—today. But what? If there was a competition for beating the tar out of each other, they'd win, but barring that . . . The courts! Why hadn't I thought about it before? Nobody called fouls at Woodbine Park. I wasn't sure my guys could win, but, man, they had a better chance without a ref blowing his whistle every few seconds.

I called Gerald and laid out my plan. "I need you to meet us at the courts to vouch for my team like you did for me all those years ago."

"I don't know, Mikey," said Gerald. "The games get pretty rough out there. Your kids could get hurt."

"You don't know my guys. Believe me, they'll be fine.

• • •

I parked on the street outside the court, and as the guys spilled out of the bus they lit into me, letting me know what they thought about my *cracked* idea.

"You done lost your mind, Coach?" said Toby.

Chey, thinking nobody was watching, gave me a quick hug and then turned toward the court. "I'm not going to let you down."

Brian, who was usually watching Chey, caught the whole exchange.

"I gotta tell you, though," she continued, "I'm with the team— this is a bad idea."

Alex had gone over the warning signs for Chey's episodes hours before. I had to watch out for fast-talking, losing focus, or becoming withdrawn. Chey would've said anything to be on the team, and I hoped she wasn't lying about gambling and not hoops causing her episodes.

As the seven of us approached the court, I spotted Gerald leaning against a picnic table. "Yo, Big Man," I said, giving Gerald a hug and an intro to the guys. "Any good?" I asked, gesturing toward the court, where two teams of five were running a fast pace.

"Same shit. Nobody's passing or playing D. Only that guy right there, the tall dude, name's Chris—works at the Popeye's on La Brea," said Gerald, pointing. "He's a monster, got moves like LeBron."

"Does he pass like the King?"

"He doesn't pass," said Gerald.

Chris drove the middle lane and dunked over two scrubs, ending the game, while my guys watched slack-jawed.

"All right, guys," I said, clapping. "Ready?"

"No way, Coach," said Brian. "They'll straight kill us."

"You better put all five guys on LeBron," said Gerald.

"*Chale, güey,*" said G, as LeBron sized us up. "No way."

"On offense—everybody touches the ball before somebody shoots," I said. "Today, we work on passing."

"What if somebody can't get open?" asked G, rubbing the tattoo on his neck.

I made sure everybody was listening because I had something important to say. "A smart person once said to me that trust is the foundation on which everything else is built. Guys, you need to learn to trust each other. Nobody wins games by themselves. In fact, you all must trust each other right *now,* or these guys are gonna mop the floor with you—guaranteed."

"He's not lying," said Gerald. "These boys play hard out here."

"Listen to the coach," said Chey, backing me like a good assistant. "Gonzalo, don't hog the ball."

G grabbed his package over his pants. "*Puta.*"

"On D—Otis and Toby, double-team LeBron," I said, clapping.

As my guys made their way to the court, I pulled aside Otis. "There's different rules out here. No ref—you feel me?"

Otis smiled.

"Don't kill anyone."

"*Mary Friedman Alternative High School*," LeBron said, reading the side of the bus. "Jungle gym's over there. This here game's for adults."

"Yo," said Gerald. "Let 'em play."

"Come on, Gerald, I ain't trying to babysit."

I sent Chey to grab my notebook off the bus, so she wouldn't see me grab three twenties out of my wallet and begin waving them around. "Sixty to the first team to eleven."

LeBron scratched his ear and looked at my guys.

"Come on, that's a week's salary at Popeye's," I said, glancing toward Chey, still out of earshot, not wanting to do anything that may trigger her.

LeBron clapped the ball between his hands as if trying to pop it. "I'll make it a good death," he said, signaling the game was on.

Chey trotted back with my notebook in hand. "Kick those old boofs' asses," she yelled before turning back to me and Gerald. "No offense."

"Hey now, baby girl," said Gerald.

"We'll lose by three buckets," said Chey.

"You're off on this one," I said.

"Not likely."

Gerald shook his head and smiled, a smile that yanked me back to when he and I first ran from court to court, to that one time in '08 when we saw Hot Sauce, AO, Mr. 720, J-Boogie, all street-ball legends, playing at the Oakwood Pavilion, or when we heard the Escalade was playing on a local court and we skipped class to see the gentle giant ball. Man, it was good to have G-man back in my life.

The game started with LeBron bringing the ball coast-to-coast for an easy deuce. "All day, baby," he shouted, pointing to Otis. "You never gonna be able to keep up, Mo'Nique."

Otis scowled and cracked his knuckles, getting a dangerous look on his face.

I could feel Chey's eyes burning an I-told-you-so hole in the side of my head. "Toby, help Otis," I called out.

"Otis, shake it off," called Gerald. "Don't let him in your head."

Brian brought up the ball, winged it to Otis, who passed it back.

"Spread them out," said Chey.

Gerald nodded to me, with a head tilt toward Chey. I was impressed with my assistant, too.

"You got no idea, Big Man. She's three plays ahead of us."

"Four," said Chey.

Brian passed to G, who passed to Toby, and when Donnie's defender moved over to double-team Toby, Toby faked a shot and fed Donnie, who sank an easy bucket. Swish! Nothing but net. And we were on the boards.

"OK," sang Gerald, clapping. "Boy's got a fine shot."

LeBron brought the ball up-court, while Toby tried to steal it. "You reach, I teach," said LeBron. With that, Otis punched the ball out of his hands.

"Yo, you drop something, prof?" asked Toby.

"That's it!" I shouted.

"You gotta hold onto that ball as tight as you do those Louisiana Shrimp Tackle Boxes!" Gerald shouted to LeBron, who flipped him the bird.

G picked up the ball and baseballed it to Brian, who fed Toby, who bounce passed it to a wide-open Donnie, who faked the shot and dished to Otis, who tried to shoot but got stuffed by a tall defender. LeBron then picked up the ball and took it down-court for an easy layup before turning back to Otis. "Tell your little girlfriend over there to stop cheering for me," he said, pointing to Chey.

"I'm cheering for a Twelve-piece Bonafide with some buttery biscuits," shouted Chey.

Gerald and Chey fist-bumped.

"I thought people didn't fist-bump anymore," I said to Chey.

"I'm like keeping it old-school for you two OG's," she said.

The other team was running a quick pace and made a few more buckets before our guys knew what happened.

"Otis, press your man, make him feel the extra seventy-five pounds you got on him," said Gerald. "Don't be afraid to lean on that sucker."

LeBron brought the ball up-court and Otis and Toby moved in for the double-team. LeBron faked left, losing Toby, but when he went right, he ran into the wall, who knocked his ass to the ground. In the boys' league, Otis would've been suspended, but on this court, a move like that bumped the scrimmage to the next level.

"All right, I see, that's how we gonna do it," said LeBron.

"That's how we gonna do it," said Otis.

"That's it," shouted Gerald. "Make 'em play *your* game."

With that LeBron set a hard pick on Toby, knocking him down.

"Come on, Toby, shake it off," I said. "Get up."

Brian and Donnie helped Toby up.

"You OK, Toby?" asked Donnie.

"I do worse to myself before breakfast," Toby said, standing. "OK, Donnie, Bri, let's clobber these clowns, for real."

"I hear that," said G, running headlong into his guy, knocking him three steps back. "My bad," he said. "Lost my footing."

"You keep it up, kid, you'll lose more than your footing," said G's defender, shoving him back.

We had ourselves one rough ball game. It looked more like a cage match than it did hoops. The smack talk continued, and the elbows flew, and Otis bulldozed anybody who got in his way, and LeBron and his team pushed back, and Donnie did his part by landing bombs.

My guys continued to pass. Everyone touched the ball before a shot, which slowed the game and confused our opponents, as that sort of teamwork was a unicorn on this court. My guys were learning patience, teamwork, and aggression—how when they're all working you could do things that surprise even yourself.

It came down to the score being ten all, and my guys had the ball. I noticed Chey was silent, studying her feet. "I was wrong," she said. "I didn't see what you saw—the aggressive play, the passing. I missed it."

"We got one basket to go, Chey. What should we do?"

"Are you upset with me?" she asked.

"What? No. Why would you think that?"

"Are you sure?" she said, a lost look clouding her face. "I messed up."

"Are you OK?" I asked, thinking she might be withdrawing—one of the signs.

"I'm not getting manic or anything. Only asking," she snapped, her attention finding its way back to the game.

The exchange made me realize how closely I needed to watch her.

Brian drove his defender into Otis and passed to G, who had a wide-open look but knew he had to pass since not everybody touched the ball. Nobody was open. Brian's defender knocked him down. Donnie and Toby were getting shoved, and Otis was basically in a UFC match with LeBron. Nobody could break loose, so G banked in a shot.

"Whoa!" said Chey. "It's a good thing I don't bet anymore."

"Yes!" I screamed, grabbing Gerald. "Whoa is right!"

G stood on the court, hangdogging. "My bad, Coach. But nobody was open. I was trying to pass."

"You gotta know when to break the rules, G. You guys won!" I wailed.

At first, my guys stood there looking at one another until Toby put his arm around Otis. "Nice game, brother." Otis stood there for a few seconds looking at Toby's arm on his shoulder. Finally, he shoved it off.

Donnie ran up to me, his arms flailing. "We won, we won, but this doesn't count as *the* win. We still have to win a league game because you promised. I can shoot in a game now, so we can win. Right? This win is great, but it doesn't count as the actual win. Right?"

"Enjoy *this* win, buddy," I said.

"But it doesn't count. We will win one in our league, because you promised."

"Yeet, yeet!" said Brian, popping and locking across the court.

"The first win is the hardest," said Chey.

I looked at my guys, who were now fist-bumping and high-fiving—all except Otis, who rubbed his palms on his shorts looking uncomfortable. I reprised my strut and headed onto the court. "Yo," I called to LeBron.

LeBron went to pull his billfold from his sock, but I stopped him before Chey could see. "You can keep it if you work with my guys on their game," I said, for his ears only.

"What I gotta do?"

"Show them how you get open—without having to foul. My guys need to learn to play without fouling."

"*Sheeit*, I don't need to foul to get open," said LeBron.

"Can you teach my guys?"

LeBron wasn't sure, until Gerald joined us on the court, and the three of us worked with the guys, showing them how to push off on a defender without fouling. Gerald demonstrated to Otis how to leverage his size with both smaller and larger opponents. Watching these two was like seeing time bend back on itself, making my past and present one, which was both disorienting and fulfilling. But most of all, LeBron demonstrated the art of smack talk. Namely, how to ruin somebody's game by getting in his head.

On the bus ride home, the guys relived plays and dished out

some smack talk to one another—even Donnie got in on the jousting, telling Otis he was so big he looked like a supersized T-Rex.

In the midst of the fun, Brian made his way to the front of the bus, sitting in the seat behind me, his hair falling in front of his eyes. He leaned into me. "You read Chey's pages, huh?"

I nodded.

Brian turned to look at Chey. "What did she write about?"

"You'll have to ask *her*, Brian."

He nodded, turning back to me. "I saw her straight hug you before the game."

"What can I do for you, Brian?"

Ensuring nobody was watching, Brian slipped me some folded pages from his pocket. "It's my assignment. Do you want to read it?"

"I do," I said, glancing at the pages folded in quarters in my hand. "But I'm not going to tell you about Chey's pages."

He hesitated. "I have to share it with someone from group."

"I don't count."

"I want to share mine with Chey, but not if mine is way crazier than hers. Maybe you can read it and tell me if I should share it with her or not, like how much worse mine is than hers?"

"I'd love to read it, Brian, but I'm not going to talk to you about Chey's."

"Fine. You don't gotta tell me about Chey's, and I don't want to talk to you about mine—like not ever. Give me a nod or a thumbs up next time you see me to know if I should share it with her or not. If I'm way crazier than her, I'm not sharing anything."

"No, I'm not gonna do that."

"OK, but maybe you will, though."

"I won't."

"Fine. You can read it, but don't feel like you need to get all hug crazy with me. I'm good there, bruh."

# TWENTY

**When I got home that night,** my old man was tilting back some Guinness watching the Lakers dominate Boston. He ignored me, so I went up to my room and sat on my bed and took Brian's typed pages out of my pocket. I desperately wanted to learn more about him, but I was afraid of what I would find in these pages, that whatever was there would prevent me from sleeping. But I couldn't wait.

## BRIAN'S ASSIGNMENT

I'm going to tell you (whoever I decided to give this to) some messed-up stuff right now. I've told this story a bunch of times to a bunch of therapists so I'm good at telling it but I haven't told any friends or even my mom about what happened that night because it's straight-up embarrassing. I'm not trying to be a teacher's pet or anything, but Dr. T has helped me a lot. If she thinks writing it out and sharing it is going to help me, or whoever is reading this somehow, then I'm down. The only thing is that whoever ends up reading this—please don't share it with anybody else like ever—especially Gonzalo.

Okay, I was driving home on Culver when something

smashed into my bumper and I jammed on the brakes like what was that? It was 7 at night and it was garbage pickup the next morning; the raccoons were out, and I guessed that's what I hit, and I bounced quick because those things are cute but dead isn't cute. No way.

But I couldn't sleep thinking about that poor bandit-faced raccoon. I finally passed out and at 3 a.m. a freaky image in my head of a cute Spanish girl with big eyes and bangs woke me up. Where did that come from, bruh? I'm not one of those pervs who dreams of little kids.

And I thought, wait, was it possible I hit her and not a raccoon. If she darted out or been running with friends or playing tag or whatever and not seen my car and I didn't hear it because my music was straight pumping? Did she pop into my head on her way to heaven? I pictured her lying on the ground crying. I'd been driving fast, fast enough to send her little body flying and into a bush or something. Would she have died on impact or died later?

I needed to go see what I hit. I parked a block away from the accident on the down-low in case somebody was looking for my ride and I walked to where I hit something, and the street was straight quiet and the houses were dark.

Something with hair on it glistened under my iPhone flashlight but I was scared to touch it like it would jump up, still alive, and bite me cuz it looked like a rat. I reached down to touch it and its fur was cold and wet and matted. I picked it up but it wasn't an animal; it was a clump of black human hair like from a little girl's head! I smelled it: oily and tart and sickly, like blood. I must've hit that sweet little girl hard enough that she skidded on the pavement and her hair got yanked out, or maybe the ambulance came and had to cut her hair off to stitch a wound. I hate to admit it, but my first thought was I was going to get in trouble. I was thinking I should go home and pretend the whole thing never happened. Total self-preservation mode, bruh. But then I started to feel guilty, and my body started to shake like when you have a bad flu. I had to see if the little girl died.

I shoved the bloody hair into my pocket and drove to the closest hospital. The emergency room was straight quiet but had a few people in the waiting area and I bolted to the window where they check you in and asked about a little girl with bangs and big eyes hit by a car. The Oprah-looking woman behind the glass told me to wait my turn but I was freaking out. What if they told me they couldn't save the girl because she laid in the street for an hour before someone found her and that if whoever hit her would've at least called the ambulance she could've been saved? What if I found out she died because I was too scared to stop, bruh?

I tried the E.R. door but it was locked. Through the glass window I saw a Mexican family. A mom and little boy were draped on the dad and somehow, I knew this was the Spanish girl's family. They came in the waiting room, and I told the father I was sorry and that I thought I hit a raccoon and begged him to forgive me. The little boy who lost his sister began to cry. I asked if she was alive. The dad didn't answer and pulled his family away, but I kept begging them to tell me what happened to her. Finally, the father straight-up had enough of me and shoved me onto the floor and screamed at me in Spanish while the little boy wailed in his mother's lap. I kept saying that I was going and that I was sorry and to please forgive me. Everyone in the waiting room was watching and I heard the father say something to his family and I recognized a word, muerte—death, bruh. Their daughter was dead, and I'd killed her.

I couldn't live with what I'd done so I drove to the L.A. River, the part where someone killed herself by jumping off the bridge onto the concrete below. I drove onto the sidewalk by the entrance of the bridge and there were no lights. From where I was sitting it could have been bottomless. When I saw a cop car pull up next to my car, I took off sprinting to the bridge. I was going to jump. The two police officers came running after me and told me to freeze but I didn't. I kept running full steam but when I hit the center of the bridge I froze because I didn't see a place to jump because the side was too high. That's when the cops cornered me and then handcuffed me as I confessed, I had drank and smoked too much and then drove and killed the little girl and how I was going to kill myself.

They took me to the station where I found out that nobody had been hit by a car that night. No girl, not even a raccoon. I pulled the bloody hair outta my pocket and I looked at it; it wasn't hair, but a clump of string caked with dirt. I stared at the string forever and I tried to make sense of the night by replaying it over and over. How could I have made the whole thing up? I was about to jump off a bridge for no reason.

I told you (whoever is reading this) that it's a messed-up story. Please don't share it with anybody, including your family. Since I gave you mine, can you please give me yours, then we would both know each other's secret story? That would only be fair and would make me feel a lot better about you not thinking I was messed up. Thanks!

• • •

I placed Brian's pages in my nightstand drawer and looked out the window at the lights of a helicopter searching the neighborhood for somebody who did something they weren't supposed to—a nightly occurrence. Brian's issues were like my mother's: real. My father always said I blew things out of proportion, that my problems were the same as everyone's, that I was weak. *Now, your mother had real issues. Bipolar is a real issue. I can't even imagine how you would handle something like that.*

I was right about Brian's pages. I shouldn't have read them before bed. Every image—his dream of the little girl, his yelling at the family in the E.R.—bit down on my skull with teeth too sharp and jagged. I summoned images of today's win to try and replace them—Otis banging his defender and G sinking that last shot—but they were stomped out by the image of Brian on the bridge trying to kill himself.

Then images of Brian traded off with that of my mother lying on the floor, her eyes half-mast looking through me. I forced myself to picture Toby with his arm around Otis, but all I could see was my mother's lost eyes. I kicked myself for telling E:60 about her suicide attempt. What was wrong with me? My heart began to pound, and I started to sweat, losing my breath.

I went to the kitchen and poured myself a drink. Finally, after the second glass of Jameson, the image of my mother dialing the phone lost focus, allowing me to get back in bed.

I looked at Fergie in her skin-tight tank top giving me a come-hither pout at the end of my bed. Fergie's obsession with my pimpled teenage butt helped me through many an adolescent night, and I wondered what she was doing now, if she lived in LA. I imagined her dream guy to be a former homeless, depressed, high school basketball coach. I closed my eyes and tried to focus but even those pouty lips were powerless against the memory of my mother on the floor. I needed to move out of my father's house, out of my childhood bedroom, but I didn't have enough cash yet.

• • •

The next morning when Brian boarded the bus, I nodded to him, and he returned the gesture. I know I said I wouldn't give him any signal, but I was in a position to help both he and Chey. He *should* share his story with her. They should know they weren't alone.

The bus was atwitter with the victory, G having spun the win into folklore, recounting his last shot in such glory as to make Jordan's '98 last-second win over Utah, one of the greatest victories in NBA history, a close second. That is until Toby stole G's ball and tossed it to Brian. G fought to get it back, while Toby and Brian ran up and down the aisle in a game of keep away.

Donnie had changed foster homes because his old fosters adopted a baby and thought keeping Donnie would be too much. His new place was now my second-to-last pickup, and when I pulled up, I knew something was wrong. He stood at the end of the drive with his chin tucked into his chest like a wounded bird and his hand over his face, but what was most conspicuous was he didn't have his ball. He tried to bolt past me down the aisle, but I held up my hand. "Hold on there, buddy, what's going on with your face?"

"Nothing," he said.

"And where's your ball?"

"Stolen," he managed to get out as he lowered his hand, revealing a shiner over his right eye.

"Did that happen in the game yesterday?" I asked, taking his chin in my hand and having a look at his eye.

Donnie shook his head. "After."

Toby and Brian rushed up to check on their teammate. "Did your new foster do that?" asked Toby.

"No, my new fosters are nice. Last night I went to that park over there," he said, pointing to a small patch of grass with a swing set and a paved half court, "to practice the spin move and shot that LeBron guy showed me, and they stole my ball."

"Who stole your ball, bruh?" asked Brian.

Donnie took a breath. "Nubbin's brother and his friends, Jovver and Russell."

"Otis, Nubbin's brother beat up Donnie," called out Brian, a rally cry.

"They should not have done that," said Otis, grabbing at the seat in front of him.

"They got out of their car and wanted to know why I was shooting in the dark. I told them I was practicing a spin move to get open because Mikey said if I could consistently get open, I'd be a monster on the court. Tim said Nubbin told him I had the best shot he'd ever seen, and that made me smile, and I couldn't stop smiling. I couldn't. Tim told me to shoot right where I was standing, and I made a shot. Then Tim said he wanted to see me do it with his friend Jovver guarding me and that if I still made the shot, he wouldn't punch me in the face. That scared me and I told him I didn't want to play but he said I had to, or he would hit me anyway. When I went to shoot, the Jovver kid fouled me, making me miss. Then Tim said I couldn't handle the pressure. He called me a 'choke artist.'"

"A *choke artist*?" I asked, taken back.

My father's nickname for me since I missed those foul shots issued from Donnie's mouth like a wild dog sinking teeth into my flesh, causing me to think of Alvarito's torn face, an image never too far away. Tim got those words from my father, who no doubt shared *my* story as a cautionary tale. My old man was complicit in Donnie's black eye. After all, he trained his team to be ruthless.

"Tim said I was a player who couldn't take pressure. But I was fouled, I told him. He called me a liar and tried to make me admit I was a choke artist, but I wouldn't, because I'm not a choke artist. Then that Jovver kid pushed me and said I *had* to admit it, but I didn't want to, and I started screaming, '*I am not a choke artist*' over and over and over and over and—"

"OK!" said G. "We get it."

The torment my father put me through with that name was one thing, but to have that pain reach Donnie tore through to bone.

"But I am not a choke artist," said Donnie as he took a seat by the window. Toby slid in beside him, talking to him quietly.

Scenarios of confronting my father for his part in Donnie's black eye ran through my head until we reached Nubbin's house. The team rushed to the open windows to see Tim and his friends taunting Nubbin in the driveway. Tim threw his brother to the pavement.

"Give it to me!" screamed Nubbin, pointing to a ball with Donnie's name all over it tucked under the Filipino kid's arm. "You don't get what that ball means to him, Jovver. Let me have it. Please."

"No," said the white kid.

"Russell, please," Nubbin begged, bringing his hands together in front of him as if in prayer. "I'll do whatever you guys want. He needs that ball."

"He doesn't need anything," said Tim.

"I mean, he's the only kid in school who's nice to me," said Nubbin in earnest. "I'm not getting on that bus without it."

"I said, *no*," said Tim.

Nubbin wailed like an Apache looking for scalps as he charged Jovver, who fell back. Nubbin lurched for the ball and grabbed it, squeezing it to his body as Tim and his two friends began kicking him in the ribs.

"Everybody stays on the bus," I shouted. "I mean it. Nobody gets off. Otis, please sit back down."

"Nobody gets off," repeated Otis, as if to the others, but I had meant him.

I bounded off the bus, prompting Tim and his friends to back off. My body was shaking as I hurried to Nubbin lying on the ground holding his side. "You OK?"

Nubbin nodded, gasping for air. "Tim must've gotten Donnie's new address from my phone."

"It's OK, Nubbin. Catch your breath," I said.

"They were all saying Tim had the best shot in the state, and I told them Donnie's was better. That's all. I mean, I didn't think they would go find him. I would've never done that to him." Nubbin looked up at Donnie, who was hanging out of the window, tears in his eyes.

"Did they give Donnie that black eye?" asked Nubbin.

I nodded.

Nubbin sprang from the ground, and I grabbed him before he could charge Tim's Navigator, which his brother and friends were getting into. "Tim!" he screamed, swinging at the air.

Now, Otis was standing on the last step of the bus by the open door.

"Everybody stays put," I yelled to Otis. "Nubbin, on the bus. Please."

As Nubbin pushed by Otis onto the bus, I banged on the driver's window of the Navigator.

Tim gave me the finger.

"Did *you* hit Donnie?" I shouted.

Tim rolled down his window a few inches and said, "Yeah, I hit that choke artist! So what?"

I lost it. I punched the window, cracking the glass. The surprise on Tim's face and the pain in my hand shot me back to reality. I turned to the bus, where my team's faces were plastered against the windows, where Otis was still standing in the doorway.

"You're so sued, bro!" screamed Tim, now filming me on his phone through the cracked glass.

What had I done? I lost control in front of my team. I looked at my hand and then back at the cracked window.

"Kiss your job goodbye," said Tim, still filming me.

He was right.

"You," said Otis, pointing at Tim. "You dead."

Tim lowered his phone. He didn't sweat me, but apparently Otis was another story.

# TWENTY-ONE

**When I pulled up at school, Dr. T was waiting for me**—a look on her face like someone had already gotten to her. As the team got off the bus, G tried to get Nubbin to tell her I saved his life, but Nubbin remained silent, holding his ribs. Dr. T asked me to follow her. The school couldn't employ a loose cannon. Even I knew that.

• • •

Dr. T came around her desk and sat in the chair beside mine. It turned out Nubbin's father called Dr. T about the incident, even sent her Tim's video of me panting behind the broken window—thank God it happened too quickly for Tim to film me punching the glass. I was embarrassed enough without Dr. T being able to see the incident for herself.

"Tell me what happened," she said.

"I know I'm fired."

"I need to know what happened." She put her hand on my armrest. "Did you punch a car window?"

"Did you see Donnie's eye?" I said. "Yesterday at the park he was over the moon, and now . . ."

"Nubbin's brother, Tim, beat up Donnie and gave him a black eye?"

I nodded. "And he called him a choke artist. Donnie's a sensitive kid. You can't say something like that to him."

"You punched the car because someone called Donnie a name?"

"I'm an idiot. I lost my cool."

She shook her head.

"I don't want him to lose the confidence he's worked so hard to get. I know what that's like."

"You do?"

I needed Dr. T to understand why I lost myself, so I took a deep breath and jumped in. "My mother died when I was Donnie's age. I just couldn't shake the sadness. No matter what I tried, I couldn't beat it. I was drowning, being pulled under by the heaviness of my thoughts. I missed my mom so much. Seven months later I missed the foul shots that cost my old man the championship. My father called me *choke artist* in front of the school. Everybody was at that game. I mean *everybody*. Between my mom's death and my father turning on me, it got scary. I stopped eating. I couldn't sleep. And I wouldn't get out of bed. I ended up across the parking lot at Friedman. Tim calling Donnie a choke artist hit too close."

"You were admitted to Friedman Psychiatric?" she asked, gesturing to her window, which looked out at the hospital.

I nodded. "The first time, I was there three months."

"How many times were you there?"

"Two more over the years. For depression. I haven't been back in a long time."

Dr. T was silent awhile. I became conscious of rubbing my hair between my fingers, and when I pulled my hand down, I realized I had pulled a few out. She gave me that look of hers, as if she were snooping around inside my head.

"I pull out my hair," I said, looking at the strands still in my hand.

"Do you have trichotillomania?" said Dr. T.

I nodded.

"Focused or automatic?"

"Both. Sometimes I pull out my hair without thinking about it, and sometimes I do it on purpose."

"Is it managed?" she asked, glancing at my head.

"I haven't had any *major* focused pulls in a long time. I hardly even think about it."

"I'm happy to hear that." Once again Dr. T was silent for a beat. "Cheers for sharing all that with me, Mr. Cannon. I know that wasn't easy."

"Can I keep my job?" I said, slipping the hair into my pocket.

"To be honest, I don't think so. But if you can promise me, you'll never ever do such a thing again—and I mean never, mate—I'll speak on your behalf."

"You shouldn't stick your neck out for me," I said. "I'm not worth you getting in trouble."

"You know you said something yesterday that really hit home for me. You said that Chey wanted to be a part of the team because she needed some purpose in her life besides working on herself to get better."

"You said you'd heard that before, right?"

"As you know, my father committed suicide."

I nodded.

"In one of our last conversations, he said he spent all his time and energy thinking about how to get better, which only made him feel worse. I don't think I fully understood what he was talking about until yesterday." She paused to take a breath. "He wasn't living his life, only struggling to make himself feel better. I should've suggested he volunteer at a boy's club or at a nursing home. He needed to get out of the house."

I reached over and touched her hand. "Don't do that to yourself."

She quickly withdrew it and made her way back to her side of the desk and sat, examining the pencils laid out by length in front of her. "Ultimately, it'll be up to Dr. Lipschitz and the board of directors, who're meeting tonight. I'm going to have to suspend you until they make their decision. But if you do end up somehow keeping your job, I need you to find a way to be more professional and in control."

I nodded. I knew that included quelling my instinct to comfort Dr. T, who still had pain around her father's death. I wanted to reach out for her hand again, but I didn't dare.

• • •

I spent the afternoon texting back and forth with my assistant coach. She told me the team was going to strike if I were fired, and I told her I appreciated the thought, but to tell the guys to work on rebounds and not to worry about me for now. She then sent me a frowny face. I didn't tell her I was summoning the courage to beg my father to ask his friend on the board to save my job. It was a taller order than convincing Dr. T to let Chey coach. My father and I hadn't shared a word since I told the world he slept through my mother's suicide attempt. I would have to swallow my anger and hurt to plead with him for help—yet again. I didn't know what else to do. I couldn't imagine not coaching my guys right now.

I called his cell a few times, but he didn't answer. Time was of the essence here, as the board was meeting tonight. I needed to go to the home of the Rams.

• • •

Through a small window in the door, I could see my father in his office. He was standing in front of a dry-erase board pointing to what looked like a complicated play and talking to his assistant, who was sitting at one of the two desks that faced each other—the smaller one. There were so many thoughts pinballing around my noggin, I couldn't grab one. I was at my old high school—with all those lovely memories—to ask for yet another favor from the man I was losing more respect for every day, a man who despite that, I felt the need to impress and connect with, a man who had zero interest in talking with me, let alone helping me.

When I knocked, my father's eyes shot to the window in the door. He didn't signal me in, but he didn't send me away, either, so I entered a room lined with trophies and plaques and framed newspaper clippings, not to mention photos of my father's various teams throughout the years, which covered the whole back wall behind his desk.

My father nodded to his assistant, who shook his head at me like a reprimand before leaving the room. My old man then gave me a serious look and sat down at his desk, leaning back in his chair. "I'm glad you're here. You and I have to get some things straight."

"OK," I said, standing in the middle of the room, unsure if I should sit.

"First thing—you've got to keep Hannibal Lecter on a leash, Bench Warmer," he said.

"What?"

"One of your rejects attacked my star player."

Once again, my old man was able to surprise me. "It was your golden child who punched my guy, a sweet kid minding his own business!"

"You expect me to believe that horseshit?" he said, leaning forward.

"Donnie wouldn't attack a dog who was chewing on his arm."

"Look, Tim's a good kid, while your guys are right out of *America's Most Wanted.*"

"Tim's an insensitive prick."

"He's the best player I've had in years, and he could've been hurt, which could cost me the record, not to mention his scholarship to UCLA."

"What exactly do you want?" I snapped. "For me to tell Donnie to stop picking on Tim? Really?"

"It's not Donnie I'm concerned about. Apparently, some other psychopath on your team threatened Tim, a kid who threw somebody off a bridge or something. I can't have my guy looking over his shoulder all season or, worse, getting hurt. It could cost me everything."

"Don't call my guys names."

"Don't be sensitive."

"I'm not messing around—that's where I draw the line."

"You're not in a position to draw any lines."

"OK," I sang out, taking a few steps toward the door. "Although you might want to tell Tim to stay away from bridges."

"Bench Warmer, wait," said my father.

I turned around.

"*Can* you back this *Otis* off? Would he listen to you?"

"He would," I stated. It was a foreign feeling, my father asking me for something. When I walked in, tail between my legs, ready to once again beg my old man for help, I couldn't have guessed he would need something from me. I mean, I never would've let Otis beat up Tim, but my father didn't have to know that. No, he certainly did not. I walked behind my old man so that he had to swivel in his chair to see me.

"I can't have anything getting in the way of my record or this documentary. I will *not* be embarrassed," he said, banging his hand on the arm of his chair.

On the wall behind him, I found the photo of my team, the one taken the year I quit. "Embarrassed like the time I missed those foul shots. Your own son blowing the championship game."

"Embarrassed like my son telling the whole world I slept through my wife's suicide attempt." His tone was vulnerable, wounded, and it made me feel guilty. "You don't know everything," he said. "You think you do, but you don't."

"Well enlighten me, please," I said, surprised. "What don't I know?"

"Look, Mikey, Richard wants to interview you—thinks you're interesting for some crazy reason, and I do not want a repeat of the other day." He sounded less confident than I've ever heard him.

"What don't I know about Mom?"

"I'm not going into that stuff now."

"I mean it. What don't I know?"

"Not now. Period. End of sentence."

I knew better than to press him when he was like this. "Fine. But I'm not gonna let it go. You're going to have to talk to me about Mom."

"Fine, not now. Now I need you to do *me* a favor for once," he said, tapping his chest.

"You need two favors—to back off Otis and to lie to E:60."

My father didn't say anything. He wasn't used to losing the upper hand.

"Well, *I* need something from you," I said, sitting in the assistant coach's chair.

My father sat up straight. "Haven't I done enough for you? You're living in my house."

"I need one more thing," I said, leaning back, confident. "As I'm sure you know, I broke your star player's car window."

"Of course I know. You haven't changed in all these years. You still can't control yourself. I had to talk Tim's father out of having you arrested."

"Tim's father called the school, and now I may lose my job."

"You should've thought about that before you lost your damn mind."

"I need you to call that doctor friend of yours on the board and have him do you another favor."

"Daddy to the rescue again. You're unbelievable. Every time I turn around, you're doing something that makes me want to say, 'he's not mine.'"

"Enough, Dad. If you make the call, I'll say whatever you want me to say in the interview. That you were daddy of the year."

My father took a few breaths, thinking. "And if I do this, you'll back off that Otis kid?"

My father and I locked eyes.

"You have my word," I said.

"Well then, we have ourselves a deal, *Coach*," he said.

"Yes, we do, *Coach*."

# TWENTY-TWO

**I received a call the next morning from Dr. T saying I still had a job.** I promised Dr. T I would be more professional and not punch anything else. This board member friend must have some real clout.

That afternoon at practice I apologized to the guys for losing my cool like an angry child and for putting the team at risk. "From now on, we all gotta think how our actions could blow back on the team," I said, making sure Otis was paying attention.

"That boy who hit Donnie need to get himself some consequence," said the big man.

"OK," I said. "Let's talk consequences. Everything we do has them. Right?"

"That boy hit Donnie, he loses himself some blood. That be a consequence," said Otis.

"Otis, if you exact revenge on Nubbin's brother you will be kicked off the team, and our season will be over, and we won't win a game. *That's* a consequence."

Otis rocked back and forth, grunting his throat clear, but he stayed quiet.

"Nubbin's brother can't get away with that, bruh," said Brian, looking at Donnie, who was staring at his shoes.

"We set out to accomplish something," I said. "To win a game. Do you want some punk like Tim getting in the way with that? Really?"

"Hell no, right, Otis?" said Toby. "We shouldn't sweat them fools. Donnie, would you rather we step to those boys that hit you or win a league game?"

"Win a league game," said Donnie. "Because Coach promised. *This is the promise which He Himself made to us*, said the Lord."

"Heard," said Chey. "We need to take care of our own business like we did at the park, and right now that means practicing. Right, guys?" Chey clapped like she was ready to get it going.

"All right," said Otis, grunting. "But let's get down to it, 'cause I feel like Donnie needs to win the *next* game."

"Yeah," said Toby, rubbing his dome. "I need to win it, too, for real."

So did I. I gathered everybody, and we spoke about the difference between the all-out-brawl of a game at the park and winning a league game—we had to play with the same intensity without fouling. Ironically, I was talking about playing with restraint and control—two things I was in short supply of.

I lined my guys under the hoop and placed Donnie with his ball at the foul line.

"Nubbin's eyeballing us," Chey whispered to me.

And so, he was—he was pacing back and forth about fifty feet from practice, glancing at us as he went.

"All right," I said, addressing my guys. "The game is won or lost right where you're standing—rebounds. Donnie is gonna miss this shot."

"No, I'm not," said Donnie.

"On purpose, Donnie. I'm asking you to *purposely* miss the shot."

"OK," he said. "On *purpose*, I will miss it. *On purpose*. I am not a choke artist."

"Donnie, I need you to hear me here, OK?" I said, approaching him. "You are not a choke artist. Got it?"

"That's what I said. I am *not* a choke artist."

"OK," I said. "I was making sure."

"Balls don't have penises," proclaimed Donnie.

Brian giggled.

"That's right, Donnie," I said. "They don't."

Donnie smiled, bounced the ball, and got ready to shoot.

"You're funny, Donnie," I said, shaking my head.

"*Funny*," Donnie repeated to himself.

"OK," said Chey. "If you boys can stop talking about penises for a second, we can practice. Donnie, you shoot and miss, and whoever gets the rebound best out of five gets out of running a mile."

My guys came to life, pushing one another before the ball even left Donnie's hands. When he did shoot, Toby backed up Brian to get position, but the ball bounced off his hands, prompting Gonzalo and Otis to dive for it. Then Brian dove on Gonzalo and Otis, and then Toby joined the pile. Everybody kicked and hit for the ball, much like they did at the park, while I blew my whistle until eventually Otis came up with the rock. "OK, good hustle," I said. "But today we are going to do it without channeling our inner Rodman. We must figure out a way to finish tomorrow's game with all five players. So, no fouling."

"And . . . so . . . yeah, anyone who fouls or holds back runs a mile. *Comprende, amigos?*" said Chey.

"What up, *chica*? Why you trying to make us hoof it?" asked G.

"Cause she straight up wants to win, bruh," said Brian. "Do what she says."

My four guys lined up again, while Nubbin paced closer to the court. Donnie missed his shot and all four vied for position, bouncing off one another's bodies so hard my shoulder hurt watching them, but they didn't foul. Toby leapt up and snatched the ball off the rim and went back up for two points.

"Toby, how'd that feel?" I asked.

"Got my dick hard, yo."

"If you guys do that tomorrow, we'll win, pure and simple," said Chey. "I'd bet big money on it. I won't of course. I'm just saying."

I asked Chey to keep the drill going, and I walked off the court. Nubbin, who was still pacing, hurried in the opposite direction as soon as he saw me. "Wait up," I called out.

He stopped but didn't turn around.

"How's your ribs, Nubbin?"

Nubbin shrugged without turning around.

"You wanna shoot with us?"

"No," he said, still facing the distance. "Donnie asked me to watch practice. That's all."

"Come on, I've seen you shoot. You don't get skills like that if you don't love the game."

"They don't want me on the team."

"You threw pee at my windshield, and I want you on the team. Who knows—maybe whatever they have against you can be fixed?"

He turned to the court as if considering it. "I mean, they don't like me," he said. "Nobody does."

"It sounds like Donnie likes you. Besides, we need a sixth."

"No way."

"Are you being recruited by someone else?"

"No."

"Are you holding out for a higher salary?"

"No."

"Those are called jokes, Nubbin."

He began to blink and started to walk again, so I kept pace. "Damn, you're a fast walker."

Nubbin kept walking, ignoring me.

"What's the real reason you don't wanna play?"

"You really wanna know?"

"I'm still following you, aren't I?"

"I mean, I'm unstable, in case you haven't noticed."

"So what? I'm unstable. The whole team's unstable."

"My father said if I played high school ball, I'd end up hurting somebody or myself. I'm not allowed to play on a team, so that's that."

"Is he right?"

Nubbin stopped.

"Are you too unstable to ball?"

"No. My father thought my being on the team would hurt my brother's chances of a scholarship somehow, that I would do something so terrible that the scouts would wonder if my brother was also messed up."

"Do you want to be on the team, Nubbin?"

Nubbin turned to the guys practicing. Chey took a shot while the guys pushed for position. "What's wrong with you?" he said, turning toward me. "I mean, are you stupid or something? I'm not allowed to play!"

"But do you *want* to?"

"Yeah, I do. But my father won't let me."

"You tell your old man everything?"

Nubbin squinted at me. "No."

This kid needed the team more than the team needed him, and the team was desperate for a sixth guy, especially one with his skills. "You won't be on your brother's team, so you won't ruin his scholarship. You wouldn't even be in the same division as your brother."

"My father would kill me if he ever found out," he said, blinking.

"All right, Nubbin, don't worry about it. It's OK, was an idea."

Nubbin kept watching practice.

"I appreciate you sticking up for Donnie. For me, that clears the whole pee-throwing thing, OK?"

Nubbin nodded, and I turned to head back to practice.

"I got something to say," shouted Otis, beelining toward us in quick, choppy steps, his attention on his own feet as if they couldn't be trusted to get him where he needed to be.

Nubbin looked as if he were about to go rabbit and spring into a hole somewhere.

"You showed me something, Nubbin," said Otis, stopping in front of us. "You took some kicks to the rib for Donnie."

Nubbin looked at Otis, frozen.

"'Cause you know what that there ball mean to him."

"Yeah," said Nubbin. "He loves that ball, asked me to steal it from him and when I did, he started screaming like I shot him or something."

"You stick up for Donnie over your family and that mean something—to me."

Both Nubbin and Otis looked uncomfortable, their attention bouncing around the ground, each other's shirts, their own hands, but they never made eye contact. I didn't move a muscle, scared to startle them off.

"I'm saying I got you, is all. Anybody give you a bad time 'bout crapping in bags or being messed up, I got you."

"Really?" asked Nubbin.

"Yeah," said Otis, making eye contact, but only for a second.

"Yeah, OK," said Nubbin. "Thanks."

Otis turned and looked at me. "What?" he said.

"Nothing," I said, trying to hold back a smile, as Otis lumbered back to the court.

# TWENTY-THREE

**The next afternoon Dr. T found me kidding with Angie** in the parking lot. I straightened up and ran a hand through my hair, which got me an eye roll from Angie, but thankfully, Dr. T was smiling.

"Nubbin, who always sits by himself at lunch, ate with Otis and Donnie," she said.

"That's cool," I said.

"I went over to see if everything was OK, and they were watching some cartoon on Donnie's phone, laughing. *Laughing*," she repeated. "That Nubbin was eating with Donnie isn't so surprising, but that *Otis* was with them—I was floored."

"*Floored*?"

"Are you taking the piss?"

"He is," said Angie.

"Out with it," said Dr. T. "Why was Otis with them?"

"As you know, Nubbin's brother stole Donnie's ball."

Dr. T nodded.

"All I know is that Nubbin tried to get it back, and Otis told him he appreciated how he stood up for Donnie over his family."

"Amazing," whispered Dr. T.

Later, when I was waiting on my bus in the school's lot for the team, Nubbin ran up and rapped on my door.

"Hey, Nubbin," I said, popping it open. "Angie's driving you guys home today. Team's playing at Pine Crest in an hour."

Studying his LeBron 15 kicks, Nubbin said, "Donnie and Otis said you read their assignments."

I guess Otis knew I read his—of course he did.

Nubbin reached into his backpack and handed me some papers that looked as if they had been crumpled and then ironed out. "If you read mine and still want me on the team, I'm in."

"OK," I said, slipping his assignment between the seat and the wall to read later.

"I mean, provided you don't think I'm too unstable to ball after those pages, I'm ready to go *today*."

"Oh," I said, realizing he wanted me to read the pages *now*. I laid them on my lap, noticing how weak the paper looked, as if the pages might tear. I guessed Nubbin had crumpled and straightened them out countless times. Feeling his eyes burning a hole in the top of my head, I glanced up. "You gonna stand there and watch me read? Really?"

"Yeah."

"No," I said. "Come back in ten."

Nubbin reluctantly made his way off the bus and proceeded to pace out front, as I picked up the first page.

## NUBBIN'S ASSIGNMENT

I don't really know who I am going to give this essay to yet, but whoever it ends up being, you may as well know, that it's true. I did take a poop in my brother's gym bag. I hope that after you read this, you won't think that I'm disgusting. You will understand a little bit of why I did it.

My stepbrother hates me. I used to think the reason he hated me was I was short. I mean, all Tim ever talks about is basketball, and to be good at basketball you have to be tall. Tim is built like how a ballplayer is supposed to be. I mean, it's as if he was born to be the best player at Westchester. My father and stepmother even built a court in our yard for Tim and his friends to play. I've watched them play countless times through my kitchen window, and it's obvious Tim is going to go pro. Everyone says so.

One time, while I watched Tim and his friends from the window, I thought of a plan to impress my brother for him to like me. Tim and his friends spent days trying to master this one difficult shot. I mean, it was way past the three-point line. They practiced over and over but they couldn't land more than three out of ten. Whenever they were off the court, I was on. I practiced that same shot until I could hit seven out of ten. I may not be tall, but I'm a great shooter. My mother used to say that God gives gifts sparingly. Even though we aren't blood brothers, it seems Tim got my share plus his, but there is no doubt that I got some shooting skills. My plan was that I would land the shot they'd given up on to show Tim that even though I was short, I was still a good player. If there was one thing my brother respected, it was a good basketball player.

When the time came, I went over to the window and watched and waited. Finally, Jovver, Tim's best friend, stopped playing and picked up his cell and was showing something to my brother. I was nervous. I grabbed my ball off the laundry machine. I had to do this before my father came home because he would stop me from shooting. He always told me not to bother my brother and his friends while they were playing. I opened the door and went right to the place I'd landed a thousand shots. I could feel them watching me, which made my face extremely hot. They were silent. Then Tim said, "We're practicing." That meant for me to go away.

I didn't even look at him. I planted my feet. I looked at the rim. I bounced the ball. I shot. I watched the ball as it went in.

"Oh shit!" said Russell, Tim's other best friend. "Fucking hobbit made that shot!"

"Tim, can I play with you guys?"

Tim grabbed the rebound and passed it to me. "Do it again, dwarf," he said like the first shot was luck.

I dribbled the ball a few times and shot. It went in. Again.

"'Daaamn!" shouted Jovver. "Wee man got some skills."

"That don't mean anything," said Tim. "Russell, guard him—let's see if you can score on somebody."

Russell handed me the ball and began to push me. "Come on, Wee Man, let's see what you got." He pushed me down. I got up right away. He could've kicked me in the balls, and I wouldn't have called a foul because Tim would've thought I was being a wimp, and you can't be a wimp and a good ballplayer at the same time.

"How come you're short?" Russell asked. "Oh, that's right, your mom was a midget, too. A dead midget." I knew better than to show Russell that what he said about my mom upset me. I mean, I understood talking smack on the court, but I didn't like him talking bad about my mother. I took a deep breath and did a crossover dribble, which totally tripped him up. I mean, he almost fell, and I easily made the shot. "Can I play with you guys?" I said.

Tim looked me up and down. "You score on me, you can play."

I knew Tim's game better than he did. I mean, most players were either righty or lefty and leaned on that hand. When Tim saw which hand a player favored, he cheated to that side. The last time my brother and I played together—two years before—I couldn't go left, and I could see him favoring my right side. What he didn't know was I spent three hours every day dribbling with both hands. I mean, I walked and dribbled—not much else to do when you have no friends. He didn't know anything about that. I faked right and went left, which faked him out. But when I shot, he blocked it.

"We're trying to practice," said Tim. "Go back to your window."

"Maybe we can play two-on-two?" I said. "I scored on Russell, and I made that hard shot twice in a row. You saw I'm good enough to play with you guys. I wouldn't be in the way. Please."

"The thing is," said Tim, "you're too crazy to play with us. You should be in a padded cell. You shouldn't even be living here."

"Yeah," said Russell. "You're a psychopath. I'm not playing with you."

"You're way scary, bro," said Jovver.

I stood there looking back and forth between my brother and his friends. I finally understood why my brother hated me, and it was so much more than my

being short. When he looked at me, he saw a psychopath, not a brother. I screamed loud. I mean, I didn't
even say anything. I just screamed uncontrollably. I
don't even know where such a scream even came from.
It was scary, like maybe I was crazy. Then I stormed
into the house and slammed the door. I never wanted
to see my brother again. I wanted to go live in a cabin
in the woods.

Okay, so here's the part you've probably been waiting for. Or maybe you've stopped reading. I don't know.
But if you are still here, I should tell you that when
I get upset my stomach goes off. I ran to the bathroom and locked the door. It was like knives stabbed
the inside of my stomach. I mean, I felt like I was
going to poop myself. I turned and saw Tim's gym bag
on the floor. I opened his bag and saw his basketball
uniform. Something about that uniform made me cry,
and I held his bag under my butt, and I pooped right
in it. I mean, I was crying like a baby. The horrible
smell got in my nose causing me to gag and to cry
even harder.

That's when I realized that my father was going
to kill me if he found out about this. I needed to
get rid of the evidence. I grabbed Tim's bag and I ran
out of the bathroom and tried to make my way down
the stairs, but my brother and his friends were now
in the house. My brother grabbed me. "Give me my bag,
psycho!" yelled Tim.

He grabbed at the bag in my hands, but I held
on tight. He pulled and I pulled back. My brother
shouted for me to give him the bag, but I kept pulling
and yanking until the bag flew out of my hands and
landed on the floor.

"What is that smell?" said Tim. His eyes were wide like he couldn't believe how bad it stunk.

I pushed through the three of them and I ran out of my house and I kept running. I ran for miles until I collapsed on someone's front lawn. No wonder Tim hated me. Nobody wanted to spend time with some psychopath who poops in someone's bag. I knew right then and there that I would never have any friends. I would have to live the rest of my life by myself. It was scary and depressing to realize this fact.

I stayed out all night. I walked around. The next morning, I waited until Tim went to school. I snuck in my front door. My father was sitting at the kitchen table. He said he'd called Dr. Tambori. He told her I should be put in a residential facility. She didn't agree. My father wanted to put me away without even hearing my side of the story, and I knew why. It wasn't what I had done. It was because my father had a better son now, not a freak of nature. Any father would want Tim as his son. I don't know if you, whoever is reading this, has ever felt replaced and like you no longer mattered, but that's how I felt that day, and that's why I pooped in my brother's bag. If you want to know the truth, I still feel that way.

• • •

I folded the pages neatly on my lap, collecting myself before looking up. Maybe Nubbin was too unstable to ball in a league, but he needed this team, maybe more than any of us. I popped open the door and Nubbin, who was waiting, stepped on.

"Welcome to the team, Nubbin."

"Really?"

"Yeah. We're lucky to have you."

Nubbin stood looking at me as if I were playing a joke on him.

"You got shorts and a T-shirt?" I asked.

He nodded, tapping the gym bag hanging on his shoulder.

"Come on. Get on board."

"If my father asks where I was, I'm going to tell him out walking. I mean, I don't think he'll ask, but if he does, that's what I'll tell him."

"The man with the plan," I said, as the team filed past him onto the bus.

"Nubbin, come sit with me," said Otis.

Nubbin sat beside Otis across the aisle from Donnie and Chey, while Brian and G stared wide-eyed at me like I was insane, which maybe I was. I wasn't sure how the addition of Nubbin was going to play out besides having another player. Sure, Nubbin had some skills but who knew how they would translate on the court, how he would fit in with the aggressive, selfless play we'd been working on, or if there would be excrement involved.

• • •

The first play of the game, Brian brought the ball up-court and passed to Otis, who passed it back to Brian, who dished it to Nubbin, who threw a defender off with a head fake and drove the baseline toward the hoop, edging toward an easy two points. But instead, just at the last second, he swung the ball out to a wide-open Donnie at the three-point line, and Donnie sank the bucket, and for the first time this season, the Mary Friedman Alternative High School had the lead.

Across the court, on Pine Crest Prep School's bench sat two coaches in blue blazers with powder blue dress shirts—the team's colors—and something like fifteen extra players. Beside them jumped cheerleaders recommending their team to *be aggressive*, *B-E aggressive*, punching out the letters with flailing pompoms to packed stands.

The Pine Crest shooting guard, number 7, popped a jumper from the foul line, while their forward, a six-foot-seven beanpole with the name Dawkins on the back of his jersey—the only person of color on the team—moved for position underneath the hoop, easily boxing out Toby. The ball bounced off the rim and Dawkins leapt up and dunked the rebound.

"Toby, get in his grill!" I shouted. "Don't let him get position."

A few plays later, number 7 brought the ball up-court while Dawkins once again moved under the hoop for position, shoving Toby out of his way. It was becoming clear that a good part of their offense was Dawkins converting rebounds. Toby put his hand on Dawkin's shoulder, checking him, when I heard something that made me all warm and fuzzy. "You're lucky you're so tall, son, 'cause you got no springs," said Toby. Number 7 missed the shot just as Toby moved in front of a confused Dawkins, who was apparently unaccustomed to smack talk, and stole the rebound, swinging the rock out to Brian.

"Hey, stilts," Toby called to Dawkins, "I hope your baby girl ain't here, 'cause I don't want to feel bad embarrassing you all day." Toby was only a couple inches shorter than Dawkins, and it was funny hearing him call anyone stilts.

"Fuck you," said Dawkins.

Otis set picks, a few give-and-goes, and generally threw his weight around, while Nubbin made some incredible passes and Donnie got a hot hand, and we matched Pine Crest basket for basket for much of the first quarter, looking like a real team. The only person having a hard time was G, who was getting owned by his man on D, who was a good six inches taller than him. I called G in and gave him a play I thought particularly well-suited for his gifts. On the next play, when G's man pushed in front of him and got position underneath the hoop for a rebound, G reached down and tugged at his guy's shorts as if he were about to pull them down. When his man reached down to keep his shorts up, G grabbed the rebound and tossed it to Nubbin. He baseballed it to Brian, who missed a layup that Toby converted into two points.

Then Nubbin caught the bug from Donnie, dropping three-point bombs from the exact same spot each time, as if he'd been practicing it. I imagined it was the same shot from his assignment, the one he was excited to show his brother. Toby, he was living in his man's head, smack-talking him like a pro, using such classics as "Yo, bro, how many times you gonna let me score?" and "I saw a tennis court across the street. Maybe you should try that." Otis grabbed rebounds and set picks, G dove for loose balls, and Brian set up plays but refused to shoot, and when he sat on the bench, Chey turned to him and said, "Bri, you gotta take those high-percentage shots—you get an open look in the paint, take it."

"I know. I know. I know. I get in my head too much when I'm about to shoot."

"I've seen you drop layups in practice. I'm talking about shooting in the paint," Chey said.

"Yeah, yeah, yeah, but if I miss, I'll get embarrassed and if I get embarrassed, I'll sink into my head for the rest of the game, and I'll be useless. I won't even be able to pass, and coach will leave me on the bench now that we got a sixth. Then, I'll start thinking about that miss all the time until I won't be able to sleep—for weeks I won't be able to sleep. I'll start drinking again, and I'll keep drinking until I wind up dead in a ditch somewhere."

I couldn't help thinking about Brian's assignment, how his obsessional thinking almost pushed him off a bridge. I wondered if he shared his pages with Chey yet. It certainly didn't seem so. I tried to drum up words that would get him out of his head, but I couldn't think of anything helpful.

Chey put her hand on his knee. "Everybody on the court knows you don't shoot, so you gotta, like, mix it up. *Comprende?*"

"*Comprende*," said Brian.

"Besides, you're not going to end up in a ditch. Not on my watch," said Chey.

Brian nodded and then returned to the court, allowing Donnie a rest on the bench between Chey and I.

"Nice work, Donnie," I said.

"I'm not scared to shoot at all, and I'm not even lying," said Donnie.

"No kidding. You're a machine," I said.

"*No kidding*," repeated Donnie.

Nubbin dribbled toward the hoop but got caught up in traffic and dished the ball through his legs to G, who sank a two-pointer.

"Go, Gonzalo," I heard from somewhere behind me. We had a fan?

I turned to Chey. "Did you hear somebody yell G's name?"

"Dr. T is here."

"She is?"

"Yeah, she's been here all game."

"Why didn't you tell me?"

Chey shrugged. "I thought you knew since you're in love with her."

"I am *not* in *love* with her," I said with a little too much conviction.

"Whatever," said Chey. "But you are."

Donnie nodded.

"Donnie, sub in for G. Now!"

"OK," said Donnie, giggling.

My palms began to sweat as I scanned the stands for Dr. T, who was waving to me ten rows back. I was almost giddy she was here, like some teenager. She was so compassionate, smart, and that skin, that lovely brown skin.

Toby brought the ball down-court and passed to Donnie, who shot, and I watched the ball sail through the air, only it looked short, as it landed in Otis's hands right under the rim. It wasn't a shot. It was a pass. I leapt off the bench, "Donnie, you are the man!" I yelled as Otis made the easy two points.

Donnie waved at me and then at Dr. T.

The game was tight, with both sides playing well until there were only a few seconds left on the clock and the score tied seventy all, and we had the ball. We had a chance to win this game, and I called a time out.

"Schizoids!" somebody shouted in the seats behind Pine Crest's bench. Then some others joined in, a whole section of fans were now chanting, "Schizoids, Schizoids, Schizoids." Otis and Donnie turned to these morons chanting and seemed to lose steam.

I clapped to get everybody's attention. "Donnie, Otis, get your heads in the game! Now!"

The whole team put their attention on me. "Guys, tonight we win this game. Donnie, this is your win. OK?"

The team shuffled their feet.

"Toby, you inbound it, and whoever gets it brings it up-court. The rest of you need to ensure Donnie gets a wide-open look. I need you guys to be patient. We have time to take a high-percentage shot, so don't rush anything," I said, my heart bucking.

You could feel the team's nerves as they ran onto the court. Toby inbounded the ball to G, who took it up-court before returning it to him at the right wing. Toby's defender swatted at the ball, knocking it from his hands, the ball heading out of bounds until, at the last second, G dove for it, swatting it to Nubbin, who cross-courted it to Otis at the left baseline. Two defenders rushed up on Otis and tied him up. He couldn't break lose and lobbed it back across court, two defenders jumping for it but not grabbing it as it landed in Donnie's hands, who passed it to Gonzalo above the foul line—everybody was touching the ball like at the park. Gonzalo saw an opening and drove toward the hoop, but a defender swatted the ball away, which ricocheted off Toby's arm into the hands of Nubbin, who faked a shot, drove under the hoop, and sank a reverse layup as time ran off the clock.

"Bloody hell!" issued from the stands above us. "Did we win?"

Toby rushed to Nubbin and seemed to be about to hug him, but stopped short, offering him a fist-bump instead. Toby then grabbed G, leaving Nubbin looking around the gym as if he were an alien who'd just materialized here. Brian did some sort of popping and locking victory dance, while Donnie and Otis high-fived and Chey marveled at the shocked Pine Crest players, coaches, and cheerleaders, whose pompoms sat limp at their sides.

I extended my hand to the Pine Crest coach like I'd always seen winning coaches do on TV. My body was pulsing, my excitement threatening to escape in the form of a hysterical scream. "Nice game, Coach," I said.

The coach looked as if he might leave my hand hanging there like a dead fish, but then he shook his head and took my hand. "Welcome to the league, Coach." I swear to God I had to fight back tears. I felt someone at my side and turned to see Dr. T waiting patiently to speak to me. "Excuse me, Coach, our fan would like a word." The coach smiled at Dr. T and put his arm around Dawkins as the two walked away.

"Cracking good game, Mikey," said Dr. T, her face radiant.

"Hey, you called me Mikey."

"I'm chuffed to bits for you and the team—for Donnie. You did it!"

At first, I tried to play it cool, as if I never had a doubt, but my glee was racing around my head like an excited two-year-old with a new fire truck. "I can't believe it. It was Nubbin. I knew he had skills, but he's really something."

"When exactly did Nubbin join the team, mate?" Dr. T asked.

"As we were pulling out of the parking lot to come here. I guess I should've asked you if he was eligible or something."

It wasn't Nubbin's eligibility Dr. T was worried about. "I would warn you about how unpredictable and destructive he can be, but I don't believe you would heed that warning."

"Nope."

"Then I'll say that Nubbin wasn't the only reason you were victorious. It was *you* and all the work you've been doing with your team. You should be proud."

I nodded, taking Dr. T's words in. We won.

"Hey, Adderall," called a Pine Crest fan, the name on the back of Brian's T-shirt. "It's time you guys report back to the ward." Brian appeared confused, but then touched his shirt as if remembering what was on the back, his excitement leaving as fast as it had arrived.

# TWENTY-FOUR

**When I got home, not wanting to give my father the opportunity to kill my elation,** I went straight to my room. Not only did we win—an idea I was still settling into—but Dr. T called me Mikey. Two triumphs in one night!

With Nubbin's mad skills, and the subpar quality of our league, we could win more games. From what I'd seen, Nubbin might even be the best baller in our division. First thing I needed to do was get the guys some real uniforms. Winners didn't show up to games in dirty T-shirts. I thought to ask the school for help, but we didn't have time for bureaucracy. We needed uniforms stat, so I withdrew the whole two grand I'd saved to get my own digs and headed downtown.

• • •

Our win was all anyone could talk about at school, and some students even stayed late to watch practice. The guys, unaccustomed to fans, reverted to the same hot-dog play as when I first saw them, which I stopped by asking Brian and Otis to grab a few boxes from the bus, where, apparently, one of them had mysteriously come open.

"No way, bruh!" screamed Brian. "These are straight tope."

The uniforms were the kind the pros wore. They were black with blue trim on the collar and three red Adidas stripes running down the side, and their shorts were half red and half blue. They were nicer than any we'd seen so far and, even with a half hour of heated negotiation, still cost me the whole two grand. Brian was right. They were tight and dope—tope. As much as I wanted out of my father's, seeing the team set on those boxes like lions destroying antelope was worth the extra couple of months.

"These uniforms are all the way right," said G.

"That's what's up," said Toby.

The guys found the ones with their names on the back. I kept the numbers they'd given themselves but decided to go with their last names instead of their diagnoses.

When Toby took off his shirt, I saw fresh, deep cuts on his shoulders with some splotches of dried blood, which made my face sweat. The cuts couldn't have been more than hours old. I thought to pull him aside but didn't know what to say to him. I was relieved when Tyrone, the towering security guard, and Dr. T approached to see what all the excitement was, and Dr. T's attention locked on Toby's cuts. She would know what to do. Tyrone, watching the guys filming one another's new duds on their phones, smiled. Until that moment, I didn't know if he had teeth.

I called Chey over and handed her a small box. "For you."

She ripped it open and grabbed her jersey, which was the same as the others, only instead of a last name, her uniform said Coach, and instead of a number:

"Percentage sign!" sang Chey. "Dr. T, mine has a percentage sign, because I'm always working the odds." Chey, for a second, appeared like she hadn't a care in the world, a kid with a new shirt.

"Brilliant," said Dr. T.

"Yeah it is," said Tyrone.

"Thanks so much for letting me coach," said Chey, rushing up and giving Dr. T a hug.

By the way Dr. T recoiled, it was clear she was unaccustomed to being hugged by a student, or perhaps by anybody.

"Sorry, Dr. T. I don't know why I did that," said Chey. "It's like I'm hug-crazy lately. We should probably talk about it in our next session."

"That's all right, Chey," said Dr. T. "You caught me by surprise."

"Awks," sang Chey, returning to her team, who practiced in their uniforms in front of their fans.

$$\bullet \quad \bullet \quad \bullet$$

The next game, not only did we show up in style, but we had fans behind our bench. Gerald and some of the boys from the park cheered us to a win: Visitors—64, Malibu Sober High School—52. Only when we returned to our bus, it was tagged. Some mental midgets painted *retards* on the sides and back window. As we were getting on, I noticed a few students and teachers gawking. "Go have a drink for Christ's sake!" I shouted. Not one of my prouder moments.

$$\bullet \quad \bullet \quad \bullet$$

The school didn't have a spare, so I had to drive the tagged embarrassment down Crenshaw Boulevard and through East and West Adams and Culver City the next morning. It drew honks, laughter, and derision from pedestrians and drivers alike, as my guys ducked in their seats, mortified. When we pulled up to Nubbin's, Tim and his friends were out front chanting, "Retards, retards, retards." It wasn't Sober High who tagged us. It was Nubbin's brother.

I turned to ensure nobody was looking to charge off the bus and take scalps. They weren't. Not even Otis, who stared at his lap. The rest of the team looked at their phones, avoiding eye contact, beat down. Chey closed her eyes.

When we pulled up to Mary Friedman, I let everyone off except the team. "What's wrong with you suckers? We won two games, and we're gonna win tomorrow night. Why are you still letting those morons get to you?"

"We won two games in a row," said Chey. "I figured people would start showing us respect after we won, or at least leave us alone."

"They're not going to because we're messed up, bruh," said Brian. "I take Clozapine and Adderall to get out of bed. We go to school at a hospital."

"None of you are retards, so who cares what people call you?" I asked.

"You're the main retard," said G. "I mean, you're more fucked up than the rest of us. We see you twirling away at your hair like a nut job, muttering to yourself. The other day I saw you pull out a strand and twirl it between your fingers for like the whole bus ride."

I thought I'd been better at hiding my hair pulling. I guess not.

"Yeah. I've heard people talking straight smack on you at school—teachers and therapists," said Brian.

"Yeah, they make fun of you for being a twenty-five, broke, living-at-home *pendejo, güey*," said G.

"They do?" I asked, feeling the sting. I thought I'd made some headway with the staff, that they were beginning to accept or even like me.

"Yo, don't that jack you up, Coach?" asked Toby.

"Yeah, it does," I said.

"Them names take root," said Otis, grunting his throat clear.

"Look, guys, Brian's right. You go to school at a hospital. People are fools. It's a bad combo. Some kids are gonna make fun of you. You can either agree with them that you're retards, let the names *jack you up*, or you can decide it doesn't matter what people say about you." I was speaking to myself as much as to the team. My father calling me Choke Artist still decimated my confidence, and it was something I needed to get over.

"What are you talking about, Coach?" asked Brian.

"Look, I could either push you guys for a name of who dissed me and beat them within an inch of their lives, or I could say to myself, *fuck them*. See what I mean?"

Nobody was following me.

"I'll give you a few names if you want, Coach," said G. "I heard them talking smack on you for fifteen minutes in the teacher's lounge yesterday."

I would've loved a few names, but I didn't think they would've helped the point I was trying to make. "I'm deciding now that whatever somebody calls me, I'm all right."

"What you mean, *decide*?" asked Otis.

"So . . . like . . . what are you going to do if a coach calls you a name?" asked Donnie.

"Or if a teacher, say of English, calls you a man-child?" asked G.

"If somebody calls me a retard or man-child, I'll think, *Hey, fuck you, dick-faced English Teacher*. See what I mean? Hey, Donnie, you're a retard."

Donnie's mouth dropped. "Fuck you, dick-faced coach?"

"You got it, Donnie. Nubbin, you're one unstable mofo," I said.

"Eat me . . . assbite."

"Way to make it your own, my man," I said.

"Anyway, you guys shouldn't be upset," said Nubbin. "It was my brother who tagged the bus and called us retards to hurt me. I mean, it's got nothing to do with you all. I'm the only retard."

"You're not the only retard," announced Donnie. "We are *all* retards."

"Your brother's such a dick, bruh," said Brian.

"You have no idea," said Nubbin.

"Did you really shit in his gym bag?" asked Brian.

Nubbin nodded.

"I hope it was a wet shit," said Brian.

"A fucking roach-coach bean-burrito shit," said G.

"We should all take shits in his bag," said Donnie, "so he won't call you names anymore."

It wasn't your usual inspirational sports movie moment, but it warmed my heart just the same.

"If we take our division, we'll play Westchester in the first round of The Tourney of Champs," said Nubbin.

"What?" I asked. Did I hear that right?

"We'd play your old man and my brother."

"How?" I asked.

"The winner of the best league plays the winner of the worst in the first round. One game."

"One and done," said Chey.

"Don't take this the wrong way guys, but we're not going to win our division. We lost our first five games."

"Actually," began Chey. "It's possible. With Nubbin, and the way we're playing now . . ."

"OK, guys, let's not get our hopes up. Our plan was to win one game, and we've already done that—twice."

"All I'm saying is that it's mathematically possible," said Chey.

I could feel the blood draining from my face. Chey was right. Anything could happen.

# TWENTY-FIVE

**That night I couldn't sleep.** I couldn't stop thinking about playing my father. The game would take place at Westchester, my alma mater, since they would have a better record and we didn't have a gym. The humiliation of *that* game on *that* court would grind me to dust. I thought about missing those foul shots all those years ago, about my father humiliating me in front of the school, his embarrassment of having a son like me. I thought about my mother, how fun and funny she was before her first break, her suicide attempt, the car accident that led to her death, and I wondered what it was I didn't know about her—what my father was keeping from me.

My heart pounded in my ears, which forced me out of bed. The game I was worried about was never going to happen, so why was I obsessing about it? Because that's what I do. There was always something to obsess about. I mean, one minute I'm worried we'd never win a game, the next I'm worried we'll win too many. As good as Nubbin was, playing my father would be a worse humiliation than any game so far for my team, but for me it would be more harmful than anything I could think of. Westchester was a private school that recruited their athletes, a team that hadn't lost a game in years. I pictured my father taunting me, calling me Choke Artist and Bench Warmer in front of my team, in front of Dr. T, pointing to a scoreboard on which he was ahead by fifty points. I wouldn't survive that. No. It would throw me into darkness with no hope of escape.

I went to my father's computer and did some research: there are eighteen games in a season for my league. We already lost five and won two, so we had eleven games left. The top two teams faced off in a playoff game. The last five years, Kovacs, the reigning league champions, won seventeen of their eighteen games, so we would never come in first place; however, the second-place team three years running won less than twelve games, so even if we lost another game and won the rest, we could still nail that second-place slot. But we would never win the championship. Kovacs was by far the dominant team in the league and was on their way to a perfect season. OK, even if we did make it to the championship, there was no way we would play my father. No way. I wouldn't have to endure the worst humiliation I could imagine. Right? Right. Why did I not feel any better?

The next morning, I got some spray paint, and the guys and I transformed the bus from an embarrassment to a work of street art. It turned out most of the team had experience tagging, and we transformed the *retard* graffiti to read *The Visitors* in the bubble letters usually found on the walls of tenements.

Dr. Lipschitz demanded the bus be repainted by professionals, but Dr. T intervened, convincing him the team discovered self-respect while painting it, that I was teaching them they could transform the names people called them into something empowering. I wasn't sure I was trying to do all that, but Dr. Lipschitz let us keep the bus the way it was, and when we pulled up to our next game, the bus drew a different kind of stare, one that had my guys puffing out their chests.

We won the next five games, beating Portal, a computer-based school, and Fondazione Italia, an Italian language school, the Albert Einstein Academy, Da Vinci Science, and the Renaissance Arts Academy. Not only did we beat them but we also spanked Renaissance by twenty points. One game, Nubbin put up thirty-nine points, a league record. We even had a growing fan base: Dr. T, Dr. Lipschitz, Chey's mom, students, Tyrone, and Gerald cheered and high-fived in the rows behind our bench.

During the games I was flying high, but as soon as we won, I crashed. We were taking steps toward the possibility of playing my father, my undoing. I'd been ignoring my old man for weeks, roommates nodding to each other in the hallway, while I banked another couple paychecks. I needed three more at least before I would have enough dead presidents to move out, which meant I would be here through the end of the b-ball season. But I kept the goal in mind. As soon as I could afford it, I would set myself up in a studio apartment closer to the school.

My pops didn't know about my winning streak, or he would have said something, and the truth was I wanted him to know. It would be the first time in memory he would have something to say about me to feel proud about. I was following in his footsteps. I was a winner. I entered the TV room, where my father was watching his favorite newscaster with the sound off, looking for something I hadn't gotten from him in a long time—an attaboy.

"It's like they're purposely teasing the viewer by not showing her ass," noted my old man.

"You want them to pan down for a booty shot?"

The news switched to sports, and my father put the sound back on to hear the reporter say the Lakers lost a close one, that it came down to the last shot but that Green missed, prompting my old man to remark that Green pulled a Mikey.

"Really? You can't just let that go. How many years ago was that?"

"Come on, toughen up."

"Do you remember what you said to me before I missed those foul shots?"

"No."

"You said, *Don't embarrass me*."

"You didn't listen."

"What is it about me you so disapprove of?"

"I'll tell you," he said, standing. "You never go *after* life. You sit on the sidelines. I mean, when things get tough, you hide under your covers like a child instead of getting angry and going out and kicking ass. You take after your mother."

"What a steaming pile of monkey shit, to quote you. You didn't give up on me because I got depressed like mom or, as you say, *sat on the sidelines of life*."

"First, you didn't get depressed like your mother—she was bipolar and had real issues. You—you can't handle when things get hard. Second, I never gave up on you."

"When Mom died, right when I needed you the *most*, you abandoned me." We were a few feet apart, both of us teetering on the edge of snapping.

"That is a lie!"

"I needed a father. How many times did you visit me in the hospital after Mom died? Twice in three months."

"I tried to make something out of you. I really did."

"Do you really believe that?"

"It's true."

"When life got tough, it was *you* who took to the sidelines. Not me."

I could tell I hit a nerve because a vein in his forehead swelled, and his lip quivered. "Look at you. You're living in *my* house, working at a job *I* got you, a job you would've lost if it wasn't for me. It pains me to say it, son, but you're a loser," he said, turning toward the door.

I grabbed his shoulder and spun him around. "I was coming in here to tell you we won the last seven games, one by twenty points! That we have a chance to win our division, that I was getting to be a good coach, a chip off the old block. I thought maybe you'd be proud of me. What a laugh."

"It's a division of losers, son. Let's not get above our station. What you and I do are two different things."

"And if we do win, we'd play you." I took a step closer. We were nose to nose.

"I feel bad for your team," he said, pointing a finger in my face. "Their lives are a swamp full of diarrhea, and who do they get to help them navigate it? Vasco de Fuck-tard. If you cared for them, you'd quit so the school could hire a coach who takes life seriously, somebody who can give them tools to look life in the eye, someone to help those kids. I never would've gotten you the job if I'd known they'd make you coach."

"That's your sage advice? Take life seriously?"

"Or end up like you. You're no coach, son."

"How about a little bet?" I screamed. "I'll bet you we kick your ass in the championship. The loser *quits* coaching." I was out of control, but I couldn't stop myself. "If you win, I'll quit, leave the coaching to 'real men' like yourself. I'll even sweeten the deal—I'll move out, out of the state. I'll never embarrass you again. How great would that be?" I shouted. "But if I win, *you* quit coaching!"

"You're crazier than your team. First off, you're not going to win your division. Kovacs is. There won't even be a bet. Second, if you ever played me, you'd lose by seventy points, and that's if I hold back."

"You're afraid. You got a lot to lose," I said, my body tingling like every cell was screaming.

"Afraid? Afraid! What is wrong with you? You can't be serious here."

"I'm off the bench, Dad. Let's you and I look life in the eye together." I stood there; my trembling hand extended.

"Fine, if by some unbelievable miracle you win your division, we got ourselves a bet," he said, pumping my hand with his own, a snarl on his face. "But son, you better pray you lose your division because if I see you in the championship, I will end you."

# TWENTY-SIX

**We played the next five games with a vengeance,** not only looking to beat teams but to hurt them. We toppled the Frida Kahlo Design Academy by eighteen points; Chinese Christian by twenty-one; Thomas Edison by three; The Art of Learning Academy by nine; and Huda Islamic High School by twenty-two. We had one more game left before the division championship against Kovacs.

The morning after the Huda High victory, after I dropped the guys off at school, I sat on the bus waiting for an interview my old man was doing on a.m. radio, daydreaming about beating him and then magnanimously letting him out of the bet. I imagined myself smiling down on him as he wept into his hands, saying, *You don't have to quit coaching, pops. I was just angry when we made the bet and would never want you to quit something you love so much.*

The interview was about high school recruiting, and when it began, my old man waxed on about creating winning teams. He spoke about Nubbin's brother, finding his excellence when he was in fourth grade, how he kept in touch with him and his family until it was time to recruit him. My father went on to explain the boys he looked for had more than skills—they needed a killer instinct, what he called a *competitive gene*. He went on to list his former players who had gone pro. There weren't any superstars, but it was an impressive list—fifteen in all.

My daydreams of beating him fell from my eyes. My father was unbeatable. He was not only going to destroy me but humiliate my team.

What was wrong with me? Coaching was the best thing to happen to me, and I threw it away. Yeah, that sounded like me. Mr. Self-Sabotage. This bet was the same thing as my quitting, running away from the only good thing to happen to me in years. Yes, we were winning, and we were good, but we would never beat my old man. Never. The only chance I had to keep my job was to lose to Kovacs—but somehow, I knew we wouldn't. It was destiny I play my old man. Our fates were intertwined. It was my father's fate to beat the record the same way I was destined to suffer one last humiliation at the feet of my old man, one last crushing defeat. I could see it as if it already happened.

I rested my noggin on the steering wheel and thought about begging out of the bet when I heard something behind me.

"I overthink everything, dude," said Brian, a few seats back. "And I mean *everything*. You've read my assignment. You know how I am. And I've been on an insane loop I can't shake, and I need to speak to someone about it now or I'm going to . . . I don't know what."

These kids were like manifestations of my issues. It was as if my overthinking problem jumped out of my head in the form of Brian. "Is it about you not shooting?"

"I'm a virgin."

"Oh."

We sat in silence while I thought of something to say. "You know, I was freaked out the first time I had sex."

"You were?" said Brian, moving to the seat behind me.

"Yeah. I had nobody to ask," I said, turning to him. "I put the rubber on early. A day early."

"I think I like Chey," he said, falling back against his seat.

"Oh."

"And could you please stop saying, *Oh?*"

"Sorry, buddy."

"I want to ask her out, but what if she says yes?"

"Gotcha," I said, wondering what a relationship would be like between them. What was the worst that could happen? Well, disaster of course, but they were both good kids, and love was always worth a shot.

"I probably suck in bed. I suck at everything. I've been thinking about asking her out for a while now, but I'm straight freaked out. What if I can't get it up because I can't stop thinking I won't be able to get it up? 'Cause that's the kind of stuff I do. I obsess and obsess and then, forget about it. Everything falls apart. And the crazy thing is I don't even know why I'm thinking about not getting it up considering I get hard every fifteen seconds. I get it up right after I jack off, and I jack off too much. My shrink told me to limit it to twice a day. And I always jack off to Chey. It's probably the same way you feel about Dr. T."

"OK, buddy, slow your roll. Let's leave Dr. T out of any conversations about jacking off. OK?"

Brian nodded. "The thing is, if Chey decides to go out with me, then I'll get in my head, freak myself out, and won't be able to get it up. I'll be more embarrassed than I've ever been, and I will have to kill myself."

"Brian, I don't want you to talk about killing yourself. I'm serious. OK?"

Brian nodded. "Well then I'll have to join a monastery, like be a monk or something. And then what if they all take a vow of silence or whatever and I have to be alone with my thoughts forever. You know what, forget it. I'm not going to ask her out. OK, thanks for your help, bruh," he said, standing.

"Sit. You're spinning into the ether. I need you to get your ass back on that seat," I said, pointing.

Brian plopped down, his face flushed and splotchy.

"Look, you need to stop thinking about your prick and think

about Chey. You *know* her. Talk with her. Did you share your assignment with her?"

"No. I tried to a few times, but I straight chickened out. I'm such a wimp."

"You can trust Chey. I think you should share it with her."

"I think I should ask her out first."

"What's stopping you?"

"If she says yes, she's gonna want to get down to it. She's no virgin."

"What if you tell her you're not ready, that you wanna wait? She'll get it."

"Dude, she'll think there's something seriously wrong with me."

"Don't underestimate her. Her waters run deep."

"She probably won't even say yes if I ask her out, so I don't even know why I'm freaking out. She's so piping hot and a genius. I'm so not in her league, but I'm in love with her. What do you do in a situation where you're in love with someone so much better than you are?"

It was a good question. Dr. T's eyes flashed through my mind. "You tell Chey it's better for *her* if you guys wait awhile before you consummate."

"Why's that?"

"Well, when the team wasn't listening to each other on the court, we stunk. We didn't know each other's . . . habits. Now you guys know one another's game. Your gut tells you when to pass, when to drop back on D, when your teammate is going to break loose."

"Dude, what are you even talking about?"

"If you guys wait, you'll know each other's . . . you'll know . . . you'll know . . ." I just couldn't find the words.

"What?" asked Brian. "Spill the tea."

"Each other. You'll know how to make her . . . happy."

Brian stared at me.

"The more you two spend time together, the more you'll get to know and trust her."

"Yeah, I got a problem with trust. I always think people are out to straight fuck me."

"Chey's on your side, buddy. That's why you like her."

"*She's on my side*," he repeated, nodding. "That's deep, bruh."

"Spend time with her, get to know her, share your assignment with her, and your anxiety and fear about getting it up will go away."

"It will?"

"Yeah, because you're not actually afraid to get it up—you're afraid to let her in."

"*Let her in?*"

"You're afraid for her to get to know you, the real you. That if she does, she'll discover you're not good enough for her and take off for the hills."

"You're freaking me out right now," said Brian. "Really freaking me out. How do you know this stuff?"

"I got the same stuff rattling around my head."

"It's exhausting, isn't it?"

"It sure is, buddy," I said.

"OK, back to me. What you're saying is, if Chey and I really get to know each other, and I can trust her, then I won't be nervous to make a fool out of myself."

"Chey doesn't want you to feel foolish. She wants you to be honest. She's been through too much for anything else."

"Heard. Thanks, bruh. I'm more nervous than I was before. Only it's a different kind of nervous, a better nervous."

"Hold onto that. No matter how terrified you get, put your head down and take a step forward."

Brian took a deep breath and nodded. "I owe you, Coach."

"You can repay me by taking a shot every now and again."

"Baby steps. Let me work on the Chey thing first."

• • •

That afternoon, Richard Knowles and his camerawoman came to Mary Friedman to interview me for my father's doc. They said they needed to film me where I worked, but my guess was they wanted to get me away from the old tyrant to crack my head open like a melon without interruption. Dr. T let me use her office. She even asked if I wanted her to stay for support, her compassion yanking the love knots in my gut even tighter. Did she care about me on the same level she did her students—or more, an ember of romantic feeling heating up? Me—I pictured us living together, how she would look in one of my T-shirts eating breakfast.

I told Dr. T I had things way under control, that it would be a quick, bland, obsequious interview. I should've known better.

I sat in Dr. T's chair and Knowles sat across from me, his Aqua Velva cologne ruining the smell of Lysol and hand sanitizer that usually permeated the room. With the camera trained on my face, the interview started by Knowles lobbing some softball questions: was I excited about the record? I was. What was it like being coached by my father? Good. Can you elaborate? Really good.

Question after question, I made my old man out to be the father I'd always wanted: good, kind, and patient. Just when I thought I'd pulled the wool over Knowles's eyes, he replaced his kid gloves with brass knuckles: "You don't want your father to break the record, do you?"

"What kind of question is that? Yes, of course I do," I said, sitting up, indignant.

"Even if you are the one playing him?"

I hoped Knowles had forgotten about my coaching, since he only brought it up that first time. "OK, OK, it's a fair question. The fact that we may play him is a long shot. Kovacs has won the championship the last few years, and so far, this year they're undefeated."

"Why did you bet him you'd win?"

I could feel my brow betraying me in little beads of sweat. The camerawoman played with a button—probably focusing on my driblets. I hoped to beg out of the bet, but now that E:60 knew about it, there wasn't a chance of my father letting me off the hook. "He told you about the bet?"

"He did. He said you were acting erratic. He was worried you were getting delusional. He told us you had a history of mental illness, that you spent time in the ward across the street."

"He did not." I could no longer put anything past my father. Nothing.

"He said you were recently homeless. He seems truly concerned, afraid for your wellbeing."

"He's concerned about his precious record," I blurted out. What was wrong with him? He told the world I was a depressive, homeless person. He aired our bet in public? Really?

The camerawoman popped the camera off the tripod and moved in closer.

"*Should* he be concerned about his record?" asked Knowles.

"I'm not going to give you some sound bite."

"If you win your division, you'll play your father in the game he is set to break the record, which means there's a chance your father will break the all-time record of consecutive wins by a high school coach by beating you, his son."

"You work that all out on your own?"

"Your division hasn't beaten your father's in fifteen years. The game's always a joke. I've heard they're trying to get rid of it next year."

"You trying to get a rise out of me? 'Cause if you are, this may be your lucky day."

"I'd like to film practice today."

"That's why you wanted to interview me here? To get some shots of my team doing layups?"

"My producers are excited about the possibility of you playing against your father, especially because it seems to me that you guys have a contentious relationship."

"I told you all that good stuff about him."

"Yeah, but it was empty talk. I'd never use it."

"Why let me go on with it then?"

"Look, we want to show the world what it took to make your father among the most successful coaches in high school history. That's the truth."

"You want a dose of truth. You're a dick. My father's a dick, and you're probably a dick too," I said to the camerawoman.

"Father against son. It's the stuff of myths. If you win your division, there's a good chance I'll win an Emmy. At the least it will play sweeps. This could be one of our biggest docs of the year."

Not only was my father going to embarrass me on the same court he did all those years ago, it would be in front of the world this time. Every person I ever met would recognize me as the homeless, mentally ill loser in my father's documentary. The role I was fated to play. I pictured old friends and girlfriends watching E:60 with family and shaking their heads, pitying me. I didn't want their pity. Anybody's pity. The room tilted and the floor pulled me toward it. I braced myself on the desk.

"Are you OK?" asked Knowles.

"No!" I shouted. "I'm not OK. Get out of here."

With that, Tyrone entered. "Everything all right in here?"

"Tyrone, please exit these guys," I said, too overwhelmed to stand.

"You heard him," he said, moving in front of the camera. "This interview is over."

"OK, OK," said Knowles. "Mikey, I'll see you at your next game. Good luck. I'm rooting for you."

I wanted to get underneath Dr. T's desk and curl up in the fetal position and cry.

• • •

After the film crew split, I decided to go hide alone in my bus to clear my head. But as I approached my big multicolored sanctuary, Chey stormed up and slapped me on the back. "Brian asked me out this morning!"

"Chey, I can't talk right now."

"Well, you're gonna have to!" she started, her eyes unable to focus, as she looked from my chin to my forehead to my nose on speedy loop. "Brian asked me out, told me you said it was a good idea."

I turned to the bus, to the promise of solitary quiet. "I don't know, Chey."

"Did I ever tell you how my last relationship ended?" she said. "He walked in on me shredding my clothes, dumping drawers, in search of tiny FBI cameras. He called the cops and got verbal diarrhea about the gambling and got me pinched. And that was like my best 'ship. I still miss him. Other guys dumped me as soon as they slept with me."

"Chey, calm down."

"I can't. I like Brian," she said, blinking back tears.

"It took me twenty-five years to realize you *should* like somebody you date."

"Instead of what, like choosing them by tit size?"

"I'm a leg guy, but you get the point."

"There's a fifty-one percent divorce rate in the US. There's a seventy-four percent chance of a 'ship failing if one of the parties has mental illness. There are no statistics computing a 'ship in which both parties—" said Chey, stopping short, looking dazed. "And my stomach hurts."

"Your stomach?"

She nodded. "It's been hurting me all day."

"Did you eat something off?"

"No," she said. "My head, too. It feels weird."

"Weird how, Chey?" I said, sobering up, putting every ounce of my attention on her.

"I don't know."

"Are you OK?" I said, grabbing her hand.

"I feel like weird."

"Sit down. Come on the bus and sit."

"I can't," she said, shaking her head, backing up.

"Chey, I need you to sit."

She flapped her arms and shook her head as if trying to shake something off, as she continued to back away from me. "I hear something."

"What are you hearing?" I said, keeping up with her.

"Like a weird voice. I don't know who she is."

"You know it's not real, right?"

"She's showing me something."

"What is she showing you, Chey?"

"A picture of myself with cuts on my face. Why on my face? Why would I do that to my face? Why? Wait," she said, her eyes darting behind me. "I see a face right over there. This is different."

When Chey first told me about these episodes, she said taking a relaxant within the first twenty minutes of hearing a voice usually quieted it to a manageable volume. If she missed that window, the voice could be with her for days. I had eighteen minutes.

"She's right there!" she screamed.

"Do you have your meds, Chey?"

"She's right behind you!"

"Chey, there's nobody there, OK?" I said, taking her shoulders and looking deep into her eyes, trying to find her, much like I saw Toby do with Donnie during my first week. "Everything is OK. The voice is not real."

"She's real," said Chey. "She's totally right there!"

I spotted G and Brian coming out of the building.

"G, Brian! Tell Dr. T we need Chey's meds right away."

Both boys hightailed it back into the school, as I scooped Chey into my arms. "You're having an episode," I said.

Chey nodded as if having a moment of clarity and pressed her face into my shoulder. "Brian won't want to date me now. He'll hate me."

"Nobody hates you, Chey. The team loves you. OK? We all do."

G opened the school's door, and I rushed into the nurse's office with Chey, where Dr. T met us with a pill and a paper cup of water. I put Chey down on the couch as she wailed, "Get away from me! Don't touch me!" I wasn't sure if she was talking to me, the nurse, Dr T, or someone inside her head, but I backed away and let the professionals take over.

The nurse pried open Chey's mouth and inserted the pill and poured in the water. Chey began rocking back and forth, shaking her head as if throwing off an attacker.

"How long has she been like this?" asked Dr. T.

"A few minutes," I said.

Chey continued to rock, a desperate, confused look on her face that made my body tremble, as the nurse sat next to her, hands on Chey's arms as if to keep her from floating away. I asked Dr. T if we could speak in her office and told her about Brian asking Chey out. "It's my fault."

Dr. T took my hand. "It's not your fault."

"She didn't recognize the attack coming on because she was messed up over Brian asking her out," I said, slumping down in my usual chair and putting my head between my knees. "Here I am trying to keep basketball from making her manic and what do I do? I make it worse."

"She went to you. Some part of her knew an attack was coming, some part of her sought you out for help."

"She was angry at me for telling Brian to ask her out."

"She wasn't angry. She was excited and overwhelmed, and she sought you out."

I shook my head.

"And you did help her. You got her the relaxant in time," said Dr. T. "I imagine she'll be back to normal by tomorrow. Nice work, Coach."

I nodded.

"Look at me, Mikey."

I looked up at Dr. T's green eyes, soft, so compassionate.

"You did great. Bloody brilliant."

# TWENTY-SEVEN

**Dr. T was right about Chey.** After spending the night and the next day in the hospital, Chey was back to herself. I wasn't. I couldn't stop envisioning her flapping her arms and shaking her head, fighting off someone who didn't exist.

It was Saturday morning, and we were on our way to a weekend outing. It was the last regular-season game. If we won, we went to the league championship to play Kovacs, and if we lost, our season was over.

Chey, sitting in the seat behind me, apologized for her episode. "Usually, as soon as I hear a voice, I pop a pill, but sometimes I like get confused." She pulled her bottle out of her bag and showed it to me. "If it ever happens again, this is what the canister of pills looks like."

I looked at the bottle in the rearview mirror.

"I've had attacks before, and I'll have them again. It's not a big deal."

"I know," I said.

"If you think it's such a big deal, you should get over it. It is what it is."

"I'm over it," I said.

"Good."

But I wasn't. She would experience that terror again and again.

Over time, would it become too much for her? Would the voices eventually win? Would she hurt herself? There was a guy in the ward with me whose voices told him to jump out the window. Would Chey's voice convince her to kill herself? Why did my thoughts always go to the Dutch, to suicide? Because of my mother, who in the end decided she wanted to live, only to be killed by a car crash? Or was it more? No. I knew the reason—I was afraid I would eventually kill myself. I was terrified the depression would become too overwhelming, that the heaviness would bury me.

We were playing Middle Park Alternative High School, whose slogan was *Where the students grade themselves*. Knowles and his camerawoman were in the front row filming everything.

The team was playing well, especially Toby, who scored seventeen points and had ten rebounds in the first three quarters. Nubbin already put up his usual thirty. Knowles kept putting the camera in my face, raising inane questions about my chances of winning. I told him our winning was a foregone conclusion, which Knowles took for confidence akin to my old man's. He didn't know I could see the future: I would lose to my father, be forced to leave my job, and I would die, probably at my own hand, on the streets of some to-be-determined state.

The game came down to a few seconds left on the clock, we were down by two, and I knew what had to be done. I needed to chop off the hands of fate. "All right, Captain, gather in the troops," I said to Toby. "I got a plan."

"I've told you a thousand times—I'm not the captain, for real," he snapped, as the camera pushed in on us.

"Do you mind?" I shouted at the camera as if it were a sentient being.

The camerawoman backed up as I looked at my guys, who were silent.

"OK," I said. "Nubbin, you draw the double-team and dish to Bri at the right baseline."

The team looked at me as if I'd lost my mind.

"Dude?" said Brian. "Are you kidding?"

"You've been wide open all game. You're the only one not being guarded," I said, self-preservation pushing past the guilt of putting Brian in this position. I couldn't see another way out. "I've seen you make that exact shot in practice a thousand times."

When the guys returned to the court, Chey pleaded with me to change the play, but I refused.

Toby inbounded the ball to Nubbin, who pushed the play up-court into a triple-team, leaving Brian wide open. He whipped Brian the ball, who caught it and turned toward the rim. Taking a deep breath, he shot in a high arc, the ball hitting the rim, then the backboard, and was about to hit the floor when Toby grabbed the bound and threw it out to Nubbin at the baseline, who, having amazing court awareness, stepped behind the three-point line and sank the shot. And like that, we were in the league championship, one game away from playing my father. It was a fool who thought he could slap down the hands of fate.

"Yes!" screamed Knowles, high-fiving his camerawoman.

Toby sidled up to Brian. "It was a good look. You'll get 'em next time, for real."

"I choked," said Brian.

"You didn't choke, Bri," said Toby. "Ball took a bad bounce. Coach is right—we need you to shoot."

"Nice work, Brian," called Chey from a distance.

Brian nodded.

What had I done? I was willing to sacrifice Brian for self-preservation. I was a horrible person, pond scum.

"Coach," called out a good-looking, curvy Mexican woman in her late thirties whose neck was covered with tattoos so faded you could no longer make them out. "I'm Gonzalo's mother," she said, continuing to make her way over. "He talks about you all the time."

Still in self-preservation mode, I asked if G's father, the pro baller, was in town, if he'd be willing to help against my father.

She tilted her head at me.

"Your husband," I said. "We could use some help from a pro baller."

"Gonzalo's father isn't a basketball player. He's a murderer. He's in prison."

I shook my head. "Oh."

"That's why it's good he has a positive role model."

"Me?" I asked, my turn to be confused.

"Yes. When a man who graduates Yale in psychology, who can do whatever he wants with his life decides to coach these boys, that's good."

I didn't know what to say.

"You didn't go to Yale, did you?" she asked.

"No."

"You'd think I'd know better by now," she said, shaking her head. "My son told me you graduated first in your class and that you were offered jobs all over the world, that you choose to teach at Friedman to coach the basketball team. Not only that—he told me you said he no longer had antisocial personality disorder, that he was healthy."

"I'm the bus driver."

"Unbelievable! I called in sick for two jobs to come see his game tonight and to meet you—the man who saw goodness in my son. What a joke. I thought he'd . . . changed."

"G's a good kid—just confused."

"He's a sociopath. He'd made me think he was getting better, that he was starting to care about me. He doesn't care about anybody but himself. And I am *so* done," she said, storming past G toward the door.

"Mama!" yelled G.

"I can't take any more lies, Gonzalo. None. You are just like your father—just like him. He's a sociopath, and you're a sociopath. I give up."

●   ●   ●

G didn't say a word the whole ride home. He just studied his phone, while the rest of the team relived their victory by recounting plays, fist-bumping, and high-fiving.

When everybody else was off the bus, G looked up at me. "I'm not like him," he said. "My father."

I nodded, not knowing what to say. What do you say to a kid whose own mother thinks him a monster?

"I did my assignment for group. I did it before it was even due. I didn't turn it in."

"Why?"

"Writing it jacked me up. Like maybe I *am* a socio. I didn't even read it myself. I wrote it and then put it away."

"What's it about?" I asked.

"I air-dropped it into your phone. You read it tonight, and tell me if I'm a socio."

"G—" I started, before he cut me off.

"It's in your phone, Mikey. I need to know what you think. Be honest. It's important to me . . . I know you read like everybody else's. Read mine and tell me if I'm hopeless, if I'm a sociopath." He hung his head, his shoulders. "Please. I need to know."

I was struck by the word, *sociopath*. Could G be one? Could G be beyond help? I dropped him off and drove a few blocks and pulled over, found his assignment in my phone, and prayed these pages would prove G's mother wrong.

# G'S ASSIGNMENT

My assignment is about how I could've been a stunt driver for Fast and Furious. I didn't even know how good a driver I was until I missed one of my family's sacred dinners. Wednesday is family dinner night. It's the only night my mother has off from her job cleaning offices.

That night, I come in the door late and she starts in with how I don't think of anyone but myself and blah, blah, blah. I said, like, simmer down, *Fabulosa*. Fabulosa was my father's nickname for my mom because she uses Fabuloso cleaning solution at work. She hated it when my father called her that, and I think she hates it even more when I call her that. But this time it angers her enough and she says "you're a sociopath, like your father." My mom knows I've been diagnosed as an anti-social, that I'm a kiddie sociopath, and my diagnosis could be upgraded to full-on socio when I hit 18. She knows that, and she'll gut me with that word when she wants to get at me. Then she starts ticking off a list, like repeated arrests—check, frequent lying—check, reckless disregard for safety of self or others—check. But she crossed a line with that—I ain't anything like mi papa, who's trying to get me into some gang even though they locked him up for it—I bounce. As I'm slamming the front door, I get this idea that's gonna teach my mama a hard lesson. Not only that, it's also gonna make me mega famous—get me at least 4 million hits—at least.

At school I saw this video of some guey jump off the Venice pier—you see this splash, and then you don't see anything. Nada. His girlfriend filmed it and posted the whole thing on YouTube and got 4 million hits, even though the pendejo died. If my mom thinks I drove off the Venice pier and died, she'll feel bad for calling me a socio.

I jack an old Honda parked on somebody's lawn, pull over around the corner and tape my phone to the dash to film myself. La pinche de mi mama wants a sociopath, I'll show her one. I fire up a live feed on YouTube. "You all wanna hear some shit—my own mom called me a sociopath," I say into the feed on my phone. "She doesn't think I care about people, well I don't care about her—not anymore." Truth is she knows I care about her and my sisters, which proves I'm not a sociopath.

I'm driving como un loco, burning through reds, screaming some cray stuff, streaming the whole time. If you're doing crazy things and talking crazy stuff on a live feed, it's easy enough to snag viewers. A bunch of kids start commenting on my feed. Some say drive faster, and some woke kids warn me to stop before I hurt somebody. Then one dude tells me he's bored and gonna bounce. I gotta up my game if I wanna go viral. Everywhere my mama goes, people would be like, hey did you see that kid drive off the pier? That's my son, she would have to say. I called him a sociopath, but it wasn't true. It's my fault. Yeah, it really is, they'll say!

I look right into my phone, into my live feed. "Is my mom right? Am I a socio? I'll give you a hint—I'm gonna drive blind," I say. "It's socio nuts. I might even die." People love to see people die; nobody's leaving my feed now.

I pull over on Pacific in Venice and I take off

my shirt and I tie it around my head like a blind-fold. I can't see. I start driving. I'm blind. And I drive for about twenty seconds when the wheel jerks in my hand and I feel myself pop up on the curb, hitting what sounds like a garbage can. "Que chingon! Awesome!" I yell into my feed. "That's nothing. That's a warm-up." People commenting on how messed up that was, but I know nobody's turning the channel—I'm guaranteeing an accident. I tell my feed I'm going again, this time I'm going faster and longer.

It takes me a second, but I find a street that's straighter than the last one, and I tell my feed I'm gonna count how long I can go without ripping off my blindfold or crashing. I'm loving how this makes me feel. Like I could die. TBH, every instinct I have is to rip off this blindfold because I am not a socio, but I gotta convince them I am, so I hit the gas.

"Fourteen, fifteen, sixteen . . ." I'm freaking, but I can't chicken out on a live feed. "Nineteen, twenty." I wonder who's watching. Kids from the hood, school, ex novias, kids in France, and Russia. It feels like I'm playing Burnout Paradise or Grid Autosport. The car pulls to the left like I'm in a groove, so I straighten the wheel out, but I bounce off a parked car and end up doing a 180. I rip off my blindfold. "Pinche puto!" I scream. "Thirty-one seconds! I'm going to the pier, see if I can skid to a stop before I go over. How's that for a sociopath, Mom!"

The feed's egging me on, calling me nuts, but then this one girl, this Psalmsister101, writes, *You're no sociopath. There's warmth in your eyes. I can see that you care about people, that you care about your mom. I can see that God is in you. I don't know, somehow* this girl's words catch me by surprise and stop me dead. She writes, *I can see the deep pain in your eyes. God will totally transcend that pain.* That's some heavy words she's dropping. Even with my putting on this show, she saw the real me. She saw my pain. She saw I'm not a sociopath. Everybody's commenting, but I don't care what they say. I'm waiting for Psalmsister's words. She finally writes, *Your mom is way wrong. You're so beautiful.* She knows me better than my own mom, better than anybody in the entire world. I want to ask where she lives and see her IRL and put my head in her lap. I'm not even thinking about kissing her, I want her to stroke my hair and tell me more about what she sees in me. But now I drive back by Washington and park and look at the stretch of three blocks to the pier. I look past the juice and flower shop, past Pacific, where the road narrows from four lanes to two, where ahead is the pier where a girl filmed her boyfriend's death, and I think about my mom and about how mega famous I'm gonna be. I can't see the pier, but I know exactly where it is in the darkness.

Way off in the distance I hear sirens. "Now or never," I say into my feed. The plan was for me to put on the blindfold and drive until I felt the wood of the pier, and then shut my phone off. Then I put the car in neutral, tie the gas pedal to the floor and stand back to watch that Honda crash through the rail into the ocean. The cops find the car, no body. They start raising questions, discover my feed, while I lay low for a whole day as the YouTube hits add up and then—tada!—I'm reborn into fame and a new understanding con mi ama.

I make a big show of tying my shirt around my eyes for my feed, and I put the car in drive and I'm off. I'm flying, not worried how fast I'm going because I know I'm stopping as soon as I feel the wood planks. "I feel the hands of God on the wheel, on top of mine. He's guiding me, Psalmsister 101," I say. I'm driving straight as an arrow down the center of the road, like maybe God's hands are on top of mine. I can feel the road, every bump, and I start thinking about Psalmsister, and to be honest, I feel bad she'll think I'm dead.

BAM. My chest smashes into the steering wheel. My face pounds the windshield. I'm thrown back against my seat, and I scream, thinking I broke my neck. Everything is quiet. For a second, I forget where I am, but then I snap out of it and pull the blindfold off, and I start looking around for the phone, but I can't find it. Out the cracked windshield, through the blood on it, I see a sign that says Parking $9. I hit the parking Kiosk. When did they put that up? I touch my head and look at the blood on my hand and I hear the sirens approaching. I get out of the car but I'm dizzy and fall. People are walking up to me, the Venice zombies. And these homeless are all scream- ing how crazy that was. But I can't stop thinking of Psalmsister. I need her to tell me again how she saw God in my eyes. I need her to tell me that she saw I was a good person. She saw it. She really saw it. No way I'm sharing this. Sorry, Dr. T. But there's no way.

# TWENTY-EIGHT

**I drove around for hours, thinking about G's assignment.** He had a father in jail and a mother who gave up on him. Yes, G needed some help. He needed to work with Dr. T and take his therapy seriously, to stop lying, but he wasn't a monster, and I looked forward to telling him that. Like Psalmsister, I saw goodness in G.

When I looked up, I was on Hope Street, where I'd found Alvarito's body. I parked and looked out the window at the clearing where my buddy killed himself, where a stranger guarded his torn remains against wild dogs, where I picked him up and then left him at the morgue. Left him. He didn't deserve that. My friend deserved a proper send off. He deserved a better *amigo* than me.

My cell buzzed in my pocket. It was Otis. He'd been arrested and put on a 5150, a seventy-two-hour hold, at Friedman for being a danger to others. I told him to hold tight, and I hung up and called Dr. T, who insisted I meet her at the school to go to the hospital together.

• • •

As Dr. T and I walked across the parking lot toward the hospital, she told me Otis had been arrested before but never called anybody. "He must trust you," she said.

I nodded, my hands and forehead becoming instantly clammy as we approached Friedman's doors.

"Being back on the juvenile ward might bring up some feelings," said Dr. T. "I wanted to ensure I was with you in case you wanted to talk."

I told her I appreciated the sentiment but that I was OK. "Besides, I told you I've been back a couple times since then."

"Yes. But being back on the *juvenile* floor might be difficult for you."

We made it through the front door and up to the waiting room to the seventh floor, which looked the same as it had when I was Otis's age, a sterile room with six seats.

We were brought to an office, in which the doctor on duty, a lanky white guy with inky-black hair, told us Otis had upended furniture and punched holes in the walls of his foster's house. She became frightened and called the police, who happened to have a social worker doing a ride-along, who was smart enough to bring him here instead of juvy jail. The only thing was, Friedman didn't have any open beds. Not only that—youth wards all over the city were full, so Otis was going to have to spend the night downtown in gen pop after all, which the doctor said was an overcrowded nightmare. I began to protest, but Dr. T put her hand on mine and quieted me with a look.

Next, we were led past some private, padded rooms with small windows looking out into the hallway. In one, a girl sobbed at the top of her voice, and in the other a boy laid on the floor playing with himself. It was in one of these rooms that I first pulled out my hair—*most* of my hair. I began to sweat and took a deep breath, as I recalled the crippling loneliness I felt as the walls pushed in on me. For my first couple of weeks here, I had few visitors—my father and a few school friends. The rest of my time was spent without a peep from the outside world.

"Are you OK?" asked Dr. T.

My eyes began to blink, and I took another deep breath. It was only when Dr. T's eyes moved up to my hair that I realized I was holding a fistful.

"I can speak with Otis on my own if you aren't feeling up to it."

I released the hair and rubbed my hands together in front of me. "I need to see him."

Finally, we were let into holding, a big room with a table and chairs and three couches facing a TV mounted on the wall, which was turned off. Otis sat on the couch against the back wall, head in his hands. There were two other boys in the room: a teenager sat on the couch in front of Otis rocking back and forth, picking at scabs on his cheek, while a younger boy, maybe a tween, sat at the table chewing his lip.

"Otis," I said, making my way over. "How you doing?"

He stood when he saw me. "I fucked up, Coach. Can you help me?"

"Anything you need, Otis," I said.

"Hey, Dr. T," said Otis, clearing his throat. "Sorry to bother you."

Dr. T reached for Otis's hand. "The doctor told us what happened, but he didn't tell us why."

Otis shook his head and his chest heaved and he let out a sob. No tears, no crying, just a single sob. "My neighbor, he left his gate open, and his dog ran off. Who forgets to shut a gate? It takes a second to shut it. That dog been gone all day. He ain't coming back. Don't got a collar, either. Every day, I go over to see that dog, bring him some treats. He ain't got anybody else, 'cause his owner's a punk who need a beat down," said Otis, his face turning dark, vengeful.

"I know you care about that dog, Otis," said Dr. T. "I'm sorry he ran off."

Otis nodded. "That dog be my first friend before the team."

I recalled Otis's assignment, how much he connected with the dog, how the dog licked his tears, and I had to stop myself from sobbing.

"I do understand why you became upset," said Dr. T.

"I been good, too. In control, except this one time. Ruth, she got scared, yelling at me to stop, but I couldn't. I couldn't stop myself. I got too angry. Angrier than I ever been. I love that dog." Otis grunted. "And Ruth—I lost another mom. That exactly what it feels like. Exactly. Can you talk to her?"

Dr. T started to speak, but Otis interrupted her. "Coach, it's you I want to speak to her. She wants to meet you, so you go talk to her about giving me another chance."

The young tweaker stood, and Otis suggested he sit back down. He did.

"I don't know what to say to her, Otis," I said.

Dr. T looked at me. "Maybe the three of us can go talk to her together," she said, standing, looking for someone in charge.

I was relieved Dr. T was on our team.

● ● ●

Dr. T convinced the ER doc to drop the 5150 and to release him into her custody. We left the bus on campus, and we drove in Dr. T's Prius to Otis's house. Otis spoke more words during that trip than the whole time I knew him. He spoke about the team, the championship game, that he shouldn't have punched walls, because he put the team in jeopardy, about how he was afraid to lose another mother, the neighbor's dog, everything. He didn't wait for us to respond, kept jumping from one thing to the next.

When we arrived at his house, we heard a dog barking, and Otis bounded out of the car and into his neighbor's yard. Dr. T and I followed, where we saw Otis hugging a big old pit and, I swear to God, the dog was hugging him back, licking his face.

The neighbor, an older guy in an unbuttoned security shirt, came out to see Otis kissing his dog on the head. "Dog made it almost two miles from here," he said. "Got to be careful with pits. Someone might try to turn Smurf into a fighter."

"You gotta keep that gate closed," said Otis. "He knows how to get outta his cage."

"He got outta the cage *and* the gate," said the neighbor. "Should've called him Papillion."

"Otis was pretty upset," I said. "He thought Smurf, which by the way is a great name, was gone for good."

"I had to work a double, didn't have a chance to give him his dinner. He must've gone looking to fill his belly."

"Maybe you two could work something out," I said, as all three humans and the dog turned toward me. "You could let Otis know when you can't get home, and he can feed Smurf. Right, Otis? You could get your own bag of food, so you don't have to go into this gentleman's house."

"Yeah," said Otis, his eyes wide. "Even if you are home and is too busy, you call me, and I'll tend to him."

The neighbor pulled at his chin, his attention ping-ponging between Otis and the dog. "You were worried about him, huh?"

Otis nodded, grunting his throat clear.

The neighbor pulled at his chin some more. "OK, yeah, I'd appreciate it."

"OK," said Otis, hugging the dog, who licked his ear. "Smurf, he like ears."

"If you wanna walk him or whatever, I don't gotta problem with that. I know I said to stay off my property, but you seem different now than the first time we met. You seemed dangerous, but now I can tell you're a good kid. Smurf thinks so, too."

"I was seeing him anyway, coming over here when you were out, and I be sorry 'bout that."

"Yeah, well that's OK. Truth is, I could use the help."

Otis looked up at me and nodded, then kissed the dog on the forehead.

• • •

Next, we went next door to see Otis's foster, and all four of us sat at the kitchen table where his foster mom, Ruth, made us jasmine tea. She was a beautiful woman with high cheekbones and a kind face. She wore a white headscarf and jeans and looked to be a sturdy sixty years old.

After some pleasantries, Otis, still riding high from being allowed to take care of Smurf, launched in. "I gotta mom in jail, who don't wanna be a mom, and I got you, who treat me like how a real mom's supposed to."

Ruth set down her delicate-looking, floral teacup and gave Otis her full attention. "You scared me, Otis. And I will not be scared in my own home," she said, her tender eyes betraying the seriousness of her stern brow.

"I'm sorry," said Otis.

"I know you're sorry, but I can't have it."

Otis looked visibly deflated, so I jumped in. "Maybe we could think of a plan, like what to do if Otis starts to go off?"

All sets of eyes focused on me.

"Otis, if your anger erupts, call me from the driveway, and I'll come and pick you up."

"Yeah," said Otis, taking up the reins. "Like if I start to lose myself, instead of throwing stuff and punching walls, I'll call Coach and he come pick me up. I'm gonna try not to lose control, but if I do, then I'll call."

"I only live a couple miles from here," I said.

Ruth looked back and forth between Otis and me. "Otis speaks about you all the time," she said to me. "He talks about you, and he talks about the team."

Dr. T nodded. "We've seen some great changes in you lately, Otis."

"So have I," said Ruth.

"You not gonna kick me out?" asked Otis.

"I want you to stay, Otis. But you gotta work on controlling your emotions. You got to work on that."

"I'm working on it," said Otis. "I am. Right, Coach?"

"That's right."

"OK," said Ruth. "And Coach, I'm gonna need your cell number. 'Cause if I see any signs of him becoming too upset for me to handle, I'm going to call you. And you better pick up, too."

"I promise," I said. "You call, and I'll be there. You have my word."

• • •

Walking to the car, I recalled the bet I made with my old man, and I started to hyperventilate. I sat in the middle of Otis's driveway for fear of passing out. We would win tomorrow's game—our division. Then we would play my father, and he would destroy us, and I would lose the bet and be forced to give up my job and move out of state. Otis and his mother trusted me to help, but I wouldn't be here when they needed me. I wouldn't be here for any of my guys. Dr. T crouched beside me and lightly touched the back of my neck.

"Are you OK?" she asked.

"Can't breathe," I sputtered.

"You're having a panic attack," said Dr. T.

"You think?" I said, a mixture of sarcasm and terror.

She put her warm hand on the center of my back, and that tenderness released a sob I didn't feel coming until it was too late. "I can't believe I'm crying. This is embarrassing."

Dr. T just held her hand still on my back. "You're upset about Otis?" she asked in her calming tone.

"Otis, Chey and Brian, Donnie, G, and my old man, how he just abandoned me in the hospital when I was a kid. I was only a kid."

249

The dog next door barked, which prompted Dr. T to help me to a standing position. The last thing either of us wanted was Otis seeing me sitting in his drive crying. She took my face in her hands. "These kids are a lot to take on, and you're doing brilliantly, much better than I would've thought possible."

"That's a compliment, right?"

"Based on your interview, I believe your success is nothing short of a God-given miracle—right up there with the parting of the Red Sea," she said, smiling. "Your team trusts you. I have to say, it's awesome to bear witness to. However, with that trust there's responsibility. Your team counts on you."

"If they knew me, they wouldn't."

"Don't be daft. I believe they know you fully well."

There was something about the way she looked at me, how intimate our conversation felt, that made me want to kiss her. I wanted to be closer to her but dreaded her rejection.

"OK. You have a big day tomorrow—the division championship," she said, her clear eyes disarming. "The whole school's abuzz with your achievement, mate. It's truly all Dr. Lipschitz can talk about."

We got into her Prius, and she turned to me. "No matter how you fare tomorrow, I want you to know that I'm truly inspired by what you've accomplished, and I'm sorry I ever doubted you."

"We're gonna win our division," I stated as fact. "I've never been surer of anything in my entire life."

"I love your confidence, but how can you possibly be so sure?"

"Destiny—we will win our league tomorrow, because it is destiny that I play my father in the Tournament of Champions, where he will destroy me once and for all."

"*Destiny*?"

"My father has been moving toward this moment his whole life. He will beat the record of most consecutive wins, and he will do so by beating his son on one of the most-watched sports shows of the year."

Dr. T remained silent a moment. "Do you truly believe *that* is your destiny?"

"Much like my old man, I too have been moving toward this moment my whole life. This will be my crowning failure. I will forever be known as the loser trounced by his father in front of the world. It will be like missing those foul shots all those years ago, only the adult version, and my shame will be shown again in rerun perpetuity."

"You have to stop thinking like that, Mikey," she said. "It's too unhealthy."

"It is what it is."

"Nothing, I believe, is what it is. The future is unpredictable."

"You're wrong. I am being dragged, kicking and screaming, toward my fate. There is no preventing it."

"What a wretched image."

"There's nothing I can do to keep us from winning our division. I tried to throw our last game by giving Brian the last shot. What kind of awful person does something like that?"

"You've undergone a lot recently. Anybody can have a moment of weakness."

"There's something wrong with a guy willing to sacrifice a kid to his own fear. But fate, she wouldn't have it. No, she wouldn't."

Dr. T took my hand, and we sat like that until a weariness grabbed hold of me, and I asked her to drive me home.

# TWENTY-NINE

**The next morning when I picked up G, he sat in the seat behind me** and said, "Well?"

"You're not a sociopath."

"I knew it," he said. "My mom is full of shit."

"No, G. *You* are full of shit. You lie all the time—you lie to me and the team, and we deserve better than that."

"But I'm not a socio, right?"

"No, you're not, but I need you to listen to me here. No more lying. Got it?"

"Great. Thanks, Coach," said G, jumping up and moving to another seat.

• • •

That afternoon we entered the Kovacs gym, which looked bigger than it had the first time we played the Division 1 Champs. It was packed to the rafters with their fans, every one of them wearing red and white, the school's colors. The E:60 camera bum-rushed us as my guys, without me saying a word, pushed past and jumped into a layup drill, practicing the give-and-go. I was proud of my players, inspired by their focus. We were no longer five guys standing around in dirty T-shirts. We were a team. Sure, the Kovacs students still called us chodes and laughed at us and stuck their pathetic student TV camera in our faces, and yes, ESPN recorded it all, but my guys weren't bothered—they were preparing to take scalps.

Their coach, noticing E:60, approached Knowles, who told him who my father was, prompting their coach to ask, "Really? He's Andrew Cannon's son? That loser?" Then he turned to me, "You think your team can get through the game without being disqualified for punching each other?"

Poor fella didn't realize he was a mere step on the ladder of fate. "I feel sorry for you, because you win the championship all these years, and the one time you lose, it's recorded by ESPN."

Turning to the E:60 camera, the coach said, "My prediction—we win by thirty points."

"Go tell it to your student camera," I said, pointing to the teenager filming us. "The pros are here for *my* destiny."

Knowles gave me the thumbs up, and I shook my head, not looking for collusion.

The game began by Kovacs winning the tip and pushing the play down-court and setting up their point guard for an easy shot, which he missed. Toby sprung in front of his defender, boxing him out and snagging the rebound, which he baseballed to Donnie, who dribbled to the three-point line and landed a bomb.

The surprise on their coach's face said it all—they were in trouble. We were not the team they played before, and the coach's face devolved from surprise to concern to afraid as my guys outscored Kovacs by ten points in the first three quarters.

At the beginning of the fourth, a few fans chanted for us to return to the looney bin, but Nubbin silenced them by getting fouled on a three-pointer and sinking the foul shot. It didn't make sense to call somebody crazy who converted a four-point play.

In the stands behind our bench, Dr. T, Dr. Lipschitz, Tyrone, a few students, Gerald, Otis's and Chey's moms cheered as we matched Kovacs basket for basket, keeping our lead.

Then late in the fourth, Destiny in the name of Donnie got a hot hand, sinking threes from everywhere, which put the game out of reach for Kovacs. And when the last seconds ticked off the clock, the scoreboard read: Kovacs—59, Visitors—88.

Our small cheering section applauded, while my guys patted one another on the backs and high-fived. My guys were Division 1A champions. Destiny had summoned my old man and I to do battle, where only one of us would survive, the big money of course being on, as my father put it, him *ending* me.

• • •

That night I lay in bed unable to stop my mind from playing potential scenarios of my father humiliating me. I picked up the photo of my mother, and I studied her smile, the laugh lines around her eyes, when the phone rang. It was Dr. T. Toby had attempted suicide.

• • •

When I got to the Kaiser ER, Toby was sleeping, tubes coming out of his nose and arms, and his right wrist was bandaged. I dragged a chair beside the bed and sat. What could've happened in the few hours after the game? Did he have a psychotic break like Chey or Donnie?

Nurses and doctors hurried past the door, and I thought to go ask them what they knew, but I didn't want Toby to awaken in an empty room, so I stayed put. Where was his mom, anyway? Did she know? Care? Why was I the only one here? Where was Dr. T? I knew she was around because she was the one who put me on the *approved* visitors' list.

After my mom's suicide attempt, when I was finally allowed to see her, she gave me this huge hug. She seemed so happy—too happy—as she smiled and joked around as if it were any other day. But no amount of joking could disguise the struggle in her eyes. Her pain, whatever it was, pushed her to try and take her life. And now here was Toby—what was his pain?

Toby moaned from somewhere deep within like he was having a bad dream.

"You OK, buddy?" I said, dragging my chair closer to take his hand in mine. The bandage seemed so tight on his wrist. I worried it would cut off his circulation.

His eyes fluttered as if he were trying to focus on me. Then he sat up and looked around the room in a daze. Noticing the bandage on his wrist, he started to tear at it. I pulled his body to mine and hugged him with everything I had as he howled out, and I continued to hug him until he fell back to sleep right in my arms, and I held him like that, waving helpful nurses away, for what must have been an hour.

When Dr. T finally entered, she had another doctor with her, who listened to Toby's chest with a stethoscope. He nodded and told Dr. T everything was stable before glancing at a clipboard, deciding something, and splitting.

Dr. T sat beside me. She didn't need to ask if I was OK this time. We both knew I wasn't.

"He rung up 911 himself," she said, her voice light. "He's never done that before."

"He's attempted suicide before?"

Dr. T nodded and put her hand on my knee. "Five times in the last two years."

"Out of everyone, he seems the most together."

"His brother was beaten to death two years ago, the stress of which caused a psychotic episode."

"Fuck," I said, looking at Toby and the tubes coming out of his nose. "Poor kid."

"It's bloody awful," said Dr. T.

Toby opened his eyes, this time his hands reaching for the tubes, prompting Dr. T to stand. "Toby, everything is OK."

Toby was more coherent now and put his hands to his sides and looked around the room, seeing me. "What up, Coach?" he asked, groggy.

"How are you, buddy?"

"OK."

"What happened?"

"You don't have to talk about it now," said Dr. T.

Toby explained how he cut himself with his mother's razor, and then he stopped and shook his head. "I'm sorry, Coach."

"You don't need to be sorry. I just…don't get it. You were on top of the world a few hours ago. We won the championship."

"My bro was murdered two years ago today."

I leaned over and touched his shoulder. "I'm sorry, buddy."

"I forgot," said Toby. "I was worried about the game. I forgot what day it was. I get home and I'm all happy, thrilled, gushing to my mom how we won our division. I see she's all doped up, and I'm like 'Aren't you off that stuff.' And she's like 'What day is it today?' She's angry I don't seem to remember or care. She tells me it should've been me that died, 'cause I was always the one in trouble, not sweet Taye, and then she starts hitting me, punching me in the chest, screaming, 'It should've been you.'" He blinked and shook his head.

I got where Toby was coming from—I mean, why stick around in a world where your bro was murdered, and your mother wished you dead?

"She knows what his death did to me, believe that. She *knows*," he said, tears dripping.

"I'm sorry, Toby," I said, my hand still on his shoulder. "Real sorry."

"Yo, Coach, can you give me my phone on that table?" he said, pointing.

"Sure," I said, retrieving it. "You want me to call somebody for you?"

"No." He took the phone. "What's your email, Coach? I'm sending you my assignment for you to see how much my bro's murder twisted me up."

Dr. T looked at Toby with such compassion, such love. She was quiet. I could see her breathing with control, maybe trying to project strength, but it was clear she was fighting back tears. This couldn't be easy for her—every time one of her kids attempts suicide, she must relive the helplessness she felt when her father took his life. "Right now, you need your rest," she said.

"I need you to know what happened to me, Coach. I want you to see the real me."

"Mikeydownlow@gmail.com."

"I just hit you up, Coach," he said, handing his phone back to me.

"Mikey will read it later, Toby. You need to rest."

"Yeah, buddy. Why not take a nap, and we can talk about it when you wake up?"

"I don't want to sleep," he said, sitting straight up, looking at the door as if he wanted out. "Yo, Dr. T, can you get the doc? I gotta ask him something."

"What do you need?" asked Dr. T.

"I gotta ask if I can ball in two weeks against Westchester. I got all messed up in the moment with my mom's nonsense, but I'm seeing straight now, for real. I put my own shit ahead of the team's, and I made a commitment not to. That's what's up."

"Don't worry about any of that now," I said. "It doesn't matter."

"It matters!" shouted Toby. "It's about the only thing that matters right now, believe that. If you read my assignment, Mikey, and you still want me to be captain, I'm all in—all the way in."

I nodded, but it didn't matter. Nothing did. A nurse entered, and while Dr. T was helping her get Toby comfortable, I bolted out of the room and then out of the hospital, past orderlies who smoked cigarettes under a gray, numb sky.

# THIRTY

**I texted Dr. T I was taking the next day off,** and I went home and up to my room and got under my covers and tried to doze off, but I couldn't stop thinking about Toby's assignment. I grabbed my phone from the nightstand and opened my email.

## TOBY'S ASSIGNMENT

**To:** Mikeydownlow@gmail.com
**Subject:** My Assignment
**Attachment:** Toby.doc

I know which memory Dr. T wants me to share because she told me. I've never told anybody except Dr. T what happened *that* day. But the thing is I don't like to let Dr. T down because she's cool. She gets where I'm coming from. She's probably the only one who gets me in any kind of real way. At first, I used to question her on every assignment, but I don't anymore. I'm going to share the time I thought my head was going to explode. It happened two years back, for real. If you think it's funny or if you are laughing reading this, I'm going to ask you stop right here, because this here is serious for me. I thought my head was going to pop, which was scary. It was like that movie Speed on Netflix. That guy from the Matrix is on a bus with a bomb on it and if the bus stops it will detonate. Except the bus was my head.

Dr. T thinks this episode had something to do with my baby bro, Taye, whose real name was Scott, but who we called Taye like in Scott-taye. I don't think it does because I had a few episodes before he died, and I've had a few after. But this was the only one where I thought my head would explode.

So here it goes. I was in the bedroom Taye and I shared when my head started to hurt badly. It felt like someone shoved a pump all up in my ear and was filling my head with air like it was a basketball or football or something. I noticed that when I moved the pressure got less, and if I stood still, the pain would build up. I walked down our hallway with the photos of my bro staring at me, into our room, and then back out again in a kind of loop like I was on a track or something. I did this to release the pressure. I did it for a long time, but I couldn't move fast enough inside the house to stabilize my head, so finally I ran downstairs past Moms in rollers reading scripture and out the front door. She didn't even look up. I wasn't about to tell her what was going down since she just buried my bro and couldn't have handled one more thing.

I ran for a stretch, but then I slowed to a quick walk, and I kept this pace for miles and miles. The whole time I was afraid my head would explode if I stopped moving, for real. I kept walking all the way until I reached Hancock Park. You know, where one house is a city block. A shorty on a scooter took one look at me, this six-foot-six brotha, and started tripping, running all up in his house. The whole time I'm saying over and over to myself, don't stop moving, as the pressure pushed against my eyes. It felt like a balloon expanding in my head about to crack my skull.

That's when a squad car pulled up behind me and asked if I was lost. I shook my head and looked down at my feet and kept walking. The car pulled in front of me at an angle like the cops do when they want you to stop. I slowed to test how it felt, but the pressure surged like water climbing up a dam. I punched myself in the forehead, but it was no help.

Both cops jumped out the car, and the driver unsnapped his holster. The other cop, the brotha from the passenger seat, paid close attention to me like they do. Then he said, "Stop!" But I couldn't, not without exploding. I kept walking. I thought to run, to bolt, but I knew they would give chase, creating a situation nobody wanted. I kept punching my forehead to try and keep things under control. "Yo, let me keep on. I ain't doing anything wrong," I said, putting my hands over my head to show him I was innocent of everything but walking, but the pressure was splashing over the dam at this point.

"I'm not gonna ask you again. Stop!"

But I couldn't. I kept moving, adrenaline kicking in my neck and fists. The driver ran in front of me, his arms extended, his palms up. I kept reaching for the sky as I walked around him. "I don't want trouble. I ain't gonna stop because I literally can't." But the cop ran up on me again, only this time holding a Taser. "I'll use this," he said. "I don't want to, but I will if you don't stop walking."

I punched my forehead to release pressure.

"Stop hitting yourself. Right now!"

The cop held up the Taser ready to strike, and as he stepped to me, I snapped around and jumped him like some jonesing tweaker. I banged his head on the pavement, screaming, "Why couldn't you let me be?" The second cop tried to grab me, but I felt invincible and Luke-Caged his ass. I punched the brotha in his throat and he started coughing and gagging.

The first cop pulled his gun, and I told him to shoot me because my head was going to explode anyway and what was the difference. People come up out their houses then, and one guy pulled out his cell and pointed it at us as I screamed my head off. Another cop car pulled up and two more men in blue jumped out, and I took off. I heard a few shots as I leapt over a fence into somebody's yard and looked for a place to hole up. That's when I realized the pressure in my head had been released. It was gone. I didn't feel as wild. My leg felt cold though, and when I looked down at my church pants, the front looked wet. I touched my thigh and saw blood on my hand. I'd been shot.

The brotha landed in the yard, his gun drawn like he was ready to put an end to this whole thing. I held my hands over my head. "Yo, I'm cool," I said.

"Put your hands behind your back," he said as the driver cop landed in the yard.

"I'm all good now, for real," I said. "My head was going to explode because of the pressure, but when you guys shot me, it got released. We all good now. I ain't usually violent. I ain't a banger." Looking back, I know I sounded nuts, but right then I felt like this explanation should've put this thing all the way behind us. The driver tackled me and cuffed my hands behind my back and said they were going to take me to the hospital.

It's crazy I can remember what happened so well, considering I was all the way nuts at the time. It was two weeks after Taye's funeral. He got himself beat to death walking home from school over some girl. When me and my mom went to identify Taye, his face was so swollen and reddish purple that if it wasn't for his bracelet, I'd never of known it was him, for real. I remember when Moms gave him that bracelet—it was the kind with a silver chain and nameplate, the kind all the kids got, which she gave to him for his twelfth birthday. At first, my mom told him she couldn't afford it, but when he opened the box, there it was. When I think of Taye, I try to remember his smile from that day, and not the swollen face and toe tag, but some pictures stick to you all the way.

I wear Taye's bracelet all the time. Never take it off. I'm always thinking of him, about his face, his big old smile, about some of the stupid stuff he says, like how he used to call me Kenobi as in Obi Wan instead of Toby. Taye. He was my little bro, my heart, believe that. I think back and try to drum up a scenario that my brother wasn't killed. If I would've known Taye took up with that banger's girl, I would've made him drop her. Last thing you need is to be messing with some banger's girl, and that's a fact. Thing is, I'll never forgive myself for not knowing about Taye taking up with that girl, not ever. I should've known, should've made it my business to know. A big brother's gotta look out, but I missed it.

Funny thing is that writing this right now has given me a bad headache, like I can feel pressure behind my eyes. I'm not saying my head is going to explode or anything, but it's weird is all. Might be a coincidence, then again, it might be all connected. I think Dr. T and I are going to have to jaw on that. Anyway, I appreciate you taking the time to read about my crazy ass.

• • •

Toby's pain, cut with his guilt and sorrow, raced in my veins as if I'd shot up with it, finally overwhelming me and knocking me out. I awoke a few hours later, battered by images of him getting shot by the police.

I rolled over to escape back into sleep but just couldn't get there, feeling as if I'd never do so again. All at once, I began to sweat, a flash of heat hitting my body like I'd been slid into an oven. I got out of bed and opened the window, but when I returned to lie back down my body went cold. I got up and closed the window again. I went back and forth, opening and closing the window, getting in and out of bed, until I stood staring at my mother's photo.

Picking it up, I pictured her swallowing those pills, tilting back her head, her throat jumping as she gulped the entire contents of the orange canister with the white cap.

Over the years I wondered about my mom's last straw, the one that made her step down into her escape hatch. What was the source of her suffering? My father blamed her bipolar, but it was more than that. Was it me? My old man? Both of us? Did her horror begin with some bad turn, an event that stirred diseased blood from her depths? Blood that rose, bringing with it the lethal thoughts and horrifying lethargy.

Now it was the thoughts of Toby in his hospital bed, the cruelty of those fluorescent lights overhead casting everything in a green, hopeless tint, which pelted me from within. I imagined him bolting up the steps of his house, taking two at a time, looking for his mom to help him celebrate his win, but instead finding a broken woman, who attacks him for forgetting his brother's death. And then his very own mom, the one person in the world who should unconditionally love him, more than she does herself, wishes him dead.

In my mind, I watched her hands, a windmill of hate, as she hits his shoulders and face while Toby stands there, taking his punishment for forgetting. But Toby can only take so much, and he decides he'll give her what she wants. If she's looking for his death, he'll serve that up on a platter. Let her feel the guilt of finding her son's body, knowing it was her words that finished him. Let her try and live with that.

Then I pictured Toby heading to his mother's bathroom to find a razor. It's the razor his mother shaves her legs with, and he likes how close this will make him feel to her as he pushes the blade into his skin. He sits on the toilet and runs his fingers over its edge, looks at his wrist, and then he runs the blade over his bulging veins, pushing the blade against his skin, feeling its bite. He feels how delicate his life is, how easy it would be to extinguish it as his mother yells for his death from the other room. He pushes the razor deeper into his flesh until blood rises from all sides, but there is only a small amount of blood—not enough, and his mother is pounding on the locked bathroom door, and Toby takes a breath and says goodbye to his mother, and he pushes it in deeper, and deeper yet.

I recalled my own time in the hospital after my mother died, after I missed those foul shots and stopped eating and sleeping. My first memory was lying in a bed, those same florescent lights making me tremble with nausea. I didn't remember getting to the hospital—whether I came in an ambulance or if my father drove me. I didn't recall my first few days, which they say is normal. What I did remember was a nurse, a Guatemalan woman with a broad face, who would lean over me with this salty-sweet fragrance, a maternal scent I would breathe in like fresh air. It was better than any medicine.

When I was thinking about getting out of bed, I heard my father's toilet flush. I pulled the covers to my chin and listened as my old man moved around the house getting ready for work.

I woke up around three in the afternoon, my room reeking from sweat. I went to the bathroom, and while I took a piss, I looked up at the medicine cabinet and remembered the full bottle of Oxy my father kept in there for his knee. Opening the cabinet, I became terrified to touch the bottle. I felt the pull of wanting to swallow every pill, that same feeling I had sometimes when standing on a bridge, that disorienting vertigo that made me want to jump head-first toward the complete silence.

Of course, my mother tried to off herself with pills, but in the end, she found something to keep her going. So did Toby. They *both* called 911. But *what* did they find? And what did *I* have to live for? All these years contemplating the Dutch, my escape hatch, those days when I considered it an accomplishment to get through the day without taking my life—now I wondered, could I actually do it? Did I really want to kill myself?

My cell rang, prompting me to shut the cabinet door and head back to my bedroom. The call was from Dr. T. Without listening to the message, I texted in sick for the following day. A few minutes later the phone rang again. This time it was Chey. I again let it go to voicemail. I didn't want Chey or Dr. T to hear my screams as the wild dogs bit down on my brain, ripped at the meat. I didn't want them to recoil at the snap of sinew as the dogs tore out flesh.

• • •

I returned to bed and lay there until six p.m. when my father came home. I followed his movement up the stairs and over to my door, where he stopped, where I could hear his labored breathing. Then the door flung open, the knob smashing the back wall. "At least you're predictable," he said. "I'll give you that, Choke Artist."

I laid there, my father glaring down at me.

"Looks like you and I have a bet, son," he said. "I heard you somehow pulled a win out your ass."

"Forget the bet," I said.

"That's it. You're going to lie down, roll on your back like some lame animal?"

I didn't say a word, looked at him, thinking about those pills in the cabinet ten feet away. I had nothing to live for—nobody who loved me. I was all alone.

"What about all that stuff about facing life head on?" my father asked. "Was it all just talk?"

I felt this could be our last conversation, the last words I would say to my old man, and I thought about how to respond, while my father stood there silent, waiting. "Son, I don't know what's going on, but you got to get out of bed now, or I'm going to yank you out, and you know I'll do it, too."

"One of my guys tried to kill himself," I said, thinking it would make him go away.

My father sat down in my desk chair and took a deep breath. "When?"

"Right after we won the championship."

"That doesn't make any sense."

I was too tired to tell him why it did make sense, how a person could be on top of the world one moment, then the next be contemplating throwing back a bottle of Oxy. My father wouldn't be able to comprehend that kind of complexity. He, like many people, saw things in black and white. He saw living and dying in black and white.

"I wanna know your secret about Mom," I said, sitting upright.

My father sat back in his chair, shaking his head. "It doesn't matter. Besides, now is not the time."

"Now is the exact time," I snapped. Whatever it was, he was scared to tell me, that much I could read on his face. Maybe he held the key to understanding my mother, and because my mother and I were so alike, I needed to hear it, whatever it was. "Dad, please! I'm begging you."

"No."

"Yes!" I cried out. "I need this."

"It stinks in here," he said, standing and opening the window and gazing outside. "It's just the wrong time. The exact wrong time."

"How can you possibly keep something about her from me? I have so little of her to hold on to."

My father continued looking out of the window before finally speaking. "I told you your mom died in the hospital after the accident."

"Yeah?"

"She didn't. I took her home the following day, while you stayed at the Wilsons' to let her rest. She was banged up pretty good, but she was OK. She had a broken arm and collarbone, but she was lucky. That was what the hospital said. A miracle. When we got home, I set her up in bed, and I took care of her. She seemed good. Only the next morning, I woke up and went to talk to her, and she was dead," he said. "I tried to wake her, but when I touched her arm it was like ice."

"What are you talking about? She died *here*?"

"The doctors said it didn't make sense. They said there was nothing wrong with her heart. They didn't understand why it gave out. But it wasn't her heart that gave up. She did. She gave up on life, on us. She didn't fight to stay alive."

"I don't understand. Why didn't you tell me she was home?"

"She needed to rest."

"I would've let her rest! Why wouldn't I have let her rest?"

"She was always fussing over you. She needed quiet."

"She didn't! She didn't need quiet. She needed me. If I were here . . . she wouldn't have given up! And if there was something wrong with her, I would've noticed."

"She loved you, Mikey, but in the end it wasn't enough. She wasn't strong enough for what ate at her."

"What ate at her? What?" I insisted, as if there was still time to save her, to save myself.

"It wasn't one thing. Life brought her down, and sometimes she couldn't, or wouldn't, pull herself back up. I don't know how much of it was her and how much was the bipolar, but it was too much for her."

"What things brought her down!" I demanded.

"Just *things*!" he shouted back, pushing off the window so he was left standing in the center of the room. "I tried to help her. God, did I try, but your mother was too sensitive for this world—she was *weak*. And you—I've tried to toughen you up to handle what life throws at you so that you didn't end up like her."

"By calling me Choke Artist!" I screamed. "By telling me I was an embarrassment! Is *that* the kind of help you gave her?"

"By making you stand on your own feet. A man has got to be able to face down this world. End of story."

"Well, you did an aces job with me. Bravo."

"I tried to make a man of you, but you fought me."

"I never fought you."

"Every step of the way you fought me. I tried to show you what life was. Back when you missed those foul shots, I was hard on you because you had to know life doesn't coddle you when you make mistakes. It punishes you. You had to know that."

"Life doesn't need your help punishing people. Besides, tearing someone down doesn't build him up."

"My biggest fear realized," he said. "That's what you are, my biggest fear realized. Sitting right in front of me, hiding under the covers. I tried to make you tough like me."

"Tough like *you*? Is that how you tried to help Mom? By making her tough like you? No wonder she gave up," I said.

My father took a step backwards, as if pushed, and gasped. "I tried to get her to fight, but she wouldn't. I did everything I could for her, you don't know."

"What! What did you do for her?"

"The last year of her life, she would cry, break into hysterics for no reason, and she would call me at work, and I would rush home to her. I'd leave practice, meetings, it didn't matter. I told her she needed to be strong, to fight what was bothering her—to face her demons head on. I forced her to go to every quack you could think of. She tried every med she could: bipolar meds, antidepressants, herbs, everything. I was always there for her, but . . ."

"But what? What?"

"She said she felt alone. She said even with me and with you, she felt alone with her thoughts, that her thoughts ate her alive."

We were the same. My mother and I were the same. "I get that," I said. "I know exactly how she felt."

"But she didn't listen to me. *You need to fight*, I would say to her. *You need to get off your ass and face down your demons*, I would say, but she didn't fight."

"How do you know she didn't fight?"

"Because she gave up."

"You expected her to cure herself by fighting against her own mind?"

"Yes! I expected her to fight for us. I told her to get angry at her thoughts, to beat them down, but she didn't have it in her. You may not believe it, but everything I did, everything I do, is to strengthen you."

His words made me murderous. How dare he say he did anything for me? I wanted to scream at him like a madman.

"It's true," he said. "You may not believe me, but it is the truest thing I could ever say."

I knew he was telling the truth—*his* truth. But his truth didn't fit with mine. "I don't want to hear any more."

"For years, there were times I was afraid to look in your bedroom, afraid you'd killed yourself. You don't know what it's like to go into your son's room afraid of something like that. I wouldn't wish that on anybody," he said almost in a whisper.

I pictured my old man standing in front of my childhood door, afraid. Bad enough his wife had died, but then seven months later his son gives up eating and sleeping and ends up in the psych hospital. I felt for my old man. I could see maybe—for the first time—his fear, his vulnerability—*his* truth.

"You thought I might've killed myself all these years because Mom tried to, and I'm like her?"

"No. Because seven months after your mother's death, *you* swallowed a bottle of pills," he said.

"What are you talking about? I did not swallow any pills!"

"Like your mother did."

"Why are you lying?"

"Why do you think you ended up in the hospital?"

"Because after Mom died, after I missed those foul shots and you turned on me 'cause I cost you your precious championship, I stopped eating and couldn't sleep."

"You swallowed a whole bottle of your mother's sleeping pills."

"That's a lie."

"I wish it was."

I leapt out of bed and got nose to nose with my old man. "I remember. I went to the hospital because I couldn't *sleep*. I couldn't sleep or eat!"

"You swallowed a bottle of her pills," he said, taking a quiet breath. "The doctor said you must've blocked it out, that it wasn't uncommon with someone your age suffering that kind of trauma."

I turned to the mirror and looked at my face, not recognizing my own eyes. I didn't remember anything about taking those pills. Not a thing. Nothing. I struggled to picture myself after my mother died, after I missed those foul shots. I remembered refusing to eat. I remembered staying in bed for days. Then I remembered screaming at my father. We'd gotten into a fight about my refusing to eat. He said he was going to hold me down and shove food into my mouth, make me swallow it. He told me to be strong. I remembered running away from him and locking myself in the bathroom. I remembered opening the cabinet and rummaging through my mother's pills, finding an orange canister with a white top, cursing her for leaving me. But did I swallow them? Did I? Could I have done such a thing and not remember? All these years studying the memory of my mother as she swallowed those pills, not recalling I did the same thing. All this time thinking about my escape hatch, not realizing I'd already used it. As I stared at my eyes, still struggling to recognize them, a feeling moved in like fog rolling over the landscape.

My father's reflection appeared in the mirror behind me. "You always ask me why I didn't visit you more in the hospital during that time. It was because I was broken. You and your mother broke me." My father appeared to age in front of me, his eyes becoming tired and beaten, losing their lust for life. "That's not going to happen again. I won't let it." With that, he turned away, then paused as if about to say something, but he didn't. He just walked away.

• • •

I stayed in bed for hours, paralyzed, working out different scenarios in which I saved my mother. She never would've given up if I were there, taking care of her. She would have found the will to keep on living if I sat up with her all night. It was my father's fault. My mom should still be alive. Why didn't she insist I come home? Maybe she had? Maybe she begged my father to get me? Did she know something was wrong with her heart? Could she feel it? How does someone's healthy heart give out? Is such a thing even possible?

My father said he pushed my mother to *fight what was bothering her—to conquer her demons*, as if her pain could be beaten like an opposing team, as if she worked hard and wanted it, she could beat her depression, her bipolar. He caused her to feel weak, as if she didn't want to get better badly enough. It was his relentless *push, push, push* for her to be strong, to get *over* her struggle, which killed her. It was his take on life—that it was something you could win by force and desire—that did her in. It was what did us both in.

One thing for sure—he was telling the truth about my swallowing those pills. I recalled it now like a movie I kept rewinding. I remember struggling to stop the self-reproach, the self-hatred, the terror of having to live alone with my father telling me day in and out to toughen up. I remember feeling pathetic for missing those shots, for not being man enough to get over what I was feeling. I remember going to the cabinet, cursing my old man and myself.

I lay in bed and watched my younger self place each pill—one at a time—in my mouth. Watched it over and over. My mother and I were the same. The incessant bile in my head would never stop, keeping me unendurably separate from the world. I got why my mom gave up. I reached up and twirled my hair in my fingers. For the first time, I understood my agony was inherited and couldn't be overcome. My mind was diseased, my soul dying. Soon there would be no soul to save, only a ponderous mass of skin and bones animated by an afflicted mind. I gathered a clump of hair in my fist. The world was too much for some of us. I needed the electrifying pain to stop the spiral. It was the only thing that could help me. I closed my eyes, and I ripped the clump out, but instead of the usual bite, I felt only a dulled pinch. Panicked, I grabbed another handful from the front of my head and screamed as I yanked it out by the roots. The sharpness burned as if my skin had burst into flame, but the sensation was only fleeting, immediately taking on a muted quality, as if from a memory out of reach. I ripped out another clump, and then another, but it was too late. I'd gone past the point of physical pain being able to help me.

I looked at the hair still clenched in my fist. My body felt weak, my limbs pinned to the mattress. Now it was my own sorrow that beat in my veins, a hollowness I would never overcome. Never. I wondered about all those years ago, how my father found out I'd taken the pills. Did he find me unconscious on the floor? Did I panic and go to him, tell him what I'd done? Well, I wouldn't make that mistake again.

# THIRTY-ONE

**I opened the cabinet and dumped the Oxy in my hand** and counted out the twenty blue and white pills. Picking one up, I could barely feel it in my palm.

I placed all twenty pills in my mouth and held them there. I tongued them around, tasting their tartness as they scratched against one another. My mother's ghost appeared in the mirror, staring through me, seeing and not seeing me. We were the same, my mother and me. We had poisoned minds, minds that couldn't be healed, minds that killed us.

I closed my eyes.

There was a knock at the bathroom door. "Mikey?" said Dr. T, her voice disorienting me, as if she were the hallucination and my mother real. "You haven't returned my calls. Are you all right?"

My mother's face vanished from the mirror. I tried to conjure her back but couldn't. All that was left was my own reflection. My bald spots were red and swollen with tiny rivulets of blood snaking down my head. There was less blood than one might think, as I was adept at pulling my hair out without taking too much scalp. I turned and spat the pills into the toilet, terrified of Dr. T finding me with them in my mouth. I didn't want to disappoint or hurt her. I wanted to tell Dr. T I was OK, but those words wouldn't come.

"You'll be happy to know Toby is feeling a bit better," she said.

"He is?"

"Of course we have some work to do, but I think he's finally ready for that type of deep work." She paused. "Can I come in?"

I leaned against the bathroom door.

"I'm afraid I must insist, Mikey."

I cleaned my head up as best as I could, but it didn't help much. I still looked like a cancer patient during chemo. I undid the lock, and Dr. T entered. I avoided making eye contact, afraid her eyes would see everything.

"Mikey, please tell me what is going on," she said.

I looked in the mirror, to my ridiculous reflection. Then I turned to Dr. T and saw the concerned way in which she looked at my inflamed bald spots. "I . . . pulled out my hair."

She nodded, gently holding my gaze. "Are you OK?"

I turned back to the toilet and wished I'd flushed it.

"Your team's quite worried about you," she said.

"They're better off without me."

"That's rubbish. They blame themselves for you skiving off work these last two days. They think they scared you, that you never knew so many nutters in your life."

"Look at my head," I said. "I'm the definition of crazy."

"I think you need to talk to them."

"I can't," I said. I glanced at the open bottle of Oxy on the counter. Of course, she noticed.

"What's going on?" she asked.

"I . . ."

She picked up the bottle and looked at me. "Did you take these pills?" she asked, eyes narrowed at me.

"No," I began but couldn't finish my thought. Dr. T moved toward me and took my chin in her hands so she could look into my eyes. At first, I resisted her, pulling back, but she held my face, forcing me to see her clear, steady gaze.

"You didn't take the pills?"

I pointed to the pills dissolving into a heavy blue cloud in the toilet. "I tried to kill myself when I was a kid. I didn't remember doing it. I took a whole bottle of pills."

"Oh, Mikey," she said.

"Apparently, I blocked it out as some survival mechanism or something."

"I couldn't take losing you," she said flatly, releasing my face and pulling me to her. I pulled back but she pulled me tighter, and I felt this embrace was for the both of us. I just let loose and cried in her thin, strong arms, letting the bottom fall out of all my efforts to shove down the pain.

"I need you to tell me exactly what's going on this instant," she said, releasing me.

I leaned back against the sink, and I just emptied my mind, the horror repeating itself in my head. "What if Toby succeeds in pushing the blade deep enough next time? And Chey—I can't stop thinking how painful her life's gonna be. I can't stop seeing her fight against her own mind. All the guys—they're gonna suffer so much in their lives, and there's *nothing* I can do about it. Nothing. And me—those overhead lights in Toby's hospital room brought me back to my own time under the same putrid fluorescence, to a time when my mother gave up on life, when I missed two foul shots and lost my father. And now I'm so scared to relive that memory—one of the worst of my life—on that same court, and this time not only in front of the school, but the world. I won't be able to survive it."

Dr. T listened, head tilted, nodding along sadly. "What else? Please tell me everything. Don't leave anything out."

"Really?" I asked. "Everything?"

"Yes. Really. I want to know," she said, reaching over and taking my hand.

I took a deep breath. "My mother gave up on life because she couldn't escape her thoughts, which were so overwhelming that even *with* people she felt alone. Just like me—I feel the exact same way. Sometimes I think my thoughts will drive me mad, and my only escape will be to kill myself. And in case all that isn't enough, a great friend of mine, Alvarito, died, and I'm terrified I'll suffer his same fate, that I will die alone, homeless, my body ripped apart by wild dogs." I tried to breathe but sobbed instead.

Dr. T reached for me again and held me, her hand on the back of my head as I pressed the side of my face to her shoulder. When we pulled apart, I looked at her and suddenly felt lighter, as if she shared my burden. And the way she stood so upright, the clarity of her eyes, I knew she could handle it.

"You're not alone, Mikey. You have quite a few people who, to put it in their parlance, *Got your back*."

I nodded.

"Actually, I'm humbled by the relationship you've developed with your team. You care for them so deeply, and the big surprise for me is that they care just as much for you. To be honest, I was relieved Gonzalo had the capacity to care so much."

I thought about G, all my guys, what my death would have meant to them, and a rush of guilt almost knocked me over. Suddenly it occurred to me I had not felt this close to anyone since my mom died. Dr. T, my team, the school—for the first time since I was a kid, I felt like I had a place.

I wished I could go back in time and tell my mother I was there for her. I would tell her she needed to make room for me amongst all her abusive thoughts. My mother needed compassion, not to be told she was weak. If I would've known she was home from the hospital, maybe I could've saved her. At least I could've tried.

"You know you're not like your mum," said Dr. T, as if reading my thoughts.

"My mother was bipolar. She had a real medical issue. Me—I'm just too weak to handle life."

"That's not how mental illness works, Mikey. Your depression can be debilitating as your mum's bipolar or Chey's psychosis. I need you to understand that."

"The guys are the ones with the real issues. I'm . . ."

"I don't believe you to be suicidal."

I thought about my escape hatch—those pills knocking against one another in my mouth—and how the very idea of killing myself made me feel close to my mother. But now I felt different. Spitting out the pills made her feel far away, as if I couldn't remember her, as if I never really knew her.

"I'm not like her," I said. "I don't want to kill myself."

"I'm going to insist you see somebody. I'm going to set up the appointment myself, and the school is going to pay for it."

"My mom had this great laugh. Her eyes used to light up when she told me stories about growing up, about my grandma and grandpa."

"I wish I could've known her," said Dr. T.

"Yeah, she would've liked you," I said, smiling at the idea of the two women meeting.

"Now we need to go speak to the team," said Dr. T. "They're downstairs."

"They're *here*?"

"Of course, it's quite unorthodox to bring students to an employee's home, but they were persuasive, and I was worried for you and for them. They're in the kitchen with your father."

"My father!"

"Yes. And Mikey?"

"Yes."

"Let's get you a hat."

• • •

Donning a Clippers hat, I stormed into the kitchen, and the guys, minus Toby, called out in unison, "Coach!" My father looked up, but they weren't talking to him. Seeing their faces here in my house slammed my escape hatch shut, forcing me back into my body. I was their coach.

"When you coming back?" said G. "You look like *mierda*, by the way."

I shook my head. "I'm sorry, guys. Toby . . ."

"Coach, you're gonna have to pull your act together," said Brian. "We straight up need you."

"We need to figure out a way we're not gonna get spanked by Prince Charming over there," said Chey, gesturing to my father. "We did not come all this way to finish the season as some kind of joke."

"I feel for you guys," started my father. "You don't have a chance."

"Dad, stop!" I shouted, the steel in my voice surprising both of us.

My father threw up his hands. "Trying to help."

"Your kind of help did mom in, did me in," I snapped. "Nobody here needs some crummy life lesson on being a man."

"Yeah. Mikey show us that," said Otis.

"Yeah, Mikey showed us," said Donnie.

"She's right. This game *is* a joke," said my old man. "My prediction is we'll beat you by fifty points."

"*You* are the only joke here," I said, our eyes locking.

"Joke's gonna be when we drop your sorry ass, *güey,*" said G.

My father looked at G, then around the room, finally landing on Nubbin. "You—I know you, don't I?"

Nubbin looked at me.

"How would you know him?" I asked, not wanting my father to place Nubbin.

"Kid looks familiar, is all."

"Mikey," said Dr. T. "You OK?"

I looked once more around the room and knew I was. "I'll see you all tomorrow morning."

Dr. T herded the team toward the door, except Otis, who hung back. "Coach, you call me you wanna talk."

I nodded. "Thanks, Otis."

Otis, who once tried to choke me, placed his arm on my shoulder and said, "I got you, Coach." I loved this kid. I really did.

# THIRTY-TWO

**That night I thought about every one of the kids' assignments.** Donnie's angel pecked my brain. I wrestled with a big ole pit named Smurf. With monstrous hands, Chey's invisible man choked me. I got why Nubbin shit in his brother's bag. I stood with Brian on the bridge wanting to jump. I felt relief for G's capacity to love the team. And I walked arm-in-arm with Toby after his brother's death. I found strength in these stories—my own and the team's.

When I roused the next morning, I went into the bathroom and examined my bald spots in the mirror. I opened the cabinet, took out a razor and gently shaved my head, careful not to aggravate the spots that were still swollen. It wasn't the first time I shaved my head to hide bald spots, but this time it felt different. I read somewhere that when a monk shaves his head it was called shedding the *idiot grass*. I felt reborn. Or at least a little less like an idiot.

Knowles's voice came at me from my kitchen. It was seven a.m., and my old man was already doing an interview about the game, which was a week away. I was terrified my guys were going to be slaughtered in front of the world, and that the humiliation would leave them scarred.

I threw on some duds and was sneaking out the front door, when my father and Knowles stopped me.

"I like the new look," said Knowles, rubbing his own bald dome. "You got a little bit of a Jason Kidd thing going on."

"I'm making some changes," I said.

"You're going to need more than a shaved head," said my old man. "We're going to be famous, you and me. A coach breaking a record is a good story but beating his son to do so will air during sweeps."

"My producer saw some footage of your last game, Mikey. She said whichever team wins will make it to sweeps. This is going to be right up there with the Bird/Johnson rivalry.

"Mikey's a big boy. He knows he doesn't have a chance to win."

Richard looked at my father and shook his head. "I don't know. Tim's brother has remarkable understanding of the game. Kid plays like he can see into the future."

"He's got excellent skills," said the camerawoman, startling me.

"I didn't even know you spoke," I said.

"That's who that hobbit in the kitchen was yesterday? I knew I recognized him. He broke Tim's arm, made him miss his whole freshman season."

"Father against son, brother against brother. This thing promotes itself," said Knowles. That reminds me—Andrew, can you round up that game footage you were telling me about? The DVDs? I need to get them to my editor ASAP."

"Sure," said my father, blinking, his attention on his lap.

I didn't think Knowles believed we could win. He was creating drama for the camera, but nonetheless his statement gave me hope. "I gotta go," I said, taking the opportunity to sneak into the garage and snag the DVDs marked *playoffs* out of a box.

• • •

Before first period, the team—who all dug my new look—and I rapped on Dr. T's door. We had some DVDs that needed watching, and she had a player. I explained to her we needed to study years of playoff footage to outthink Westchester.

"We never outthunk anybody, dude," said Brian.

Dr. T stopped tapping on her keyboard and regarded the determined-looking brood, which consisted of everybody but Toby, who was still on the mend, assembled in her doorway, and she grabbed a few notebooks and passed them out. "What precisely are we looking for?" she asked.

"We'll know when we see it," said Chey.

And we all sat and watched, and we kept watching. Dr. T even cleared her day and excused the guys from classes, and Chey narrated each game, pointing out patterns and my old man's go-to plays.

Watching my father age from year to year reminded me of his mortality, and I pictured him afraid to open my bedroom door. I hated to admit it, but I started to feel for him, to feel the empathy he should have had for my mother—for me. Then I pictured him running up the score on us to prove some point, and I instantly got over my compassion.

DVD after DVD, Chey searched through games looking for I don't know what, muttering how smart my old man was. At six p.m., we were on the last DVD, and beginning to lose hope, when she said, "Fuck me. Your old man is playing safe."

Everybody stopped.

"For the last two years your father stopped taking risks. He wants the record so bad he changed his game. In the final minutes, if it's within a few points, your pops has Tim hold the ball at the top of the key, waiting to be challenged. The rest of the players set picks, or whatever, moving their guys out of the way while Tim drives toward the hoop drawing a foul—he does that ninety-two percent of the time when the game's close. It's a simple, safe play, but effective because Tim is great. When your father feels the pressure, he's predictable as LA smog."

"Brilliant," said Dr. T. "Chey, you have a real talent for spotting patterns."

"Thanks, Dr. T."

"I wonder if you see any patterns in your own life?"

"Are you serious right now?"

"No. I am not, Chey," said Dr. T, winking at me. Dr. T had gone for the funny, and I loved her for it. I also loved that her humor seemed different than mine. She didn't use it to keep people at a distance. I liked that. I would have to give that a try.

Chey threw Dr. T a high-five.

Chey's insight was right, but it had a flaw. We couldn't use it unless the game was close, and it wasn't likely to be.

Dr. T, with the help of Chey, created Excel sheets on each opposing player, listing their strengths and weaknesses. And for the next week, my guys walked around studying their Excel docs like anxious brokers looking for market trends, and during practice, we used the info to role-play. Nubbin proved remarkably adept at playing his brother, and I admit, I was beginning to believe anything was possible.

• • •

The day before the game, Dr. Lipschitz summoned me to his office and told me the entire board was coming to see us play, where he would pitch them on getting us a gym.

"That's fantastic," I said. "Why do you look like your puppy got steamrolled?"

"They are a prideful bunch and won't be feeling generous if the game is an embarrassment to them."

"Look, I'm not promising a win here, but we've been studying my old man's team, and I think we got a chance to keep this thing tight."

"How bad would tomorrow night's game be without Nubbin?"

"What?"

Dr. Lipschitz shook his head. "Nubbin's out."

"Out?" I said, leaping up. "What does that mean?"

"It means he won't be playing," he said, leaning back in his chair—more like slumping back in his chair. "Did you tell Nubbin to lie to his father about being on the team?"

"Shit," I said. "I told him not to tell him he was playing."

Dr. Lipschitz shook his head. "He's calling for your termination. I tried to reason with him, but look at it from his point of view. You punched out one son's window, and you told the other to lie to him."

"I should've punched *him* out for choosing one son over the other."

"Mikey, you've done a lot of good for these boys and this school, and I'd hate to lose you, but Nubbin's father plays golf with the CEO of the hospital and school and has her ear. Not even your father will be able to help you here."

"Is there anything I can do? Anything?"

"You could win. People tend to forgive winners."

• • •

At practice that afternoon I broke the news to the team, who were smacked into silence—not a word. "I told Nubbin to lie. You guys deserve better from me," I said. "I'm sorry."

"Yeah, well my *cholo* father's not a professional baller," said G.

"No shit," said the entire team in unison.

"You guys knew that?"

"Yeah," said Chey. "Only we didn't care."

"Fuck you, *cabróna*."

"I don't get why you even needed to lie," said Chey.

"I don't even know. I lie all the time, and that's the truth. My own mama thinks I'm a socio. But Mikey read my assignment," he said, smiling, "and he said I wasn't one."

"We can't trust you, G," said Chey. "We all got issues, but with you, we can't believe a word you say, and that hurts the team."

"All right, guys," I said. "Let's not beat up G. We got a real problem here we have to discuss."

"We do," said Chey. "In Woodbine Park, before we won our first game, you said we needed to learn to trust each other, that nobody wins games by themselves, that if we couldn't count on each other, we were gonna be spanked by that Popeye's dude. You said our loss was guaranteed if we didn't. Right?"

I nodded.

"Well, I'm totally upping our trust to the next level here. I'm sending you all my assignment. You guys are going to have to know and have absolute faith in me if we have a chance of surviving this game without Nubbin, and I'm going to have to completely trust you."

"If you think it'll help, Chey, I'll straight up give everyone a copy of mine as well," said Brian.

Chey nodded to Brian. "We need to know each other down to the bones so we're in sync," she said. "There can't be anything between us."

"Sharing my story made me feel closer to you guys, if that makes any sense," said Donnie.

Toby, looking healthy, clapped the ball between his hands and looked down at the bandage on his wrist. "I miss my bro."

"What was his name?" asked Otis.

"Taye. He was my heart."

Otis put his hand on Toby's shoulder.

"Chey's right," said Toby. "I want you guys to read mine, too, for real."

"Me too," said G. "I should be the one benched for lying—Nubbin only lied once. I'd take the hit for him if I could."

"I bet his old man ain't ever even seen him ball," said Toby.

"What did you say, Toby?" I asked.

"If he actually saw Nub ball, he'd change his mind about him, believe that."

"Chey, you run practice today," I said.

• • •

I knocked on Nubbin's front door, and I kept knocking until he answered.

"I'm sorry, Coach," he said. "I mean, I had to tell my father I was playing before the game. He went nuts. I kinda panicked and told him it was your idea."

"You don't get to apologize for telling the truth, Nub. I should, for putting you in this position. I didn't think it all the way through."

"Are the guys angry at me? They're like my first friends."

"They don't blame you, and besides even if they did, they'd get over it. Friends forgive each other. You forgive me?"

He nodded.

"Good. Is your old man home?"

"Yeah, but he hasn't changed his mind over anything in a hundred years," said Nubbin.

"I know the type."

Nubbin led me through huge rooms with high ceilings and art on the walls. The living room boasted a life-size African villager breastfeeding, and I have to admit, the wealth was intimidating, but I was determined—I had to be. His old man was sitting poolside smoking a cigar and watching his favorite son swim laps by a giant replica of the *David*.

When he saw me, he popped up like he wanted to hit me, dropping ash on his button-down. "You've got some balls coming here," he said, wiping ash off his shirt. "Get out of my yard, or I'll have you arrested."

"Dad, I mean, give him a chance," said Nubbin.

"Nubbin, back in the house. Now!"

"Listen to him at least," pleaded Nubbin.

"First of all, check your tone. Second, I'm not going to ask you again."

Nubbin looked at me and shrugged before retreating inside.

"You got every reason to be angry," I said, holding my hands out in front of me in a gesture of acquiescence, "but I need you to listen."

"I'm calling the cops," he said dialing his cell. "I'm beginning to see why your father calls you an embarrassment."

"I Need Love" by LL Cool J lit up the yard, issuing through speakers everywhere.

"Nubbin!" screamed his father. "Get the door!"

"Great doorbell. Classic," I said.

"You *are* a fool."

"Call the cops, Dad," said Tim, who had stopped swimming to glare at me.

"You told my son to lie to me. What kind of man does that?"

With that, the sliding-glass door to the house opened, and out walked Knowles. "That's Richard Knowles from ESPN," I said.

"I know who the hell he is," said Nubbin's father, pushing past me with a little bounce in his step. "*Richard Knowles* in my house. That piece you did on the top ten ballers of all time was pretty good."

"*Pretty* good?" said Knowles.

"Isaiah Thomas should be on that list."

"He's up there, but top ten?"

"Hell yeah," said Nubbin's father. "I'm James Tillet. You here to interview Tim?"

"I'm here to talk to you about your sons," said Knowles. "They're *both* great ballplayers."

"If I have my way, Tim will play for the Lakers."

"Nubbin—" Knowles began.

"I hate that nickname. His name's Gordon."

"He has a real head for the game."

"You're kidding me—Gordon?" said James, crossing his arms, turning toward the window where his son was watching. "He's too short and too violent. I was happy to hear he didn't hurt anybody."

"I've never seen Gordon lose his head in a game," I said. "Never even fouled out."

"And he knows how to compensate for his height," said Knowles.

"Really?" asked James, looking back and forth between us. "Are you two kidding me?"

"I told Mikey's father it was going to be a *game*," said Knowles. "Gordon's a great player with a terrific shot, but what is so impressive is how selfless he is. There's this kid on the team, Donnie, who has the best shot I've ever seen, and your son has this talent of drawing in defenders for Donnie to get open. It's remarkable."

It was satisfying to hear Knowles talk about my guys. I felt warmth settling in my chest.

"I'm not saying Mary Friedman could win, but at least it would be a game. Without Gordon, I'm afraid it will be a blowout. To be frank, it would be better for ESPN if your son played."

"Wait, let me get this straight. You told Coach Cannon how good Gordon is?"

"I think it scared him."

"Really?" he asked, shaking his head, turning toward Tim, who'd gone back to swimming. "Coach Cannon came over here this morning, told me Gordon was out of control on the court, that he could end up hurting Tim again."

"Unbelievable!" I scoffed. "He's never even seen him play."

"Gordon is the only thing that could put his record in jeopardy," Knowles said. "Coach Cannon is looking to hedge his bet."

"No. There's a lot of animosity between the brothers. A few years back, Tim called Gordon a name and Gordon attacked him, broke Tim's arm. Gordon's too unpredictable—it's a part of his illness. I can't risk him attacking Tim on the court. I will never forgive myself if Tim gets hurt and can't play. Coach Cannon said he was expecting somebody to come from the Lakers' camp. Between Tim's pro future and the coach's record, I'm sorry. I can't take the chance."

"I need Gordon to play," said Knowles, his tone flat and firm.

"I'm sorry. My mind's made up."

"Look," said Knowles, leaning in toward Nubbin's father. "You're thinking about this all wrong. This doc *could* put Tim on every pro recruiter's radar. It's E:60. Everybody who matters in pro ball will see it."

"What do you mean *could*?"

"Depending on how it's edited," said Knowles. "Your son may not even be in it."

"What do you mean, *how it's edited*?"

"Could be a great opportunity for Tim," Knowles said, standing. "Then again, it could be an opportunity missed."

"Are you threatening me?" said James, also standing.

"Unpredictable what hits the cutting room floor, so to speak. Thanks for your time," said Knowles. "Hopefully, I will see you and *both* your sons tomorrow."

James looked at me.

"ESPN. E.S.," I said, "P.N."

"Get out."

# THIRTY-THREE

**When Knowles and I left, I couldn't tell which way Nubbin's father was leaning.** The next day, Saturday, when I went to pick up Nubbin for the big game and nobody answered his door, my heart leapt off a cliff.

The first round of the Tournament of Champions was played at the home court of the team with the best record, and we arrived at Westchester two hours early for my guys to get used to the court, and so I could try and beat down my nerves before the game. The gym was twice the size of any we'd played in, the stands behind each bench large enough to seat the Mary Friedman students four times over. Championship banners streamed from every corner of the ceiling, and the same ferocious ram from my childhood, the team's mascot, still bucked in blue and gold center court. Only now there was a Nike swish under each hoop, my father's impending fame apparently commanding a sponsor. It never occurred to me how this gym felt more like a college's than a high school's. The bounce of the ball, our voices, all sounded inconsequential in this colossus.

For an hour, we ran plays and stretched in the relative quiet, while I wrestled with my history. It lived in the wood of the floor, up in the stands, the walls, even in the air, a history that was queuing up for a sequel. With every shot my boys took, I relived missing those foul shots, heard my father call me Choke Artist that first time, felt the fresh stab of the loss of my mother. I was never one for praying, but I put a knee down and I asked the Big Kahuna for help. I asked that He keep watch over my guys, to keep the game close enough that they could walk out of this gym with their heads held high and not revert to where they started this season.

We were cold, bricking most of our warm-up shots. To bolster the team, I shared an old John Wayne quote: "Courage is being scared to death and saddling up anyway."

"What is a John Wayne?" asked G.

As I was explaining the Duke, the gym doors opened, and in came Knowles with his camerawoman, who both turned back toward the door in time to film my father and his team strutting in with a confidence I'd never known.

"Hey, crack babies," called out Jovver. "You ready for the worst beat down in history?"

"You ready for me to pull your liver out your mouth?" said Otis, lurching for him.

Toby stepped in front of Otis, "On the court, big man."

"Keep your boys on a leash," snapped my father, as he approached, camera in tow. There was to be no handshake between my father and me, no wishing each other good luck—not even for the camera. "We are going to trounce you, son, and we are going to keep grinding until there is nothing left, until you have submitted. And then we are going to thrash you some more."

With that my father led his team away, and Westchester Private began to practice with the precision of a pro team, as more of their fans filled the bleachers behind their bench. I turned to our empty bleachers and pictured how pathetic our twenty fans were going to look, when the gym doors opened. A few seconds later, Dr. T walked in and threw me a smile that cut through my anxiety like a lightning strike.

She then led in two hundred patients, a third in hospital gowns, a third in street clothes, and yet another third in some combination of both. Doctors, nurses, and orderlies led this rowdy herd toward me, and row after row, they filled every seat behind our bench, while my father and the Westchester fans stared in shock, and my guys watched in awe. We had more fans than Westchester, and it was glorious.

The ref, whom I recognized from a few of our games, entered in his black and whites and shook my hand, as my father rushed over, pointing to our boisterous fans. "They'll be too disruptive. We have ESPN filming here today," he said, pointing to two other cameras being setup. There were to be three E:60 cameras filming today. "You have to remove them."

"Oh please," said the ref, brushing my father off as another official approached.

The championship was a two-official game—one ref from each league—and my father turned his attention to his ref. "This game is too important to allow these mental patients to ruin it."

My father's ref looked at the Visitors' stands, while a few patients attempted to perform a wave.

"Look at them," continued my father. "The game hasn't even started yet."

"They're practicing the wave," said my father's ref, shrugging.

"Unbelievable!" shouted my old man, turning toward the front door in time to see Nubbin's father entering the gym—alone.

Nubbin's old man made his way over to us and quickly pulled my father aside. I sat looking at these two men, feet away, whispering to each other. They were two peas in a pod. But something wasn't right. They seemed to disagree. James gestured toward Knowles, who was huddled with his camerawoman.

"Are you *kidding* me?" barked my father, no longer in the whispering mood.

Knowles waved back at the two men.

"I didn't have a choice," said James, turning toward the door, where . . .

293

Nubbin had entered the gym . . . in uniform.

"Nubbin!" I screamed, prompting a few patients over my shoulder to do the same.

"Nub-bin, Nub-bin, Nub-bin," they chanted, prompting others to just yell. The patients seemed to understand how much we needed them here. I turned toward them and began to clap, and they all followed suit, and we had at least a hundred people applauding Nubbin's entrance. The look on his face was irrefutable—it was as if he'd somehow awoken in one of LeBron James's dreams.

The team tripped over themselves to get to Nubbin, showering him with fist-bumps, chest bumps, and even a few hugs.

"I forgot how big this gym is," said Nubbin, jogging over to us.

"This whole thing is a circus," said my father, turning to me. "This is going to be the worst day of your life, son, and that's saying something."

"Or the worst day of yours," I said. "You usually study your opponents. You don't know the first thing about us."

"Let's go, Friedman!" shouted Tyrone in the stands, as he rallied the patients into chanting, "Fried-man, Fried-man, Fried-man!" We were no longer the Visitors. We had a name.

The players took their respective spots center court for the jump ball to start the game, while Brian, Chey, and I could barely hear each other over the rioting behind our bench. "I want to say," said Chey. "This is awesome."

It sure *was*.

The ref jumped the ball. Tim pushed off Nubbin, sending him flying, while Russell tipped Tim the ball. He swung it around to Jovver, who tossed an alley-oop to Tim who slam dunked over Toby. It was a play meant to send a message, and it sure did. My guys just stood there, slack-jawed. We'd never seen anything like that in our puny league. Chey turned to me and shook her head, "We're beyond doomed."

"OK, guys," I said, clapping, noticing my hands were trembling. "Shake it off. A dunk is worth two points—same as a layup."

Nubbin brought up the ball, but Tim stripped it at half-court and took it all the way for a reverse dunk, prompting the Westchester fans to jump to their feet and chant his name.

Once again Nubbin dribbled the ball up-court, and when he was by our bench, Tim said, "Heard you were good for the league. Let's see what you got." Tim gave Nubbin some space, inviting him to try and get by him, but when he did, Tim swiped the ball out of his hands to Russell, who took it down-court for an easy deuce. "Remember your place, little man," said Tim, while Nubbin began to mutter and blink his eyes.

"Don't listen to him, Nubbin!" I called out. "Don't let him get in your head."

The next play Donnie's defender shoved him, sending him to the ground, which somehow the refs missed.

"Get up, Donnie. Shake it off," I said, clapping. Donnie remained on the ground, refusing to look at me. "Keep your eyes on number eleven, ref," I shouted. "He pushed my guy." And I watched as Donnie got himself to a standing position and walked down-court, looking at the exit as if he might bolt. My team was falling apart and there was nothing I could do about it.

Only four minutes into the game, I called a timeout and told my guys to slow down the play, to remember the basics, to get position, to set up screens, to feed the open man, but they were too overwhelmed to hear me over the Westchester fans chanting, "Tim, Tim, Tim."

This time G brought the ball down-court, but once again, Tim stole it and threw it to Jovver, who landed a three.

Westchester was too good. I felt my hand reach up for hair no longer there. I had to settle for rubbing my eyebrows. I was fooling myself to think we could play close against my father. It was like a high school team playing a college. I turned to Chey, "Any ideas?" She shook her head, silent.

My guys, God bless them, tried but they couldn't make anything happen: Toby battled Jovver for rebounds, but couldn't get position. Donnie struggled to get open, but his guy was manhandling him. Brian and G attempted to set up plays, but the coverage was too tight. Westchester continued to score, while we had yet to get on the boards. That is, until G stole a ball and raced down-court.

"Pass it!" I screamed. "Toby's wide open under the basket!"

But G drove toward the hoop, getting stuffed by Tim.

"Yo, pass the ball!" screamed Toby.

G ignored him, getting back on defense.

At the end of the first quarter, the score was twenty-two to nothing, and my father called to me from across the court, "It's only going to get worse, son." One of the E:60 cameras pointed at me, no doubt focusing on my eyes as I watched my team and all the work we had done crumble.

Nubbin turned to his father, whose head was buried in his hands, and I thought about how I quit my high school team, about quitting jobs, relationships, about quitting everything, about living on the streets, about Alvarito, about the bet, about how I was about to lose this job, and I hoped Nubbin would be able to shake today off, but something told me this game would forever change him like a game changed me.

Once again, Nubbin brought the ball up-court, and his brother rushed up on him, but this time Nubbin was too quick, moving his body between his brother and the ball.

"Remember what we practiced," I shouted, standing.

Nubbin signaled to Otis, who nodded and got into position. Then Nubbin drove his brother right into the wall, knocking Tim on his ass, and Nubbin sank a jumper—a perfect shot! But my father's ref blew his whistle, calling a foul.

"No!" I screamed. "It was a perfect screen. Open your eyes, ref!" The ref blew his whistle and pointed at me, giving me a warning. The one basket we made didn't count. Unbelievable. The ref informed me my next outburst would be a technical foul. My father was right. It *was* worse than I could've imagined.

I glanced into the stands and saw Dr. Lipschitz staring in shock, and Dr. T had a look on her face as if she'd just witnessed a terrible accident.

The next play, Nubbin dribbled the ball up-court and once again Tim knocked it away. Only this time Brian dove for it and slapped the ball to G before sliding out of bounds. G whipped it back to Nubbin, who landed a three-pointer at the top of the key. Chey and I leapt out of our seats. We were on the boards. No matter how bad it got, we weren't going to be shut out.

Nubbin looked up in the stands to his father, and I looked too, catching the man nod to his son. That little nod must have inspired Nubbin because he came to life, and over the next five minutes, he scored a few more baskets—but not enough to make any difference. It was brutal. We couldn't stop Westchester from scoring at will.

With only a minute left in the first half, Donnie's defender knocked him down again, and this time the ref blew his whistle, as Otis knocked Donnie's defender on his ass. The ref blew his whistle a second time, prompting Toby to sprint across court and wrap his arms around Otis to prevent a brawl. My guys were getting frustrated and about to blow up, and I didn't blame them as I watched the last seconds burn off the first half, the score forty-eight to eleven.

• • •

I tried to make it to the locker room without talking to anyone, but my father wasn't one to miss out on a film-worthy sound bite. "You're still the little boy who missed those foul shots, aren't you?"

"And you're still the father afraid to look in his son's room."

"I hope you enjoy your last game as coach," he snapped, storming off, leaving me standing there, struggling to collect myself, when I looked up and saw Toby.

"What was that about this being your last game, Coach?" asked Toby.

"My father and I made some bet, and if I lose, I gotta quit coaching."

"Why would you risk your job?"

"Because I'm an idiot. It's what I do. As soon as something good happens, I self-sabotage," I said, putting my hand on his shoulder. "Let's keep the bet between us for now, OK?"

Toby nodded, touching the tape on his wrist.

"I read your assignment, Toby, and I gotta lot of love for you—don't ever forget that. OK?"

"OK. You still want me to be captain?"

I nodded.

"Then I'm the captain."

• • •

In the locker room, my guys sat on benches wearing the same beaten-down looks they had my first game as coach. We were right where we began, and I pounded my hand on the lockers. "Fuck!"

"What the shit, *güey*," said G. "You trying to give us a heart attack?"

"I'm proud of you guys," I said. "All of you."

"We're getting killed," said G.

"Nobody's getting killed," I said. "When we started, we couldn't even finish a game. Now, look at us. We won our division."

"We were better off when we lost every game, bruh," said Brian.

"We got no business being here," said Nubbin. "I mean, these guys are too good."

"Otis, you set a great screen. It was a bad call. Toby, you're hitting the boards. Donnie, you're fearless. Nubbin, you're keeping cool but bringing the heat. Maybe you guys can't see how far we've come, but I can."

With that, Toby moved to the center of the room. "I got something to say."

He had their attention.

"These fools have been calling us mongoloids, tardos, crack babies, crack-tards, fuck-tards, and worse than that, they beat up Donnie."

"Dude, you getting to a point?" said Brian.

"Yo, Chey, what were the odds of us winning that game in the park, for real?"

"I would've lost a ton of cheddar on that game. Seriously, I would've given us a .07 percent chance to win. But Mikey saw something in you guys I missed."

"Right! He saw we had balls—big elephant balls," said Toby. "The guys who walked onto Woodbine Park and bested those fools in street ball are the ones who are gonna win this game, yo. My guy's done reaching over me without getting an elbow in his ribs. Otis, Nubbin's brother should have nightmares about you tonight. Donnie, Nubbin, we're going to need three-pointers to get back in this. Tomorrow when Westchester wakes up with every part of their body in pain, they gonna remember the hurt we put into them today. The first half Westchester forced us to play their type of ball. Second, they play ours."

"Big elephant balls!" screamed Donnie, jumping off the bench.

"That be the kinda shit I'm talkin' 'bout," said Otis, punching a locker so hard the room shook.

"Now let's go fuck some shit up!" screamed Toby.

The guys stormed out of the locker room, wailing like Arapahos looking for Custer.

"Toby," I called out.

He looked back at me.

"Good speech," I said.

"I'm the captain," he said, giving me a nod and heading out to lead his team.

"You know our big elephant balls aren't going to get us there, Chey," I said. "They're too good."

"I know," she said. "But it was a good speech."

"You've got Westchester's profiles, plus the stats from the first half in your noggin."

"They're not going to help, either," said Chey.

"Everything you've gone through, the gambling, watching games with your old man, the breaks, fighting to be on this team, has led to this moment, Chey. This—right here—is *your* fate. Street ball's not going to get us there. You are."

"There's less than a three percent chance of us getting within twenty points."

"What were the odds of us winning the division?"

"I would've said zero."

"Three percent sounds good."

Chey bit her lip and scrunched her eyes shut. Her eyes popped open. "Jovver can't go left, drives right ninety percent of the time."

"Let's fuck some shit up," I said.

"Yeah, let's fuck some shit up."

"I'm proud of you, Chey."

"Don't be such a dork."

• • •

The two teams once again approached center court for the jump, and once again Russell tipped the ball to Tim, who took off down-court, but Nubbin was quick and caught him, forcing Tim to slow down the play at the top of the key. Tim dribbled between his legs and switched directions, keeping the ball out of Nubbin's reach.

Suddenly, Otis punched the ball out of Tim's hands, and Nubbin grabbed it and whipped it down-court to Donnie at the three-point line. Swish! It was our turn to make a statement: the second half won't be like the first. I'm sure in Westchester's league nobody ever punched the basketball, and this made me smile.

"You think they got the message?" said Chey.

"I do," I said.

Chey signaled to Otis, who ran up to Tim. "I got four fouls with your name on them. And they gonna hurt."

Tim took off down-court, while the Friedman fans wailed. They must've been practicing during the half because they performed a perfect wave.

Next, Jovver passed to Tim, who missed a shot. Toby grabbed the rebound and scooped it to Nubbin, who dribbled down-court to the top of the key to set up a play. He dribbled between his legs, keeping his eyes on Tim guarding him.

"Let's see what you got, Psycho Midget," said Tim.

Nubbin threw a head fake and then whipped a no-look pass to Brian, who bounce passed to G. He missed the shot, prompting Toby to scream like a warrior as he slammed into Russell's body, converting the rebound and drawing a foul. Toby had himself a chance at a three-point play, and he took his place at the foul line.

"Punk's got no shot," said Russell.

"Can you feel the change, son?" asked Toby. "'Cause I'm beginning to feel it. Donnie, what about you? You feeling a change in tide?"

Donnie nodded and smiled. "I literally feel it."

Toby, the captain, sank his foul shot, and across the gym, my father ran his fingers through his hair and looked up at the scoreboard. In the stands, Nubbin's father stood.

We continued to take it to Westchester with everything we had: Toby threw elbows, Otis bumped and held and intimidated anybody who got near him, especially Tim, while G talked smack like it was his native tongue, and up in our stands I saw Gerald fist-bump LeBron, who must've rushed over to the gym as he was still wearing his Popeye's uniform.

Chey devised plays that worked our players' strengths and Westchester's weaknesses. My favorite one was a Picket Fence, where all four of our guys lined up on one side of the court, leaving Nubbin to drive one-on-one against his brother. When Donnie's defender moved over to help Tim, Nubbin bounced it behind his back to Donnie, who sank a wide-open two-pointer from the foul line. When I asked Chey how she knew it would be Donnie's defender that would come out for the double-team, she began to talk percentages and patterns, and I smiled and nodded.

With Chey's plays, and my guys playing hard like they did in the park, we matched Westchester basket for basket for the rest of the third quarter.

"We're not making up enough ground," said Chey.

"You're killing it."

"Yeah, yeah, yeah, I know, you're proud of me. But we have to stop them on D if we're going to catch them. Either that, or every shot has to be a three."

Tim, trying to slow down the game, dribbled at the top of the key when Nubbin stripped the ball and raced off down-court. But his brother was fast and looked to be about to catch him when he ran into a brick wall named Otis and fell flat on his back.

"Ref, that was a foul!" shouted my old man.

"Are you kidding," said Knowles, clapping. "It was perfect—absolutely perfect."

I was so excited I put my arm around Donnie beside me on the bench. Remembering myself, I yanked it back. "Sorry, Donnie. I didn't mean to touch you. I got excited."

"It's OK, you can put it back."

I reached over and hugged his shoulders and squeezed him, feeling all the love I had for this kid.

"Too much," said Donnie. "*Way* too much."

I looked up to see my father watching me, shaking his head.

On the court, Tim took a shot over Nubbin, landing a swish. "You got no springs, little man."

On the next play, Nubbin shot a three-pointer over his brother, prompting G to trot up beside Tim and throw down an oldie but a goodie: "I saw a picture of your game on a milk carton."

"Fuck you," said Tim.

"Don't let him get in your head," shouted my father, prompting a big old smile from Nubbin.

"What are you smiling at?" asked Tim with a scowl.

"I'm having a good time," said Nubbin, bopping away.

Otis, as promised, continued to foul Tim, and as promised, the fouls hurt, and Tim began to fall apart as he took low-percentage shots and rushed his passes.

The score was sixty-eight to thirty-eight when the fourth quarter began. Toby and Brian each had three fouls; G and Otis four, and we couldn't risk anybody fouling out. "Guys, we need to keep up the intensity, but we can't foul anymore," I said.

"We already up in them fools' head," said Otis. "We don't gotta foul anymore."

"It's true," said Nubbin. "My brother's off his game. I mean, we can catch them."

When we stepped back on that court, the b-ball Gods woke up, and they were in a generous mood. Donnie, Nubbin, and Toby all got hot hands at once—it was the first time all season, and they couldn't miss. I'd never seen anything like it. Every time Westchester moved to double-team, we passed it off to another hot hand at the three-point line. Every time Westchester scored two points, we scored three.

We double-downed on the smack talk, and Westchester continued to fall apart, and my father continued to yell and rake his fingers through his hair and look at me as if he'd no idea who I was or what I was thinking. With three minutes left on the clock, we were within twelve points, and my father called a time out, prompting the patients in the stands behind us to leap to their feet and chant—I had no idea what they were saying, but it hit my ears like the sweetest song. Even with all that noise, I could still make out my father yelling at his team, "I did not come all this way for nothing! I *need* this *record*! It's *mine*! Guys, will you get it for me?"

"Yes!" they fired back.

"Then let's *finish* this pathetic excuse for a team. Tim, show me you're a champion, because right now I'm sure UCLA is second-guessing themselves."

My father's speech lit his guys up and they marched onto the court and Tim landed a three-pointer. When we got the ball, Nubbin answered his brother with a three of his own, and James jumped to his feet, smiling, and clapping for his boys. On the next play, Brian stole the rock and threw it to Donnie, who shot the ball without even looking at the basket. Splash! Three points!

Chey turned to me. "I've like never seen him this hot."

"What are you thinking, Chey?"

"You're going to love this," she said, calling over Donnie and whispering in his ear.

The next play Brian fed Donnie the ball at half-court, and Donnie turned and shot a nearly impossible shot. Swish!

My father screamed out in pain. "Somebody guard that kid!"

Knowles jumped out of his seat, pumping his fist. He felt it. Something special was going on here.

Our guys pushed and shoved Westchester, and they fed Donnie every chance they got, and it didn't matter where on the court he was, as soon as he touched the ball, he shot, and he scored. With one minute left on the clock, Westchester was up ninety-two to eighty-seven.

"Guys, we got time," I said to my crew at our bench. "We need five points—Chey, what do you think?"

"Donnie's getting triple-teamed, so let's fake to Donnie and hit

Toby at the baseline. Toby, you haven't shot in a while, so you're going to be wide open."

I extended my hand in the middle of our huddle and each player and one assistant coach layered their hands on mine, and we all shouted, "Friedman!"

With fifty-nine seconds left, with his brother on him like a shadow, Nubbin drove up-court and shot a no-look pass to the three-point baseline, where Toby, wide open, landed a shot, hitting nothing but net.

Now I could make out what the stands behind me were chanting: "El-e-phant balls! El-e-phant balls! El-e-phant balls!"

It was eighty-two to eighty, and Tim dribbled the ball up at the top of the key, holding onto it like we'd seen him do year after year, DVD after DVD.

"Guys, we're ready for this," I called out. "Outthink them."

My father looked over and squinted at me. Nubbin signaled the guys as he moved out to force his brother's hand. Then Tim, like on the DVD, drove toward the hoop, and all four of our players stepped into his lane, and like we practiced, Brian snagged the ball and we all yelled, "Time out!"

The ref blew his whistle, but you couldn't hear it over the patients going bonkers, yelling and chanting, doing the wave, high-fiving, hugging. Everybody in the gym was on their feet: Knowles, Dr. T, Gerald, Dr. Lipschitz, the Westchester fans—everybody. There were thirty seconds left on the clock, and we were down by two, and we had the ball.

"Who wants the last shot?" I asked our huddle.

Everyone decided it should be Nubbin, who nodded like a true champion, and when my guys trotted onto the court for the last seconds of the game, I took a deep breath and turned to Dr. T, who was watching me with a big smile, and I felt every bit of all right.

Brian inbounded to Nubbin, who drove up-court against a tight full-court press. He was being double-teamed by Tim and Jovver.

There was no way he was going to be able to shoot, so he passed it to G at the top of the key. G put the ball on the floor and drove toward the hoop but got caught up in traffic and snapped the ball out to Toby underneath the hoop, but Westchester was all over him. Toby threw the rock to the only open guy on the court—Brian. And with twenty-four seconds left on the clock, Brian looked down at the ball in his hands.

"Shoot!" I screamed.

Brian turned to the hoop and shot but was hacked in the arm by Russell. The ref blew his whistle, and with twenty seconds left on the clock, we were still down by two. Brian had to make both foul shots to tie the game.

My father and I looked at each other. We were back in the same position we were in all those years ago, the moment our relationship severed, the championship riding on two foul shots.

Brian, terrified, stood in the spot he'd been fouled, as players lined up, waiting for him to make his way to the foul line.

"Good foul!" shouted my old man. "Kid hasn't taken a shot all day."

"Yo, don't listen to him, Bri," said Toby.

"You got this," said Otis.

"Remember to keep your eye on the rim," encouraged Donnie.

Brian looked to me for help, the same look I'd given my father back then. "Bri!" I shouted, waving him over.

Brian approached the bench, all blood retreating from his face. "I'm in my head. I'm straight freaking out."

"Brian, I've thought about being in this exact position every day for the last ten years." I looked up at my father studying me. "I got a joke for you."

"A *joke*?"

"You hear about the b-ball player who spent all day sketching chickens?"

"What are you talking about, Coach?" he asked, his eyes darting to the scoreboard, to the camera, and then to my father, who had his hands on his knees, staring at the two of us.

"Brian, I need you to focus," I said. "He spent all day sketching chickens. Why?"

Brian concentrated, closing his eyes.

"He was learning to *draw fouls*," I said.

He opened his eyes. "That's stupid," he said.

"No, you're missing the whole point. It's a great joke, but it's more than that, and I need you to go make those foul shots and come back here and tell me *why*. Why it's one of the *best jokes* ever told."

"I—"

"This is more important than the game. He spent all day *sketching chickens*."

He turned to Chey. "Sketching chickens," she repeated, nodding.

The ref blew his whistle and Brian, confused, walked to the foul line. The ref handed him the ball, and Brian bounced it and took a deep breath.

"Chickens, buddy," I called out.

And Brian turned and shot, and the ball hit the front of the rim, bounced up in the air, hit the backboard and landed. We were down by one point. One of the patients began to stomp his feet, and then everyone else joined in, and our side of the gym sounded like a stampede.

Chey grabbed my arm. "The chickens—you did that to keep him out of his head, right?"

"In moments like this, Chey, we realize how *funny* life is. We must get the joke. We have to."

Brian, eyes wide, received the ball and bounced it.

"Choke Artist will never make two in a row!" shouted my father, who hadn't changed in all these years.

"Come on, Brian," I called out. "Tell me about them chickens!"

Brian took a deep breath and turned back to me. I put my hands under my arms and clucked, and Chey followed suit. We both clucked, and the patients in the stands changed out their stomping for clucking. Within moments, two hundred people were clucking like chickens. Brian smiled, even laughed a little, as he took it all in.

"You got this, Brian!" shouted Chey, also laughing. "One hundred percent chance you make this shot. Hundo P."

He nodded at Chey, and when Chey nodded back I saw a flash of something pass between them—there was a chance for them after all. Then he turned and he made the shot, and we had ourselves a tied game.

The patients wailed and clucked and screamed as Toby huddled the team together on the court. When he was done, they all looked up at me, and I knew he'd told them about the bet, that they needed to win to keep me as their coach. It was the right call, and I loved him for making it.

Jovver stood, getting ready to inbound the ball.

"Nubbin!" screamed Chey over all the noise. "You know it's going to your brother. You know it."

Of course, Chey was right, and Jovver inbounded to Tim. Only Nubbin jumped in front of his brother, snatching the ball, and bobbling it out of bounds with nineteen seconds left on the clock, as the noise in the stands behind me hummed in my chest.

Jovver, once again, stood at the line, and the ref handed him the ball. He whipped it to Tim, who snagged it out of the air with the quickness of grabbing a bird in flight, and he dribbled down-court. He had time for one play, and he bounced the ball at the top of the key. I studied his face, but this kid was opaque, and I couldn't tell if he was going to shoot or drive. My guess was he was going to drive because he knew Nubbin couldn't foul him—any foul would put Tim at the foul line, which would cost us the game.

There were fourteen seconds left on the clock when Tim drove, and Nubbin, as if he was in his brother's head, predicted the cross-over dribble and knocked the ball from his brother's hands, where

G picked it up and baseballed it to Donnie running up the sideline. Donnie grabbed the ball and without hesitation, still running, shot, the ball sailing through the gym in a high arc, hanging in the air as you could feel a collective intake of breath before smacking the front of the rim and springing back up, hitting the backboard and landing. We'd won! The Visitors, Friedman, Crack Babies, whatever you wanted to call us—we'd won the game.

The stands behind me exploded in screams as a ref's whistle pierced the air. My father's ref signaled that Donnie's foot was out of bounds. My ref raced up to him, and the two men huddled center court while the stands behind my father shouted in hope.

My father was on his feet, doing what we were all doing—trying to read the refs' lips, as the two men argued with only eight seconds left. The cameraman next to me rewound his footage and studied it in his little screen but said he didn't have a clean shot. It wouldn't have mattered anyway. There were no instant replay reviews like there were in the pros. The refs made the final decision.

"I was in bounds," said Donnie, rushing up to me, arms flailing and eyes wide. "I looked. I was in bounds."

"I believe you, buddy, no matter what they say."

My father's ref blew his whistle again and said Donnie's foot was out of bounds, and he handed the ball to Westchester, and the fans behind my father roared to life, while my side howled in concerted pain. I looked at Donnie. "It's all part of the game. Don't let it get in your head. We still got a shot."

Jovver stood at the sideline, the ref handing him the ball, and once again, Jovver whipped it to Tim, who drove toward the hoop, his brother on him like a shadow, careful not to foul. Toby, spotting he was heading for an easy layup, jumped up and stuffed him on his release, and once again a whistle sliced through the gym—this time from my ref.

Everybody was on their feet making more noise than I would've thought possible, causing my ears to burn.

"Smart foul!" screamed Chey in my ear, clapping. "It was a hundred percent chance he would've made that layup."

Across the court James stood, cheering and applauding, while my father paced up and down the sideline. There were two seconds left on the clock, and Tim only needed to make one of his two foul shots to win the game. My father cupped his hands and yelled something, but I couldn't make it out, as the players took their positions and Tim stepped up to the foul line and bounced the ball.

My guys signaled one another, pointed down-court, and planned the course of action if Tim missed both shots. They had hope.

Tim bounced the ball three times, closed his eyes, and took a deep breath as the patients wailed. He then took another deep breath and leveled his attention on the rim. It was impossible to concentrate with all the commotion. Finally, he shot—hitting nothing but net. It was a great shot.

Westchester's fans cheered; a cheer dwarfed by the one over my shoulder. Yes, Westchester won, but you wouldn't have known from the reaction of our fans. Both sides were up and applauding.

The camerawoman followed my father as he rushed up to Tim. It was an inspirational sight, a coach hugging his star player, the one responsible for helping him break the record. Somehow, I thought this should or would bother me, but it didn't. I was happy for my old man as he was lifted onto his team's shoulders and paraded around the gym. Knowles gave me the thumbs up—he had one great finish to my father's story.

My guys watched the celebration in disbelief—we had come so close. From over my shoulder, the patients were giving us a standing ovation, chanting, "Fried-man, Fried-man, Fried- man," and I signaled my guys over.

"We could've won," said G. "We could've actually beaten those *pendejos*. Donnie's foot was *in!*"

I shook my head. "A ref's call is part of the game, boys, but forget that for a minute—look," I said, gesturing to the applause raging behind us. "Guys, I want you to remember this. There's gonna be times when you'll need to recall this moment, when we all came together and played like champions. Nobody will ever be able to take this from you." My guys were young, but they'd struggled enough to know I was right. They turned to the stands, and they basked in the glory being showered onto them, and I watched as the miracle of this close game took root in each of them.

"The chickens were to keep me out of my head, right?" asked Brian.

I smiled.

Over Brian's shoulder, I spotted Tim approaching, and I understood our moment was over. Otis, feeling the same way, grabbed Nubbin. "You want me to put your brother in that garbage can over there?"

"Let's see what he's got to say," said Nubbin.

"Nubbin," said Tim, shaking his head. "You threw it down like Chris Paul, man. Great game."

"You too," said Nubbin. The two boys stood there, appraising each other, silent, when James rushed up and grabbed his two sons, hugging them. "My two boys," he sang out. "That was the best game I have *ever* seen. *Two* champions! That's what I've got—two champions."

The ref handed Tim the game ball. "You've been voted MVP."

Tim looked down at the ball in his hands, then up at Donnie. "Yo," said Tim, passing Donnie the ball. "Your foot was in bounds, little man."

"It was," said Donnie, vindicated. "I saw it."

I turned to James. "You've got an impressive family," I said.

He nodded. "Tim, let's go find your mom. Let Gordon celebrate with his friends."

Tim gave his brother a hug before joining his father.

"Mikey," called out Dr. T, running over. "They're going to build us a gymnasium!"

"People like winners," said Dr. Lipschitz with a shrug and a smile, approaching alongside a guy in a bougie suit.

"Great game, Coach," said this dude. "I'm Akeem. I got you the job here."

"Right, my father's friend," I said as we shook hands.

"Here's the son of a gun now."

My father was on his way over, trailed by Knowles and being filmed by the camerawoman.

"Congratulations, Andrew," said Akeem.

"Thanks, Akeem," said my father.

"Your son gave you a run for your money, huh?"

"Second best coach in the family," said my old man.

I nodded at my father. "Congratulations, pops. You did it."

"A lot of coaches I play are predictable," he said. "Not you, boy. You are anything but."

"I'm gonna take that as a compliment," I said.

"What about the bet?" asked Knowles. "You're not going to hold Mikey to it, are you? You guys need to face off again next year."

"If he even wins his division next year—anybody can have a lucky season. Now winning your division two years in a row—that would show me you were a real coach, son."

"I'd like the chance to do that," I said.

"Mikey can stay on as coach, for real?" asked Toby, standing at my side.

My father nodded. "Yeah. He can."

"Can I get you two to shake hands for E:60," said Knowles.

My old man extended his hand. I thought about this man, my father, afraid to open my bedroom door, the man who thought he was toughening me up, the man who wanted me to be like him. I reached out and took his hand in mine and we shook, and then his team whisked him away, Knowles behind the fray.

Dr. T turned to me. "How're you holding up?"

"Surprisingly, well," I said.

"You know I've got your back, don't you, Mr. Cannon?" said Dr. T.

"I do," I said and smiled. "And that's *Coach* Cannon, thank you very much."

"I imagine your mum would be well chuffed today."

"I believe she would."

The camerawoman nudged me from behind. "Your boy's foot was in bounds. Knowles is gonna see that in the editing room. No telling what makes the final cut." I nodded but said nothing as we looked over at my father's celebration. Knowles signaled for her to get some footage of it. "Duty calls," she said, nodding back at me before making her way to my old man.

I turned to look at my guys, playing around, joking, throwing their arms over one another's shoulders. Chey's mother ran up and hugged her daughter, followed by the rest of the team's families congratulating their kids.

"Coach," I heard beside me.

I put my arm around Toby, who'd attempted suicide two weeks earlier and who would possibly do so again, this kid who I loved. "I'm proud of you, Captain," I said, squeezing him so tightly that for a moment it feels like I might be able to save him.

# THANK YOU!

Thank you for reading *Head Fake*. If you enjoyed it, please consider leaving a review on your retailer of purchase, Amazon, Goodreads, and/or Bookbub. Nothing helps an author more. Your review will encourage readers to pick up a copy.

# FOLLOW SCOTT ON SOCIAL MEDIA

**www.scottgordonbooks.com**
(sign up for the newsletter to be informed of events and new books)
**Goodreads:** https://www.goodreads.com/author/ show/49560258.Scott_Gordon
**Facebook:** ScottGordonBooks
**Instagram:** scottgordonbooks

# ACKNOWLEDGMENTS

I will start by thanking my wife, **Samantha,** for her fierce support and faith in me. And for her advice on, well, everything—most of which was greatly appreciated. And for always going for the funny. I couldn't have written this novel without her.

A very special thanks to the kids I worked with over the years, who taught me infinitely more about life than I could have ever taught them.

My family, who always believed in me.

I also want to thank:

**Doug Kurtz,** for his thoughtful guidance, and for the many nuanced ways in which he said, "You should write that part better."

**Julie Miesionczek Maloney,** for her spot-on advice, for answering my texts, and for pointing out that the British use contractions.

My agent, **Jill Marsal,** for reading *Head Fake* straight through in one sitting. And for calling me.

**Gil Bellows,** who believed in this story since its inception, and who is going to shoot it as a film, or better yet, as a series. Right, Gil?

**Michael Goldberg,** for being my unofficial, unpaid Marketing Guy.

**Kali Londono,** who believed in the story in all of its forms.

**Rob Samborn,** for his help navigating this crazy book business.

**Ronald Meyer,** for being a mentor for so many things, for so many years.

**Tiffany Coleman** and **Brooke Terpening,** for their ongoing support and notes. We will be critiquing each other's work forever.

**Danielle Lange** and **Diane Evans,** for proofreading at breakneck speed. And Danielle again, for proofreading twice.

**Scott Gordon's** fiction has appeared in the *Green Hills Literary Lantern (GHLL)*, *Modern Times Magazine*, *Pennsylvania Literary Journal*, *The Satirist*, and *Mobius Magazine*. In addition to writing fiction, he has written and directed films and television series, including *A History of Black Achievement in America*, *Great American Authors*, and more. Scott spent years working as a Youth Advocate for juvenile offenders with mental illness. *Head Fake* is inspired by the strength and courage of the kids he worked with. Originally from New Jersey, Scott lives in Los Angeles with his wife, Samantha, and their two rescue pups, Mel Brooks and Khaleesi Bee.

scottgordonbooks.com

Made in the USA
Columbia, SC
07 August 2024

39707094R00198